SOVEREIGN
A DARK COWBOY ROMANCE

RAYA MORRIS EDWARDS

Sovereign
By Raya Morris Edwards

SECOND EDITION

Editing by Morally Gray Author Services

Cover by Maldo Designs
Cover photo: Michelle Lancaster @lanefotograf

This book is for anyone who ever wanted spanked and called a good girl by a hot cowboy. That's not too much to ask, right?

TRIGGER WARNINGS & TAGS

This is a dark BDSM romance that contains heavy content only appropriate for adults regarding abuse, dubc*n, nonc*n, trauma, death, and other intense or potentially triggering topics. If you have any triggers at all, please go to the link below and read through the list.

Please go to the author's website rayamorrisedwards.com for the full and detailed list.

CHAPTER ONE

KEIRA

"Keira!"

I jump and the coffee cups rattle against the counter. It's late and I'm exhausted after preparing and serving a full meal for everyone at Garrison Ranch. It took me the usual two hours after dinner to clean the kitchen and load all the dishes into the dishwasher. I was about to head upstairs to bed when I heard truck tires come up the drive.

My husband, Clint, told me to go back into the kitchen. Unsurprised, I obeyed, but I lingered just behind the doorway. Listening to the unfamiliar voice of our late night visitor.

It's deep and smooth with a thick undercurrent of gravel. The hairs on the back of my neck stand up although I'm not sure why. I lift my arm and goosebumps are popping up across my skin.

I lean my head against the wall and close my eyes. Their footsteps fade out as they head upstairs to Clint's office on the second floor. It doesn't bother me anymore that my husband shuts me out of everything, including who comes and goes in my own home. I know exactly what I'm good for in his mind and it's not being his equal.

Clint's footfalls ring out again and I make a mad dash for the island countertop. It's empty so I pretend I'm taking forks and knives from the drawer. His boots pause in the doorway and I look up, brushing back my hair.

My husband is a tall man with dusky blonde hair and steel gray eyes. He's handsome, but I stopped feeling anything when I looked at him a long time ago. Maybe less than a year after our wedding.

"Make up some coffee for our guest," he says.

I nod and slide the silverware back into the drawer. "Decaf?"

He glances up at the clock over the stove. It was his grandmother's and then his mother's. I fucking hate it. I wish I could open the back door and pitch it so hard I never have to look at it again. It's yellowed and the wooden frame has cracked from hanging above the stove. But the reason I hate it so much has more to do with how badly his late mother treated me after the wedding.

Before the wedding, she'd been nothing but sweet. But as soon as the ring was firmly on my finger, she stopped speaking to me except to hurl insults. It was a relief when she died.

I used to wonder what I did to make his family hate me. But after a while, I came to accept that nothing made sense anymore. Clint had once loved me too. Now he's disgusted every time I open my mouth.

"Of course," he says.

"How many cups?"

He shrugs. "Make up a tray. And put something to eat on there as well."

He leaves before I can ask him what. I wipe my hands on my apron and unwrap the leftover biscuits. Even Clint doesn't have a bad word to say about my biscuits. They're fluffy, layered perfectly so they can be split open hot and soaked with butter and raspberry jam. I pop them in the oven for a few minutes as I make coffee.

Then I load everything up and slip my house shoes off to carry them upstairs in my socks. I don't want to risk falling and spilling everything.

Clint would lose his shit.

I'm wearing a modest, long-sleeved dress that goes to my knees. At least I don't have to worry about Clint calling me a slut. He likes to do that when I wear anything that shows an inch of skin.

Outside the oak door, I balance the tray in one hand and knock once with the other.

There's a short silence. Then:

"Come in."

I enter, allowing myself one glance over the room. I see a pair of steel-toe boots by the chair in the corner. Clint sits at his desk between the two windows on the far wall. There's a short pile of folders before him, one of them open. I can tell it's paperwork for cattle.

"Set it down on the desk," Clint says, without looking up.

Uncomfortable, I cross the room and put the tray down. My eyes flick to the side, locking on the stranger's boots. They're bigger than normal and the leather is worn. Whoever he is, he's a broad man, I can tell from his feet.

Gathering my courage, I let my eyes run higher.

My heart stops.

He has a pair of pale blue eyes beneath dark, lowered brows. His face is broad and masculine, his jawline defined and covered in a short beard. His nose is heavy with a bump on the bridge, like maybe he broke it once. There's a firmness to his expression and face, but no emotion.

He glances at me and glances away. Then he does a double take.

Our eyes lock and I can barely breathe.

Heat curls in my lower belly. We stare at each other for a second that feels like an eternity. My eyes take in every detail of his face hungrily. The dark, wavy hair, a bit falling over his forehead. The button up that leaves a V of bare skin at his throat exposed. The smattering of hair rising above it that sparks my curiosity.

My gaze flicks down.

He's got a thick, muscled body that fills out his work pants and shirt perfectly. But it's not the physical that stops me in my tracks.

He feels like when the winds change to bring in a storm. Maybe it's because his aura is dark like the cool shadows in the pines. Or clouds rolling over the mountains, soft at first, and then bringing swift destruction.

I shudder. He hasn't said anything to me, I have no reason to be intimidated. But I am. There's an edge of darkness to him, like a gravitational pull. It's overwhelming.

"Can you pour the coffee?" Clint says.

I glance up and he's scowling the way he does before he pulls me aside to chew me out. Except he won't do that here because we're being watched. Obediently, I pour two cups and pass one to my husband and one to the newcomer. He reaches out to take it and my eyes fall on a ring on his smallest finger.

There's a silver symbol on it. I tilt my head and make out three letters. SMR.

My brows shoot up to my hairline. I know who this man is. No one else would wear that insignia on a ring like that. He's Gerard Sovereign, the owner of the wealthiest cattle and horse ranch in the state. Sovereign Mountain Ranch borders our land, but I know better than to go there.

I'm not sure why, but we're not friendly with them. I know that much from Clint.

They say he has everyone in his grip. That all roads lead to Sovereign Mountain at some point.

Clint talks about Gerard Sovereign like he's the devil. I half expected him to have horns. But he's handsome, heavily muscled like one of the draft horses we use to pull hay in the winter. His eyes are on me and I get the impression he doesn't lose control easily. His lack of expression is a testament to his restraint.

Especially because I saw his body tense when he looked me in the eyes.

"Do you want cream?" I whisper.

He shakes his head, once.

Clint doesn't take cream in his coffee either, so I turn to leave. My husband clears his throat and I freeze, turning.

"Stay," he says. "We've got someone else coming in a few minutes."

Heat creeps up the back of my neck. He does this to me occasionally and I fucking hate it. It's humiliating having to stand there like I'm on his payroll and wait for one of them to have some need that needs fulfilling. My lashes feel wet as I back up and sink down in the chair in the corner.

Gerard follows me with his eyes.

"Is that your wife?" he asks, his voice soft and deep.

Clint nods, glancing up. Something sparks between them that puts me on high alert. Their gazes lock, like two wolves squaring off. Then Clint turns his eyes back to the desk like it never happened. He passes Gerard a pen and paper without raising his head. I study Gerard's impassive face and I think I see a flicker of amusement.

"Why do you want to know?" Clint says, his tone forced. He's trying to be casual.

"She doesn't need to stay," Gerard says.

Clint glances at me and I swallow hard. "She's fine. It's not like she has anything better to do."

My chest aches. Before our wedding, he never spoke to me like this. Now it's the only way he talks to me and what scares me is that I'm used to it. I get up in the morning with an empty brain and put my hands to work because it's what he wants. It's not like I can leave, I have nowhere to go and no money to my name.

So I cook for the entire ranch, I clean the house spotless, and I fuck him when he wants it.

When he's finally asleep at night, I roll onto my side and take the painted wooden mare from my bedside table. My mother was from Sweden and when she came to America, she brought one of her childhood toys. A red and white wooden mare, beautifully carved. It's running hard, three feet off the ground.

I never met my mother. She died not long after I was born.

At night, I trace the bridle painted to look like a string of stars. The paint is still crisp. Before my father passed when I was seventeen, he had it repainted and sealed with varnish. It was his farewell gift.

After losing my farm and my freedom to Clint, all I have left is the painted mare.

I look up from my corner and he's watching me again. Clint is by the file cabinet in the corner with his back to us. Gerard leans back in his chair, spreading his legs. My fingers clench in my lap.

What is he looking at?

"I have the paperwork here," Clint says, turning and crossing back to the desk.

Gerard drags his cold eyes back to my husband as he holds out his hand and accepts the file folder. Something crackles between them, like they'd much rather be anywhere but in this room together. A tiny shiver moves up my spine. I'm fine-tuned to read my husband's emotions and it's very obvious he's uncomfortable with Gerard.

Downstairs, a car door slams. Clint leans back and glances out the window.

"There's Jay," he says. "Keira, go down and bring him up."

A muscle twitches in Gerard's jaw. He snaps the folder shut with one hand and sets it down.

"I'll go," he says.

Clint frowns. "No, Keira's fine."

Gerard clears his throat. "I mistook her for your paid help with the way you treat her, Garrison."

The room goes deadly silent again. Clint's steel gaze snaps to me like I had something to do with Gerard's words. Heart pounding, I curl back into the chair. Am I going to pay for this later when we're alone?

Clint rises abruptly and crosses the room, yanking open the door.

"I'll get him myself," he snaps.

His footfalls echo down the hall and the room goes deadly quiet. Gerard's lips part and his eyes drag over me. Starting at my feet tucked under the chair. Traveling up my thighs. Lingering on my breasts, throat, and mouth. Then our gazes clash.

The air crackles.

Beneath my dress, my nipples tighten. Heat stirs in my lower belly and curls down until I feel it between my thighs.

It's quickly followed by shame. I'm married, I shouldn't be looking at other men this way. And yet...I can't stop looking at Gerard like I'm starving.

I *am* starving. Clint gives me crumbs of attention. He fucks me, but he doesn't bother going down on me. Or even staying up while I use my vibrator. He says it's not his problem that I can't come while he's fucking me. That's not even the worst thing though. It's the lack of emotional intimacy that really hurts. No hugs, no late night talks, no comforting me when I cry.

All that neglect means I'm left empty.

And Gerard Sovereign looks like an entire meal and then some.

"You're going to get me in trouble," I say, my voice cracking.

"I'm not afraid of your husband," he says quietly.

Before I can stop myself, my mouth opens and I say the one thing I never admit to anyone else.

"No, but I am."

His face goes hard. "Is your husband a mad dog?"

Confused, I glanced back at the door. Listening for footsteps. When I drag my attention back, he's got me in his crosshairs. His eyes aren't just blue as I previously thought. He's got a darker ring edging his irises that makes his stare even more piercing.

"What?" I whisper.

"Mad dogs bite," he says. "There's no cure for it but a shotgun."

My jaw goes slack.

"Are you...threatening Clint?" I whisper.

"Does he need to be threatened?"

I'm struggling to find words. No one has ever spoken to me like this while they unabashedly eye-fuck me.

Oh God, I'm blushing.

Flustered, I brush my hair from my face and straighten my shoulders.

"You should stop," I say firmly.

He cocks his head. "Stop what? You're the one who has bedroom eyes."

I tear my gaze away and fix it at the ground. My complexion is too fair to conceal the heat in my face. It's making pink splotches down my neck and chest.

"You need to stop it," I say, more sharply this time. "My husband gets jealous."

"Again. I'm not afraid of him."

I study him warily. His face is hard to read, but I can feel that he's got a vendetta against my husband. Maybe they had a soured business deal once upon a time. But whatever it is, I hear the subtle distaste in his words when he talks about Clint. Like he's something disgusting that needs to be scraped from his shoe.

"Maybe you should be," I say.

He leans forward and I peek at him through my lashes. "Mrs. Garrison, I could bend you over this desk and fuck you with your husband watching and he wouldn't say a goddamn word."

My jaw drops. The silence rings in my ears. He leans back in his chair like he didn't just say something shocking. Before I can answer, we both hear footsteps in the hall. I scramble to fold my hands and tuck my feet back under the chair.

The door opens and Clint enters with a wiry, graying man in dress pants and a shirt. I recognize him as Jay Reeds, his lawyer. Automatically, I rise to let him have my chair and go to stand by the door. Hands folded and eyes on the ground.

This time, to conceal my bright red face.

CHAPTER TWO

GERARD

I've never hated anyone the way I hate Garrisons, especially Clint. But the moment I lay eyes on his redheaded wife, I'm glad I agreed to meet with him.

Tonight was supposed to be a quick transaction. We're the two biggest ranchers in the state and having to do business together is inevitable. I anticipated a brief meeting where I scrawled my name on paper and walked out without speaking more than I needed to.

But then she walked in.

Nervous, tired, trying to make herself as small as possible so he doesn't look her way. I know exactly what kind of man he is, so it doesn't surprise me that his wife acts like a scared rabbit. But it does surprise me that the moment I lay eyes on her, my body reacts like a live wire.

She's got an hourglass figure with curvy hips and breasts. When she turns, I get a good look at her round ass, big enough I could get a handful and still have plenty leftover, and my mind goes into overdrive. Imagining what it would be like to sink my teeth into her bare ass hard enough to make her scream.

I thought I felt desire before now, but the way my body burns when I look at her face is something new. She is, without a doubt, the most beautiful woman I've ever seen. On screen, on page, in real life.

Until this moment, I didn't know what it felt like to experience chemistry. But I feel it now, and it makes the hair rise on the back of my neck.

The way I need her doesn't care about decorum. It's pure, it's primal.

The unevolved part of my brain is telling me to put a bullet in Clint and drag his wife back to Sovereign Mountain.

It's tempting, but not exactly socially acceptable.

I steal a glance at her. Taking in her oval face, full mouth, and wide blue eyes. Her brilliant red hair is braided loosely and secured with a bit of string. Freckles dust over her cheeks, nose, and down her chest. I wonder if she has them on her breasts.

Fuck, she's exquisite.

My pulse races and sweat trickles down my spine. I force any expression from my face and lean back like I'm unbothered by her presence. We're on either side of the room with Clint and his lawyer talking between us and the tension is so thick I can almost see it.

I stay silent as they go over the contract of sale. I wrote it and I know what I want from it. They have to come up with a counteroffer while I'm waiting.

"Keira," Clint says, glancing up. "Get Jay whatever he needs."

Jay waves a hand. "I'm good, too late for coffee, too early for whiskey."

Clint nods and goes back to the paperwork while his wife stands awkwardly by the door. He's an evil cunt—he always has been—but I didn't realize how good he is at subtle humiliation until now. His intention is clear.

She's his property. If he wants her to stand there all night, she will.

I stand abruptly. "I'm going to use the restroom. Could you show me where it is?"

I'm looking at Clint. He glances up, beckoning to Keira.

"Take Mr. Sovereign downstairs," he says.

She gives me a look. It's subtle, but it lets me know she's onto me. Amused, I follow her out the door and down the hall. My eyes fall as she descends the stairs. Watching her ass jiggle beneath her tight skirt.

"It's down the hall," she says.

We're in the doorway to the kitchen. I glance down the dim hall, to the open door of the bathroom at the end.

"I'm not sure I can find it," I say.

Her brows crease. "It's right there."

"Where?"

She walks halfway down the hall and points. Before she can turn back around, I plant my hand against the wall to block her path back. Her entire body freezes and her tongue darts out to wet her mouth. From this angle, I can see the faint suggestion of her cleavage.

Her breath hitches. Her lips part.

"You weren't looking for the bathroom," she whispers.

I shake my head. My hand comes up and tucks one strand of hair behind her ear. She smells like a woman, like shampoo and perfume and lotion. I'll bet her skin is so fucking soft.

I'll bet it marks easily.

"You need to leave," she says, her voice catching.

I pull back. She darts into the kitchen, putting the island counter between us like a blockade. Her body is drawn up tight and she's got her hands tucked behind her back. I can tell she's used to being submissive.

That's interesting.

But not altogether surprising. Clint is a bully, among other things, so it doesn't surprise me that his wife shrinks at the sight of men. I study her face, wondering if he hits her.

It's not really the Garrison's style. They're better at emotional torture.

I would fucking know after what they did to me.

"Do you drink, Mrs. Garrison?"

She licks her lips, catching the bottom one on her teeth. "I do a shot of whiskey now and then."

"Pour me a shot," I tell her.

She obeys at once. For all the wrong reasons, she's well trained. But she has what it takes to be obedient and that interests me. I keep silent as she pours a shot of whiskey and brings it to me. I take it, ignoring the sharp scent.

"Come here," I say.

She shifts closer, glancing at the stairs through the doorway.

"Open your mouth," I murmur.

Her eyes widen. "What are you doing, sir?"

The way she calls me sir solidifies the question I've had in my mind. Do I want her enough to wreak havoc? Or do I just hate Clint Garrison so much that his pretty wife is a temptation?

"Trust me," I say. "I won't hurt you."

She doesn't seem to be afraid, but it's hard to tell. She shifts closer and I reach out and bury my hands in her soft curtain of hair. Right at the nape of her neck. My fingers fist and I gently pull her head back. Her breasts heave and—lucky for me—the top button of her dress unfastens under the strain. I get a glimpse of the prettiest cleavage I've ever seen.

Soft, full. Freckled and perfect.

I'm fully hard, but she can't look down, so who the fuck cares. Slowly, I bend her head back until she's looking up into my face. She's breathing hard and both her hands are wrapped around my wrist. Holding on for dear life.

"Open your mouth, sweetheart," I tell her.

She hesitates, but then she does as she's told. Her lips part and reveal a pink tongue and white teeth. My cock is so fucking hard it's going to have a zipper print on it.

Slowly, I drizzle the shot into her mouth. Her throat bobs until it's gone. We both freeze, the glass still tilted over her face. Her eyes dart to mine, so wide the whites flash. Before she can fight me, I release her and take a step back to give her space.

She claps her hands over her mouth, like we've done something terrible. I turn the shot glass upside down and set it on the counter.

"I'd better get upstairs," I say.

I leave her there, standing in the kitchen as dazed as if I spun her around and let her go. My boots carry me up the stairs and back into Clint's office, but my mind couldn't be further from the dim room where he sits at his desk. He's so smug that I agreed to discuss a deal with him because we both know ten years ago, I wouldn't have given him the time of day.

I lean back in my chair, crossing an ankle over my knee. Clint and Jay are both still reading over the contract. I know he's expecting me to rip him off, I see his eyes move over the words again and again.

The contract doesn't matter to me anymore.

Not after meeting Keira Garrison.

I came here tonight in what I thought was a lapse of judgment. Westin, my right hand, said I was hurting the business by refusing to work with the Garrisons. He understood why, but facts were facts. So I agreed to sell cattle directly to them for a higher cut per head than what I'd get ordinarily. Westin wrote up the contract and I brought it here under a brief white flag.

I hadn't expected her.

Vaguely, I knew Clint was married to the daughter of a local rancher who passed away a few years back. But my path never crossed with the Garrisons by design—the Garrison family and mine are our own brand of Hatfield and McCoy—so I never laid eyes on her before tonight.

Fuck me, she's everything I've ever wanted.

Those bright blue eyes are enough to make me forget I have any morals left. It's the leftover bits of my conscience that stop me from just taking her. I'm an ice cold motherfucker, but I'm not the kind who fucks another man's wife while he still has a heartbeat. As I watch Clint, it dawns on me where I know that scared look on her face.

A long time ago, a different Garrison man broke someone I loved. And I saw the pain on her face then, just as I saw it on Keira's face tonight.

She looks like a bird in a cage. A redbird with clipped wings.

15

I can feel how tight my jaw is as Clint hands back the signed papers. He's gloating, but I ignore the glitter in his eye. Pocketing the contract, I shake Jay's hand and we walk outside to my truck. Clint hangs back for a second, as if he doesn't know how to send me off.

I put my hat on and give him a quick nod. "I'll see you tomorrow for the sale."

I leave him standing on the porch and drive out into the night. My knuckles are white on the wheel as I head home. All I can think about is the redhead back in that house and what she's doing right now. Maybe she's curling up to sleep, her hair loose over her pillow. Or maybe that son of a bitch is fucking her right now.

My fists tighten. The leather steering wheel is going to have indents.

I have my doubts that she's being satisfied. I've never met a Garrison who gave a fuck about anyone but themselves.

There's a place just before I turn into the long drive that leads to my ranch where I can see for miles. I turn the bend and pull off at the overlook. Silence falls. I rummage in the glove box and come up with a stale cigarette.

I don't smoke, but I need a cigarette after meeting Keira Garrison.

I step out onto the gravel and light it, inhaling deeply. The tingling calm seeps through my veins and my eyes roam the dark horizon. The stars hang heavy, there's no light pollution to fade them. I can't make out the ground, but far away I see the opening between the cliffs.

Tomorrow, Clint, myself, and our men will go up to the cliffs and bring the cattle down. I'll sell, he'll deposit the money into my account, we'll shake hands without meeting eyes, and I'll never see Keira again.

That thought makes me fucking sick.

I've heard people talk about soulmates, about the one person out there made just for you. But I never believed it. And I still don't. But I do believe in chemistry, and I felt that electricity spark in my veins as we sat in that office together. I've never had my body respond to anyone that quickly before. And now I have to live with that.

I have to know everything about her or I won't be able to rest.

The cliffs keep my eyes occupied as I finish my cigarette. They're a dangerous area, especially at this time of year when the weather can turn easily. Where all it takes to send a herd of cattle stampeding through the narrow opening is a storm rolling over the hills without warning.

It would be a fucking pity if something were to happen tomorrow.

I stab out my cigarette and get back into the truck. Once I'm home, I go to bed, but I don't sleep. All I can think about is the way she called me sir. Lids lowered, husky voice going right to my groin.

I lie awake until dawn.

CHAPTER THREE

KEIRA

After Gerard Sovereign leaves, I rush upstairs and shut the bedroom door.

My heart pounds. My mouth tastes like whiskey. I rarely drink so it hits my brain right away and warmth creeps over my nerves.

Never, not once, has Clint made me feel like this. Teased, desired, and thoroughly seen. He dragged those pale blue eyes over every inch of my body. If I wasn't married, I know he'd have done the same with his hands.

God, he has big hands. Thick, square at the tips. Neatly trimmed nails, scars on his knuckles, and calloused palms.

My back arcs, pushing my ass against the door. I'm acutely aware the space between my thighs is empty. All I can think of is how good his fingers would feel pushed inside me.

My fist clenches, bunching my dress. Pulling the skirt up to my waist. My other hand slips beneath my panties, searching. My breath sucks in as my fingertips slip over the seam of my pussy. Playing in the wetness there before slipping over my clit.

I can feel my heartbeat there. My clit is so tender that I feel pressure ache through my sex as I start rubbing it. I haven't masturbated in so long. Not since the last trip Clint took out of town.

When he fucks me, it leaves me dry. The rest of the time, I'm too tired for desire.

But tonight, I'm soaked.

And it's all for a man I barely know.

Downstairs, I hear the men leave the office and go outside. My fingers move faster, my hips thrusting up against my hand hungrily. An orgasm rises and coils closer and closer. Sending heat surging through my lower belly and thighs.

The memory of his hand in my hair flashes through my brain and I come, hips shuddering so hard I almost fall.

Guilt floods me so fast I barely have time to recover. I stumble into the bathroom and wash my hands. My eyes snap up and meet my reflection's glassy stare. My cheeks and nose are pink. My hands shake as I scrub them hard.

For the first time in years, I look alive.

I'm so shaken, I just sit on the bed and wait for Clint. My husband doesn't come up for another hour and I take every minute of that time to compose myself. Guilt still creeps in as he enters our room and closes the door.

He takes his boots off.

"What are you looking at?" He scowls.

I shake my head. "Nothing."

I try to arrange my face to be casual. I know he's pissed from Gerard's comment. I just pray he doesn't take it out on me.

To my relief, he's quiet as he strips for bed and takes his shower. I wash up in the sink, worried I'll set him off if I ask him to leave the shower on for me.

He hates when I wear flannel to bed, he mocks me for giving up when I'm only twenty-one. So I always wear a cream slip even though he rarely fucks me anymore. I have no idea why this matters except I think he gets off on controlling me in meaningless ways.

He comes out of the bathroom in his sweatpants, drying his forearms on a towel.

"What did you think of Sovereign?" he asks.

I freeze. Did he see something?

"He seemed fine," I say quickly.

His ash blond brow arcs. "Fine? What does that mean?"

My hands twist under the quilt. "I don't know, it was hard to tell. He didn't speak very much."

He snorts and tosses the towel aside. I watch it land in a heap by the basket, but I don't say a word. My eyes snap back to him and his gaze narrows. Unease curls through my stomach. He's never hit me before, but I've always been afraid of it. He's a big man and he's strong from working the ranch.

"Come here," he says.

My heart thumps.

"Get your ass over here, Keira," he says, his voice hard.

Mouth dry, I crawl on my hands and knees to the edge of the bed and sit back. I can't keep the fear from my face and he scowls as he looks down at it.

"Jesus, I just want to fuck my wife," he growls. "You don't have to look like you're going to cry."

I shake my head. "Sorry, I'm just tired. That's it."

He knows that's not true, but he doesn't care. He takes me by the wrist and pushes me down on his side of the bed. For a second, I think he's going to fuck me missionary, but then he flips me onto my stomach. He rarely looks at my face while we have sex.

I used to wonder why that was because I'm pretty enough, but then I realized that while I might be attractive in real life, I don't look like the girls on his phone. I'm not airbrushed and surrounded by perfect lighting. My body is curvy, I have dimples and stretch marks. And freckles, I have a lot of freckles.

None of the women he looks at look like me. Realistically, none of the woman he looks at look like that either. Not that it matters to him.

He enters me and the pain makes my back arch. His breath heats the back of my neck as he works his hips.

"You're dry as fuck," he grumbles.

I squirm, trying to spread my legs further. "Can I have lube? Please?"

He doesn't like it when I ask for it. It pisses him off, like I'm rubbing it in that he doesn't get me wet. He pulls out roughly and spits in his hand. It's enough I don't see stars when he pushes himself back in, but it dries up quickly. Right away, a friction burn starts and I have to grit my teeth to keep quiet.

I stare at the painted mare on the bedside table.

She's beautiful, lithe like a thoroughbred. When she runs, she steps high. Her bridle glitters like snow under moonlight.

I lie still, even after Clint finishes. He starts snoring a moment later and I shift to my side, still watching the painted mare. She's an angel watching over me. At least that's what I like to hope.

The next day, my husband goes with a dozen other men to Sovereign Mountain. They're rounding up a few thousand cattle and purchasing them before auction. That's what he tells me before he puts his hat on and drives off.

The morning goes like any other morning on Garrison Ranch. I prepare breakfast, serve it, and clean everything up. I have a few spare moments so I steal upstairs and tidy our bedroom. The painted mare is tucked in my bedside table, wrapped in a handkerchief so there's no chance Clint sees it. He thinks it's childish, so during the day I put it away. At night, I ignore his comments because I can't sleep without it watching me.

I expect Clint back around four so I head down to the kitchen and start making dinner at two. The kitchen is hot and my head is stuffy. I didn't sleep well last night after what happened in the kitchen.

After Gerard Sovereign put his hand in my hair, after he told me he could bend me over the desk and fuck me in front of Clint.

A little part of me wishes he had.

It's the part that kept me up, staring at the ceiling until dawn. I have circles under my eyes when I get up and wash my face in cold water and go to make breakfast. I don't know why I feel so guilty, I didn't do anything. I didn't touch or kiss Gerard, I barely spoke with him. Clint might be a cheater, but I'm not. I know he's slept with other women since our wedding, but I won't become him.

But that heavy feeling of guilt stays with me until four rolls around. I have three roast chickens in the oven and a pot of potatoes boiling on the stove when I hear a car pull up the drive. Clint is home.

Pit in my stomach, I creep down the hall and push the screen door ajar. But it's not Clint's truck in the drive, it's Jay's sedan. I freeze, watching as he steps out of the car with a briefcase in his hand. His tall, lined face is tense and there's a grim set to his jaw.

Something's wrong.

I push the door open and step out.

"Where's Clint?" I ask.

He freezes, one hand fussing with the button of his jacket. "Let's go inside, Mrs. Garrison. We should talk."

My heart thumps. "Where's Clint," I repeat forcefully.

He clears his throat, shuffling his feet. "Ma'am—"

"Where is he?" I snap, shocked by my own tone.

"He's dead, there was an accident," Jay blurts out. He's looking anywhere but my face, like he's guilty for telling me.

My pulse slows. Clint always moved fast and recklessly. It doesn't surprise me that it was an accident that took him, but what shocks me is that I feel nothing but surprise that today was the day. A long time ago, I thought I loved him, but months of verbal abuse, neglect, and infidelity killed that. I didn't realize until now just how badly Clint hurt me.

But I know it now because he's dead and I feel nothing.

"Okay," I say, clearing my throat.

His brows draw together. "Can I come inside?"

Numbly, I lead the way into the kitchen. He stands awkwardly in the doorway while I turn off the stove top. The potatoes stop bubbling and float half done in their milky water. I wipe my hands and pull a stool out, indicating he should sit.

"Do you have questions?" he asks hesitantly.

I put the kettle on and take a mug down. "Coffee or tea?"

"Coffee."

He lays his briefcase on the table and waits. The kettle whistles and I pour it out, stirring instant coffee into his cup. Then I make up a mug for myself because I need something to do with my hands.

"How did it happen?" I ask.

"Um...he was rounding up cattle and they spooked. He fell from his horse and into the stampede."

I sink into the stool opposite him. The coffee sears my hand and I let it.

"Where is he?"

"They brought him to the coroner," Jay says. "He was...clearly gone by the time they brought him to the hospital so they just sent the body on."

My lips crack and I lick them. "What time did it happen?"

"Around one."

I nod, sipping the coffee. It's cheap, but it's soothing. "Alright. What happens now?"

He seems relieved to get off the subject of Clint's body. His fingers fumble over the briefcase and then he appears to decide against opening it. I frown, watching something I can't recognize pass over his face.

"Clint left everything to you," he says, eyes averted.

I feel something finally—disbelief. "What?"

He keeps glancing over the room like he's guilty. "Um...Clint left you Garrison Ranch, the portion that belonged to him, and all the money in his account to you."

My jaw is slack. It takes me a full minute to get control of myself and formulate my thoughts.

"Clint hated me," I whisper. "There's no way he left me shit."

I didn't mean for the words to come out so harshly, but right now I have no filter. Jay releases an uncomfortable sigh and leans back, steepling his fingers.

"I can't tell you why, but I can tell you it's true."

My mind whirls and all I can think about is last night when Clint got angry because I didn't obey him fast enough. I glance down, noticing I still have a little mark where he gripped my wrist to push me down onto the bed.

My eyelids are sticky when I blink. Nothing makes sense.

"I can handle all the paperwork for you," he says.

It feels like he's a million miles away. I nod and he's saying something I can barely process. He tells me the Garrison brothers, Avery and Thomas, will likely contest the will. But I shouldn't worry because he'll handle the case. I don't have to do a thing but show up in court when he tells me to. My head keeps nodding and at one point he puts paper down in front of me and I sign it without reading a word.

This has to be a cruel trick from the universe.

There's no way my cheating, abusive husband is gone and I'm conveniently left with his ranch and all his money.

He asks me a few more questions I can't remember and he says he's sorry for my loss. He means it, Jay is a good man, not like Clint. Before he goes, he takes my hand and asks me if I'll be alright if he leaves me alone. My mouth is so dry I can't answer so I just nod hard.

I stand at the foot of the stairs and listen while his car drives off. Then I tiptoe around the house and feel how still it is. Dust sparkles in the evening sun that splits through the blinds. Horses nicker in the field. I can hear the birds trill from the marsh on the other side of the road.

This house is mine.

Clint will never desecrate it with his sharp voice or loud footfalls again.

I stand there frozen for what feels like forever before I remember dinner is still cooking. Anger pours through me and I stride to the kitchen. Wrapping my hand in a towel, I yank the half done chicken out and pile it on the stove. I'm not fucking making dinner for anyone tonight. They can feed themselves.

Everyone can fuck off and leave me alone for one night of peace.

The bottle of whiskey I poured from last night sits on the counter. I grab it and the shot glass beside it. Unwashed. I bring it to my lips and push my tongue inside, cleaning up the half dried bit of whiskey. The guilt from meeting Gerard Sovereign is gone.

Last night I was afraid.

Today I'm free.

No one comes in for dinner because I never ring the bell. Surely they heard the news already. If they haven't, they'll figure out soon enough.

Whiskey in hand, I go upstairs to our bed and take the painted mare from the drawer. She stares at me with dark eyes, perpetually in motion. Forever on the run.

I take a shot. I'm twenty-one years old, I've been married since I was eighteen. It's only been four years, but it feels like I wasted eons. Today I'm going to drink until the emptiness is gone and tomorrow I'll figure this mess out.

I push myself up against the headboard, whiskey between my knees.

What do I do now?

I could try getting laid by someone who cares if I finish or not.

A wry smile twists my lips. My hands shake as I pour another glass and shoot it. It burns like fire again and again until I've had so much I'm worried I won't be able to stand. Half the bottle is gone when I finally roll it onto the empty side of the bed. My head spins as I peel myself from the bed and wobble to the silk slip hanging behind the door.

I strip and pull it on. I'm so drunk I can barely untangle my braid, but I manage to get it free and shake my hair out. My heart thumps at breakneck speed. Gerard buried his hands in my hair, right at the base of my neck, and just that touch made me feel things I've never felt.

Fear, excitement.

Unadulterated lust.

When he held me by the nape, my body came alive. I'd never been touched like that before. Roughly, but without malice—the complete opposite of Clint. My fingers slip down my body and clench so hard my knuckles go white. Crushing the silk in my grip until my nails scrape my skin. Holding me the way he held me.

That's what I need. To be loved so hard it hurts.

CHAPTER FOUR

KEIRA

SEVEN MONTHS LATER

I step out of the courthouse and feel the heaviest weight I've ever carried fall from my shoulders.

I did it.

All of Clint Garrison's ranch is mine, including what he took from me when we married. It's taken me a long time to acknowledge that he annexed my land into his ranch. He had me so convinced it was normal. Just like opening a joint bank account.

It wasn't until I lifted my eighteen-year-old hand from the paper after signing away everything I had left of my family that I realized what I'd done. The Garrison Ranch owned Stowe Farm. I had nothing and my new husband was the legal owner of everything. He even marched me down to the courthouse and made me change my name.

Mrs. Clint Garrison.

Within a week, he erased Keira Stowe from existence.

The courthouse door slams behind me. My brother-in-law, Thomas, strides out. He stops to put his Stetson back on his head and shoot me an evil glare from beneath the brim. My heart thuds, I step back. My back collides with a warm body and I whirl, my fists clenching.

My other brother-in-law, Avery Garrison, stands behind me. Avery has always hated me.

My mouth is dry. I used to wonder if Clint knew the way his brother looked at me. The way he'd walk past me in the barn and accidentally hit me against the wall with his hip. Or that his hand would graze over my torso before I realized what was happening. Maybe he'd wanted me and that was why he hated me so much. Likely he just enjoyed torturing things that couldn't hit back.

Well, today I'd hit back.

"Leave me alone," I say, trying to stand as tall as I can.

It doesn't do much. I'm five-three. The Garrison brothers are well over six feet and pack on more muscle than beef cattle. I'm in my sundress and heels and when I step back, my shoe catches on the courthouse stairs. My entire body hurtles backwards and my arms windmill.

I hear their laughter as I grip the guardrail and fall onto my knees. Pain shocks down my legs. My folder of papers spills out onto the dusty pavement.

My hair falls forward and shields my face. I know my knee is bleeding, but I ignore it. Tears stinging my lashes, I scramble to gather my things. From the corner of my eye, I see Avery's boots draw close. He kneels down and I freeze, pulling back.

"I'm going to call the police," I whisper.

"Go ahead," he says, shrugging. "If they were going to help you, they'd have done it already."

I know he's right. Since Clint died and left everything to me, I've been harassed relentlessly by Avery and Thomas. I find my fences clipped, my cattle bitten by dogs, my barn that I know I left locked wide open in the morning. On one occasion, Avery pinned me against the wall in a bar and poured a beer down the front of my dress. Not one person in that bar did anything to stop him.

The Garrisons are South Platte's darling family. The only ranch bigger and wealthier than theirs is Sovereign Mountain, and Gerard Sovereign doesn't meddle with our affairs. He rarely leaves the mountain save for the occasional city planning meeting or auction.

I've lived here my entire life and I've seen him once.

Avery's jaw tightens and he spits onto the sidewalk. Ever since Clint's death, I've been locked in a nightmare legal battle with the remaining Garrison brothers. They say the will is a fake. My husband's lawyer says it's real as they come. And now the judge declared it so.

But Avery doesn't set much store by what the judge says. I flinch and draw back, trying to control my anger. The law might be on my side, but outside the courtroom, I'm helpless against him. When Clint gave me the ranch, he painted a bright red target on my back.

Avery rises, kicking one of the papers towards me. I stay where I am, eyes on the ground. Glued to the place where his saliva drips into a crack in the sidewalk. My chest simmers, but I know better than to antagonize him.

The sound of their boots die away. Slowly, I take my heels off and gather up the papers. My knee burns as I limp down the cold sidewalk to the corner where I parked Clint's old truck. I shift inside and push the seat back so I can stretch my leg out and inspect the damage.

It's not bleeding as badly as I thought. I lick my finger and dab the blood. The little shock of pain makes my eyes well up with more tears. I'm frustrated, angry enough I want to scream and punch the seat beside me. But sad enough that all I'll actually do is go home and cry into my pillow.

I take a deep breath and brush my hair back. It's a quiet day in the city, but inside I'm churning with a million different emotions. It's been seven months since Clint died on Sovereign Mountain.

Seven months since Jay Reed walked into my house and told me that Garrison Ranch is mine.

All of it. The land, the horses, the cattle, the money in Clint's bank account.

Anyone with half a brain would have turned around and sold all of it back to the Garrison brothers. But all I could think about was how much I fucking hated their entire family and I was determined to never let it fall into their hands again.

They took my farm once before. They'd treated me like a servant in my own home.

Never again.

I shift the truck into gear and pull out onto main street. The papers from the judge sit beside me in the seat. They should be the nail in the coffin of the war between myself and the Garrison brothers, but I have a feeling this is just the beginning.

A shudder moves down my spine. It's getting dark and I hate driving alone on the back roads. Clint and I had a short and miserable marriage, but at least he'd kept me safe in this remote wilderness.

It feels like it takes an age to get back to the Garrison Ranch. I pull slowly up the drive and jump out, taking my farm boots from the bed of the truck. The floodlights from the barn illuminate my path as I head to check on the horses.

They're all fast asleep. I breathe in the sweet hay as I move silently down the center of the dark barn. I do a slow loop and lock the barn up, pausing a moment to lift my head and look up at the sky overhead.

I was born under this sky. Under the heavy net of diamond stars with the mountains standing like guardians around me. I'll probably die here.

What happens between now and then is a mystery.

Eyes burning from exhaustion, I trudge across the driveway and climb the front porch steps. My keys slip through my fingers and clatter on the floorboards. I'm grumbling under my breath as I pick them up, but my entire body freezes when I realize there's something taped to my door.

A black envelope with a silver monogram. I glance over my shoulder.

The night is chilly and empty.

Quickly, I yank the envelope down, unlock the door, and burst into the warm kitchen. Thankfully, I left the heat running from the night before. We're still in the time of year when it's balmy during the middle of the day, but the night has a bite to it.

I kick off my boots and pad barefoot to the kitchen table and sink down. The envelope is made of thick, expensive paper. I turn it over and stare at the silver letters on it.

SMR.

SMR?

It hits me all at once and I feel stupid. Sovereign Mountain Ranch. Of course, I've seen those letters before. On that night seven months ago—when Gerard Sovereign sat in my husband's office. My stomach flutters and I'm not sure why.

Maybe because the memory of his bright eyes is burned into my brain. Maybe because he'd looked me dead in the face and said, "Mrs. Garrison, I could bend you over this desk and fuck you with your husband watching and he wouldn't say a goddamn word."

Heat curls in my lower belly. I clear my throat and press the back of my fingers to my cheek. I'm glad to be alone, just as I was when...I've thought about him before. Because, as ashamed as I am, once Clint was gone, and I had time to spend on my back upstairs with my rose vibrator, the image that never failed to get me off was those words falling from his lips.

And the realization that he meant it.

And in my fantasy...I let him.

I rip the envelope open and a card falls out. One side is black with SMR in gunmetal gray and the other is white scrawled with masculine handwriting in black ink.

Miss Garrison,

I'm extending an invitation to talk with you now that you are the owner of Garrison Ranch. Please join me for a business dinner on Wednesday, the 14th of September, at six-thirty.

I will see you then.

Sovereign.

His email address is printed at the bottom along with his phone number. There's something so arrogant about him signing only his surname like that. It's a scrawl, it takes up space, it's big and loud. It eats up my tiny name that isn't even correct. I'm *Mrs.* Garrison, not Miss. It feels like he's trying to make me smaller than him.

I flip the card over and over in my fingers.

Am I afraid of Gerard Sovereign?

Should I be?

When Clint died, he left me the largest plot of Garrison land with the original house on it. And all the land he'd taken from me when we married. It puts me between Avery and Thomas's land on the front and west side.

On the north and east side, I'm right up against Sovereign Mountain. I'm stuck between the three wealthiest men in the state. Like a fly in a spiderweb. They all have the police in their back pockets and no one would help me if I found myself in danger.

It's a wild country…and I've heard what the people of South Platte say about Gerard. He's a necessary evil, so they do business with him, but when he walks into a room, it goes quiet.

After meeting him, I understood that part.

There's no law on Sovereign Mountain but his. It's the reason I barely got any information around Clint's death. I only knew that he'd been thrown from his horse and run over by cattle while purchasing livestock for auction. The police won't go out to these remote places, and the coroner is a close friend of Gerard's.

I get to my feet and double check that the front door is locked. Then I leave the kitchen light on and move through the silent house and up to my bedroom.

I undress and curl up beneath my quilt. My iPad is charging on my bedside table and I swipe it open, typing his name into the search bar. It's slow—the internet is terrible out here—but eventually it brings up a page of photographs of him.

They're all from newspapers. In the first one, he's standing with the mayor of the city at a ribbon cutting event. They've both got black Sovereign Mountain hats on. Below it is a photo of him holding a check beside the city commissioner. A hundred thousand dollars for the emergency worker's fund.

The city might not love him, but they're all happy to take his money. Funny how that works.

He's handsome, I have to give him that. Heat creeps up my throat again. He's got a Hollywood face, chiseled with low brows and a square, stubbled jaw. In the photo, his dark hair is tousled and his ice blue eyes stand out against his black lashes. There's a grim set to his jaw that I see in the men who've worked the land their entire lives.

Like nothing phases him anymore.

Like he's seen it all. Death, taxes, and everything in between.

My eyes shift over the photo of him standing with the mayor. Gerard Sovereign towers over him. He's easily six and a half feet of solid muscle, broad shoulders, and thick forearms. He has thick, heavy body that make me wonder what he feels like naked.

My toes curl. I set the iPad up on the bedside table, propped against my water glass. Then I flip onto my side and pull the quilt to my chin.

The painted mare still sits on my bedside table. She's always there, like a guardian angel, keeping me company, every night since Clint died. Sometimes I take her with me when I leave the house, just so I'm not alone. Tonight, I wrap her in my handkerchief and tuck her into the drawer.

The photo of Gerard swims before my eyes. He's in a pair of work pants and a Henley rolled up to expose his forearms. His clothes are broken in by his body, hugging him in all the right places. Faded by the sun.

Would it be so bad...to just look while my hand slips under the covers? It's not like anyone would ever know. The house is empty, the painted mare is put away. My pulse increases, but it's in the most pleasant way that sends warmth down between my legs.

Fingertips skim over my thighs.

My eyes lock on him, tracing down his thick neck to his broad shoulders. Down his hard stomach to his groin. There's a very faint rise under his zipper, like whatever he's got in there is too big to conceal properly.

If I could have him any way I wanted—my fingers find my wet sex—I would let him take me the way he said he had wanted that night. Bent over in front of him. Skirt pushed up...his big hand in my hair pulling my head back until it hurt. I'd let him show me just how much strength he has in that big body.

My fingers speed up.

My lashes flutter and between them I see flashes of him on the screen before I shut them and give into the fantasy. I never came with Clint, and now that he's gone, I find it's so much easier to finish when I'm not constantly worried about his temper. Pleasure surges after just a few minutes and washes over me, arcing my body.

Then it's gone. I peel my eyes open, flushed and sweaty.

I should feel ashamed, but I don't. Instead, I get up and go to the window, drawing aside the curtain. I can see the hill where my land meets his in the distance.

I wonder if he thinks about me the way I do him.

I wonder if his hand wanders too.

CHAPTER FIVE

GERARD

Westin Quinn, my oldest friend and manager, calls me at night, right as I'm getting undressed for the day. As soon as his name appears on my screen, I know it's bad news. I answer, reaching for my pants and pulling them back on.

"There's a break in the fence," he says. "On the Garrison side."

"Fuck," I say. "Any cattle out?"

"No, but there's one stuck in the fence. They think, anyway."

He hangs up. I shrug into my flannel and push my boots back on. My black hat sits on the desk, the Sovereign Mountain insignia burned into the leather. Settling it on my head, I move downstairs and out the front hallway, grabbing my coat on the way through.

It's fuck-all cold. That's what Westin calls it. Even though it's only September, I can tell we're in for the kind of winter that makes me question my sanity living out in northern Montana. The leaves are golden, the grass is pale brown. I can smell weeks of snow on the horizon.

It'll be a hard winter, but if everything goes according to my plan, I won't spend it alone.

I stride towards the barn. The thought of Keira Garrison in my bed has sat at the edge of my mind since the night we met.

I'd gone to Garrison Ranch expecting to have a brief business transaction. I hadn't expected to walk away on fire.

Now I'm so much closer to making her mine.

One look at that pensive little redhead and I was fucked. I'm not a soft man, most of my emotions are covered with thick calluses. Out here, where the sun burns in the summer and the winter wind can take the tips of a person's fingers off with frostbite, I've learned to love the silence and isolation.

I've learned to become part of it. Then I saw her—my enemy's wife—and I felt something.

A splinter in my steel facade.

I barely remember what we talked about—although I recall drizzling whiskey into her mouth in the kitchen. The clearest memory I have is stepping out of the house when the meeting was done and realizing that I'd never in my life wanted anything as much as I wanted Clint Garrison's wife.

But I'm not a fucking cheater.

I look up, broken from my thoughts as Westin walks Shadow and Rocky, our geldings, out into the yard. They're already saddled up and ready to go. I catch Shadow's bridle and swing up, settling my weight. Westin does the same and we head through the yard and out to the path that leads to the west side of the pastured fields.

Neither of us speak until we locate the break in the fence. This area is too rocky to be accessible by truck, so we have only the electric lantern to work by. There's a shed several yards away where we keep supplies for repair. I walk the fence line while Westin drags wire and cutters out and tosses them to the ground.

"I don't see any cattle caught in the fence," he says.

I lift my head, inhaling. There's no scent of coyotes, but we're downwind. I scan the dark horizon. I don't worry often about wolf kills, but it can happen up here in the mountains. It's possible something got to the bull first and dragged it off before we arrived.

"Could be dogs," Westin says.

"Could be," I agree.

We had an attack earlier in the year. Dogs from the Garrison farms had broken through the gate and taken down one of our calves. I went to Thomas Garrison's farm with the remainder of the animal's carcass and a shotgun.

"I'll shoot anything that comes over that property line again," I told him. "Man or animal."

I don't like the way the western pasture feels tonight. It's the only pasture that borders the Garrison Ranch. It provides direct access to my land as well as a shared source of water that comes down from the mountain.

Westin shrugs and starts unraveling the wire. I join him and we work in silence. Bringing the broken portion of the fence together and pulling it tight. When we're finished, we head back down the mountain, both barely awake.

"What happens if she never replies to you?" he asks.

Westin is the only person who knows everything. When I got home after meeting her, I couldn't sleep. So in the early morning, I went outside and he found me sitting on the porch staring at the silhouette of the mountains. He asked me what was wrong, and I told him that come hell or high water I was going after Clint's wife. He didn't judge me, just like I don't judge him.

"She'll answer me," I say. "And if she doesn't, she will as soon as she realizes she isn't safe."

He clears his throat, brows pensive. "Are you afraid the Garrison brothers will get to her first?"

Yes, the truth is, I am. But I can't force her hand...yet. I have to give her an opportunity to come to me before I take her forcibly. She doesn't know what the Garrisons are capable of, that if she stays on her dead husband's land, she's in danger.

"I'm watching her," I say.

"How? Don't tell me you did something weird like assign a guard to her house?" Through the dim light, I see him roll his eyes.

"No, I installed a security camera outside her barn."

"Jesus," he says, but he doesn't berate me about it. He knows if she didn't really mean something to me, I wouldn't have done this.

He's used to the shades of gray we operate in at Sovereign Mountain. There's no way anyone builds the largest ranch in Montana in two decades without stacking the deck and playing a few dirty hands.

And he knows I won't stop until I have what I want.

We didn't get to sleep until past midnight. I wake so early that my eyes burn as I dress for the day and go into my office to check my emails. My laptop is still open on my desk by the window.

I sink down and her name jumps out.

Keira Garrison.

It took her long enough. I rarely have patience for procrastination. Everything in my life runs efficiently and promptly because I've made it do so.

But for the redheaded Garrison girl, I seem to have all the patience in the world.

I have the biggest ranch in the state and everyone asks for favors eventually. That means that all roads lead to Sovereign Mountain at some point.

I'm confident her road will bring her here as soon as she realizes she's out of options.

I crack my neck and click on the email. That last name bothers me to no end. In my last several months of research, I discovered she was the reason my land now directly bordered the Garrison ranch. Before that, I'd shared a boundary with Stowe Farms. She was the Stowe daughter who had inherited the land and married into the Garrison family. She was the reason that land had been annexed into theirs, putting me squarely against their ranch.

Keira Stowe sounds better, and I wonder why she hasn't gone back to her maiden name. Her husband is gone.

Thoroughly gone.

I watched the accident happen. I stood over his broken body and helped load it into the truck to take to the hospital.

Her email loads on the screen.

Dear Mr. Sovereign,

I've thought it over and will accept your request for a business meeting.

I look forward to speaking with you Wednesday.
Kind regards,
Keira Garrison.

The corner of my mouth tugs up. She's trying to be formal, but she's probably never had to arrange a business meeting before. I wonder if my invitation made her nervous. Or maybe she wanted to make me wait.

I cock my head. Normally I don't like to chase. But for this woman, I'll make an exception.

Every night for seven months, I've fallen asleep to the thought of Keira. The irony that I'm pining after a woman with that surname isn't lost on me. Garrison used to be poison on my tongue.

Now I whisper it while I come.

Keira Garrison.

I snap the laptop shut and rise, leaving the office and going back to the bedroom. In the upper dresser drawer is a folded piece of silk. My rough fingertips catch the fine fabric as I unwrap it to reveal a silver chain with three clamps at each end.

I've been collecting things since that night.

Imagining how they'd look on her body. I take up one of the nipple clamps and into my mind flashes the image of it on her breasts. Pinching her pink nipples while I lower my mouth and trace the exposed tip.

I lay the clamps aside and take up the silver collar. It's simple with a circle that will rest between her collarbones. Marking her as taken, as mine.

Someday soon, she'll wear this and I can pleasure her the way she deserves. With my tongue on her pussy, my cock buried in her mouth...in her cunt. But for today, I do what I do best and practice patience. Sliding the drawer shut, I take up my coat and leave the bedroom, hoping chores will give me some relief from my thoughts.

But she's on my mind every second for the rest of the day.

CHAPTER SIX

KEIRA

On Wednesday night, I put on my best dress. I don't go into the city and it's hard to get delivery this far north, so I don't buy a lot of clothes. But I do have a thin cotton sundress made of pink print. The material clings to my body and the ruched neckline makes my breasts look a lot bigger than they are.

I turn in a circle in front of the mirror. I don't normally wear pink, but this shade isn't bad on me.

It's chilly out so I put on a blue sweater and my boots. Then I leave the house and take the truck out onto the main road.

I've never been to Sovereign Mountain, so I put the address into my phone and follow the directions. It's not more than thirty minutes from the entrance of Garrison Ranch, but it feels like hours. I don't see a single car the entire time.

I hate that he summoned me like this. It makes me feel helpless.

I start sweating with the heat on and I struggle out of my sweater, pushing it aside. My fingers tighten on the steering wheel. Knuckles white.

I'm not helpless. I have money in my bank and a lot of land to my name.

I deserve to be treated as his equal.

The driveway up the mountain is long. I lean forward in my seat and go slow. Never sure when the next curve will creep up on me. When I see the pavement even out and turn into a gravel parking lot, I finally sink back and release a sigh.

Not out of relief because my heart is pounding.

I park the car.

The engine dies as I pull the key out.

I scan the empty yard around the house. It's a typical Montana ranch house. Fairly new and sprawling over the size of three normal houses. It has two stories and a wrap around porch on both levels. The wood siding is smooth and stained a rich, dark brown. Over the front door is a plaque with the SMR emblem burned into it.

I get out. The cold bites my skin, but before I can turn to grab my sweater, the front door bangs open.

A huge black dog bursts out and skids to a halt at the edge of the porch. It has bright blue eyes, thick fur, and a pointed nose. I wonder if there's some wolf in there somewhere because it clocks me at once.

I freeze, my heart in my throat.

Of course he has what looks like an attack dog on his porch. I shrink back against the truck and feel around for the door handle.

The screen door pushes out. I snap my eyes from the dog and my body tingles as he appears in the doorway.

He's just as handsome as when I last saw him—maybe more. His square jaw is set, his mouth pressed in a thin, grim line. His beard is short and his dark brown hair slightly wet. Like he washed his hands and ran them wet through the waves. His dark brows, sitting low over his eyes, are not quite a scowl. More a brooding stare.

His broad, muscled body is covered in a dark Henley, the buttons undone, and a pair of worn work pants and boots.

My eyes keep going to his chest. Heat stirs deep in my belly as I notice ink rising up above the collar of his shirt. He's got tattoos. Of course he does.

Suddenly, I feel naked. I'm a curvy woman and the thin sundress only makes that more apparent. I should have worn something that covered my cleavage. My breasts are fighting against the thin fabric.

It's too late for that. I'm here.

He steps out onto the porch and crosses his arms over the broadest chest I've ever seen. His jaw tightens and I think I see a faint glimmer of something like amusement in his face.

"Does your dog bite?" I ask, my voice hoarse.

He whistles once and the dog sits.

"She won't bite," he says. "Myself...I can't promise anything."

My breath hitches. His voice is deep with a hint of gravel. Just as I remembered it. The corner of his mouth turns up and he steps down from the porch, clicking his fingers for the dog to follow. It sprints up ahead and sits directly before me.

I extend my hand. She licks it and her tail wags in the dust.

"She's pretty," I say, petting her silky head. "What's her name?"

He pauses a few steps away. "Big Dog."

I jerk my head up, but before I can speak, I'm overwhelmed by how close he is to me. I can see all the little details of his body. The scar on his knuckles. The faint lines by his eyes. The droplet of water hanging in the waves. The thick hairs on his chest, between the open buttons of his Henley.

He looks big, warm, and solid.

I shiver and his eyes dart down. His gaze is like the brush of hot fingertips. Lava pools in my veins and pushes blood down to where I feel it the most. For a shameful second, the last time I touched myself fills my brain.

I thought about him. Why? I have no idea. Perhaps because I'm so touch starved.

But I thought about him, I fantasized about him turning me around and bending me over the table.

Flipping my skirt.

Dragging his rough palm up my thigh. Slapping my bare ass hard enough I cry out. Peeling my panties from my wet pussy and pushing them down before his fingers sink—

"You alright?" he asks.

I jump. My body feels oddly sensitive. Heat radiates from my face and I shake my hair back, trying to pretend I was just lost in petting Big Dog's head.

"You should name her something else," I say.

He smiles. It's a polite, short curve, like he doesn't know how to do it properly.

"Really?"

"Big Dog implies a Small Dog," I say.

He jerks his head, holding out his hand to point the way to the house. Heart thumping, I follow him up the path and enter the front hallway. The ceilings are tall and the floor is dark wood. Probably harvested from the ranch. I scan the decor as I follow him down the hall, appreciating how tasteful it is. Either he or an interior designer somewhere has a good eye.

He pauses and I almost crash into him. We're at the edge of a spacious living room with ceilings nearly twenty feet tall. Gerard leans in and whistles. From the couch comes a grunt and a tiny black dog that looks like a fox jumps to the floor. It's graying and stiff, but it manages to make its way to us.

"That's Small Dog," he says. "He's got one foot in the grave."

I kneel and Small Dog lets me scratch his chin. "You could give them real names."

"Do you name all your horses and dogs?"

"I don't have a dog." I look up at him. "But I name my horses. Every single one."

He smiles, that polite smirk. "Why?"

I straighten. "All creatures great and small, you know. They deserve to be noticed."

His eyes narrow, but not angrily. It's more of a contemplative look that swallows me up and drags me to the depths of his eyes. In the dark, they're the color of a waning sky. Blue with a hint of gray.

"Are you hungry, Miss Garrison?" he asks.

"Yes, sir," I say quickly.

"We're having roast," he says. "You can wait in the four season porch while I change."

I consider telling him that my name is *Mrs.* Garrison, but I don't have the courage to be confrontational. I still have no clue why I'm here, and that's fraying at my nerves.

He ushers me across the living room and I'm wide-eyed. Taking in the huge, lofted ceilings, the fireplace so tall I could walk into it, and a row of cow skulls over the mantel. Everything is big, even the couches, but that doesn't surprise me. He's a big, broad man and he's built the world to fit him.

He moves me through a rounded doorway and into a dining room. He described it as a four season porch, but that's a bit of an understatement. Everything is dark, expensive wood and the windows that look out over the lake are thick glass and reach from the floor to the ceiling. An oval table takes up the center of the room.

He pulls out a chair. I sit, taking my purse off and putting it in his open hand. It looks tiny in his palm and I can't help but stare as he sets it aside. What size are those fingers? A thirteen maybe? Bigger? It's hard to say.

"Excuse me," he says. "I'll be right back."

He pours me a glass of wine and leaves, his footsteps rising as he heads upstairs.

Movement stirs in the corner of my eye. I glance over and Big Dog is peering into the dining room, head cocked. I lean down and hold my hand out. She doesn't budge, so I click my fingers. The look she gives me is almost disdainful.

"Here, girl," I say.

Big Dog backs up a step and sits. Small Dog is nowhere to be seen, but I think I can hear faint snores coming from the next room.

Maybe his dogs don't like me after all. I flip my palms. They're damp and I notice my heart is pounding. My dress is sweaty under my arms. I hope my deodorant holds up.

The truth is, it's not just being here.

It's what he said, how he looked at me that night seven months ago. Like he wanted to devour me whole.

Maybe it's because the first and only time we met, I told him something I'd never told anyone before—that I was afraid of Clint.

I'd mulled over my accidental admittance for weeks after that. Hoping it never came up again. Hoping he would fade away as quickly as he'd appeared in my life so I never had to address my confession.

So much for that.

Flustered, I click my fingers again. Big Dog yawns, but keeps her hunches firmly glued to the floor.

"Come here," I say, holding my palm out.

"Dogs aren't allowed in the dining room."

I jump, whirling. He's standing at the far end of the room. He must have come from the back entrance, as quietly as a lion stalking its prey.

"Really?" I say, gathering myself. "They never beg for scraps?"

He clears his throat. "My dogs know better."

"That's no fun," I say.

He crosses the room and pulls out the chair beside mine. I hear it creak as he sits down. My eyes drift to the side and run over his chest and shoulders. God, he looks good. His biceps are the size of my head. His chest is wide enough I could comfortably use it as a pillow.

"It's good manners."

"So I'll take it they don't sleep in the bed with you?" I say, jerking myself back to reality.

"They're working dogs."

I glance back to the couch, where Small Dog is sawing logs.

"Is Small Dog retired?" I ask.

"No," he says. "But he's never won employee of the month."

I laugh and his head snaps up, those pale eyes glittering. Like I did something right. At that moment, a woman in her sixties appears pushing a cart.

She pulls up beside me, and I offer her a smile which she doesn't return. There's suspicion in her eyes as she sets down a plate and lifts the lid to reveal roast beef, vegetables, and whipped potatoes.

45

"I've never had beef from Sovereign Mountain Ranch," I say. "Let's see if it holds up to Garrison cattle."

"It holds up," he says. "And Maddie makes the best roast you'll ever have."

"Thank you," she says, a hint of pride in her voice.

She finishes serving us and leaves. Gerard pours himself a glass of water, ignoring the wine. Then he sits back and spreads his knees. I try not to stare, but it's hard when his body takes over the regular sized chair and makes it look small.

"Let's cut to the chase," he says.

My mouth feels dry and I try to wet it with a sip of wine. "Okay."

"You are underwater in debt, Miss Garrison."

A ripple moves through me, but I'm unsure if it's shock and disbelief.

"No, I'm good," I say slowly.

"I take it your husband never told you that he took a mortgage out on your ranch and I own the bank he did it with," he says.

"No," I squeak.

"And it hasn't been paid in months."

"Okay," I say frantically. "I can pay it. Just get me the paperwork."

His lids flicker. He plants one arm on the side of his chair and I'm temporarily distracted by the bulge of his bicep. It's incredibly hard to focus on my world crashing down while he's wearing a t-shirt that doesn't properly fit him.

"You can't pay this," he says.

He's not mocking me, he's just stating a fact.

"How much?" I lick my dry lips.

"A quarter of a million dollars," he says.

"In total?" My voice cracks.

"No, that's the payments from the last year and a half," he says. "The mortgage is a total of twelve million dollars. Your husband sold off portions adjoining my land, or it would be a lot more."

He'd sold part of the ranch?

My body is cold around the edges. My heart beats so fast it feels like it's trying to jump right out of my ribs.

How could Clint have done this? The Garrison Ranch was doing so well, our bills were paid...at least I'd assumed they were. Why had he risked everything and gotten into such a sickening amount of debt?

Was this why I'd been left everything in the will?

Because it was worth nothing?

My hands clench and my vision goes dim at the edges. I turn and Big Dog's face swims in my vision. Gerard leans in and his rough hand cups my elbow, gripping it hard.

"Miss Garrison," he says. "Are you alright?"

I turn on him. "*Mrs.* It's Mrs. Garrison."

The deep furrow between his brow appears and his mouth presses together. I try to sit up, but my head spins. My torso feels like it's sinking beneath water and I can't get my lungs to expand.

"I can't breathe," I gasp.

The last thing I remember is reaching in my pockets for the painted mare.

But she isn't here, I left her on my bedside table. I came here alone.

CHAPTER SEVEN

GERARD

She faints and I catch her, letting her body slump into my chest. For a second, I sit there holding her, but she doesn't wake. I roll her over and check her pulse. She's breathing, but deeply.

She's totally out cold.

Fuck.

I hadn't meant to do that. I gather her soft body in my arms and carry her through the living room where Small Dog lifts his grizzled head and stares through his milky eyes. I send him and Big Dog a look and they both stay where they are, watching me as I carry her upstairs.

The guest rooms are done up, but I don't bring her to any of them. Instead, I keep walking down the hall to the door at the end and push it open with my boot. She's in a flimsy, little sundress. She needs the warmth of my fireplace.

I lay her in the center of my bed and pull the woven blanket up from the end, wrapping it around her lap. Then I turn the gas on and the fireplace showers the room in warmth. I shoot a text to Maddie, asking her to make tea and toast and bring it up to my room.

When I turn, my chest tightens.

I'd left her husband's house seven months ago haunted. Something about this girl has split fractures through my rock solid world.

Whatever it is, I've thought about this moment for a long time. I wanted her here at Sovereign Mountain. In my room, in my bed. Just not under these circumstances.

She stirs and her lids flutter. She's got the prettiest pair of blue eyes and dark gold lashes. Her red hair falls around her shoulders in a cascade. I'd caught a hint of its scent when I'd lifted her. Sweet and smelling faintly of pomegranate shampoo.

"Feeling alright?" I ask.

She looks around. I know my room is probably overwhelming with its tall ceilings, roaring fireplace, the window that showcases the sweeping mountains, and the bull skull above the hearth. I glance back to where her eyes are glued behind my head.

I preserved the skull from the biggest bull we ever had at Sovereign Mountain. It was an anomaly, a Goliath of an animal. I'd kept it for breeding and when it died, I'd sent its head away to be scraped clean.

Now it hangs over my fireplace. A trophy of success.

"Where am I?" she manages.

Her chest heaves and I allow myself the luxury of one look. She's curvy and I know that, despite how big my hands are, her tits would fit in them perfectly.

"My room," I say. "You passed out."

Her eyes widen and she tries to sit up, but I shake my head. To my surprise, she obeys. Sinking back on the pillows.

"That's right," she says weakly. "I owe you a hundred million dollars."

"Twelve million."

"It could be my immortal soul at this point."

What about her body? I cock my head. Her dress is flimsy and I can see her curves straining against it. What size are her tits? It's been such a long time since I fucked anyone, I'm not good at guessing anymore.

"I have a way out for you," I say.

Her eyes dart up. "If it's not total forgiveness or death, I probably can't pay it."

I laugh, shaking my head. "I need to be able to talk to you about this without sugarcoating it."

She nods. "You can. I'm sorry I fainted. I think I'm just hungry."

"Maddie is bringing you food and tea."

She sighs, nestling back and gripping the blanket. She looks good in my bed.

I drag a chair around to the side of the bed, flip it, and sink down backwards. She stares at me and I see her throat bob. Her cheeks go faintly pink and she looks away.

"Your brothers-in-law are going to come after you," I tell her. "I'm breaking confidentiality by telling you this, but they will try to buy you out. And if they can't buy you out, they'll hurt you. They'll frighten you into submission until you cave to them. If you're not dead."

She gasps. "Avery and Thomas aren't like that. They're bullies, but they're not dangerous."

She's so innocent. She hasn't sat across from the Garrison brothers and faced the glitter in their eye as they presented their offer to buy her out. The only thing that kept me from blowing their heads off were the dozen bank officials seated with us.

"She'll sign," Avery said. "One way or the other."

I didn't make it to where I am by putting my head in the sand. I can read men like him like an open book. He would start by financially pressuring her, then he would threaten. Then he would hurt her. I saw his family hurt women like Keira without a second thought.

She doesn't understand the danger she's in.

"Avery and Thomas Garrison are not your friends," I say. "It's my professional opinion that you shouldn't speak or interact with them. You leave that shit up to me."

Maddie knocks on the door and I go to take the tray. Her forehead is furrowed and she sends me a curious look, but I just thank her and shut the door. Sliding the lock down so we're not interrupted.

I put the tray of buttered toast, soup, and hot, black tea with cream before her. I expect her to balk, but she starts eating right away. Tearing the toast and sopping it in her soup before pushing it into her mouth. As I sink back into my chair, I can see the glow return to her face.

"I want you to live at Sovereign Mountain," I say.

She goes still for a long moment. She's got butter on the tip of her thumb and she slowly licks it off. Flashing the tip of her tongue.

"Why?" she asks.

"For protection."

Her brow rises slowly. "Are you trying to take my land too?"

I shake my head. "Technically, it's my land until you pay the mortgage. No, I want something else, Miss Garrison."

She keeps eating toast, watching me owlishly. She must have been starving, she barely got a chance to eat downstairs.

"Okay," she whispers. "What do you want?"

"You," I say. "In exchange for my protection and a hold on all repayments until our contract is over."

Her jaw drops and she goes crimson. We sit there in stunned silence for a moment and when she wipes her hands, I see them shake.

"I'm not paying you with sex," she says.

"It's not like that," I say. "I want you as my submissive."

She levels a blank stare on me. Okay, so we're starting from square one.

"Do you know what that means?" I ask gently.

She blinks, jerking her head. "Yes, I know what it means. I've watched movies and read...you know, books."

I smile. "Dirty romances?"

She shrugs. "So what if I did?"

It strikes me as...cute, although I'm not the sort of man who usually finds anything cute. I've been on Sovereign Mountain for so long that most things are just...grim. I haven't seen anything as beautiful, as soft, and, well, cute, as she is up here in a long time.

She shifts her thighs, squeezing them together for half a second. I catch the movement and I know what it means. She's turned on by my proposition.

Now I just have to get her to admit that.

Maybe if I can get her to play once, she'll see how good I can make her feel. That I can offer her so much more than just protection.

"Is that what you like?" she asks hoarsely.

"Do I like being a dominant?" I ask. "Yes, that's why I want you as a submissive. I pick and choose my partners carefully and I've wanted you as mine for a while."

It's not the whole truth, but she doesn't need the exact details. She swallows hard. Her fingers tug at the blanket. Tearing the threads.

"This is really important for you," she says quietly. "I guess I wasn't aware people did this seriously."

"People take BDSM relationships seriously," I say. "Some more so than marriage."

That makes her chew on her lower lip. "It's not legal, is it?"

"No, not at all. It's an honor system."

"You strike me as the sort of man who takes that seriously."

"Deadly."

She stares at me, still making a meal of her lower lip. Then she shakes her head hard enough to make her hair fall over her breasts. That's probably a good thing because now they're out of sight and out of mind.

"How long do I have to stay?" Her brows draw together.

"I think a year would buy you all the former Stowe land," I say. "During which, you won't pay anything on the mortgage, I'll handle that. And you'll be safe here."

"And if I want out?" Her voice is small.

"You can leave, but your payments will resume. And I can't protect you out there."

Her eyes glisten and I know she's fighting back tears. A part of me wants to have mercy on her, she's innocent. But the bigger part knows this is the only way. If I don't get this woman somehow, I'm going to lose my mind. She's all I can think about.

I can't live like this anymore.

"No, no, I can't do that," she says huskily, wiping her eyes.

"Why?"

"You don't know me."

"I probably know you better than you think."

That is an understatement. I get to my feet and cross the room to my workspace. I have a copy of the proposed contract on my desk. Her eyes bore into my back as I flip through it and make sure it's in order.

"Take a look at it," I say, walking over and tossing it into her lap. "I think you'll find it more than fair."

She picks up the folder, but doesn't open it. "So my brothers-in-law get a real meeting, in an office, about the future of my ranch. And I get a meeting in your bed with my body as collateral? Seems fair."

I gaze down at her, admiring her spirit. "It's not fair. I never said it was. And you know why it's different between us."

Her breath hitches, her lips part.

"Why is it different?" she says. "Sir."

I sink to my knees by the bed, just a little shorter than she is, and look up into her face. "Because I want you," I say quietly. "Because you're in danger and you need my protection."

"If you were a good man you'd offer me protection for free," she whispers.

"Who told you I was good?"

She swallows hard enough I see her throat bob and her knuckles go white on the folder. My eyes fall to the rise of her thighs beneath her thin dress. I'm so close...all it would take for me to see what I've fantasized about for months is for me to spread those thighs and pull her panties to the side.

Is she wearing any? She doesn't seem like she'd go without, not in a dress that short.

I'm hard and I stand, not caring if she sees what she does to me. "I'll let you sleep and mull this over," I say. "I'll take the guest room tonight."

She bites her lip, like she's considering something. "You can...sleep here."

I lift my brow, looking down at her, trying to read her face. "You trying to fuck me, Miss Garrison?"

She flushes dark pink and shakes her head hard. "No, but it's a big bed. We won't touch."

I laugh once. "I'll take the guest room."

Her eyes follow me as I gather up my sweatpants and head for the door. I have a lot of patience and self control, but not enough to spend the night beside her and not break. She makes a little noise in her throat and I pause in the doorway. She's curled up against my pillows, arms wrapped around her bare thighs.

Eyes big, like she doesn't want me to go.

"You need anything, I'll be in the room at the far end of the hall," I say.

She nods.

"Um...thank you," she whispers.

"I haven't done anything for you yet," I say. "But give me what I want and you'll have plenty to thank me for."

She shifts, chewing the inside of her mouth. "How do you want me to thank you, Mr. Sovereign?"

Is she baiting me? I narrow my gaze, stepping out into the hall. It's become clear in the last few minutes that she wants me, but she's confused. She doesn't know if she can trust me yet.

Probably because I just asked her to trade her body for protection, a bit of forgiveness, and a plot of land.

"Read that contract," I say. "Goodnight."

I shut the door and stride down the hall. Instead of going to the bedroom, I push open the doors to the game room and shut them behind me. I'm not a smoker, but fuck...every time I go near her, I feel like I need a cigarette. I know there's an old pack in here somewhere and I retrieve it and kick open the balcony doors.

The stars are bright. Up to my left are the distant bumps of the cliffs, barely visible. The night feels just like it did seven months ago, when I pulled off on the side of the highway.

I think that was the moment when I decided to make her mine.

I've been patient. Now I see the fruits of my labor so close I can almost sink my teeth in and feel the juice drip down my neck. I see that she wants me too, even if she doesn't know it yet, and that makes me want to snap and eat her alive.

Instead, I wait. Patience is my only virtue.

There will be no sleeping tonight. I doubt there will be until I'm in my bed with her beside me, so I stay where I am for a long time after my cigarette is done.

Watching the moonrise over Sovereign Mountain.

CHAPTER EIGHT

KEIRA

It's early when I wake. I'm still in his bed and I can smell him on the sheets. It's a masculine scent mixed with something more natural. I bury my face in the pillow and breathe it in. My head spins and I sit up sharply.

What am I doing?

I'm still in my thin sundress, but the room is warm and the gas fireplace is still crackling. I shudder as my eyes shift up to the bull skull staring down at me. It reminds me of him. Big, rough around the edges, and intimidating.

I get up and pad silently over the cool hardwood floors to the huge window. Outside, everything is covered in a light layer of frost. The lake steams and a group of ducks float in tranquil silence by the dock. I can see the corner of the barn and the paddock to my left. There's a handful of horses out, one of them a brown and white paint mare.

A shock goes through me.

She looks just like my painted wooden mare. Down to one white sock, a spot over her back and halfway down her face. The only difference is her mane is white instead of auburn.

Is this a sign?

Heart pattering, I turn and duck out of the bedroom and creep silently through the huge house. From somewhere downstairs, I can smell someone cooking in the kitchens. Everyone else, I'm sure, is out in the barn or the fields already.

I slip on my boots in the hallway. Gerard must have brought them downstairs after I fell asleep. I can't remember much after I had my tea and I wonder if he drugged it. I slept better than I have in years.

Probably since before my father's death.

The cool air bites my bare legs and arms. The yard is empty and my shoes crunch over icy grass and mud. I pick my way to the paddock and the horses ignore me, all except for the paint mare. She lifts her head and stares at me from below her forelock.

As I draw up to the fence, she lets out a heavy breath that clouds the air.

We stare at one another and I think I'm in love.

Gravel crunches behind me. I know who it is without turning around. Warmth like a blast of heat covers my shoulders and back, and a heavy weight settles over me. He puts his jacket on me and it smells like him.

I pull his coat closer, feeling shy as I turn to face him. He leans on the fence, the muscles in his arms apparent beneath his shirt, and narrows his eyes at the paint mare.

"She's not fully broken," he says.

I clear my throat. "Where did you get her?"

"Won her at a game of poker," he says. "Some addict gambled away everything he had, plus his horse. I wasn't going to take her, but I saw the way she shied from him. There's no need for an animal to shy from your hand unless it's not been treated right."

"She was abused?" I whisper.

He nods once. "I work with her a few times a week. Progress is slow."

I stare into the mare's eyes, my stomach turning. How could anyone look at such a beautiful animal and want to hurt it? I sniffle and run my hand over my nose and he glances down at me.

"She's alright now," he says.

"What's her name?"

"She doesn't have one."

Why am I not surprised? This is the man who came up with Big Dog and Small Dog. He'd probably call himself Tall Man With Hat if he could.

I feel the corners of my lips tug back in a smile and he looks over and notices. His mouth thins and he turns, but not before I see a glimmer of amusement in his eyes.

"What would you call her?" he asks.

I stare at the paint mare and she stares back. "Angel, maybe. She looks like an angel standing in the frost, with all the steam coming off the lake."

He cocks his head, studying me. "By that logic, should I call you Redbird? I saw you walking across my yard, looking like one of the redbirds at the edge of the woods in winter."

My heart skips and I turn to look at his profile. There's something personal about the word when he says it like that. It feels more intimate than the brush of his hand against my bare skin. My mind spirals, wondering what it would feel like to be in bed with a man like him. Pinned between his hard body and the sheets.

"You don't know me like that," I whisper.

"I could."

I swallow and drag my eyes back to the mare. My pulse thrums and my head feels light. He's an enormous presence just standing beside me in his t-shirt with the misty cloud of his breath hanging before his lips in the chilly air. The implications of his contract are unfathomable. If he can make my body react like this just standing beside him, he could break it if he had a chance to be alone with me.

Door locked. Sheets on his bed pulled back. Big, heavy body between my thighs and hard mouth on my neck.

Beneath my dress, my body curls with heat. It spills through my chest, up my neck, down my thighs. It centers in my core and I feel the urge to let out a little sigh.

I'm rooted to the frozen ground.

Do I want him?

I can't trust my taste in men anymore. After all, I picked Clint. He was quick, talkative, and had a temper like a snake striking. I liked how witty and intense he was. Now, I find I like that Gerard is the exact opposite, not the kind of man I ever saw myself wanting. He's guarded, he moves slowly, as impenetrable as the mountains around us.

He's been hurt. No one builds walls that thick without good reason.

But he doesn't strike me as cruel the way Clint was.

"Maybe you're right," I say, my throat tight. "Maybe I am a redbird."

His brow twitches. "Why is that?"

"I feel...fragile. Like every gust of wind blows me in a different direction."

I hate that I'm being vulnerable with him, but he's listening. And so is Angel. For the first time in fucking years, I'm being heard. It feels extraordinary.

"My wings aren't strong," I whisper.

Clint taught me that. When I lived in the shelter of girlhood, my father told me I was strong, brave, and worth the same as any man. Then came the painful years of growing into a woman and learning that all those words were just a smokescreen to hide a harsh truth.

The world was made for men like Clint, like my father, like Gerard. Not for women like me.

That had become clear to me at age eighteen when I talked back to my husband. He took my hair—the same auburn waves my father had taught me were beautiful and rare—and held me still with a fistful of it. That was the first time he used a part of my body as a weapon to subdue me, but not the last.

"Don't fucking talk to me like that if you can't back it up," he snapped that day.

I wanted to obey him, but the problem was, I wasn't saying anything that wasn't the truth. Usually, I was expressing frustration at my crushing workload. Or simply loitering nearby, hoping for some small scrap of attention from him. But he'd push himself into my space until I felt small. Trying to goad me into hitting first.

"I'm not a man," I begged once. "Stop trying to fight me like one."

He never hit me, but he liked to tell me that a lot. He was a good man for not beating the daylights out of me and I was the bitch who deserved it. That scared me enough to keep my real thoughts to myself.

"You're fucking lucky," he'd hiss. "You're lucky I'm not the kind of man who puts his hands on his wife."

I still don't know what I did to make him hate me with such venom.

I shudder and drag myself out of my memories. This man, standing in his yard with the sun creeping over the mountains, is far more pleasant. I clear my throat and take off his jacket, holding out to him.

"I should go," I say

His eyes fall on my body and I swear I'm on fire. How does he strip me bare with a single glance?

"Let me feed you first," he says.

I shake my head. "I really think I need to go."

He clears his throat. "I'll walk you to the truck."

He holds the coat with one arm and his other drifts to my lower back. Is this normal? Clint usually walked up ahead, his legs much longer than mine.

We stop outside his truck and he opens the door. I turn to say goodbye and he takes a step closer, pinning me between his big body and the front seat.

"Sure I shouldn't take you down the mountain, redbird?"

I stare up at him. My mind is an empty slate. I've never felt such a magnetic attraction to anyone. It doesn't help that one of his hands rests on my hip, and it's making me wonder if he could break me in half.

He has the kind of body I'd like to curl up with on a winter's night. And I'm feeling so cold right now in my thin dress with frost melting on my shoes.

I swallow, lowering my lashes.

"Why do you want this?"

"This?"

"You said you wanted me," I rasp. "As your submissive. Why?"

He's silent and when I look up, he's gazing over the cab of my truck. That's how tall he is. After a moment, he clears his throat and narrows his ice blue eyes.

"It's not complicated," he says. "You're a beautiful woman."

His guard is back up, and I know he's using it to hide the truth. Does he want me because Clint died on his land? Is this some kind of honor code where he feels an obligation to care for me and this is his odd way of doing it?

I don't put much weight on that theory.

With one arm, he lifts me into the driver's seat and spreads my sweater over my lap. Before I can react, he turns the car on and slips something into my passenger side. I glance over and scowl. It's a folded envelope.

That damn contract.

"Just read it, redbird," he says.

He shuts the door, and I watch him head back to the barn. He's in his work pants, boots, and a Henley the color of his eyes. The morning sun glints off his dark hair.

My hands grip the steering wheel until my knuckles go white. I guide the truck down the driveway and around the bend, going slow down the hill in case there are patches of ice.

The road is scraped and salted.

I glance around as I drive, taking in the pastures of clean, healthy cattle and horses. I've spent my life on ranches and I've never seen one so well cared for. He's meticulous and he has a firm grip over Sovereign Mountain and all the surrounding counties.

There's natural dominance and care to the way he does everything.

Is that why he wants a submissive and not a girlfriend? Because that way everything is spelled out for him in a contract? Maybe he really does just want to sleep with me, but he doesn't do the messiness of hookups. That's too bad for him because if he'd been straightforward and never brought up a contract, I'd have fucked him stone cold sober.

It doesn't occur to me until I'm back at Garrison Ranch that despite him not being able to name his horses or dogs, he found a name for me without trouble.

Redbird.

CHAPTER NINE

GERARD

I can't sleep. The night she leaves, I lie in the same spot she slept in my bed. When I turn my head, I swear I can smell the soft pomegranate scent of her hair.

Seven months of waiting, watching, obsessing. Weeks of planning and she walked right into the belly of the beast and spent the night. Like I'm someone she can trust.

And I still can't sleep.

It's past midnight when I get up, put on my clothes and coat, and head to the barn. Shadow stands with his head hanging over the stall door. When I run my hand over his neck, he blows hot breath out in a white cloud. His whiskers prickle my palm as he rests his muzzle in my hand.

"We're both up," I say. "Let's clear our heads."

I tack him, mount up, and hang the electric lantern in front of me in the saddle. Shadow and I have taken late night rides for years. He's a quiet, stoic horse who enjoys the stillness of the mountains while everyone is asleep.

Tonight, I have an itch, and not even the moonlight and frosty air scratches it.

It's an hour later when I see the rise of smoke in the distance from Garrison Ranch. At first, it looks like it could be coming from her chimney. Then I realize there's far too much for that. I squint and click my tongue, sending Shadow forward. He feels my mood shift and his gait goes jumpy, forcing me into a posting trot. We crest the hill over the river and he skids back, rearing up on his back legs for a second.

My center of balance is thrown back. My instincts kick in and my abdominal muscles tighten as Shadow's front feet hit the ground. We can both tell something is wrong, and it's making him want to move. I keep my weight steady, forbidding him from running.

At first all I see at the bottom of the hill is a blur of orange. Then I blink and it comes into focus.

Fuck.

The barn is burning.

Flames spill from the front door, eating at the wood. Casting shadows across the yard.

She's alone in that house, probably asleep oblivious to the danger she's in. Or she's in the barn trying to save her horses. She said she'd named each one, there's no way she'll leave them inside.

I rip my hat off and dig my heels in. My legs tighten and Shadow shoots forward, slipping to a gliding gallop. The path down the hill with the fence to my right is clear and Shadow takes it easily. The wind bites my face and my eyes water.

We careen around the corner. The yard gate is shut, but Shadow doesn't stop. His hoof beats thunder over the dusty ground and he soars over the fence, landing with an earth-shattering impact on the other side.

We skid to a halt by the truck. I dismount before he's at a full stop and throw his reins over the horn in case he needs to run. He'll go home if he spooks, he knows his way around the mountains.

The barn crackles. The heat sears my face as I run up the porch and try the lock. It doesn't budge, so I back up and throw my shoulder against it. The wood groans, but stands firm.

Fuck this. I kick it in, right above the knob, sending wood shards flying.

As I enter, I almost collide with a small, soft body. Keira darts back, her eyes wide, and hits the light switch. She's in her nightclothes, a short white slip, and her hair is a tangled mess of red. Her eyes are frantic. She reminds me of my unbroken mare, Angel, when I first brought her to Sovereign Mountain. Wild with terror, unreachable.

"My horses," she gasps.

"Get into the yard," I order. "Stay with Shadow."

Her feet are bare and she's barely covered, but she obeys. I practically carry her down the steps and when she sees the barn, she starts fighting me. Her chest heaves and her nails come out. Shredding my shirt as she tries to get away. I keep pushing her further from the barn and house, forcing her to where Shadow waits.

"My horses," she screams. "My horses are locked inside."

"I know, I'll get them," I say, pulling her back. "But only if you stay with Shadow."

She twists and I grab her wrists, yanking her against me. Our eyes lock and I send her a look that makes her go still. She's crying and I'm not sure she knows it. Tears stream unchecked down her face.

"Please," she whispers, chin shaking. "Please."

"Stay here," I say, my voice low and urgent. "Do not move. Or I'll have to pick between saving you or the horses. You know which I'll pick."

She nods, running her hand under her nose. I pick her up and put her up on Shadow and she grips the saddle horn. Shadow is a giant at seventeen hands tall and her body looks so small up there. But it's the safest place for a quick getaway, and I know he'll bring her back to Sovereign Mountain.

He gives me a sharp nicker. I move past him and head for the barn.

I hear her quietly sobbing as I circle the building. The side door is still intact. I take off my jacket and wrap it around my hand before touching the metal door. It slides back to reveal crackling flames on the far side by the front door. The horses hit their hooves against the

65

doors, throwing their heads. The whites of their eyes catch the fire like coals.

Ignoring the sweltering heat, I bolt to the far end closest to the flame and rip the bar off the first stall. The chestnut horse inside bursts free and tears into the darkness outside. One after the other, I free each one. Their thundering hooves fill the air as they race into the void.

They'll seek shelter in the mountains and I can go after them later.

The barn is too hot and the smoke is so thick I can barely see. My skin burns like it's been striped raw and my eyes stream. My shirt is soaked in sweat and dusty with ash and I can feel the heat through it.

I need to get out now.

Yanking the last stall door open, I send the final horse out through the back door. I'm right behind it, circling the barn and skidding to a halt. A second set of flames fills my vision, smaller than the first, but just as deadly.

The back of the house is on fire.

How is that possible?

It hits me right then that this wasn't an accident and I have a pretty good idea of who's responsible. This wasn't an electrical fire or a careless cigarette. Someone did this and their target is alone right now. Sitting on my horse in her front yard.

My chest tightens.

Not again.

They took everything from me once. I won't let them do it again.

I break into a full run and see her, climbing down from Shadow. She couldn't be obedient this one time?

She starts running towards the house on her bare feet and I catch her before she gets to the porch. Wrapping my arms around her waist and lifting her from her feet.

She screams, arcing. Her fists pound my back.

"It's all I have," she wails. "Please, Gerard, it's all I have."

It's not.

She has me. Whether she likes it or not.

I carry her ruthlessly back to where Shadow waits and put her down. She wrenches herself back and attempts to dart towards the house, but I grab her wrist and pull her into my chest. Turning her so she can't see the flames eating the back of the house.

"It's just bricks and wood," I tell her. "It's not worth it, redbird."

She sobs, hyperventilating. Her chest heaves in until it's concave and she's barely able to breathe. Her hands shake in my grasp, her eyes wide like a deer in headlights. I brush her tangled, sweaty hair back and cradle her face.

"Breathe for me," I urge.

"It's all I have," she gasps out. "I've never had anything until this. I have no home...I have no one."

I grip her shoulders and pull her against my chest. Her entire body goes still. I wonder if she can hear my heart pound against my ribs as her breathing eases. She's no longer struggling for air the way she was, but I feel her shake like a leaf in the wind.

"I will take care of you," I say into the top of her head. She smells of smoke and pomegranates.

There's a long silence.

The fire crackles on.

"Why?" she whispers, sniffing. "Why will you take care of me?"

I want to have the words. God, I wish I had them. But that part of me is calloused and dead. If I had the ability to speak my emotions, I could say all the foolish things I'd felt since I'd laid eyes on her. That she was the first woman in twenty years who'd made me feel human again. That I was used to loneliness and she was the opposite of that.

But I don't know how.

That's why I need her to sign the damn contract.

Then she'll be mine. Then I can sink with her into the type of intimacy that I understand.

One with structure. Rules to keep her safe.

But without the safety of those rules, that contract, I can't do anything but hold her body against mine.

The barn burns on and fills the dark sky with smoke. Sparks shower like fireworks over the yard. I step back and lift her chin, wiping her sticky face. Her eyes are glassy like she's slowly checking out. I hope she's not going into shock.

"You're cold as ice, redbird," I say hoarsely. "I'm taking you home."

CHAPTER TEN

KEIRA

My cheek presses against his chest and the wind stings cold on my back. My eyes sting so badly I can't open them. The front of my body is warm where he burns through his shirt and my back is numb. He had a coat when he arrived. It must have fallen in the barn.

In my curled hand, pressed against my chest, is the painted mare. She was the only thing I took when I ran down the stairs.

His hand is on the back of my head and his arm is locked over my spine. Keeping me tight to his body. Beneath us, his enormous bay gelding runs like he's never been allowed to. I feel the sleek rhythm of his gallop, four beats like a drum through my body, and it lulls me like the rocking of a cradle.

Inside, I'm empty.

No fear, no sadness.

Just a void that hurts worse than anything.

Sometimes Garrison Ranch felt like a prison, but when I inherited it, it became my home. I know the name of every horse that's now wandering through the darkness. I can ride that property line with my eyes shut.

Now my home is gone after only seven months of being mine. Washed away in my scream of terror and black smoke billowing up to the sky. I doubt there will be anything left when the sun rises.

We don't stop until we're in the barn at Sovereign Mountain. Gerard hits a buzzer just inside the door and a moment later, I see a light flick on in the gatehouse on the other side of the driveway. I lift my head just as he dismounts, taking me with him and setting me on my feet. I sway and his arm slides around my waist.

Am I in shock?

I lean into him, seeking his heat and he curls me into his chest. A dusty blanket is wrapped around my body and I hide the painted mare deep inside. It feels childish to be holding a toy. Footsteps sound. Around the corner comes a tall, fit man with chestnut hair. His belt isn't done and he's fastening a flannel with the buttons lopsided. I can tell by his messy hair and red eyes that he was fast asleep.

"Is that the Garrison girl?" he asks.

Gerard nods. "I need you to cool down Shadow and put him away. He's breathing hard and he's soaked."

"What happened?"

He lifts me in his arms and I flail, grabbing onto his shoulders. "Someone, and I have a pretty good idea who, burned the house and barn. I got her out and released the horses."

"Garrisons?"

"I wouldn't be surprised."

I hear them, but dimly. The idea that my brothers-in-law would try to kill me and my horses sounds far-fetched.

The man doesn't stay for introductions. He takes Shadow's reins and heads to the back of the barn. Gerard carries me across the driveway and around the back entrance of the house. I hear the dwindling clip clop of Shadow's hooves. My eyes flutter shut.

"Who is that?" I whisper.

"Westin Quinn, my property manager," he says.

"Is Shadow hurt?" I murmur.

He shakes his head and gives a short laugh. I can hear the rumble deep in his barrel chest. Warmth blossoms inside and starts to melt the numbness.

"Shadow's gone on harder runs than that," he says. "He'll get cooled down and spend tomorrow resting."

"Are you hurt?"

"No, redbird, I'm not hurt."

He kicks the back door open and enters the hall. His housekeeper, Maddie, appears at the end of the hall, wringing her hands. I know I must look terrible. Dirty, sweaty, in just my night slip. I probably smell terrible too.

"Can you make a tray up like last time?" Gerard asks.

She nods. "Right away."

His boots ring out as he carries me up the stairs and into his bedroom. A sense of safety creeps over me as he sets me down. He walks past me and pushes open a door on the opposite end of the room, revealing a bathroom.

"Let's get you cleaned up," he says.

I hesitate. "May I have privacy?"

He turns on the shower and steps out. I slip into the bathroom, but he pushes his boot in the door when I go to close it.

"Leave it cracked," he says. "I don't want you passing out in the shower alone."

There's no point in arguing. He's one of those belligerent men with a head thicker than wood.

I nod, pushing it until it's just ajar, and duck behind it. I know he could easily see through the opening and catch my reflection in the mirror, but I don't care. I'm cold and shaken and I want to sleep so badly. I want to take two Benadryl and fall into a stupor that lasts hours.

I fold the painted mare into the blanket from the barn and lay it on the chair. Then I strip naked and drape my slip over top, hiding her away.

My head aches as warm water spills down my sore body. When I close my eyes, all I can see is orange fire and the shadows of my horses disappearing into smoke.

Grimly, I wash my hair and body until I don't reek. When I step out, I notice there's a light gray sweatsuit sitting on the floor. I try it on, surprised to find it's my size. The soft fabric is a balm to my shocked body. I lift my hand and turn it, studying the little Sovereign Mountain insignia embroidered on the left cuff.

He's got his name on everything, now he's got it on me.

Shyly, I leave the bathroom. He's on his phone, standing by the fireplace. My stomach flips. His profile is gorgeous. Big arms and hands. A flat stomach and broad chest that rises to a thick neck. Hair slicked back with sweat and short beard shading his jaw until it looks like stone.

He sees me and sets aside the phone.

"Gerard," I whisper.

He clears his throat. "What is it, redbird?"

"What about my horses?" My throat feels raw and my eyes burn.

He moves across the room and touches me and my whole body warms. His rough palms slide up my forearms and cradle my elbows. He's so tall I have to crane my neck back to look up into his face.

"I promise I'll send out my best in the morning," he says. "Horses are smart. They'll be fine until we find them."

There's a knock at the door and he goes to retrieve the tray from Maddie. Like last time, he doesn't let her in. I wonder if he lets anyone but me into his bedroom.

I'm hungry and limp as the shock wears off. Exhaustion makes me bold, and I crawl into his bed, sitting up against the pillows. If he's surprised, he doesn't show it. He just sets the tray in my lap and points to the food.

"Eat," he says. "I'm going to shower."

He shuts the bathroom door and I look around, stunned. Sovereign Mountain feels different than last time. More like a real home. Maybe because before I had a choice to stay or leave, but now I have nothing to go back to. Either I stay here with Gerard

Sovereign or I take the little money I have left, beg him to defer my debt, and try to find another place to call home.

A minute ago, I was so tired I couldn't keep my eyes open.

Now I'm buzzed.

I sink down and start eating the buttered toast. My stomach growls, but the hot food goes right to my soul. Soothing my shock. It's gone by the time the bathroom door opens and he appears in a pair of sweats and a t-shirt. His hair is wet and pushed back. A trickle of water moves down past his ear and etches along his neck.

Every ridge of his stomach is visible through the worn, gray t-shirt. It's tight on him. I'm sure most clothes barely fit that broad body. Maybe he has to order them custom.

He notices me staring and tosses the towel in his hand aside.

"You still hungry, redbird?"

I shake my head, wordless.

There's something about the way he said that word that sets me alight and soothes me at the same time. His voice is hushed and hoarse. It's so familiar. Like in another life he said that word to me and it's still echoing through my memory.

"Say it again," I whisper.

His pupils dilate.

"Redbird," he says.

My body wants comfort, and he looks like a sanctuary. It's been such a long time since I've craved sex, perhaps because Clint stopped wanting me and turned elsewhere. Nothing is more humiliating than begging for attention from a man. So I stopped early on and let him come to me when he wanted it. After a while, it was a relief when he didn't reach for me.

I won't beg for Gerard Sovereign either.

If he wants me, he'll take me.

He picks up the tray and sets it aside. Behind him, the bull skull glowers over the fireplace. His body moves close and fills my vision, sitting down on the edge of the bed. My breath hitches and his eyes drop as my breasts heave.

"Do you need to see a doctor?" he asks.

73

His words feel so out of place in the tense room. I shake my head.

His hand comes up, touching a thick strand of my hair. My eyes flutter closed. He'd called me a redbird, a spark of color against the winter. Has he lived in the cold for so long on Sovereign Mountain that he needs a sign of hope?

That's what a redbird is—hope.

I crack my lids and study his face, tracing the laughter lines with my eyes. I count a few strands of gray hair by his ears. He'd look better with it cut very short. He's got one of those hard, bullet heads I find so attractive and I want to see the shape of it.

I want to run my nails down the back of his scalp, and slip my fingertips over his broad, muscled shoulders. He's so effortlessly powerful and right now, I'm broken.

I'm tired of being strong. I tried for so long and I'm fucking done.

"Fuck me," I breathe.

His eyes snap up. "What?"

Before I can lose my nerve, I pull the sweatshirt over my head and toss it to the ground. I hear his breath hitch and a flush creeps up his neck. His gaze falls and stays glued to my naked breasts.

His hand comes up and I tense, my body tingling. But it moves past me and taps the nightstand. The lights flick off and we're left with nothing but the fireplace. It floods the room in an orange glow that cuts heavy shadows down his face and nose.

He clears his throat. "If that's what you want, redbird, I won't tell you to change your mind."

My body is empty, especially that place between my thighs that hasn't been filled in so long. When I shift my hips, I can tell I'm soaked just from the thought of sex with him. I want him to break through to me like he broke down my front door.

"I won't change my mind," I whisper.

He puts his hand against my back and it's so big and rough it sends heat down my spine that centers in my sex. Our bodies move together like we're connected. His other hand slips up the side of my waist and brings me into his embrace, wrapping me in the weight and warmth I've craved for so long.

I let my head fall back over his forearm and his mouth comes down on mine. His lips part and when I taste him my body comes alive. I'd thought it was wide awake before, but that was nothing compared to the burst of sensation moving through my veins.

I've never been kissed like this. His mouth is hard and soft all at once and he tastes faintly of mint. He probably brushed his teeth after his shower. Or maybe he's just that perfect.

When he slips his tongue into my mouth, I moan around it. My hips work and blood pounds through the emptiness between my thighs.

I need it filled.

He breaks off the kiss and his rough palm cradles my left breast. My eyes roll back as he palms it, running his thumb back and forth over my nipple. Teasing it until it hardens beneath his touch. My hips jerk and his eyes fall, watching the tremble in my thighs.

"I've been tested," he says. "We can fuck without a condom."

"I'm not on birth control," I pant, "But I've been tested too."

He picks me up and flips me onto my back on the bed. My sweatpants are off and he's between my thighs under the blankets. The heavy weight of his body shifts over me and it's so much better than I imagined. All that power between my legs makes my head spin.

He bends and catches my nipple in his mouth. Sucking first one and then the other before pressing a kiss on the base of my neck. Each touch sends a tendril of the most delicious pleasure down my stomach. It centers deep in my pussy and I let my head fall back. Wishing he'd slip those big fingers into me and fuck me with them.

Instead, he reaches down to the tie of his sweatpants.

My hand shoots up, bracing against his chest. His winter-blue eyes flick to mine.

"I don't want to get pregnant," I breathe.

"I won't knock you up, redbird," he murmurs, kissing beneath my ear. "I've been snipped."

That isn't what I expect to hear, but to my horny brain and desperate body, it's the best news in the world. My hips lift and I rub them up against his...oh God...up along the ridge of his hard cock beneath his sweatpants.

Fuck, he feels so big and hot.

His hand pushes between us and my lower back arcs as his fingers slide into me. God, yes, it burns like sweet fire. Two big fingers stretch me, slipping gently against my sensitive inner walls. He's looking for something and when he finds it, I moan as he strokes that spot with precision.

I've found that spot myself, but I've never had it touched by a man's fingers. It's so incredibly intimate, especially with his eyes locked on mine in the dark.

I know he feels the slickness and the slow tightening of muscles around him. My desire can't be a secret because he's knuckle-deep in it. Feeling my body from the inside.

His fingers leave me and I almost cry with how empty I am. Then his hips sink down against mine and I feel him push his sweatpants down. My heart pounds. My breasts heave against his chest. I spread my thighs and wrap my ankles around his hard lower back.

He pauses, reaching into the nightstand drawer. Before I can speak, he's uncapped a bottle and he's gently rubbing lube over the entrance of my pussy.

"Am I not wet enough?" I whisper.

"You're soaked," he assures me. "But I don't want to hurt you."

He sets the bottle aside. My stomach quivers with anticipation and my fingers dig into his shoulders. He breathes out, bracing his elbow beside my head. The outline of his head and shoulders fills my vision completely.

He reaches down and I feel it. The hard head of his cock against my entrance.

The tip is warm and smooth and feral need rips through me. More wild than anything I've ever felt. I lift my hips, rubbing my pussy up against the underside of his cock. Begging him to slide it into me and settle it against my deepest point.

I need the emptiness to be gone.

He braces his knee and pushes. Pain splits through my hips and my muscles tense in response. What the fuck does he have down there? A battering ram?

"You're tight, redbird," he murmurs.

Has it really been so long that I've gotten this tight? I just nod because he's pushing the head of his cock into me, forcing me to stretch to take him. A sharp little burn starts at the intrusion and quickly splinters into pain. Tears spring to my eyes and my head falls back. I gasp and dig my nails into his shoulders.

"You're hurting me," I pant.

Our eyes lock.

"I know, redbird," he says.

He pushes again and I arc back. The pain ebbs once and morphs into something else I've never felt before. My head spins as the most intense kind of pleasure blossoms inside. A heady blend of ecstasy and torment.

"Is it too much?" he asks.

I shake my head.

His mouth grazes mine. Mint and Sovereign.

"Good girl, I knew you could take it."

Can I take it? It's probably better I didn't see his cock beforehand because I'd have balked. Now I can only cling to him and let him break me into a thousand pieces.

I focus on my breathing and my muscles ease. Just enough for him to push the rest of the way in. His hips settle against mine and my weak legs spill open on the bed. Shaking too badly to wrap around his waist. He takes my nipple into his mouth and teases it gently, sucking and circling it with his tongue.

The burn leans into pure pleasure. I'm not a virgin, but this is all new to me. This is all consuming. We're on fire and the heat melds us together. Fusing our bodies where they're joined.

I feel my pussy pulse around his intrusion. Easing just enough I'm not cramping anymore. His hips rock and he strokes gently up against my cervix. I never imagined I would like that feeling, but it's new, it's painful, and so incredibly intimate.

I've never been intimate like this, with anyone before.

Sex was just mechanics.

But this...this is being ripped open and laid bare.

He could have warned me. Clearly he knew because he'd used a lot of lube, so he'd expected to be too big for me. I want to be pissed, but I'm too turned on by his lack of concern. He'd known I could take him. He made the choice for both of us without me.

There was something sexy about that. And a little shameful.

I didn't want to be forced.

But I do want him to force me.

How can that be? Confusion swirls in my head and chest. I'm feeling things I've never experienced before, and I can't identify them. I don't have time because he draws out slowly and my mouth parts in a silent cry as he thrusts back in.

"Please," I pant.

He looks as if he can barely feel my fingernails raking down his back. His big body ripples and he thrusts again, forcing me to take him. Pleasure and pain swirl and the only thing I know for sure is I need release. If I can just come, I'll fall over the edge to total pleasure.

His gaze flicks over my face. Then his hand slides between us and my spine arcs as his fingertips find my clit. I'm slippery with lube and his touch moves over me like silk. Our gazes lock, but I can't read him.

My lips part. My eyes roll back.

Pleasure crashes over me in a torrential wave and my entire body shudders. I can't control the spasms as I buck up against him, fucking myself onto his cock. Not caring that he's hurting me. Waves of cramps ebb into waves of desire under his thrusts.

All I want is to be ruined.

My orgasm slows. He shifts and his hand comes up to grip the headboard. The wood groans. He draws his hips back and I feel the power of them as he begins fucking me in earnest.

I cry out.

The bed hits the wall in a steady, loud beat. Sending a shudder through the room. His hand holds the headboard so hard I wonder if he'll break it. The veins on his forearm stand out beneath his tanned skin. Sweat etches down his chest.

I'm either going to come or die.

I'm not sure which.

I've never taken anyone, or anything, this big. And never like this—so brutal and unrelenting. He has a distinctive signature to the way he fucks and it reminds me of a freight train. A relentless beat that throbs through me like the turning of a steel wheel on railroad tracks.

Bang.

Bang.

Bang.

Somewhere inside is a dull throb that aches with every stroke. It's so sweet and it's spreading through my hips. He's bottoming out, the head of his cock stroking up against my cervix as he fucks.

My lashes flutter open and he's so close, his eyes burning with need.

"You're doing so well," he rasps.

I whimper, incoherent.

He relents, shifting his hips so he can look down and see between us. I wish I could see what he does because I know it must be extraordinary. His lips part and his hot breath kisses my face.

"God...girl, you are a pleasure to fuck," he gasps.

He bends and his mouth brushes over the tears tracking down my cheeks. The hot tip of his tongue tastes them. I feel the stutter of his hips, like he's considering easing up on me. My nails dig harder into his back.

"Don't stop," I beg hoarsely. "Make me feel something."

CHAPTER ELEVEN

GERARD

I give it to her the way she wants. Usually, I don't fuck without a dynamic already established, but there's no world where I'm waiting a single night longer. For the last seven months, I've been patient. I've moved the players and the pieces of this game, edging her ever closer to me.

And now she's here, she's willing, and I can't hold back anymore.

Tonight is the first night of the rest of my life with her. She doesn't know it, but this is a consummation.

My fingers circle her clit. Her freckled face flushes and her eyes flutter shut. Tears stream from beneath her lids.

I taste them and kiss her mouth. Salt and sweetness combined on my tongue.

Her spine rises and her body pushes up against mine. Her fingers curl into the pillows. I feel the tremble of an oncoming storm, I see it quiver down her belly and tighten her thighs. Her eyes fly open and lock to mine.

"Oh, God," she whispers.

"Sovereign," I correct gently. "Say my name while you come on my cock."

The depths of her eyes are hazy, but her lips tremble and I hear my name tumble out on her breath. Sovereign. My hips drive against hers. Her hand flies up and slides up the back of my neck. Tangling in my hair so hard it hurts.

She comes, and it's the most beautiful thing I've ever seen.

My orgasm hits me out of nowhere. She's still going, her hips bucking up against my groin, when I feel it rush down my spine. I fall against her, catching myself just in time, and she gasps as she realizes what's happening. Maybe she feels it, the throb of my desire, the warmth emptying up against her deepest point.

We both go still. Our breathing fills the silent room.

"Are you alright, redbird?" I murmur.

She stirs and nods, her hands going to my chest. Her finger trailing through the hair and down to my stomach. Warm tingles follow her touch as it continues down...down...to where we're still joined together.

Fuck. Me.

I feel her finger and thumb attempt to wrap around my length and I fight not to thrust against it. Her eyes widen and I shift my hips back, the head still inside, and let her stroke over the base of my cock. Her exploratory fingers are gentle—I can't remember the last time I was touched so gently.

"You're not what I expected," she says.

I bend and nuzzle her neck. "Neither are you."

Shifting my body, I pull out slowly. She winces and a tremor moves down her thighs.

"I'm going to be sore," she says. "You could have mentioned you have a monster cock."

I laugh, running a hand over my face and sitting up. Her eyes widen as I grip her thigh and move it apart, giving me my first look at her sex.

My groin tightens again even though I've just finished. She's beautiful. And she's bleeding a little, a single smear of crimson on her inner thigh and another at the entrance of her pussy.

I touch it with the backs of my fingers. She's swollen and when I move my fingertips to her opening, she winces. I spread her gently and her stomach tenses, sending my cum trickling onto the bed.

"I'm messy," she whispers.

I stroke up her thigh. "Let's put you in the shower again."

I lift her to her feet and we get into the shower together. It's big so we have space, but she huddles back against me like she's cold. I slide my arms over her breasts and stomach and pull her against my chest. Her soft ass settles over my cock and I let my face sink into where her shoulder meets her neck.

"Why did you get a vasectomy?" she asks.

"That's a question for another time," I say.

"Okay, sorry I asked," she whispers. "I just thought you seem young for that."

I turn her around, brushing soft strands of auburn hair back. She's tied it up in a bun and the stray bits are curling in the steam. "How old do you think I am, redbird?"

Her eyes flick over me and she bites the inside of her mouth. Her forehead draws together and I have the urge to trace the line with my fingertip.

"I don't know," she admits. "You have lines on your face, but they're the sexy kind. It's hard to tell if they're from age or from working outside."

"I like your honesty."

"You have gray hair, but I only saw two."

"So what do you calculate?"

She cocks her head, staring up at me from beneath her hooded eyes. "Maybe...you know what, just tell me."

"Thirty-eight," I say.

Her lips part. "Oh...that makes sense."

I study her quietly, wondering if the gap between our ages is a good or bad thing in her mind. She notices my silence and a slow smile starts on her lips. She cocks her head and sucks in her lower lip like that will keep that smirk off her face.

"You don't know my age either," she says.

I shake my head.

Of course I do, I know when and where she was born. I've seen her birth certificate. But I play along because if she finds out how much I already know about her, she'd be horrified.

"Guess," she says.

I shake my head again. She rolls her eyes and something bolts down my spine and makes my dick pulse. When I have her name on that contract, every time this little redhead sasses me, I get to punish her and make her come until she cries.

"I'm twenty-one," she says. "Almost twenty-two."

I knew it, but hearing it from her lips is different. I've seen her life laid out in certificates, bills, receipts, court documents. Each one more tragic than the last. She's far too young to have suffered so much.

I study her as she watches my face for a reaction. "You're young."

She shrugs. "I was emancipated at seventeen because my father died and I was so close to eighteen. Clint and I married two days after my birthday. At the courthouse in the city."

"Did...why did you marry him?" I ask.

She shrugs. "I thought I was in love with him."

"And you weren't?"

The sigh that escapes her mouth is heavy. Weighted with years of tension.

"I think it faded when I realized all he wanted was my farm," she says. "He absorbed my family's land. I know it was a lot smaller than your ranch or his, but it was my father's legacy and he left it to me. I was really stupid to fall for Clint and sign it over to him. When it sank in that maybe I'd been played, I kind of hated him."

"The farm belongs to me," I say. "Sign that contract and we'll see what happens."

Her brows arch. "So you get to spank me and I get my farm back in a year. Which belonged to me in the first place."

"It's about a lot more than spanking."

She turns back around like she's pouting, but I'm too distracted by that perfect, heart-shaped ass to care. "I'll read the contract in the morning."

I touch the little bump of spine at the nape of her neck. She shivers and I trace all the way down to her ass. My hand dips and cups the soft curves for a second before pressing between her legs. She's slippery with my cum and her arousal and my finger pushes up into her body easily.

Soft heat envelopes the tip. Her head falls back and she moans.

"You have a lot of spirit, redbird," I say.

"I'm thinking I'll sign your contract," she whispers. "As long as there's nothing extreme in it."

"As in?"

"You know, urine and that stuff."

"No, there isn't. That's in the hard limits section. I'm not interested in it."

"Good."

"But the point of you going over the contract is so you can negotiate it with me."

She sighs. "Alright. Let's go to sleep and we can talk in the morning."

CHAPTER TWELVE

KEIRA

My eyes skim over the paper. In no particular order, sentences leap out at me. I'm holding the desk with one hand and sipping coffee with the other. Trying to pretend I'm unbothered while reading the paper, despite the crimson flush creeping up my neck.

The dynamic will remain in place at all times when the submissive and dominant are alone. Outside of those spaces, both participants will behave in a manner that is respectful to the consent of those not involved.

The submissive will refer to the dominant as sir when alone.

The submissive agrees to a maintenance spanking of medium intensity every week on Sunday night, regardless of behavior.

The dominant will provide aftercare for every session regardless of the dynamic or punishment.

There's an entire section on the back of that page labeled COMMUNICATION. I take a breath, straighten, and flip the page over. I expect something equally as surprising, but I'm intrigued by what I find.

The submissive will keep a journal accessible to the dominant at all times. The submissive agrees to be completely honest in writing down their thoughts and emotions. The dominant agrees to never use this material as a reason for punishment.

The submissive agrees to be completely honest with the dominant. Lying or refusing to communicate is considered a heavy offense and will result in punishment.

The dominant agrees never to use the submissive's honesty against them or as a reason for punishment.

My head spins. Maybe Gerard Sovereign should consider being a relationship therapist. Kinkiness aside, these sound like pretty good communication rules.

I take a sip of coffee and glance up. I'm sitting at his desk in his room, overlooking the lake. I took the painted mare from the bathroom and now she's sitting on the corner of the desk, watching me. There was a light fall of snow last night and Gerard is out breaking the ice on the animal's water. He promised to return for breakfast after handing me a coffee and the contract and ordering me to sit and read it.

I flip the page.

Punishment includes spanking over the dominant's lap with a hand or implement. The submissive may not fight or speak unless a safeword is needed.

My breasts tingle. My mind drifts back to the way his hand feels...so big and rough. I have a feeling being spanked with that palm would hurt like hell in the best way.

Other punishment includes delayed gratification, and other safe, agreed upon methods of implementing pain or humiliation.

The dominant will never publicly humiliate or verbally punish the submissive in front of another person. All punishments are to be strictly private.

I have to take another break to focus my attention back out the window. I hear distant laughter and the steady clank of machinery behind the barn. The ranch is operating with perfect efficiency. Now I realize why that is.

Gerard has an attention to detail that amazes me. He's thought through this contract and written up clauses for everything. As someone that struggles not to be messy and chaotic, I'm impressed.

My eyes return to the contract and shift to the next section. This one is labeled DAILY TASKS, ETC.

The dominant will pick the submissive's bra and panties the night before and they will be worn. Failure to abide by this will result in punishment.

The submissive will offer herself to the dominant each night before bed.

The submissive agrees to free use.

The submissive will take care of herself reasonably by eating well, exercising, bathing, and wearing proper clothes.

I'm not sure how I feel about that last part. I flip the page and there's a section called FINANCIAL before me.

The dominant will provide the submissive as much money as needed or desired.

The submissive will never conflate sex and financial compensation. Nor will the dominant.

The submissive will not pay for anything during their time in the contract. When money is needed, the submissive will request it from the dominant.

Hold up...does that mean I won't have my own money? I narrow my eyes and run them over that last line again. Then I grab a highlighter from his desk and swipe it over those words.

Behind me, the door opens and I hear his heavy boots on the floor. My hand shoots out and pushes the mare out of sight. I turn and he's standing by the door, his pale eyes washed out in the light from the window.

He looks so good it makes my heart patter against my ribs.

I clear my throat.

"Interesting contract," I say. "What's free use?"

He shuts the door and walks over to me. I'm sitting down and he's so tall that I'm eye level with his lower stomach. My eyes drop and I can see the faint rise of his groin. Even soft, I can still make out a hint of the monster in his pants.

His fingers slide under my chin. Tilting it up.

"If I walked up to you right now," he says. "Took my cock out and fucked your mouth until I came and then went down to breakfast...that would be one example."

My jaw drops. He slides his thumb up and between my lips. The taste of soap and the feeling of his rough skin fill my mouth.

My pussy aches. He runs his thumb over my tongue in a slow circle. His eyes are glued to my lips and there's a flush at the base of his throat. I like this feeling of being used as he gently strokes the inside of my mouth. Petting me like I'm nothing but a toy here for his pleasure.

Is this what I could feel like if I sign that contract?

He thrusts with his thumb and I feel saliva slip down my chin. It's humiliating, but I keep perfectly still. I don't even move my eyes from his face to see if he's fully hard.

He pulls it out and licks it clean. I'm speechless, rooted to the spot.

"You hungry, redbird?" he asks.

I nod.

"Let's go eat."

Head spinning, I follow him downstairs with the contract in hand. We enter the four season porch, which is empty except for two covered plates of food at the far end closest to the windows. He guides me to the seat beside the head of the table and I sit down meekly. The folder goes on the chair beside me.

I'll have to discuss it with him and I'm dreading that.

He pours coffee. I grip the hot mug in my hand, shifting my eyes out the window. It's so cold there's ice on the glass and I'm grateful I'm inside and not back at Garrison Ranch. There's surely nothing left of my house at this point.

"Have you found my horses yet?" I ask.

He shakes his head once. "No, not yet. We're looking."

My brows scrunch. I feel distantly guilty that I'm in a warm house, in a soft sweatsuit, with a hot cup of coffee in my hands and my horses are out there roaming in the cold.

"It'll be okay," he says.

I nod and bite my lip.

"Your horses know what they're doing," he says. "I wouldn't be surprised if they bring themselves home."

"I won't be there though," I say.

"I have someone watching the ranch. They'll let me know as soon as they see anything."

He pulls the cover off my plate to reveal eggs, sausage, biscuits, and gravy. My stomach rumbles and I pick up my fork and wait. Watching him to see if he's going to eat too. It's already weird enough for me that I'm not eating in the kitchen and I need him to start so I feel less awkward.

He just sips his coffee. I put down my fork.

"Do you have questions about the contract?" he asks.

I nod. "Yeah, I have a lot."

"Fire away."

I lean back in my chair. "I want to keep my bank account. I don't mind if you want to pretend I don't have it, but I'm not letting you strip what little money I have from me."

His jaw works and he dips his head. "You may keep it, but there's no need to use it. I'll pay any and all expenses you have while you're here."

I blink, surprised it was that easy.

"Why aren't you eating?" he asks. "I can have Maddie make you something different."

89

I shake my head, grabbing my fork. "Sorry, I was waiting for you."

He gazes at me for a long moment, but clearly decides not to pursue his thoughts. Guiltily, I start eating. I'm not sure why it's so embarrassing. Maybe because for the last handful of years, I've eaten standing up at the kitchen sink. Shoving my food in as quickly as possible before the men in the dining room needed service.

All it had taken was for Clint to come looking for me once for me to realize I needed to be available until dinner was finished.

"What did you do at Garrison Ranch?" he asks.

I shrug. "I cooked and cleaned. Clint ran it like a bed and breakfast during parts of the year for conferences and business meetings. I was the housekeeper and the cook and he handled the financial stuff."

"That's a lot of work," he says.

I shrug, taking a sip of coffee. "I got used to it."

"Maddie has a whole kitchen staff to help her with that."

"Garrison Ranch is smaller than Sovereign Mountain."

He cocks his head, one hand rested on the table. "Still, that's a lot of free labor your husband got out of you."

I'd never thought of that before, but yes, he had gotten a lot of free labor out of me. He would have had to pay multiple people a lot of money to do my job. I'd gotten up at five in the morning and worked until eleven at night for free. For the privilege of eating a quick meal over the sink three times a day.

Suddenly, I feel both stupid and incredibly grateful that he'd never tried to get me pregnant.

"I made the best of it," I say shortly.

"You won't do any housework here or cooking. Unless you want to, but I prefer you don't. Maddie rules the kitchen, she's paid well for it."

I consider him. Now that my stomach is full and my coffee has hit my veins, I'm thinking more clearly. Last night, I'd fallen asleep open to signing his contract because I'd lost everything. Shock and grief pushed me right into his bed and made me more than willing.

But now that I've had time to recover, I'm determined not be taken advantage of again.

"I want to go over the contract sentence by sentence," I say.

He dips his head.

I draw myself up. He's three times my size, and he's got me right where he wants me. Holding me up like a puppet by the strings. But I still have my dignity and my resolve.

"How about tonight?" I say.

"Now."

His tone is firm. He reaches across the table and touches my elbow. My entire body tingles and the memory of him inside me comes crashing back. Now, in the light of day, I'm not sure why I let him fuck me. Was it this animal magnetism that glowed from him effortlessly? Or just the high of adrenaline?

Whatever it was, it's hitting me again.

I slept with Gerard Sovereign.

No...I *survived* sleeping with Gerard Sovereign with nothing more than soreness and a bit of blood in my panties.

He starts eating. Nothing seems to bother him. I finish my food and wait for him to set his clean plate aside. He wipes his hands and sits back, knees spread. He probably can't cross them properly with what he's packing.

"Let's see that contract, redbird," he says, holding out his palm.

Obediently, I pass it over and he flips it open on the table. It falls to the page where I've highlighted a section in yellow. My stomach somersaults as I realize which part it is.

His eyes fall and they flick back up to me.

"No oral?"

I want to squirm in my seat, but I have to behave like an adult. We're having a very adult conversation and I can't crack under his steel gaze. His mouth thins and his eyes remain on me, pressing me for an answer.

"I don't mind giving you oral," I say. "But I'm...honestly, I don't really like getting it that much."

His face doesn't change. A bit of wavy hair comes free and falls over his forehead. I can't help but think a haircut would look amazing on him. He needs it short to compliment the brutal cut of his jaw.

"I don't believe you," he says.

My jaw drops. "Excuse me? I think I know what I don't like."

"Did Clint take your virginity?"

This time, I squirm in my chair. "Yes," I admit. "I was eighteen when we married."

His face goes hard and something glitters in his eyes that makes my stomach cold.

"Did he fuck you when you were underage?" he asks.

I shake my head. "We waited."

His jaw works. "So...he fucked you at midnight on your birthday?"

My cheeks heat and I draw myself up. "No. It was later."

"That day?"

Defeated, I nod.

He clears his throat, the sound rumbling in his chest. "So you only ever slept with your husband?"

Without realizing it, I'm chewing the inside of my mouth hard enough to draw blood. It spreads over my tongue and jerks me back to reality. My face is so flushed it's probably glowing.

"Yes," I whisper.

"Most likely your husband was just bad at going down on women," Gerard says. "Before we cross it off, let me eat you out so we can take this off the hard limits list."

My brows rise. "You're confident."

"Yes, I am," he says.

His eyes drop to the second highlighted line and his brow arcs. "Let's add anal to the soft limits list as well. I'm not willing to forgo it."

My stomach swoops like I took a tumble. "If you have anal with me, I might die," I say.

He laughs and his gaze lights up. "You won't die. I can train you to take it."

"I don't want to be trained."

He flips the page and sits back again. His gaze falls on me, thoughtful. "That's too bad. You'll have to train to be my submissive. We'll have a month where we work together to figure out our limits, our likes, dislikes. At the end of it, we'll write amendments to the contract. Then I'll collar you."

I feel my eyes widen. How is he saying these things so casually? He must be so deep in this lifestyle it's second nature to him.

"What...do you mean?"

"If you want to be my submissive, redbird, you'll wear a collar. During the day, when others are around, I'll put a discreet collar on you. When we're alone, you'll wear a leather collar with an O-ring. You'll sleep in it, play in it, and when you need to shower, you'll come to me and I'll remove it."

I'm speechless, my mind whirling. What stands out most starkly aren't his words, but the reaction my body has to them. There's a vivid image in my brain of myself kneeling at his feet while he buckles a leather pet collar around my throat.

I swallow and between my thighs, my sore pussy tingles.

"I...I don't know how I feel about that," I whisper.

He leans across, his face intense. His hand slides under the waistband of my sweatpants. Before I can react, he's pushing his fingers between my legs and swiping the tips over the seam of my pussy. When he draws his hand out, I see the glisten of my arousal.

"I think you know how you feel about me," he says.

He licks his fingers, slowly. Like he's savoring the taste of me. Never in my life has a man wanted to taste me and it's a power trip to watch him.

"What do I taste like?" My voice is barely audible.

His eyes snap to mine. The air between us crackles.

"Like pussy."

I was expecting something more eloquent. But my surprise is wiped away as my body reacts to him saying that word. I thought I didn't like it, but hearing it fall from his lips puts a new spin on it.

93

He's so big, rough, and male. The word slips from his mouth like a piece of silk.

Suddenly, I don't want to fight anymore. I reach across the table and take the contract from him and flip to the next highlighted section.

"Tell me about the diary. What's that for?"

"Aftercare and communication."

That sounds harmless. "Okay...um, there was one other thing," I say. "Why do I need spanked every Sunday?"

His mouth twitches. "Because I don't enjoy brats. A lot of submissives act up trying to get a rise from their Dom when the dynamic isn't enforced often. Some subs want to be spanked every day. I think to keep you respectful, we'll try a spanking every Sunday night after dinner. If you need it twice a week, we can make an amendment."

My lips part and my hips shift. I'm soaked, I can feel it in my sweatpants and I wish I had panties on. If I sit up and there's a wet spot, I'll die of embarrassment.

"Won't I get...used to it?" I whisper. "I thought it was a punishment."

His eyes glimmer, arousal and amusement in their depths. "You'll know the difference between being spanked for maintenance and for punishment."

My mouth feels so dry. "What's the difference?"

"When you're spanked for maintenance, you'll cry and come," he says. "When it's for punishment, you'll just cry."

"I don't want to cry," I say automatically.

He cocks his head. "Why's that, redbird?"

He has this way of saying things when he's this close to me that's more intimate than sex. It isn't helping me that whenever he calls me redbird, it feels like being naked in his arms.

I draw myself up. "I never have the time."

That's a lie. I cry easily and often, but Clint hated it so much I learned to keep it secret.

He leans back. "No time to cry? That's too bad. You look like you could use a good cry."

"I'm not weak," I whisper.

"No, this is about release, not weakness," he says. "Once a week on Sunday nights, I'm going to spank you and let you cry it out until you feel better."

"Do you cry?" I shoot back.

"God's honest truth?" He tilts his head back like he's thinking deeply. "The last time I cried was at my mother's funeral and I was eleven. My father told me he'd hit me if I cried in public again, so I haven't done it since."

My jaw goes slack. It's the first piece of information he's volunteered. My mind latches onto it hungrily, trying to imagine Gerard before he was the hard, closed off man sitting before me.

"Was your father abusive?" I whisper.

He shakes his head. "No, he just drank until he turned into somebody else. Now, sign the contract."

I pause and mentally check in with myself. I don't feel scared, my body isn't tensed up the way it always was with Clint.

He reaches into his pocket and takes out a metal pen with blunt ends.

I look up at him.

And down at the pen.

"What happens if I change my mind?" I whisper.

His head cocks. "Then you're right back where you started."

I hold out my hand and he places the pen firmly in my palm. It's cold and smooth and heavier than expected. It feels like a little Pandora's Box, tempting me to just pull the cap off and sign my name.

What's the worst that could happen?

I study his face. He has me right where he wants me and I'm dismayed that I don't mind. Last night was the best sex of my life and now he's offering me an entire year of that.

Slowly, I realize I've been asking myself the wrong question. I should be asking what's the best that could happen.

The best would be good sex, having him listen to me like I'm the only person in the world, letting him call me redbird, falling asleep in his warmth every night.

I want to experience that. Even if it doesn't last beyond this year.

He leans forward in his chair. His two fingers tap the paper.

"Sign it, redbird," he says quietly. "Sign it and let me give you everything."

How does he read my thoughts so easily? Ears burning, I uncap the pen and put it to paper. My hand shakes, my signature is sloppy.

But I manage to scrawl it across that dotted line. And it feels so different than when I did this with Clint.

For the first time, it feels like opening a door instead of closing it.

CHAPTER THIRTEEN

KEIRA

We go to bed early, but he doesn't fuck me. I slip into bed wearing one of his worn t-shirts and he gets in next to me in just his sweatpants. I wait for him to roll me over and push himself into me, to leave me aching again, but he doesn't.

Instead, I feel his hand slide over my hip. Holding me gently. When I peek over my shoulder, he's asleep.

Curious, I shift onto my back. The blanket is around his waist. I have my half pulled up to my chin because it's freezing outside, but he radiates heat. I reach out and touch his bicep. I didn't get a good look at it before, but he's got a black and white traditional tattoo of a bull skull on his chest. It extends to his upper arms and stops above his elbows.

My fingertips contact his warm skin, tracing the sightless eyes of the skull. The thick muscle under it is relaxed. A slab of skin, muscle, and bone. I shudder. I've always been wary of big men the way I am with big animals.

They're unpredictable and when they go off, the damage is like a bomb blast.

I nestle my head deeper into my pillow and pull the quilt up to my chin. The problem with Gerard is that, despite how he reminds me of a bull, I'm not scared of him.

In fact, he looks warm and inviting.

And I'm cold.

I inch closer. He doesn't move so I shift even closer. He rumbles in his chest and his hand moves out, his palm gripping my hip and flipping me. Like I weigh nothing, like a pancake on a griddle. He pulls me back against him without waking and I'm enveloped in his heat.

It's like sinking into a hot bath.

Oh God, it feels good to be held. The hand that drapes over my waist might suffocate me, but I don't care. I've waited too long for this.

My father loved me and taught me to be strong. To stand on my own. My husband ignored me and I taught myself not to need him.

In Gerard Sovereign's arms, I feel my walls crumble. I haven't felt safe since my father died. But here, at the top of the mountain, in this kingdom he's built, I feel untouchable.

It's early when I wake, the sky is still dark. Gerard moves around the room, already dressed. I can hear the gentle tread of his boots on the ground. It comes closer until he's right in front of me in the firelight.

He crouches and shakes me gently. "Wake up, redbird."

I cough the hoarseness from my voice and lift my head. "What is it? What's wrong?"

"Nothing," he says. "We're going to the blacksmith shop."

He rises and my stomach flutters as I sit up.

"What are you going to do to me?" I whisper.

His mouth turns up. "Nothing, redbird. I won't surprise you with punishment. I'm making something for you and I want you to sit with me while I do."

That explains nothing. I get up, shivering in my t-shirt and he hands me another sweatsuit. Where are they getting these suits in my size? And when can I have my real clothes?

He watches me as I pull on the clothes. Then he pushes me back down on the bed and gets back down on one knee. I'm on high alert, unsure what he's doing. But he just pulls a thick pair of woolen socks over my feet and tucks them in.

He carries me downstairs and out the door. Overhead, the sky is deep blue and the stars twinkle like diamonds. There's light pollution from the barn, but otherwise, we're in total darkness.

I've seen stars like this my whole life, but at the top of Sovereign Mountain, they take my breath away. Every color is brighter, deeper, bolder.

I let my head nestle against his shoulder. He took a checkered green and white blanket from the hall closet and wrapped it around me. Between his heat and the blanket, I'm deliciously warm.

He carries me past the barn to a long building on the opposite side. It's a newer structure, although everything is in perfect repair here, and I can see the light is already on inside. He carries me over the threshold and places me on a table just inside. The door shuts and we're in total silence.

It's warm, a wood stove crackling on the far side. The floor is cement and I follow it with my eyes to the left end of the long structure. There I can make out an anvil and a forge in the darkness. That side is darker and I feel the cold radiating from it.

I tear my eyes back to him. He opens the vents on the wood stove and fire blazes. Pausing before me, he pulls the blanket around my body and takes a thermos from the bag over his shoulder. He shakes it once, flips the lid, and fills it with steaming coffee. I hold out my hand eagerly, but he keeps it back.

"Ask for it, redbird," he says.

I feel a faint heat creep over my cheeks. "May I please have some coffee?"

He shakes his head. "What do you call me?"

I want to squirm. This is so embarrassing.

"May I please have coffee, sir?" I correct.

He dips his head and puts the cup in my hands. "Good girl. You're bright and quick. This month should be easy."

I hope it is for my sake. I snuggle back against the wall, crossing my legs on the wooden table, and cradle the coffee in my hands. He strips down to his Henley and pushes the sleeves up to his forearms.

I have to curb my stare because....goddamn. He has nice arms and every time he takes them out, my brain goes empty.

He goes to the far side of the room where he takes a long, wide strip of leather from a plastic box. There's a set of cubicles on the wall beside me and his eyes skim them. Then he takes out what looks like a scalpel and lays the leather out flat on the table.

"You're pretty handy," I venture.

"How do you mean?" His eyes don't lift as he takes a thin measuring tape out.

"I didn't know you could work with leather," I say. "What are you making?"

"Everything you'll need," he says. "Today we're working on the cuffs for your wrists."

I stare at him, heat creeping down my spine. He glances up and our eyes lock. Electricity crackles in the dim blacksmith shop.

"I thought you'd buy those," I whisper.

He shakes his head. "Custom is better. More comfortable. Hold out your hand, redbird."

"Yes, sir." I'm surprised by how easily the words slip from my lips.

This time, he doesn't praise me, he just takes my hand and wraps the measuring tape around my wrist.

There's something thrilling about him winding it around my wrist. I glance up, but he's unbothered. He takes multiple measurements and scrawls them across a piece of brown paper. His handwriting is neat and he's left handed, so he writes from above. The veins on the back of his hand shift and I squeeze my thighs together.

His gaze flicks over me. "Alright, redbird?"

I nod, biting my lip. His eyes drop and linger on my mouth, and I feel like I'm in a spotlight. Nervous, I take a sip of warm coffee and cough as the acrid taste fills my mouth.

"That's strong," I manage.

His mouth twitches. "I'll let you teach me how you like it next time."

"I like a lot of cream and sugar," I say.

"However you like it is how you'll have it."

He takes up his pencil. I watch him put marks on the leather in silence. Occasionally, he uses a clear plastic tool like a ruler to keep the lines clean. I lean my temple against the wall and sip my thick coffee, trying not to grimace.

"What do you like, redbird?" he asks out of nowhere.

I stare at him, unsure what he means. "Like...to do?"

He nods.

"Well, I didn't have a lot of time for hobbies," I admit. "But when I was a girl, I loved riding. I had a bay mare my father gave me and he used to let me ride the perimeter of the ranch to check it sometimes."

"Your father gave you a lot of freedom?"

I shake my head. "My mother died in a car accident a week after I was born. He was pretty scared for me most of the time."

His head jerks up and his lips part. There's a long awkward silence and then he clears his throat.

"Sorry for your loss," he says gruffly.

Did I upset him? He goes right back to tracing leather like his strange reaction never happened.

"Go on," he says.

"I...um...I went riding a lot. After I got married, my horse died. Just from old age. I asked Clint for another horse, but he said it was a frivolous expense."

His brow raises, but he stays silent.

"I really liked riding," I muse. "I used to take my horse up to the mountain ridges behind Stowe Farms in the morning and come back at night. My father gave me a gun for my tenth birthday to protect myself against cougars. And men, probably. He'd let me go out as long as I came back by five."

His jaw works. "Can't say I'll give you that much freedom. But I'll give you Angel."

I sit up straighter. "Really?"

"You want her, she's yours."

I blink, staring at the firm press of his mouth. I wish he'd joke and smile, but he's as hard as the packed earth beneath the field grass in summertime.

"What about a gun?" I say daringly.

He turns his head, glancing at me with those winter-blue eyes. "Now what would you do with a gun, redbird?"

I shrug. "Protect myself."

He goes back to cutting the leather. "You have me. No one will hurt you when you're under my protection."

There's an undercurrent of possessiveness in his voice. I'm not sure if he even realizes it, but I hear it for a second. His shoulders have been tense since I told him how my mother died. I see a glimpse of the man who held me back from running into my burning house.

"What do you like to do?" I ask, trying to change the subject.

"I like riding too," he says slowly. "I like making money. I like fucking you. Palm out."

I obey and he measures a cut out strip of leather around my wrist. He nods and I pull back.

"What do you want your safeword to be?" he asks abruptly.

Off guard, I stare at him, but I can't think of a single word I'd feel comfortable shouting out during sex. I know a little bit about safewords, and I know they have to be something unusual. But I don't want to pick something ridiculous.

"Um...any suggestions?" I ask.

"We can't use red because you're my redbird," he says. "How about crimson?"

I nod. That feels different enough, but not embarrassing. "That's good to me."

"Have you been physically punished before?" he asks. "Do you have any places you don't want me to touch like that?"

I shake my head, blushing. "I don't think so, sir."

"Why were you scared of Clint? Did he hit you?"

The way he changes subjects gives me whiplash. I blink, shaking my head hard.

"No, he didn't. He said I was lucky that he never put his hands on me and I think that was his way of threatening me. Reminding me he could hurt me if he wanted to."

"You still haven't answered my question. Why did he scare you?"

I take a quick breath and set the empty coffee cup aside. "I was worn down. I hated when he'd get angry because he'd shout and get in my space. Sometimes he'd grab my hair. He never hit me, but he made my life hell when I crossed him. I was just tired, and I did wonder sometimes if he would snap."

He's silent, the way he always is when I reveal something less than savory about my late husband. I realize that outside of me, Clint and Gerard were barely civil. Friends, never. Business partners maybe, but there's clearly no love lost between them.

"I'm glad he didn't," he says. "Hold your palm up."

Timidly, I obey. He moves closer and I have to force myself not to clench my fist. His hand comes up and his rough fingertips trace over the lines by my thumb. His touch is light and it sends a shiver down my spine.

"You have calluses," he says. "You shouldn't have to work."

"Why?" I frown.

He cocks his head. "You're too pretty to be anything but a plaything."

It's not the most misogynist thing I've heard from a man out here in the male-dominated hills of Montana, but it still lifts my brows. Then I remember that it's training month, and I can't tell if this is him...or if this is my Dom.

I'm struggling with that part of the contract. When does it start and when does it end? Is this him or is this him in his role?

I swallow and my dry lips part. Truthfully, I don't know how to play these games.

"Thank you," I whisper. "Sir."

He growls, deep in his chest. His hand curls around the back of my neck and he pulls me in. His mouth contacts mine and my entire body lights up. Lava floods my veins and gathers deep in my pussy. Everything tingles, down to the soles of my feet.

He tastes so good that I follow his mouth when he pulls back. Hungry for more.

"That's my girl," he says. "You're learning."

My chest glows at the praise. So I guessed right. We are playing.

He sets the tools aside and pulls me close to the edge of the table. "Lean back on your elbows and spread your thighs."

I hesitate. His head cocks.

"What are you going to do?"

A muscle in his cheek twitches. "Did you or did you not sign that contract?"

Dry mouthed, I nod and obediently lean back. Resting on my elbows and letting my knees fall apart. Without breaking eye contact, he tugs my sweatpants down around my knees.

Cool air washes over my legs and bumps rise on my skin. I'm not sure if they're from the cold or from the way he's looking at me.

He strips my pants off and rolls my socks up to my knees. His firm hands grip my thighs over the cuffs.

My heart hammers. It's been a few years since I've been on the receiving end of oral. And I was telling him the truth when I said I hadn't enjoyed it. Clint was rough and impatient. Trying to come from his tongue had been a uniquely frustrating experience.

Gerard presses my thighs apart. He leans in and his hot breath washes over my sex. My hands clench and my heart flutters.

His other hand slides up, gripping the back of my neck. He's so big he can lift me across his forearm and eat me out at the same time. I sink into his grip. His hot breath scorches me and his tongue skims over my pussy.

Oh.

This isn't in the same universe as what I've experienced before. He licks the outer edge of my sex and heat explodes. I have no anxiety about this the way I did the few times Clint did it. My brain is empty and the only place I can feel anything is between my legs.

My inner muscles clench. Wetness trickles into the cold air.

"Fuck, redbird," he breathes.

All I can do is moan.

The tip of his tongue forces inside me. My hips buck, but he holds me down. Pushing his tongue into my sensitive opening almost an inch. Making my eyes widen and a whimper force its way up.

I want to grip his hair and ride his face. But I have a pretty good idea of our dynamic and we're not there yet. I know what he's doing and I'm determined to pass his test. To show him I can be good for him.

I hold perfectly still. The sight of this big man, musclebound shoulders bent, face buried between my legs is enough to make me come. I hold off, trying to relax and breathe the orgasm back.

He's too good at this. That itch of pleasure that signals my impending orgasm grows unbearable.

"I'm...I need to finish," I whisper, barely audible.

"No," he says.

A spark of annoyance moves through my chest and I squash it down. He spits on his fingers and eases one—the middle—into me. My eyes roll back. It fills me so well and I find my hips working. Riding his hand as his tongue laps over my swollen clit.

Oh God, I'm so close I can barely breathe. My hand flies up, bracing on the wall. My other hand grips his hair before I know what I'm doing.

He pulls back like I've burned him.

"Palms flat on the table," he says.

He's not angry, but I see that he's dropping a boundary. Like a dog raising its hackles. Right away, I plant my hands on the table.

"Yes, sir," I whisper.

"Good," he says. "Tell me when you're right on the edge. Understood?"

I nod hard, desperate for his tongue on my pussy and the rasp of his jaw on the inside of my thigh. He goes back to work and I practically purr.

His fingers stroke that sweet spot inside me. His tongue moves in slow circles. Silence falls except for the wet sound of his fingers and my heavy breaths.

He brings me closer and closer. Working my pussy the way he works his cock. Decisively, with perfect rhythm, like he knows what the fuck he's doing.

Clearly he does because it barely takes any time for pleasure to surge. Helpless, I feel myself riding the wave higher. My fingers tighten on the table, knuckles going white.

"I'm going to come," I gasp.

He pulls away. One second I'm right at the edge of the best orgasm I've ever had, and the next, I'm empty and throbbing with need. He steps back and wipes his fingers on a rag and puts my pants back on.

I stare, shattered.

"What was what?" I whisper.

He lays the leather down, bending to make sure the lines are even. The scalpel-like blade slices through it and leaves a clean cut behind. He holds it up and I can see he's pleased with it.

"When I tell you to do something, do you hesitate?" he asks.

He's so calm. I shake my head quickly. Am I being punished?

His jaw tightens. "No, sir."

I catch on, sitting up. "No, sir. I'm not supposed to hesitate."

"That's correct," he says, glancing at me. Ice blue eyes flicking over me. "I'm not angry, I'm pleased. You're a good girl, but you need training."

I stay quiet because I'm feeling something new and overwhelming. The truth is...I like this dynamic. It feels secure, despite me having no control other than my safewords.

For the first time in years, I feel like a person again. Not just a machine that spits out free labor. And I know the bar is low, but it means a lot to me, what he's doing this morning.

No one has ever given me their undivided attention before.

The only downside is...God, I want to come so badly. I'd get down on my knees and beg for an orgasm, but I know I won't get it. He's laid down a boundary. I'm learning he's not the sort of man who concedes his ground.

"I'm sorry," I say.

"I know," he replies. "I'm almost done here for the day. You'll have breakfast, then spend some time unpacking what I purchased for you upstairs. I'll meet you at noon."

My stomach flutters and he notices my flushed cheeks. The corner of his mouth turns up. He's so sexy, in a gruff, masculine way, and when he smiles, I see his humanity.

Like he wasn't always thirty-eight, scarred, tattooed, and encircled in walls.

"Why? What happens at noon?" I whisper.

"I'm going to edge you again," he says.

I can't bite back the noise of disappointment in my throat.

His eyes flash. "You'll learn how to behave," he says, not unkindly. "Tonight, if you are good for the rest of the day, I'll let you come as many times as you want."

CHAPTER FOURTEEN

GERARD

I leave her at the breakfast table later that morning and meet Westin at the truck. I've known Westin for two decades, he's my right hand, and he's fully aware of everything going on with Keira. We're as close as brothers—his family is my family.

He puts away his horse and joins me in the truck, reaching for my thermos of hot coffee. Steam rises off the top and he leans back, stretching his legs out. I don't need him to evaluate the ranch, but I'd like a witness for our visit to Thomas Garrison's farm.

"Fuck-all cold for September," he says.

We pull out onto the road and head towards Garrison Ranch. My head is cloudy with what I did to Keira in the blacksmith shop. It's been a long time since I went down on a woman, but I know what I felt is different.

My cock twitches in my pants. I shift and clear my throat, glancing up to see the faint trail of smoke still rising over the hills.

"Are you gonna keep missing morning chores?" Westin asks.

"I was with Keira," I say.

"Could have guessed," he laughs.

We don't talk until we're pulling up in front of Garrison Ranch. Westin swings out and his boots hit the gravel as he settles his hat on his head. I circle the truck and follow him up the remainder of the drive.

The barn is gutted. We're both silent as we circle the house and meet by the still intact front porch.

"The house isn't bad," Westin says, resting his hands on his hips. "It looks like the part that burned was probably the original farmhouse. You can see the seam there."

I follow his gaze and nod. It's clear the house was once an older farmhouse with sizable additions built onto the southern and western sides. The burnt portion is the older part. It looks like the fire flickered out, perhaps due to flame resistant materials in the newer side.

Westin loiters around the side and I head up the porch. The front door creaks open as I step into the hallway. Everything smells of smoke and my eyes smart. I take my bandanna and pull it over the bottom half of my face, lowering the rim of my hat.

I move through the charred portion to the untouched upstairs. The first room is clearly made up for guests with a crisp quilt and no sign of dust. I glance over it, impressed. Miss Garrison was quite the homemaker.

I hear Westin downstairs on his phone and I lean over to look out the hall window. He's standing with one foot against the truck tire, a cigarette hanging from his mouth.

Good, I want to be alone right now.

My boots creep along the floor and carry me to the largest room on the second floor. I push the door open and stop short.

It's clearly the room she shared with Clint. But she hasn't changed anything. He's been dead for seven months and his boots are still behind the door. His flannel is hanging over the chair in the corner.

Like that motherfucker was going to walk in here at any moment.

I enter the room and shut the door and flick the lock.

Despite the smoke, there's a faint feminine scent. I run my fingertips over the end of her side of the bed. Up to her pillow and lift it, bringing it to my face. Sweet like pomegranate shampoo. My cock twitches again, and this time I reach down and adjust it.

The bedside table is made of cedar. Over it hangs a painting of bluebells that match the embroidered blue flowers of the bedspread. There's a lamp and a short stack of books on top. I pick one up and flip it over. It's a diary with a strip of leather tying it closed and a pen tucked underneath. I untie it and skim through the pages, but they're empty.

She never wrote anything in it.

I push the diary in my back pocket and pull her bedside drawer open. There's a makeup purse, a bottle of lotion, and a velvet drawstring bag. I open it and my brows lift.

Inside is a pink, rose shaped vibrator.

Arousal surges down my spine. She laid here on her back with her legs spread. Her slender fingers held this toy to her clit and her hips bucked as pleasure tore through them. I pull the blankets down, revealing the fitted sheet.

There's a faint stain, right at hip level.

I'm so hard my eyes swim. This is the bed she shared with her husband, maybe the bed she'd lost her virginity in on her birthday. When she was too young to be used like that.

But it's also the bed she slept in alone for the last several months.

Blood surges. I fucking hate that I wasn't the first man to have her. It should have been my name she cried out all along. I shouldn't care because she's mine now and she'll never walk away, but I do because I'm a jealous motherfucking bastard.

I unzip my pants and take my cock out.

My hands wrap around my erection and my fist grips her vibrator. How many times did she push her pretty, tight cunt against it and come? Was that stain from lubricant or had she squirted hard enough to soak the sheets?

I brace my knee on the bed. I'm primed from eating her out this morning and it takes less than a minute for pleasure to shoot down my spine. Cum explodes from my cock and hits the bed she shared with her husband. Soaking over the stain she left from pleasuring herself.

My head spins. My cock tingles as I push it back into my pants and fasten my belt.

I have good, solid reasons to hate every member of the Garrison family, but I've always hated Clint the most. I hope that whatever part of hell he's burning in, he knows I fucked his wife.

I hope he knows I'm about to go home and edge her until she cries.

There's still water in the pipes so I wash up in the bathroom. Then I toss her vibrator and leave with nothing but her diary in my pocket.

Back in the truck, Westin is having another cigarette. He hangs up the phone as I approach and yanks open the truck door.

"That was the cleaning crew," he says. "They can be out Thursday."

I nod, settling in the front seat and pull back onto the road. We have a few hours left and I need to go see one of my least favorite people.

"Can I ask you a question?" Westin says, rubbing his stubbled jaw.

"Sure," I say, not looking over.

"Is this girl just about revenge?" he says slowly. "Or is this something more?"

I simmer on that for a minute even though I know the answer. My redbird belongs to me. She has since the night we first met in her husband's office, whether she knows it or not.

But I can't deny she's uniquely situated to be part of my revenge as well.

"Why?" I ask.

"Because this could get ugly," he says.

I trust Westin's opinion, but I also recognize that he's not me. He doesn't live with this burning anger in his body. He's never felt the deep sting of injustice the way I have for most of my life. He's never watched the people he hates take everything from him.

And he's not fucked up for the redheaded Garrison girl in my bed.

My knuckles go white on the steering wheel. I take a beat to sort through my thoughts.

"I'll handle this part of my business," I say.

"I get it," Westin says. "Just don't hurt yourself. You've got enough scars as it is, Sovereign."

He never calls me by my first name, most of the men who work for me don't. When we were boys, he called me Gerry. Then, after everything went to hell, he found me in a bar one night trying to drink myself to death, and something changed.

"Come on, Sovereign," he said. "Let's get it together."

I didn't realize it then, but he was giving a new name for a fresh start. He took me to a motel and cleaned me up. The next morning, he bought me breakfast and marched me downtown to the basement of a church in South Platte. I was at rock bottom so I went along with it because it couldn't get any worse.

"My name is Sovereign," I said. "I'm an alcoholic."

Westin stuck by me for the next few months. He cleaned me up and took me back to his mother's house. There I recovered and paid my bills by working on their ranch. After two years of hard labor alongside Westin, his father offered us a plot of land that bordered the Garrison Ranch. Westin was adamant he didn't want to manage a ranch, but I accepted it without question. I didn't have anything to fall back on the way he did, this was my one chance to make something of myself.

I'd never had anyone believe I was anything but trash before that. Westin finally agreed to work alongside me, so long as he didn't have to bear the brunt of management. I leapt at the chance to build something, to finally have a piece of land to call my own. From that small plot, we created Sovereign Mountain Ranch. The wealthiest cattle and quarter horse operation in the state of Montana.

Westin told me to forgive and forget what the Garrison family had done to me, but I couldn't. They'd destroyed my family and one day, I would return the favor. If it took me until I was eighty, I'd wait until the opportune moment to strike back.

Then I met Keira Garrison and suddenly everything felt urgent.

I was at peace with eating my revenge ice cold, but not with leaving her with that man.

My thoughts carry me in a haze down the road. We pull up before Thomas Garrison's ranch and I cut the engine. My pistol is at my hip, where it always is regardless of where I'm going or what I'm doing. I flip the holster strap open—just in case—and get out of the truck.

A sheepdog bursts around the side of the house and yaps at me. The screen door creaks open and Thomas's wife steps out. She's in jeans and a white t-shirt and I see Westin's eyes linger on her curves. Westin used to date her a while back, but then Thomas swooped in and got to her first. She's a pretty thing with curly blonde hair and sharp, brown eyes.

She has a scowl on her face. "What are you doing on my land, Sovereign?" she snaps.

Westin swings out of the truck and lifts his hand to me. "Hold on, I believe this is earth I've plowed. Let me handle this."

Oh, this will be good.

Westin moves up to the bottom of the steps. The sheepdog bounces at his mistress's feet, aching for a chance at him.

"Where's your husband?" Westin drawls.

She jerks her head towards the barn. "He just got in. What do you want?"

"We want to talk with him," he says, tilting his head. "Nothing you should worry about, darling."

Her jaw tightens. "Don't call me darling unless you want to lose your fucking balls, Westin Quinn."

I cock my head, squinting through the sun. Westin plays it straight in most areas, but he's got no respect for the Garrison brothers. He'd just as soon fuck one of their wives for no reason other than to kick the hornet's nest.

Given my current circumstance, I can't say I'm any better.

Through the barn door, I catch sight of the youngest Garrison, Thomas. He's the least guilty in my eyes because he was young when everything went to shit, but he's got their blood in his veins. And now he's put a black mark on his record by burning down my woman's house.

He sees us and his eyes narrow. All the Garrison brothers have tall faces, sandy hair, and gray eyes. Thomas still looks like a teenager

113

even though he's in his twenties, and he already has the glitter of a bully in his gaze.

"What you doing on my fucking land, Sovereign?" he barks.

"Wait in the truck," I say.

Westin puts his hands on his hips. "Don't do anything you regret."

I cross the yard to the barn and a few feet from Thomas. Every time I see one of their faces, it sends my mind back to every dark memory I have. There's always been a Garrison involved, from my first experience with death, to cheating, and back to death again.

My muscles are tight up my spine.

"I've been out to Clint's ranch," I say.

"Yeah? That right?" His eyes narrow. He spits to the side. "That Stowe slut still living out there?"

Anger tears through me like a wildfire, but I keep my face impassive.

"No, Keira is with me," I say.

He freezes and he's not as good as I am at hiding anger. It flashes over his face like a thunderclap. It takes him a moment to get control of it. Then he shrugs.

"Hope you like Clint's leftovers," he says.

I fit my hat back on my head. "If you come around her ranch again, I'll shoot you. She's under my protection on Sovereign Mountain. I own her, just like I own more than half your family's motherfucking land."

He's trying to goad me into talking about her body, but that's between me and her now. The fact she slept with my enemy means nothing to me anymore. Not after the way she cried and came when I fucked her in my bed the first time.

But I won't talk to Thomas Garrison about my woman's body. If I had my way, I'd cut out his tongue to keep her name from his mouth.

I cross the yard and pull open the truck door. "Stay off her land. I've got people watching it."

He flips me off. "Take your slut and her ranch. Fuck off."

He's bad at bluffing. That's why he has an ocean of debt from the casino he's concealing from his older brother. I know how hard the

Garrison brothers fought in court to contest Clint's will and keep Keira from owning their largest plot of land. I know how much it means to them.

And I know that me fucking Clint's widow is salt in their wound.

I shut the door and turn the truck around, heading back to the main road. Westin sits beside me with his brows raised, waiting for me to talk. I keep silent for a good twenty minutes. It always takes me a while to get a handle on the hatred that flows through me when I speak to a Garrison.

"How'd it go?" Westin goes.

I clear my throat. "You should go after Diane."

"Jesus Christ," Westin mumbles. "You're crazy."

"You could do with taking a page out of my book and going after the things you want."

He glances sideways at me. There's a hint of sadness in his eyes. "I hope your past doesn't fuck up your future, Sovereign."

We're both quiet the rest of the way home.

CHAPTER FIFTEEN

KEIRA

Up in the bedroom closet, I find a stack of boxes and bags that weren't there yesterday. My name is written on the side of each one in black marker. I drag everything out into the middle of his room and start unpacking it all.

It's clothes, shoes, outerwear. And for some reason, a box that contains a beautiful leather bridle. My name is engraved into the underside of the browband. I run my fingers over it, hoping this isn't some kink he has because this is definitely a real bridle.

Meant for a horse. Not a person.

I set it aside and go over the clothes. Somehow, he guessed my size exactly. Or maybe he measured my body in my sleep. I shiver as I pull on a Henley and a pair of jeans, turning to admire how they hug my ass. I've always had good curves and they're finally getting appreciated. By both the jeans and Gerard.

I spin, watching my reflection in the bathroom mirror. For the first time in a while, I don't look tired. My eyes glitter and my hair is soft and falls down my back. Loose over my shoulders instead of tied up to keep it from the greasy stove.

I remind myself that this is temporary. The contract will end or one of us will want out.

At least...that's what I assume.

After some of the things he's said and done, I'm starting to question his motives and his intent.

Maybe he didn't mean for me to be just temporary fun.

But if that's the case...then what does he have planned for me?

The thought leaves me cold like the frost that gathers on his bedroom windows. I shudder and collect the bags of the clothes and drag them downstairs to the laundry room off the kitchen. Maddie helps me wash and dry them, but she barely speaks except to ask if there's anything I'd like added to the next grocery order.

I can't tell if she's just shy. Or she doesn't trust me.

I am a Garrison after all.

Upstairs, I mull it over. The empty eyes of the bull skull watch me as I fold my clothes and put them in the empty drawers of his dresser. The coats and shirts, I hang up. The panties and bras, I can't find a place for so I push his boxer briefs to one side and put them in the drawer together. There's something exciting about sharing an underwear drawer with him.

It's almost noon when I'm done. I leave the quiet bedroom and move down the hallway, turning the corner near the doorway of the game room at the far end. I've never been inside, but I know there's a hot tub on the balcony because I've seen it from the yard.

Out of nowhere, a solid wall crashes into me and I yelp. A hand covers my mouth and I'm spun around. Blue eyes meet mine as he backs me against the wall. My chest heaves, my breasts brushing the front of his shirt. Sending tingles to the soles of my feet.

We both stand frozen, then he releases my mouth.

"Gerard," I gasp. "You startled me."

The corner of his mouth twitches. "Where are you going, little girl?"

The way he says those words gets me flustered. Little girl. It falls lazily from his mouth, but there's an edge of softness that makes me want to lean in and beg for a kiss. He always tastes so good when he comes in from outside. Like winter and fresh air.

"Down to lunch." My voice is a whisper.

His hand slides down my outer thigh and up the seam of my jeans. Heat curls in my lower belly.

"Down to lunch, sir," he corrects. "Address me properly when we're alone."

I nod, but I'm so distracted I can't think straight. My zipper hisses as he pulls it down. I'm in the panties he bought for me. Pale blue silk. He pushes his hand into my pants and his fingertips brush my clit through the fabric.

My stomach quivers. The muscles in my thighs tighten.

"What do you say?" He steps closer.

My head falls back against the wall. "Yes, sir."

He lifts his two fingers and taps my lips. I part and his big middle and pointer fingers slip into my mouth. Filling it completely. My stomach tightens and arousal floods my pussy, making the tender folds of my sex ache.

He pulls them free and my eyes shut as he pushes them under my panties. I know I'm soaked, but I'm not prepared for the heavy groan that reverberates in his chest as he slides his touch over the seam of my pussy.

"Do you need relief so badly, redbird?" he murmurs.

I nod. "Please, let me come. I'll be good."

His eyes darken. "I'll let it go this time, but don't try to change your punishments. If I'm edging you, you accept that you won't come until I say. Understood?"

Embarrassed, I nod. He can be so stern about things and I'm not sure if I like it.

"Use your words when I ask you a question." His low voice is firm.

My eyes widen. "I'm sorry, sir."

"Good girl." His tone shifts. It's huskier, lower, and it fills the air between our bodies.

I bite my lip. His fingers stroke my sensitive pussy, drawing all the blood down between my thighs. I fist my hands and let my head fall back.

I should be angry. But I'm too busy wrestling with how much I'm enjoying his denial. This is a completely different world than being ignored by Clint. Gerard is denying me, but he's not withdrawing his closeness. I feel safe that he won't reject or hurt me. It's such a new feeling and it takes my breath away.

He slides his middle finger over my clit again and again. My hips ride up against his hand.

"Oh," I gasp. My stomach goes tight and I feel myself about to fall.

He pulls back and licks his fingers and draws my pants back up. The air between us feels like a brewing storm. Thick and sultry. My God, I'd let him push that enormous cock into me and fuck me however he wants if he'd just give me some relief.

His brows are lowered in thought. He takes something from his back pocket and holds it out.

I take it, realizing with a jolt that it's my diary. The empty one my father gave me, the one I never had anything good enough to fill it with.

"I want you to use this as your diary," he says.

I chew my lip, unsure how I feel about that. "My father gave me this."

He shrugs once. "It's just a book. Paper and empty lines."

I nod, but I'm not entirely sure. I've always been good at putting my feelings into a box and burying them deep inside. This empty book has sat in my bedside table for years. Is now really the time to mark the pristine pages?

The last time I considered writing in it was on my wedding day. Now I'm grateful I didn't taint the pages with my disaster of a marriage. My fingers close on the book and I make up my mind to leave it for now. I have time to decide.

"You went to my house," I say.

He nods. "I needed to assess the damage."

He heads down the hallway and I follow him, my legs still wobbly. I'm soaked between my thighs, but I do my best to ignore it.

"Is it bad?" I ask.

He doesn't answer. We descend the staircase and enter the large dining room accessible via a doorway below the loft stairs. I'm taken aback for a second, looking around at the huge table packed with men. I scan the rows, hoping to see another woman, but it's all testosterone as far as the eye can see.

Clint had the same set up. All the men who worked on his farm ate in the dining room for breakfast, lunch, and dinner. They lived in on-site housing and I was expected to cook and clean for the endless people streaming through the ranch house.

All at once, I realize I'm in the wrong place. I draw back, clutching the book to my chest.

"I'm going to go," I say.

He frowns, pivoting on his heel. "Where?"

"I'll eat in the kitchen with Maddie," I say, frowning.

Is he expecting me to eat with the men?

"Maddie doesn't eat in the kitchen. She sets the food out and then she eats with her husband in their lodging," he says. He's still looking at me with that heavy crease across his forehead.

"Oh," I say, looking around. I notice that a few dozen of the men are staring at me curiously. I back up to the doorway and he follows me, blocking their view.

"I didn't give you permission to leave," he says. "Where did you eat at Garrison Ranch?"

"In the kitchen," I say.

"And before that?"

I'm so uncomfortable I'm squirming. "With my father in the dining room."

"Then you'll do the same here."

He takes my hand and leads me through the room to the table on the far end. I notice the man from the other night who cooled down Shadow.

He glances up and waves. Gerard ushers me to a seat beside him.

The man leans over and extends his hand. "Westin Quinn."

I shake it. He's got calluses like Gerard. They probably all do.

"Mrs. Keira Garrison," I say.

His brows shoot up and he glances at Gerard. He's gathering up our plates and turning to head to the buffet table. I jump to my feet to help and he shoots me a look that's so hard and commanding I sit back down at once.

"How well do you know Sovereign?" Westin asks.

It takes me a second to realize he means Gerard. "Not well. I was surprised he wanted me to come stay here."

He laughs. "All roads lead to Sovereign Mountain."

I'd heard the phrase before. It was never a good thing. It usually implied desperation and unwillingness. I glance over the room and the atmosphere feels relaxed, everyone seems well fed and happy. Maybe the distrust the people in town feel towards Sovereign Mountain is unwarranted.

Gerard returns and places a plate of thick stew poured over mashed potatoes and a slice of bread before me. It smells amazing and the roasted meat is so tender it's falling apart. He hands me a fork and sets a drink down. Then he sits.

"So how bad is the house?" I ask.

"It'll need cleaned and the older portion repaired," says Westin.

"Did you go?" I ask.

He nods. "The house is salvageable. The barn will need rebuilt."

Gerard shoots him a look and he falls silent. I wonder if he said something I wasn't supposed to know, or if Gerard is just territorial. They both eat in silence so I clean my plate because I'm starving. It's been hours since the egg on toast I had at breakfast.

I've always lived with men, watching them like they're zoo animals. Wondering what it would feel like to have been born with the kind of confidence they have to take on the world.

No fear. That sounds like heaven.

Our pocket of Montana is a wild place. My father taught me I was worth the same as a man, but he never shied away from telling me I'd have had an easier life if I'd been born male. He taught me to ride and shoot, to defend myself, but I'm still half the size of most of the men in this room.

If I didn't have Gerard Sovereign for protection, I'd be a deer among starving wolves.

CHAPTER SIXTEEN

GERARD

She's so desperate that night when I flip her onto her back and spread her legs, she gives in without saying a word. Her thighs clench when I dip my head to kiss her lower belly, she shudders and strains up towards my mouth.

I can smell how wet she is.

It's the first time I've gone down on her in bed. There's something luxurious about it. Outside, the wind howls through the trees. Inside, we're warm, and there's nowhere to be on a night like this but in bed together.

She sits up against the pillows and I push my face into her lap. Her pussy is so soft—I'm not used to things as soft and fine as her—and she builds slowly as I lick her clit. Her long fingers with her oval nails play with my hair and trace the tattoos and scars on my shoulders. The taste of her is sweet and I want it on my tongue forever.

Her toes curl and her thighs clench when she comes.

"Oh God," she gasps.

She lays in bed afterwards and watches me undress. Her head is propped up on the heel of her hand and her eyes are distant. I wonder where she goes when she's quiet like this. When I lay down with her, she shifts close and tentatively leans over.

I kiss her and her lower back arcs in. The taste of her mouth and the pomegranate scent of her shampoo fills my senses, reminding me I haven't come. When I pull back, she follows my mouth. Hungry for more.

I fucking love the way she wants it.

Her hand wraps around my cock. Her fingers don't meet as she starts jerking me off. Our eyes lock and I brush back her hair to kiss her again. Pleasure moves down my spine and before I can come on my stomach, I flip her onto her back and push the tip of my cock against the entrance of her pussy. I let out a low groan as I come. Filling her, putting my cum where it belongs.

She's flushed when I pull back. When she moves to get up, I take her wrist and pull her back down.

"No, you leave it inside you," I say quietly.

She's flustered, pink cheeked, but not displeased. Her body curls up against my chest and I pull the blankets up to her chin.

The next morning, Westin and I get up earlier than usual and take the truck to Garrison Ranch. The sun is still cresting the mountains when I swing out of the truck and cross the driveway. Jensen, the head of the local construction crew of South Platte, breaks off from a group of his men and heads over.

"How's it look?" Westin asks, coming up behind me.

Jensen pivots and waves a hand at the barn. "That's all fucked. But the house is mostly fine except for the back section. Are you wanting us to tear that away and build onto it? Or do a restoration project?"

I squint, taking in the scarred exterior of the Garrison house.

"Restoration...right?" Westin glances at me.

I shake my head. "Tear it down."

We circle the house and Jensen kicks at the charred back stoop. "What are you thinking you'll put in its place?"

"I don't mean tear down the damaged part," I say. "I mean, tear the entire building down."

They both reel back and stare at me, but I'm already circling the barn. Taking in the piles of charred wood, ash, and melted equipment.

"Sovereign," Westin says, appearing at my elbow. "You might want to think about this before you do something like that."

I glance up. "I own the mortgage. It's my house."

He steps in front of me, eyes narrowed. "It's Keira Garrison's house. If you do this, she'll have nothing to go back to."

"I know," I say.

His jaw squares. Jensen appears beside him. Neither of them seem surprised by my announcement, but I can tell it's not sitting right.

"Any sign of her horses?" I start walking around the rubble and head to the edge of the yard. The hills behind the house are quiet. The day after the fire, I moved her cattle into my pastures and put her people on my paycheck. All the worker housing sits empty.

"Nope," says Jensen, leaning on the fence. His hat comes down low, shielding his eyes as the sun cuts over the mountain. "Are you sure you want us to tear this place down? It's worth a lot."

"I can eat the cost," I say.

"But...can she?" Westin asks.

I turn, crossing my arms over my chest. "She's in debt over her head. The only way she gets to keep anything is if I let her. She's already fucked."

"So your solution is fuck her too?" Westin says, appearing on my other side.

I push off the fence, adjusting my hat lower to keep the sun from my eyes. "My solution is to keep her alive."

They shut up right away. Both of them know me and they know what I've been through. They also know how evil the Garrison brothers can be. Jensen brings me the paperwork and I spread it out on the hood of the truck. Westin lights a cigarette and I hear them talking as I go over each piece and sign my name.

I'm leaving a paper trail.

It's not like she has anywhere to go if she finds out.

The drive back to Sovereign Mountain is quiet. Westin has a short span of attention and better things to do than try to persuade me my behavior is immoral. He jumps out of the truck when we get back and heads to the barn. I take my hat off and walk around the yard to the pasture where we keep Angel. Hoping for a glimpse of red hair.

She's inside the paddock. Leaning on the fence with her cheek against the top rung. Big Dog is sleeping on the ground and she offers me a glance without raising her head.

I draw up to the other side and Keira jumps. Her expression shifts as I lean in and kiss her forehead. When did she stop looking at me with wariness? Because right now her sky blue gaze feels like warm sunshine.

"How's it going?" I ask.

She nods, smiling. "Really good. We've just been doing laps around the paddock."

Angel nickers, throwing her head. I send her a look to let her know I'm onto her—I've worked with this horse and I know she's a menace. She's more like me than I care to admit.

Keira turns and rests her hands on the fence. The way she's looking up with her fiery hair falling down her back is doing things to me. My palm is itching to slide up her face and brush her waves back.

"Where'd you go today?" she asks brightly.

"Your place. We're working on handling the damage to the house," I say.

"Again?"

I nod. "Last time I stopped by your brother-in-law's place on the way back."

"Which one?" Her face falls. "Why?"

"Thomas. I went to warn him I don't want any Garrisons on your land."

"*Your* land," she says flatly.

"We'll see, redbird. The world changes fast."

Her eyes dart up. "Sometimes I don't understand you."

I slide my hand around the back of her neck, pull her close, and kiss her over the fence. Her breath hitches and she moans in her throat. She likes being kissed, maybe just as much as being fucked. Her entire body melts and I feel her blood pump fast in her veins.

When I break away, she's flushed and her eyes are glassy.

"You don't have to understand me," I say. "Everything, all in good time."

I leave her there and go inside to wash my face up in my bathroom. My shirt is damp with sweat despite the cold and I strip it off. From outside, I can hear Angel nickering and thundering in her paddock. Big Dog lays by the gate, always at her side.

I go to the window, wiping my hands and forearms on a towel. Keira stands at the center and Angel trots in a circle, the lead attached to her halter.

She's making progress.

They both are.

CHAPTER SEVENTEEN

KEIRA

I've saved this diary for years hoping for something significant enough to happen that I can write in it. Yesterday morning, I was sitting in the window watching the smoke rise from the chimneys where Gerard's staff live. It was cold enough that bits of frost covered the edges of the window glass. There was a redbird in the tree. I could hear laughter from the barn.

Maybe what I need isn't a cataclysmic event. I've had enough of those in my life. Maybe I've been waiting for life to slow down so I can see it well enough to put it on this page.

He's going to read this. That makes me uncomfortable, but I promised to be honest. The truth is, I haven't had a moment to slow down since I was a child. Every day was just another notch in the tumbling of seasons around the calendar.

I'm safe here, for however long I stay or he chooses to keep me. So far the sex has been a small price to pay for my protection. He's gentle when he chooses to be and when he doesn't, it's the sweetest storm.

It scares me, but not the way Clint scared me. I've never met a man who lives with the same intensity as Gerard. He's a mountain, a force of nature. And if he's reading this right now, that's not always a good thing—so don't let it get to your head, sir.

I think what surprises me most about this arrangement isn't the sex or the man, it's that I haven't wanted to leave Sovereign Mountain once since I came here.

I've never been safe before. I could get used to this.

I just wish I knew what happens next.

CHAPTER EIGHTEEN

KEIRA

The days inch by at a snail's pace. Maybe time is slow because I'm so used to being busy. Other than working with Angel, my only tasks are to wear the clothes he picks out for me and fuck him at night.

I'm not keeping track of the days as they inch by. My phone sits unused in my dresser drawer. There's hardly any signal at Sovereign Mountain and I have no one to text or call. The internet works almost never. The realization that I just disappeared from the world is sobering. I had friends in school, but after my father died and I dropped out to live with the Garrisons, they'd faded into the distance.

Gerard sleeps next to me, but he hasn't fucked me since he ate me until I came. Sometimes he'll push his fingers into my panties and stroke my pussy absently. At night, I wake and he's got his palm over it. Holding the heat of my sex in his hand.

During the day, he works outside the house. Occasionally he has to do something in his office that's just off the bedroom, but he hasn't invited me in, so I don't ask.

I start to see the patterns of Sovereign Mountain. He runs the whole thing, the sun rises and sets with him. Westin is his right hand and advisor. They always confer in the driveway in the early morning. Both standing in the cold in their flannels and jackets, steam rising from their lips. Billowing out beneath the brims of their hats. Then they part ways and the ranch runs smoothly for another day.

I hold up my end of the bargain. I obey him, I say yes sir and no sir. Shyly, I start offering him sex or oral at the end of the day. He praises me, but he doesn't fuck me as often as I anticipated he would.

What are we waiting for?

Then, all at once, the structures of our dynamic come into focus. I'm in the bedroom, late one night, under the covers with a book I pulled from the shelf downstairs. It's a war memoir. Maybe it's too heavy for before bed, but it pulls me in even though I don't usually read nonfiction. I'm heavy eyed when I finally set it aside and reach for my cup of water.

The door opens and Gerard enters. He locks it, as he always does.

"What is it?" I ask.

"It's Sunday night," he says.

At first, I'm not sure what that means. Then it floods back to me and my cheeks explode with heat. There's no sound but the gas fireplace in the corner. The great bull skull towers over us both. The air between us crackles as we stare at each other across our bed.

His bed. Not mine, I'm still a guest here.

"Okay," I manage. "What would you like me to do...sir?"

He crosses to me and sits on the edge of the bed. His rough fingers graze my chin. "You're such a good girl. But you need this, I think I haven't played with you enough this week."

"Did I do something wrong?" I ask.

"No, I'm just easing you in. My absence is never a punishment. If you need punished, you'll know right away."

I appreciate his honesty. He rises and disappears into the bathroom and I hear the shower run for a while.

He returns in nothing but a pair of sweatpants. My eyes run over his hard stomach and my sex aches at the way the waistband hangs from his hips. He's so lean there I can follow the veins down the trail of hair until it disappears.

He goes to the closet and when he returns, he carries a folded square of leather. I pull myself up against the pillow to watch him unfold it. Revealing a set of implements. They look brand new.

"Tonight, I'll use my hand," he says. "But I want you to look at those and tell me what you're willing to experiment with."

There's something so confusing and humiliating about vetting the items he's going to spank me with. I kneel beside them and pick up what appears to be a paddle and run my fingers over the handle. It's light, but long enough to be laid across my ass. I know in his hand, it'll hurt.

"Did you make these too?" I ask.

He shakes his head. "I have someone who makes them custom. Nothing I use on you has ever touched anyone else."

"What do you prefer?"

He cocks his head, picking up a ruler. It looks small in his hand. "I like the riding crop. It's good for beginners because it sounds worse than it is. The sound of it will get you wet."

I'm bright red. My stomach flutters.

"You can use it if you want," I say.

"I will when it's done. I'm making one for you."

I run my eyes over the ruler, the hairbrush, the paddle, and the thin switch. I'm unsure what to expect with them, but I'm willing to try each one before banning it.

"I'm comfortable with experimenting with any of those," I say.

He nods and rolls the leather up. Then he sets it aside and returns to the bed and sits on the edge. His gaze bores into me and I lower my eyes and realize he's rock hard. I can see his heavy length hanging in his sweatpants.

My mouth goes dry and my pussy does the opposite.

"When I spank you with my hand, it will always be over my lap on the edge of the bed," he says. "You'll remove your clothes and lay over my knees. You won't struggle or fight me. If you're good, after your maintenance spankings, you'll get to finish."

Breathless, I nod. "Yes, sir."

He extends his palm. "Go on."

Shakily, I get to my feet. His eyes follow my every move as I tug my sweatshirt off, leaving me in nothing but my panties. My fingers clench as I hesitate. Chewing my lip and waiting for instruction.

"You'll be spanked without padding," he says. "Panties down."

Oh God, I wish I could moan out loud. I push my soaked panties down, hoping he doesn't see the wet spot.

"Fold your clothes and lay them on the bedside table," he orders.

I obey and return to him, standing with my hands at my sides. My nipples ache. I know my cheeks are burning. There's no way he doesn't know how aroused I am.

"Come," he says.

His warm palm slides over my hip and he guides me over his lap. I settle my hips over his thighs, realizing he's too big for me to rest my elbows on the bed. I'm hanging awkwardly a few inches above the quilt. He notices and he pulls a pillow below my chest for support.

My breath comes heavy and fast. My eyes squeeze shut.

His fingers run over my bare ass. His palm rubs gently, massaging the muscles, being careful not to touch my exposed pussy.

"I want you to know that you're a good girl," he says. "This is for when you're tempted to disobey me. Do you understand?"

"I understand," I whisper. "Sir."

He caresses my ass and upper thighs. Taking his time with every inch of naked skin. I'm breathing hard and doing my best not to squirm. He said I was to keep still, so I'll do my best. His hand slides up my nape, up against my scalp, and closes. Holding my head in place by my hair.

He spanks me once. It barely stings, but I feel it in my pussy. I bite my lip.

"Good girl," he murmurs.

My brain goes blank. I can take a lot if it means he'll praise me like that. With a voice as smooth as fine, dark whiskey, edged with rough gravel beneath.

He spanks me harder this time, three times in a row. My eyes widen and I grip the pillow. He waits, like he expects me to react, but

I don't. I suck my breath in as he starts spanking me with little blows, just heavy enough to sting, but not enough to really hurt.

"Do you know your safeword?" he asks.

I nod. "Yes, sir."

His grip tightens in my hair and he spanks me hard where my left cheek meets my upper thigh. I gasp this time and my eyes water. My skin is starting to feel warm where he's striking me. But it has nothing on the heat pulsing between my legs.

He spanks both sides of my ass in rapid succession. More like quick swats, like he's trying to deny me the pleasurable thuds that send vibrations down to my clit. He's making sure it hurts before it feels good. I want to call him a sadist in my head, but if he's a sadist and I'm wet from what he's doing...does that make me a masochist?

I'm not sure I'm ready for that label yet.

My inner muscles clench and I feel my pussy leak. It drips down my sex and I know it's on his thigh. Staining his pants.

My ass is warm and I'm struggling to keep still. He doesn't let up, he just spanks me evenly on both sides again and again. The same way he fucks—without reprieve. I wish he'd given me something to bite down on because my jaw aches from clenching. My fingers grip the pillow and I force myself to focus on my white knuckles.

I can breathe through this.

My lips part and without my consent, a whimper bursts out. He goes still for a beat and I freeze. Was that the wrong thing to do?

"I'm sorry, sir," I breathe.

His palm moves over my burning ass and up my lower back. His other hand doesn't loosen in my hair, it holds my head down so I'm unable to raise my eyes higher than the pillow.

"It's alright, redbird," he says. "You may whimper. Just no backtalk."

He spanks me again, hard enough I cry out. Something thick rises in my throat and I realize it's a sob. Part of me is humiliated that I'm crying. It doesn't even hurt that badly. I've had worse period cramps in the last few months. But there's something so vulnerable about allowing him to hurt me.

It's safe.

It's pain, but not the kind I'm used to. This pain is closer to the intimacy of pleasure. Like a whisper against my throat in the dark. Like the soft thud of his hips meeting mine as he ruts into my body.

My mind latches onto the memory of the bed hitting the wall.

Thud. Thud. Thud.

Every one of his thrusts calculated to hit every inch of my inner walls. I pinch my eyes shut and I realize I'm getting used to his palm on my ass. My hot muscles are relaxing and calm rises up my spine.

Sweet, painful release.

I feel it before I realize what it is. My pussy tightens as his hand cups it, sending heavy vibrations through my lower body. My clit throbs as it contacts the rough fabric of his pants over his hard thigh. Back and forth with each spank.

One tear and then another slip from my eyes. My throat clenches and a sob bursts up. And another until I'm crying into the pillow. But I barely notice because suddenly I'm aware that I'm right on the edge of coming on his thigh. I freeze, realizing I don't know the boundaries around orgasm during punishment.

"Sir," I gasp.

He pauses. "What is it?"

I'm a ball of mortification, but I force the words out because he told me that failure to communicate was one of the worst offenses. If this is being spanked for maintenance, I'm nervous to imagine what real punishment is like.

"I'm going to come...I can't stop it, sir," I whisper.

"Fuck me," he says reverently.

His fingers graze the entrance of my cunt. His fingers feel rough on my raw flesh. He tugs my head back by the hair and slips his middle finger down to my clit. I know I stained his thigh, I can feel it.

He uses my arousal and circles my sensitive bud. Using slow, even pressure until I feel my muscles clench and spasm, releasing a well of pleasure. It's not the most tumultuous orgasm I've had, but it's the clearest.

I feel every ebb and flow of blood, every release of muscle. The blood surging through my body and culminating in my sex throbs, heightening every sensation. Etching out every bit of pleasure until I'm limp across his lap.

"That's my girl," he says.

He lifts me up and sets me on my feet. My knees wobble and I can't meet his eyes.

"Can you walk to the dresser?" he asks.

I nod, inhaling shakily.

"Go and get the bottle in the top drawer out," he orders.

I obey, bringing the small bottle of lotion to him and putting it in his outstretched palm. My arousal stings my inner thighs. The emotion in my chest is gone and all that's left is calm.

"Lay down and flip over," he says.

I do as he says and I feel his weight sink the bed behind me. Then cool lotion spreads over my ass and thighs. The relief is immediate and my eyes flicker shut as he gently rubs it in.

"Tomorrow, I want you to write in your diary," he says. "Tonight, I want you to process."

"I wrote in it already," I whisper. "But not really about sex."

"Good girl," he praises. "Write some more, leave it out for me on the desk when you're done. And write about the sex too."

I'm glad he's giving me time to understand my emotions. It was such an endorphin rush, such a wave of adrenaline. And now I'm drained of all the tightness in my chest, all the anxiety and worry that built up over the last seven months.

I nod and then remember I'm supposed to affirm him aloud.

"Yes, sir."

He shifts up behind me and pulls me back against his warm body. Being comforted by the person who just held me over his lap and spanked me is confusing. He gave me pain and now he's giving me comfort.

It's so vulnerable it makes my chest ache.

My eyes close.

I'm going to have to watch this man. Without me realizing, he's going to have my walls down faster than he got my panties around my ankles.

CHAPTER NINETEEN

GERARD

She's curled up somewhere deep in the blankets the next morning. I drag myself from the bed and get ready for the day. She must have been up during the night because the diary is on my desk. I pick it up and flip it open.

She's settling in.

A small smile tugs at the corner of my mouth.

I lay the diary where I found it. She's doing so well. I'm trying to ease her into this. I can tell she's doing everything she can to follow the rules as she understands them.

I'm proud of her, she's got the fundamental qualities that make a good submissive.

I select a pair of cotton panties and matching bra. They're simple, but they'll be so fucking sexy on her body. And my name is embroidered into the band of both. Marking my property.

She sighs when I tug the sheets down. After I spanked her pretty ass red, she fell asleep against my chest, still naked. The longer she's with me, the more feral my reaction is to seeing her bare.

I roll her onto her stomach. There are small purple and pink marks on the underside of her ass.

She stirs and I sink down onto the bed.

"Let's go, redbird," I say.

She grumbles and rubs her face into the pillow. Her eyes crack open and she stares at me through a haze.

"Are we going to the blacksmith shop?" she whispers.

"No," I say. "We're going for a ride."

That perks her up instantly. She sits up and rubs her eyes, yawning. Seeing her fully naked in my rumpled blankets is doing things to me. I'm going to have to start fucking her daily. She's had enough time to get acclimated.

"Where?"

"I have someone ride the west border and to the upper pasture every morning," I say. "Today it's my turn and I'm taking you with me."

She pauses and I lift my hand and lay it on her waist. She's got beautiful curves. I touch the line of her abdominal muscle and run my fingertip down over her lower belly to her clit. I gather her wetness and use it to stroke her. Until her breasts heave.

"Do you want me?" she whispers.

I nod. "Tonight."

She chews her lip. "I thought you would fuck me more often, sir."

She says those words with a sigh. I can't hold back a short laugh as I withdraw my hand. She's horny, and I can't blame her. I've teased her, I've made her sleep in my bed, but I haven't fucked her for almost four days.

"Did you find the bridle I left you?" I ask.

Her forehead creases. "Yes, what is that for?"

"You wanted to work with Angel so I ordered you a bridle for her," I say. "She's able to wear it, but I wouldn't try riding her yet. Give her a little longer."

"Oh," she says softly. "Thank you, sir."

"Let's go ride," I say.

She pulls on her warm clothes and boots. With the dogs at our heels, I lead the way out to the barn and she sits on a stack of hay bales and watches me saddle up Shadow. He's watching her over his shoulder, his big, glassy eyes glued to the way her auburn hair glitters.

This woman has enchanted my animals. Big Dog and Small Dog follow her around the house all day. They couldn't care less when I get in at night. They're in the living room, curled up at her feet or draped over her lap. If I didn't make them sleep in the living room, they'd be trying to crawl into the bed with her. And now Shadow is staring at her like she hung the moon and stars.

Maybe they're just feeding off my energy.

I bring my secondary horse, a chestnut mare with white socks, from the back of the barn. She's big enough to carry me, but smaller than Shadow. Keira's face lights up when I lead her out.

"What's her name?" She slides to her feet and extends her palm.

"I just call her girl," I say.

That frown appears instantly. "You need to hire someone part time just to name your animals for you."

I look down at her with faint amusement. She's running her palm over the mare's neck. The horse nuzzles her head and nips at the strands of red hair over the back of her jacket. They all seem to like how her hair looks in the light of the electric lantern.

"Can I call her something different?" she asks.

Her blue eyes turn on me, wide and begging. Without thinking, I nod. Just to see that smile flash over her lips.

"Bluebell," she says, stroking down the horse's side. "We always had fields of them in the spring."

I don't protest. I watch as she brushes Bluebell down and I help saddle her up. The saddle is heavy and she struggles to get it above her head. She doesn't try to get up on her own, she just lets me lift her and watches silently while I mount Shadow.

We ride to the outer yard, leaving the dogs at the barn door. The sun is just kissing the horizon, sending streaks of pale blue across the early morning sky. The air is cold, but with a promise of sunshine later. I don't trust it—I know we'll have a snowstorm before November.

The view of the western side of the ranch is breathtaking. We pause for a moment and she lets out a little sigh. I glance over and I see a new emotion on her face. It looks like freedom, like joy.

I should take her out riding with me more often.

"Have you always lived at Sovereign Mountain?" she asks.

I shift my weight and Shadow begins trekking down the slow hill. She falls into step beside me, riding easily with one hand on her thigh. The faint wind whips her hair back even though she's wearing a knit cap. I should get her a real hat to contain that brilliant hair.

"No," I say. "I'm from the east."

Her brows rise. "Really? Where?"

"Boston," I say gruffly. I don't like talking about the past.

Either she can't read social cues or she just doesn't care. She leans forward curiously, studying my face.

"Why did you come out here?"

"My parents moved out," I say. "I had aspirations to be a fighter. So I stayed."

It was true, I had trained in Colorado, but only for a year in my teens. Then I'd been shot in the thigh during a summer job back in Montana and my aspirations to box died.

She opens her mouth and I clear my throat.

"You tell me about yourself," I say.

"I already have," she says. "I don't have an interesting story."

"Tell me about your relationship to the Garrison family."

Her eyes dart to my face and she works her jaw. I can tell it's not something she wants to delve into. But I don't really care. I need to know her version of her history with the Garrison family.

"Did you know the senior Garrisons well? Abel and Maria?" I press.

She nods. "Abel was very insistent that I marry Clint. I felt that...maybe he would have kicked me out if I didn't."

Wait...what did that mean? I turn and my expression must be sharp because she notices it.

"I lived with them after my father died," she says quickly. "I worked on the ranch and they helped run Stowe Farms. We weren't

140

much of an operation, mostly unused land, by that point. When I married Clint, Garrison Ranch absorbed everything and they tore down the barn and house. It's all pasture now. And...then they died on that trip overseas. I felt really guilty about feeling relieved, but Maria was so difficult to me."

I knew most of that, but I hadn't known she was living with Clint's parents before her marriage. It was no wonder she folded so easily. The thought of it turns my stomach. She was young, not even legal, in a house full of people who wanted her property. I had no doubt Abel and Maria knew exactly what they were doing by pushing their son onto her. Not caring that she wasn't old enough to consent.

At least I had some lines I wouldn't cross. I'm not a good man, but I gave her more of a choice. And she's old enough to give full consent.

We pause as we crest the hill. The horses blow steam into the air and the sun has risen enough to see the field stretched out before us. Far away, barely visible to the eye, is the line that separates my land from the Garrison's.

"That's the border," I say, jerking my head.

Her eyes narrow. "I thought it extended further in."

"It did," I say. "But I bought it off them."

Her brows shoot up. "I can't imagine the Garrisons selling to you."

"They sold to the bank," I say. "I own the bank. And now, in the last year, I've absorbed seven thousand acres of Garrison land."

She gazes at me and her lips part. My eyes wander and I remember how soft they are. How they wrap around my fingers. How they parted in the blacksmith shop as I licked her soft pussy.

Fuck...she's a pretty thing.

My thoughts turn quickly darker. Her skin marks easily. She's delicate, but she's also sturdy from working on the farm. I could lay my belt across her ass until she bruised and she'd probably let me. This little redhead is a slut for pain, that much is obvious.

I got a taste for dominating her the other night, and now I'm hungry again. I want her tied up in my bed, ass flushed red, cum seeping from between her legs. Tears dusting her thick lashes.

"What are you staring at?" she whispers.

I shake my head once. "I'm not friendly with the Garrisons, Keira. We have a dark...bloody history. There's no love lost."

I can tell she wants to pry, but instead she stays quiet.

"Don't speak to any Garrison," I say. "And you don't need to fear them. If anyone goes after you, I'll consider it theft of my property and deal with it accordingly."

She knows we're so far out the law is a loose memory. The penalty in these parts for hustling cattle and horses is a quick shot to the side of the head. And a shallow grave in the mountains. Her eyes widen and her throat bobs.

"What do you say?" I press.

"I understand, sir," she says in a rush.

"Good girl."

The thing that surprises me most about Keira is that, whether she knows it or not, she wants this as badly as I do. Maybe she didn't know it before, but she seems to want the security of obedience from someone she trusts.

If that's the case, I'm doing something right because she's offering her obedience to me.

It's almost ten when we get back to the house. She's cold so I send her inside while I brush down the horses and put them out to the pasture. When I go to drop some things off in the bedroom, I find the bathroom door ajar. The shower is running and thick steam wafts through the crack.

Something catches my boot. I look down to see her clothes on the floor.

I don't like messes. Everything in my house must be neat.

Bending, I pick up her shirt and jeans. Her panties fall out and I catch them before they hit the ground. The pale pink cotton feels like silk in my rough fingers. I turn them over and there's a little wet stain where her pussy sat. I bring it to my nose and inhale.

Sweet...pure pheromones.

Something animal wakes in me. She's not on birth control and I can smell she's ovulating. The scent is a little sweeter and it hits me like a brick wall. It's like an electric shock that blows my pupils and turns my senses all the way up.

I want to wrap my cock in her panties and jerk off into them. To paint my cum on every intimate thing she owns.

The bathroom door creaks open and she's standing there, patting her hair dry. Looking clean and flushed pink from her shower.

"Come here," I say.

She obeys, setting the towel on the bedside table. There's hesitancy in her steps, but I can also see her nipples tighten.

I don't stand on ceremony. She gasps as I spin her around and bend her over the bed. Her fists clench the sheets.

My belt clangs as I undo it and unleash my cock. It's hard, straining to be inside her, and wet at the tip. I see the tremor of muscle in her back as I spit into my hand and rub it over my length and her entrance. She's wet, perhaps from arousal, perhaps from ovulation. It's hard to tell.

I push in. She can take me.

"Fuck—Gerard," she gasps.

My hand comes down on her ass and she yelps as I thrust my cock into her pussy. Not caring that it doesn't fucking fit. I grip her face, forcing her lips open, and push her panties between her lips.

"Don't use my name when I'm inside you," I say. "It's sir or nothing."

Between us, her pussy stretches to take me. I know it hurts her, but instead of crying out, she's moaning. Her face is shoved into the bed and she's pushed back against me. She wants the pain, the fullness. Her needy, tight cunt needs to be used.

I hit resistance. She's tensed up. I slide my fingers between her thighs and stroke her clit. Her pupils dilate and her naked breasts heave. Slowly, her muscles relax enough I can thrust the rest of the way inside.

She wriggles her hips to wrap her legs around my waist, but I take both ankles and flip them over my shoulders. She's folded in half beneath me and there's nothing between us to hold me back. I pump my hips out and thrust hard, getting all the way to the soft resistance of her cervix.

Her spine arcs, her eyes roll back, and she screams around the panties between her teeth.

If I wasn't snipped, this woman would be pregnant. There's no fucking way I'd pull out of her.

Wetness slips down my cock. She's such a sweet, perfect slut for me. She lives for the feeling of being forced, of being filled. I feel her muscles relax all the way and each thrust gets easier as she gets so wet I can hear it.

I keep working her clit until she tenses in my arms. Her spine locks back and her head falls in a cloud against the sheets. She screams around the gag and her eyes roll back as she shakes hard.

Her body goes limp. I flip her easily to her hands and knees and mount her from behind. She's small enough I can slide my hand up between her breasts and wrap it around her throat. Holding her still so I can rut into her pussy.

I've never felt anything like her cunt. Soft like silk, soaking wet, and so tight it grips me and caresses every inch of my length as I fuck it.

The bed frame slams against the wall. She whimpers with every thrust. My orgasm draws closer and I push myself into her again and again, chasing it without a thought in my head.

I feel her tense. My orgasm shoots down my spine and I push in deep and go still. Feeling the pleasure throb through my cock as all my tension releases into her body.

She moans as I pull out and sit up. Her pussy is swollen and my cum seeps out and drips from her clit. Her inner thighs are slick with arousal and I bend, licking it up. Savoring the sweet taste of my submissive's cunt.

She pushes herself to her knees, still facing away from me, and spits the soaked panties out. I gather her wet hair and stroke it. A little purr of satisfaction sounds in her chest.

"Good girl, redbird," I say.

There's a short silence and she sighs.

"What are you doing to me, sir?" she whispers.

I could ask her the same thing. I spend all my free time thinking about her like a lovesick teenager. She's got me so horny I can't keep my cock in my pants. I grip her hair, wrapping it once around my fist. Dragging her head back to make her look at me.

"What do you mean?"

She blinks up at me. "I was never this slutty until I met you."

I laugh. "You hadn't been fucked properly."

She nestles her head back against my chest and I let her feel my warmth. Just long enough I know she's feeling alright. I draw back and turn her around.

"I want you to get down on your knees and thank me for letting you come," I say.

Her eyes widen and she stands. "Sorry, sir. I didn't know."

"No, you don't have to do it every time," I assure her. I tuck my cock in my pants and fasten my belt. "Go on."

Her cheeks flush and she wobbles before sinking down to her knees. She tucks her heels under her ass and uncurls her palms on her lower thighs. Like the perfect girl she is, she drops her head and keeps her eyes to the floor.

"Thank you, sir," she whispers.

"For?"

"Thank you for letting me come," she manages. "Sir."

She's so humiliated she probably needs to come again, but that can wait. I crouch down and lift her chin. Her big blue eyes flick to mine and she studies me, trying to read my face.

"You're doing well," I say. "The cuffs for your wrists are almost done."

She nods. "Thank you, sir."

We have a few weeks left before I collar her and the amended contract begins. Part of me is looking forward to it, but the other part doesn't care because it changes nothing. Maybe we'll end up staying in this dynamic, maybe we won't, but whatever happens, Keira Garrison will sleep in my bed from now on.

CHAPTER TWENTY

KEIRA

I go out to the paddock behind the barn early one morning. Big Dog and Small Dog reluctantly follow me out into the cold and sit puffed up on the porch. The sunlight is cool, still shaded behind the mountain. Tiny flakes of snow spiral from the sky. So few I have to look twice to see if they're really there.

Angel is quiet as I put her tack on and lead her out to the paddock. We've been practicing a lot lately. I spend a few hours with her every day and she's learning to trust me now. I'm not sure I'm ready to get on her yet, but that will come with time.

How much time?

How long will I be here?

Angel pauses outside the barn, blinking her dark eyes up at me. I stroke down her velvety nose and she buries it in my glove.

The painted mare sits heavy in my pocket.

Other than the mare, the only thing my mother left behind was a book of Swedish fairy tales. I read it cover to cover, so many times it fell to dust. Right now, I'm reminded of a story about a woman who goes out into the wild to rescue her father and is snatched by a dark mountain spirit. She has to answer a riddle to get by his bridge, but in the end he lets her pass for a single kiss.

I think back to how Gerard looked when I left. Still sleeping, the blanket pooled around his waist. He's taken a lot more than a kiss, but I'm still not allowed to leave his mountain.

It tickles me to think of him as a mountain spirit. Long claws, even taller than he is now, bright white eyes.

Speak of the devil.

I hear his boots on the frozen ground. His presence fills the space like smoke. Angel lifts her head and rests her chin on my shoulder, staring past me at him.

I turn. He's leaning on the fence, one boot on the first rung.

The corner of his mouth turns up. Without breaking his stone visage, he whistles. For a second, I think he's trying to get Angel to come, but then I realize he's wolf-whistling at me. Heat creeps up beneath my coat and scarf. I don't know what he's looking at, every inch of me is covered.

"Come here, redbird," he says.

I release Angel and she stays still as I cross the hard, crunchy ground to the fence. He tilts his head so we don't knock our hats off and I stand on my toes to let him kiss me. He tastes faintly of coffee. His face is smooth—he must have shaved it this morning after I'd left.

"No beard?" I ask.

He shakes his head. "Not today, but it'll be back in a day or two."

I think I feel a crack in his cold so I offer him a smile. "You make me think of a story I read when I was little."

"Really?"

I relate the story to him briefly and his brow rises. There's a faintly amused shadow over his mouth. He looks at me like that a lot. When I fall silent, I start to wonder if he'll be offended by his portrayal as a dark woodland spirit. But he just reaches out and tugs my braid and taps my chin with the side of his curled finger.

"I see how it is," he says.

"How what is?" I frown.

"My price is much higher for passage."

"I know that."

147

He leans in, his breath a cloud. "Don't lie and say you don't enjoy it."

A shiver moves down my spine and I can't think of anything but the last time he fucked me. When I walked from the bathroom and he pushed me down on the bed. My toes curl in my cold boots.

"Show me what you've been doing with Angel," he says.

"We've been working on lunging," I say. "I'll get on her in the barn and let her sit with that, but we haven't been riding in the pasture."

"Good girl, that's smart," he says. "Gives her space to obey, but not feel restricted."

He takes the lead rope from the gate and hands it to me, following me inside the paddock. I'm a little nervous with him watching me, but I'm confident Angel can at least do this. He stays by the gate, arms crossed over his broad chest. Hat pulled low.

I pause in the center of the paddock. Angel backs up obediently and lines herself up with the fence. She waits, gazing at me through her forelock. I take the loose end of the lead and swing it in slow circles. Right away, she breaks into a clockwise walk around the perimeter of the fence. Pride fills my chest and I want to look at Gerard, but Angel deserves my focus.

I switch hands. Angel pivots and moves counterclockwise.

"Good," Gerard says. "Bring her in to you."

I stop swinging the rope and loop it over my arm. Angel turns and starts walking slowly in my direction. She comes to a halt, drapes her head over my shoulder, and follows me back to where Gerard stands by the gate.

"She's doing really well," he says.

I open my mouth to reply, but out of nowhere there's a sound like a gunshot. Angel throws her head so fast I only have time to fall back against the fence. Her eyes flash white and I see panic set in as she whirls. She takes the paddock at a gallop, kicking up ice and dry grass and heads back at us.

Panic sets into me too and I scramble back, but it's too late. Her chestnut and white body swings around and her hindquarters fill my vision.

At the last minute, I feel his body over mine. I hear his grunt as he takes the weight of Angel's body against his. Big Dog barks from somewhere outside the paddock. And I see Gerard grit his teeth as he's slammed against the fence.

His hat falls off and his eyes flash, but he stays calm. Angel throws her head and Gerard's body ripples as he shoves her back. Pushing half the weight of a horse off him.

Oh my God, that's both terrifying and impressive.

Angel bolts to the far side of the paddock and stops. She's heaving, her skin shivering.

I turn to run to Gerard, but he's already standing, dusting his hands off. He's got a dirty print on his back, but otherwise he's unharmed. My feet are frozen to the ground as he walks back over to me.

"I'm so sorry," I burst out. "It won't happen again. It was my fault."

He glances up, eyes calm. "It's fine, redbird. She's a horse and horses spook."

My clenched hands uncurl. Heat floods my body in an uncontrollable wave. If that had happened with Clint, he'd have berated me for days. He'd have made me feel terrible and taken away my horse as punishment, telling me I didn't deserve to train her anymore.

"It was probably a car backfiring by the employee residences," he says. He takes his coat off, hanging it over the fence. "Let me get Angel."

I stand by the gate, speechless. He's in his Henley and he's rolled the sleeves up just enough to show his wrists. I can see the outline of his undershirt beneath. There's a faint sweat stain around the buttons. I can tell he runs hot, even in the winter.

I watch the muscle move beneath his shirt as he centers himself in the paddock. Angel balks, backing into the fence. He kneels down, making himself smaller, although he still comes up to my shoulder when he's on his knees.

He whistles. Angel stands perfectly still.

"She doesn't like men," he says quietly.

I like that he doesn't fault her for it, he's just stating a fact. He holds out his palm. We wait in silence for several minutes. I'm trying to keep myself under control, but how patient he's being is driving me wild.

Seeing him get thrown against the fence scared me, but seeing him lift half a horse off his body set me on fire.

I want to pull him into the barn and drop to my knees.

Angel moves, slowly. She rounds the paddock and drops her head, coming close. He reaches into his pocket and takes out a handful of grain. Her eyes flicker and she moves in, nibbling it from his palm.

He stands slowly, letting her body drape against his. She rests her neck in the curl of his elbow and he pats her shoulder.

"Good girl," he says.

He gathers her reins and leads her back to the gate. I push it open and we head for the barn without speaking. Together, we strip the tack from her and brush her down, putting her away for the day. She'll be anxious for a while, but later in the evening, I'll put her out to pasture for a few hours.

He picks up her saddle and disappears into the tack room. Heart thumping, I follow, shutting the door as best I can. The frame is uneven, leaving an inch of space.

He turns and I swallow hard.

Our gazes clash and the air burns with electricity. The barn is heated, but it's not as warm as the house. That doesn't bother me as I take my hat and coat off, dropping them to the ground. His brow rises slowly, his pale eyes taking in my every move.

I haven't initiated sex with him since that first time.

It's terrifying.

His face is unreadable. My fingers feel weak as I pull my sweatshirt over my head, leaving me in just my bra and jeans. I'm nervous, but it's overpowered by the wave of desire soaking me. I've never been attracted to power before, I've always been afraid of it. I wonder what the difference between his strength and Clint's is and why I'm not cowed.

He takes a step closer.

"You saved me," I whisper.

It sounds silly when I say it out loud in the quiet of the barn.

"Did you expect me to let you be crushed?"

I lick my dry lips. "I just didn't think you would take the hit yourself."

His jaw works.

"I can take it."

He closes the space between us, backing me up until I hit the wall. My eyes dart down and I see the hard ridge beneath the front of his work pants. My fists clench. God, I want to undo his belt and take him in my grip. Hold his desire in my hand, feel how much he wants me.

His eyes run over my face, light blue as the sky and heavy lidded. He clears his throat.

"I'm not fucking you," he says.

I swallow my disappointment. I know better than to let it show on my face.

"Why, sir?"

He reaches out and forces the door shut and releases it. It swings open.

"Because one other man seeing your body is one man too many."

He steps back and hands me my sweatshirt. Confused, I pull it back on and let him settle my jacket overtop.

"There's no one in the barn, sir," I say.

He cocks his head, leaving the tack room. I follow him to the doorway and he looks up at the sky. Sometimes I wish he would just speak so I didn't have to guess what's going on behind those hard eyes.

"What are we waiting for?" I whisper.

He lifts his hand. There's a beat of silence and the breakfast bell rings out.

"The barn will be full in a moment," he says.

Disappointed, I turn to go, but his arm shoots out and he grabs my wrist. I open my mouth, but before I can speak, he's pulled me against his chest. His hand slides up my cheek and buries in my hair. He takes his hat off and bends, his mouth brushing mine.

My whole body tingles. I love kissing him, he's so good at it.

And I can tell he knows it.

When he pulls back, I'm a panting mess. He presses his mouth to my forehead for a second and I'm so weak I can barely stand.

"Your cuffs are done," he says. "I laid them by the bed."

I stay still, not wanting to leave. He extracts me from his arms and turns me towards the house, giving me a little spank to get me going. I give him a look—which I'm careful to keep respectful—and he smiles. It's tempered, but it's real.

Back in the bedroom, I find the cuffs on the bedside table. Reverently, I lift them and run my fingertips over the embossed, dark brown leather. Over the center is a line of bluebells and above and below it run two rows of intricate braiding. At each end, where they come together, is half of the Sovereign Mountain emblem. I push the edges together to make it whole.

I know what it means.

His.

He's so selfish and jealous—I feel it even though he never cracks and shows it with his face or words. He doesn't have to, my presence here is proof enough.

I change into my slip and sit back on the bed to fasten the cuffs around my wrists. I've never had anything custom made for me before. The amount of care and attention to detail amazes me.

But what do they mean?

Are they just for sex? Just because he likes fucking women in restraints?

I thought things were going to be different after reading and signing the contract. I thought our relationship would be purely transactional. That he'd get what he wanted out of me in the bedroom and I'd be kept safe. That he wouldn't step between me and danger or press kisses to my forehead in the barn doorway.

But here he is, putting cuffs made of bluebells around my wrists.

And he's barely fucked me.

Apparently he's not very good at sticking to the rules of his contract. I'm not either because I don't understand when we're playing and when we're not. Sometimes he says something that jars me and I have to remind myself that he's playing a part.

Or is he?

Whose words does he speak when he fucks me and tells me I belong to him? His or my Dom's?

That night after dinner, he strips my clothes off and cuffs me to the headboard. My heart pounds as he takes a thin switch from the dresser and braces one knee on the edge of the bed.

"Let's test what you can take," he says.

He's still dressed and I'm fully naked. My ankles cross and my toes curl, anticipating pain. I hear the hiss before I see it and pain sears over my nipples. Fuck, that wakes me up. My eyelids fly open and I cry out, my spine arcing.

"Good girl," he says.

He doesn't stop because I don't safeword him. At first, the pain of the switch across my breasts makes me want to scream. But he gives me a strip of leather to bite down on and I keep it in, diving headfirst into being out of control. The pain numbs and leaves behind the sweetest burn I've ever felt.

It travels down my belly to my clit.

My brain disengages. All I can feel is the slow build in my clit, the slippery arousal between my thighs.

And the ceaseless sting of the blows across my breasts.

He stops and sets aside the switch. I'm so close, teetering on the edge of orgasm. My lashes flutter and he hears me whimper.

"What, redbird?" he asks.

"I was so close," I pant.

He makes a sound in his throat that's pure desire. A growl and a groan intermingled. I bite my lip as he flips me onto my knees, my wrists crossing. His zipper hisses and he enters me so hard from behind I see stars. Sometimes the pain is just pain, but tonight it's so much more.

He takes me by the throat and holds me against his chest. His cock is deep inside, but he isn't fucking me. With his other hand, he slaps my right breast. Right at the tip where it hurts the most.

I spill over the edge, my body jerking so hard in his grip he almost drops me. He throbs and I moan, my head falling back as I pulse with him, pleasure shattering through my hips. I'm dimly aware of him pulling the cuffs from the headboard and wrapping the chain around his fist.

Then he throws me on my back, holding me down by the wrists, and fucks me like an animal. I lay there, stunned and exhausted from my orgasm, and let him. I've never had sex like this and every time with him is different. It's deeper, it's harsher, it feels so much more intense.

We're both quiet when he's done. After a while, he picks me up and carries me into the bathroom. I sit weakly on the sink while he rubs lotion into my breasts. His rough fingers taking care with the tender pink stripes across my nipples.

"How do you feel?" he asks.

I clear my throat. "I feel like I have nothing left. I came harder than I have in my entire life."

His fingertips graze my sensitive nipples. His mouth is a firm line and his lids are heavy.

"You astound me," he said finally. "I never expected you to want this as badly as I do."

My breath hitches. "It's a lot...but I've never felt so...raw."

He's quiet for a long time as he rubs my breasts. Despite how hard I came, I feel my sex tingle. And ache.

"It's not the pain," he murmurs. "It's the way it breaks down your walls and lets me in."

He wipes his hands like he didn't just say something vulnerable. He's such an enigma. Musclebound, shrouded in mystery, and so handsome it feels like looking at the sun.

We lay on our sides in bed, our bodies almost touching. There's a vein in his neck that thrums with each heartbeat.

I touch it with my fingertip just to feel how alive he is.

CHAPTER TWENTY-ONE

GERARD

I go into the city later that week. I make the two hour drive once a month and set up meetings all afternoon so I can get everything done as efficiently as possible.

Today, I need to see some bank officials about a certain mortgage. She's kept up her side of the deal, so I need to keep mine.

It's the only time I get dressed up. When I come out of my bedroom in a dark gray, tailored suit with an open collar shirt, I find my redbird curled up in the bed even though it's the middle of the afternoon. She has a book in her hand and her lids are heavy. When she hears my step, she startles and her head lolls.

Her eyes snap open. "Oh my God," she breathes.

Her jaw is slack. She pushes her back against the headboard and the book slips to the floor.

"What?" I turn and glance behind me.

Her mouth parts. Her cheeks are a distinct shade of pink I've come to realize arrives before the soaked spot in her panties.

"Oh," I say, taking a step closer. She tenses and I kneel on the edge of the bed. She shivers as I kiss the side of her throat and down her shoulder.

She moans. "You look good," she whispers. "Sir."

I sink down to a sitting position and she leans in. Her hands graze my chest, touching the triangle of bare skin where my shirt collar parts. Her nimble fingers tug the top button and she strokes my bare chest. I stay still and let her explore me, enjoying how wide her blue gaze is.

She tilts her head, looking up at me through her lashes. In the last two weeks she's been with me, she's gotten comfortable expressing herself. She offers her body to me in the morning and at night. She's always soaked when I slide into her cunt.

The way she moans drives me wild. They're breathy, like a series of little gasps. The sounds get faster as I drive her to orgasm. Her lower belly quivers, her thighs go tight. When she comes, she's so fucking wet it leaves a stain spreading across the sheets every time.

I'm not a sadist without pleasure. And how easily she comes for me is the best high I've ever felt. Her pleasure is like syrup and it flows without stopping some nights. I've never had much of a sweet tooth, but I find myself savoring her every night before I sleep.

The pain balances it out. Like salt in caramel.

***

Last night, I spanked her across the palm and fucked her with my hand until she came all over the hearth. Right below the bull skull with the heat of the fire on her back. Not for punishment, but for training. I have to be able to find her limits before I administer real punishment.

She's a good girl. I send her to the dresser for the leather case of implements and she goes obediently and brings it to me.

"On your knees," I tell her. "Palm up and out to the side."

She obeys, sinking down before the fireplace. The bull skull watches over her, eyes empty. The fireplace glitters against her naked back and her beautiful, full ass. She shifts onto her heels and curled toes.

Her head sinks back and she looks up at me, hesitantly

Eyes so big I'm lost in them.

"May I look up, sir? Or should I look at the ground?" she whispers.

"I want you to watch your palm," I tell her.

I retrieve the ruler and she tenses, but instead of using it on her hand, I kneel before her. "Open that dirty little mouth."

Her full lips part, flashing her pink tongue at me. I slide the ruler between her teeth. Tentatively she bites down. It pushes the corners of her mouth back and I find myself wondering how pretty she'd look with my cock in her throat.

Tears running down her cheeks. Spit dripping from her chin. Trying so hard to be a good girl and take as much as she can.

My cock thickens against my zipper. I take the switch out and she holds perfectly still, but I see a quiver run down her naked stomach.

It strikes her palm, just hard enough she tastes the bite. She gasps around the ruler and her poor palm flushes. I apply it four times to her hand and she doesn't move her arm an inch. When I'm done, I kneel and kiss her palm as I slide my fingers into her soaked pussy.

She moans around the ruler as she comes. When I've soothed her and put her to bed, I go back to the fireplace and kneel to run my fingertips over the little spatter she left where she knelt.

Traces of her.

***

I used to be a stickler for privacy. I fucked, but never brought anyone home to my room. Now I take pride in the way she's made her mark on my private spaces. Her clothes are in my closet, my pillow smells like her hair. Her makeup and bottles are lined up on my sink. The last time I showered, I found one of her red hairs wrapped around my dick.

"Sir."

I jerk my head, tearing myself from the memory. She's leaning in so close I feel her breath on my lips. Her lashes are lowered, dark feathers against freckled skin.

"What is it, redbird?" I say, my voice hoarse.

"Where are you going, looking like that?" she asks.

There's something in her voice I've never heard before. It sounds a bit like a pout. Is she resentful I'm going into the city and not taking her?

"I have business meetings," I say. "Sovereign Mountain has a lot of moving parts and I own other operations."

She tilts her chin up and stares into my eyes. Inches away like she's trying to imprint my image into her brain.

"Are you sure?" she whispers. "Sir."

I stand and she shifts to the edge of the bed, sitting back on her heels.

She's pouting her lips with a hurt look in her eyes. She knows what pulls at my heartstrings.

"Remember the part in the contract about communication?" I ask firmly. "If you don't speak up and tell me what's wrong, I will punish you."

She hesitates and I see the gears turning in her head. Then she shakes it and flops onto the pillows. "I'm just wondering...if I'm the only one."

There's a little crease between her brows. Oh, she's jealous. I dip my head to conceal my smile and she scowls. Maybe I should punish her for that, but I don't care to right now. I click my fingers and hold my hand out and she takes it reluctantly and allows me to lift her to her feet.

I brush her hair back. "You're lucky you were a good girl last night. Otherwise I'd take your panties down and spank you."

Heat creeps over her face. "I'm not trying to be bad. It's just...Clint used to go into the city like this. And sometimes he'd smell like someone else when he got back."

I don't tell her that I already know about Clint Garrison's infidelity—it's part of the reason he was in so much debt. Cheating is an expensive hobby. I saw his bank statements when I pulled some strings to look over his will post death. I noticed she went to the gynecologist's office more than normal. Most likely obsessively getting herself tested.

But I'm not supposed to know any of that. She won't forgive how deeply I've intruded into her personal life in the last year if she finds out.

"Come here," I say.

She obeys, and her eyes are on the floor as she approaches. I lift her chin with the side of my curled finger.

"Eyes on me," I command. Her gaze flicks up. "There is no one but you. When I get home tonight, I expect you to be in bed, naked and waiting."

She pouts, I see the push of her lower lip, and her forehead creases in a scowl. I bite back my displeasure. If I had more time, I'd take my belt off and make her count until she's whimpering an apology. But I'm late as it is, so I just turn and leave her sitting on the bed. Her pretty face scrunched.

I'm still thinking about her words as I leave Sovereign Mountain. I don't like her jealousy—it feels too much like defiance.

And I don't enjoy defiance for defiance's own sake. It's always been a trigger for me. I need the structures of BDSM because, to me, it's a holistic practice of trust. Defiance without consent feels like a violation of that.

I know her submission intimately and I feel that she stepped out of its bounds. Maybe just to test her limits for the first time.

Is that what she wants? To feel my resistance?

My shoulders are tight the entire drive into the city. And I can't get that angry, little scowl out of my head.

CHAPTER TWENTY-TWO

KEIRA

For the first time since meeting him, I'm pissed off.

I understood when I signed the contract that this was an impersonal arrangement. He gets gratification and I get protection and deferment of debt. He doesn't owe me the truth about where he's going or what he's doing.

I get that.

But after everything we've done together, I can't help feeling possessive. So I allow myself the luxury of pouting in bed for a while after he leaves.

The afternoon stretches on. I get bored of sulking and take a nap. When I wake, the house is empty and it's evening.

He'll be home soon.

My stomach flips, but I ignore it. Instead, I climb out of bed and pad naked down the hall to the game room at the far side of the hall. It's always been shut, but I've investigated it once. I know it has a set of double doors that lead out to the balcony where the hot tub sits.

I slip into the chilly space, my toes curling on the thin carpet. There's a gas fireplace on the right side, and I hurry over and flick it on. The fire roars up and I bask in it for a moment. Stomach fluttering.

He told me to be naked and waiting for him in his bed.

But a little part of me is feeling rebellious. I pull open the door and cold air hits my naked body. Taking my breath away. The stars hang overhead, the milky way a glistening trail across the sky. Shivering, I tug the cover off the hot tub and hit the button on the side. It takes less than a minute for it to start churning.

Experimentally, I poke my finger in. It's lukewarm, but heating up rapidly. I climb over the side and sink into the delicious water, letting it cover my shoulders. It smells clean and faintly like chlorine.

This is heaven.

If only I had some wine.

I clamber from the tub and scurry back into the game room. In the kitchenette I find a bottle of chardonnay in the wine rack and a stack of fluffy towels. I gather both and sink back into the tub, leaving the porch door wide open.

The view from over the railing is breathtaking, but I can't think of anything but how he told me to be naked and waiting and I'm disobeying him. He's on his way home...maybe he's already downstairs. I've never seen him angry before—I wonder if this will make his stone exterior crack.

Why do I want it to anyway?

Maybe because he makes me feel everything, but shows me nothing of himself. I've laughed in front of him, I've sobbed in his arms. He's seen me stripped naked, in every vulnerable position I can think of. Yet he's offered me little more than a flash or two of vulnerability in return.

I want to feel what's behind those pensive eyes. He's full of secrets, I can tell. And I want to pry open his walls.

Faintly, I hear his truck pull up the drive. My stomach twists and I freeze. The door slams and it snaps me out of my panic. I might be his submissive, but I'm not a doormat.

He can take a little pushback.

I pull myself from the hot tub and move to the railing. Down below I see him lock the truck. He pauses in the driveway and checks for his keys. My stomach clenches and my eyes eat the sight of him

161

hungrily. He's taken off his suit jacket and his sleeves are rolled to his elbow. His tousled dark hair is brushed back, but a few strands hang over his forehead.

Brashly, I lean over the railing. My two fingers find my mouth and I whistle. Loud enough for him to hear, but not loud enough to wake the horses.

He pivots and his head jerks up.

I know I have to be a sight. I'm completely naked, except my wet hair hanging down my back, and my tits are hard against the cold. His brow jerks, but his face stays the same. Then his mouth thins, he fits his hat back on his head, and strides up onto the porch and out of sight.

A thrill of terror moves down my spine.

My ass tingles at the memory of how much his maintenance spankings hurt. My toes curl against the cold porch. Maybe I made a miscalculation.

I freeze at the railing and then I snap into action and burst through the game room and into the empty hallway.

Naked and soaking wet, I tear down the hall and head for the bedroom. Maybe if I get on my knees, into the submissive position, he'll forgive me.

I round the corner and he's right there. Over two hundred pounds of solid muscle. His eyes are dark and his jaw is set.

Suddenly I remember that my husband died on his land.

And I never really found out how.

A bolt of real fear moves through my body. Maybe he's been shielding me from himself for a reason. He takes a quick step towards me and I gasp, stumbling back against the wall. From the soles of my feet comes the most delicious shudder that moves all the way up my thighs to my core. It's quickly followed by shame.

I'm wet from fear.

And maybe...a little part of me likes the thought that he's that dangerous. The feral, animal part of my brain that hasn't evolved in thousands of years wants him. He's the biggest, baddest motherfucker in our corner of the world. I'm completely ashamed to admit it, but some, unevolved part of me wants to roll over and open my legs at that thought.

Quick, like a snake striking, he pins me to the wall with his hand on my throat. My mouth pops open in shock and he kisses it, hard and long. Filling my senses with the taste of his mouth. My head spins and I can't breathe. His fingertips press harder and harder, trapping blood to my brain.

He's panting slightly. His pupils are blown. Black against ice blue.

"You are a dangerous woman," he says from between his teeth.

I'm dangerous? Has he looked in a mirror?

I gasp, a strangled sound coming from my throat. He eases up and I inhale, coughing.

"I'm sorry," I manage.

He's so close I can feel the heat rising from his fully clothed body. Kissing over my naked, wet breasts and thighs. His mouth parts, flashing his bottom teeth.

"My redbird," he says softly. "Thinks she can disobey me."

His fingers ease, stroking down the side of my throat. Sending tingles down to my breasts and making my nipples harden.

"How should I punish you?" he says.

Fear bursts in my stomach and goes right to my pussy. Tender blood throbs in my clit and confusion swirls. Why do I feel like I'm going to come right here in the hall, without even being touched? Am I sick? Am I fucked up?

"I could do anything I want with you, Miss Stowe," he murmurs. "No one stops me. Sovereign Mountain is mine and you are my woman."

My eyes widen. If he'd said these things to me another day, without deadly calm in his eyes, I would have thought this was just play. But he means his words. This realization is quickly followed by a heavy throb between my thighs and my fingers twitch. I'm aching, I'm right on the edge. So close I wonder if I'm going to come just from his words.

My lashes flutter. I know my face is flushed pink.

"My name is Garrison," I whisper. "Not Stowe."

He leans in. "I will fuck your dead husband's name out of your mouth," he says. "Then I'll decide what I want in its place."

I'm trying to make sense of his words, but his hands tighten on my throat and my thighs squeeze together. Rubbing at that tender place where my pleasure is coiled, pounding like a drum. I throb once and my eyes widen, fixing on his.

His brow arcs and he glances down.

"Don't you dare come," he warns.

My breasts heave, my body twists. I'm going to pass out if he doesn't give me air soon, but I can barely think about that right now. I can't unlock my thighs and the pressure is pushing me higher and higher. The calm in his eyes shatters and wildness replaces it. Like he's gotten a taste of something and he can't control himself.

"Don't you do it, little redbird," he says, his voice low.

My eyes roll back. Pleasure rips through my lower body and a little gasp bursts from my throat. He releases my neck as my orgasm hits me and the combination of oxygen to my brain and pleasure turns my legs to water. I sink to my knees, my palms flat on the floor.

It hits me what I've done as my orgasm ebbs.

He has rules and I broke them. Not just by coming without permission, but by not being in bed, ready to offer myself to him when he returned.

I fucked up.

I look up at him, towering over me. Hat still on his head. I have a feeling that whatever happens tonight, I'm about to see his walls come down for the first time. I thought he showed me flashes of honesty before, but they're nothing on what's simmering in his eyes.

"I'm sorry," I whisper.

Too late. I can tell without him saying a word.

CHAPTER TWENTY-THREE

GERARD

Her full, soft mouth trembles. Her eyes are huge. They follow my every move as I strip my belt off.

"You can safeword me—or hit my leg if you need out," I say. "But it's better if you just take it."

She won't safeword me. She's a filthy little slut and now that she's gotten a taste of what I can give her, she'll go right over the edge with me.

I see how hungry she is to feel alive. To taste fear and pleasure at the same time.

Her potential is limitless.

I crack the belt in my hand once and she flinches, but she doesn't back away.

Her pupils blow as I slip the looped end around her throat and tighten it just enough she feels the burn. She gasps and I take a second to look at what a pretty picture she makes. On her knees, naked and flushed. Her mouth is swollen and I know she's soaked between those soft thighs.

I'm going to get her off until she cries.

One handed, I unzip the front of my pants. The whites of her eyes flash and she pulls her head back.

"Quiet, be a good girl," I tell her, pushing down the front of my pants. "You've taken it in your cunt. You can take it in your mouth too."

Her pink tongue darts out and wets her mouth. I unleash my cock and it hangs heavy right before her lips. I'm so fucking hard and hot, I might blow my load all over her perfect face.

"I don't know if I can," she whispers.

I slide my hand under her chin and tilt it up. "Open up. You're going to do your best for me."

She nods and I tug the belt tighter, bringing her face close. Her tongue flicks over her lips again and she opens her mouth as I push the head of my cock into it. Hot, silky wetness wraps around the tip and my vision blurs. I've thought about her mouth for so long. And it's a hundred times better than in my fantasies.

I keep the belt taut. My other hand slides up her hair and grips it in my fist.

"Breathe on the out," I tell her.

I fuck into her mouth, not giving her more than half my length. Her throat fights me and tears spill from her eyes immediately. I know she can barely get air. But she's not trying to resist me, she's just taking it. Pretty mouth slack so I can fuck it.

My hips pump. Spit gathers on her chin and drips on the steel tips of my boots.

She chokes and I ease up on the belt. Just a trace. Her breasts heave as she gasps for breath around me. I give her a moment, then I fuck her mouth relentlessly. Putting her back in her place with every moan and gag that comes from her throat.

"Is this who you are?" I say from between gritted teeth, "Just a place for me to get off? A pretty little bitch with bruised knees and a belt around your neck?"

Her lashes flutter and her eyes roll back. I push in so deeply her throat convulses before pulling out to let her breathe. My fist grips my cock as I tug her head back.

"Open your mouth and put your tongue out," I order.

She obeys, tentatively. Her face glistens with saliva and tears. A bit of makeup is smudged under her eyes.

She's never looked more beautiful.

Fuck. I would die for this woman.

Cum shoots from the tip of my cock and splashes across her face. Shocked, her eyes snap shut, but she keeps her tongue fully extended. Catching the next pump of cum. Painting her face and dripping down her neck to the belt until I'm empty.

I release her, stepping back and taking my hat off.

She falls onto the heels of her hands, gasping. I sink down on one knee and take her by the chin and turn her face up.

"Open your eyes," I order.

She obeys, fixing them on me. They're glittering like she's feverish. I slide my hand down her neck to her right breast and pinch her tight nipple hard enough she moans.

"Do you need to come again, redbird?" I ask.

She nods eagerly. Cum slips down her chin and I catch it with the side of my finger and feed it back to her. Forcing her lips apart until she gives up and cleans it from my finger with her tongue.

"May I have a break?" she whispers.

I stand, backing up. "No," I tell her. "You'll get a break when you earn it."

My hat hits the floor. She blinks at it and her eyes snap up to me as I back slowly down the hall. I can see she's trying to figure out what I want.

I come to a halt just inside the open doors to the game room. She wanted to play fucking games tonight, so I'll give her what she wants so hard she won't be able to sit tomorrow.

"Put my hat between your teeth, girl," I order. "And crawl to me on your hands and knees."

Her cheeks are bright pink, but she does as I ask. Taking my black hat and putting the brim between her white teeth and full mouth. I can tell it's heavy for her, but she's being such a good girl and holding it steady.

"Now crawl," I say again.

Her beautiful face glistens with cum and tears. Her eyelids are heavy with desire and her cheeks are flushed. The brim of my hat pushes back the corner of her lips like it did when I made her hold the ruler. Reminding me of how she looked with her mouth full of cock.

She crawls slowly down the hall on her hands and knees. Her soft ass sways side to side as she makes her way slowly to me. Those big, blue eyes are loud. She doesn't need to speak a single word for me to know she's eating this up—dirty, little redbird.

I sink to a crouch and whistle. A short, stilted sound I use to call my dogs.

She pauses, and I know she understands what I'm doing.

"Did I tell you to stop?" I say.

She shakes her head, managing to keep the hat in her mouth.

"Then crawl," I order, rising.

She keeps moving, her eyes glued to me. Just as she's about to reach where I stand, I back up into the game room. Her brows crease and she follows me as I keep moving back and in a slow circle around the pool table.

How far will her obedience go?

I pause by the bar. "Get up and put my hat on the counter."

She rises and places my hat down. Carefully. Then she turns and tucks her hands behind her back, waiting for my next order. My cum is dried on her face—a work of art—and her knees are pink. I hope they bruise. I want evidence of tonight under her skin.

Fuck, I'm so hard it feels like I didn't just come all over her face.

"Bend over the pool table and put your hands behind your back," I tell her, jerking my head towards the empty table.

She turns and I get the best view of her soft, round ass jiggling as she walks to the table. She bends over it, going up on her toes, and her hands slide behind her lower back. Fingers intertwining.

I consider her for a second. There's an ocean of things I could do to my redbird. I should punish her without pleasure. I should keep to the rules we set down when she first came here. But she's such a good girl and maybe, if she behaves for me, I can find it in myself to forgive what she did tonight.

I cross to the table, hat in hand. She lifts her chin, her breasts pushed against the tabletop.

Fuck. Me.

I lean forward and she tilts her chin up and I fit my hat on her head. Her lips part and she blushes as I step back, cocking my head to enjoy the sight of my redbird. Naked, smeared with cum, wearing my hat.

Clint Garrison is rolling over in his grave.

The corner of my mouth turns up. "You keep still like that."

"Yes, sir," she whispers.

I circle her and she arches her lower spine. Pushing up her ass, begging for my cock in her cunt. I grip her thigh and pull her soft, pink pussy open. It's glistening with arousal, so much it's creamy around her entrance. My cock aches and I fight back the urge to unzip and push it into her slick opening.

She moans as I touch her pussy. Playing with the softness there before dipping my fingertip inside. Her toes curl against the carpet.

"Do you have something to say, redbird?" I ask.

She shakes her head. "No, sir."

"Nothing?" I push my finger to the middle knuckle before withdrawing.

Her inner muscles tighten. "I just...I feel so empty."

I slide my hand up her spine and spread my fingers on her upper back. She tenses and then she moans as I draw back my other hand and slap her across her right ass cheek. It shakes and I grip it hard and spread her open. My thumb brushes over her asshole.

She freezes. We both know anal is on the table. It was written into the contract and she agreed to at least try it.

"Sir," she whimpers.

I lean over her and she spreads her ass and legs, pushing her sex up to me. Her ankles curl around my outer thighs and one foot hits against the gun in my thigh holster. Usually I carry on my hip, but today I had to remove my weapons to get into the bank where I had

169

my meeting. I'd disassembled my holster and reassembled it to fit on my thigh afterwards.

"Why do you always carry that thing in the house?" she whispers.

I slap her across the ass again and flip her to face me. She bites her lip, muffling her yelp. Her pussy clenches, dripping onto the pool table. I know she's dying to come so badly she'd do anything for me. My hand hesitates. Then I flip the holster open and take the handgun out. Her body freezes and she jerks her head, the hat falling to the side.

"Sir," she whispers.

The high I get from sex like this is exploding in my brain like a drug. I drag the flat side of the barrel up her inner thigh and pause right before her delicate sex.

The cold metal lies in sharp contrast to her body. She's all soft curves and pretty angles. Maybe that's why the gun in my hand looks so good against her skin.

Hard against soft.

The unblemished against the scarred.

My mask is slipping. It's fallen and shattered at her feet. Do those blue eyes see me for who I am?

The world slows and I have to make a choice.

Do I stand behind these walls, watching her from the inside? Or do I stop building walls between myself and the world? Do I let her in and show her the man I am?

In this moment, I want to lower my defenses more than anything. I'm tired. I've built so many walls my hands are bloody.

I lift my eyes to hers and I see deep inside them a single flame. Flickering, calling me to fall into her depths. To show her all the ugly rage, the hunger for vengeance, the spite, and my selfish obsession over the woman in my arms.

So I fall, because I'm tired of pretending I'm not broken. And I hope to God that this woman gives me grace—that when she sees me clearly, she won't turn away.

CHAPTER TWENTY-FOUR

KEIRA

He's fucking psychotic.

My head spins. My breathing feels shallow. Maybe it's from all the blood pooled between my legs. I can feel it throb in my clit and I'm so sensitive right where I need him most. I swear the emptiness is going to be the death of me.

Then he took his gun out and put it to my inner thigh.

Right below my sex. Right where I've dripped down my leg.

I should be afraid, but something else overpowers it. My senses are sharp, but my better judgment is dulled by lust. I need Sovereign in a way I've never needed anything before. I'd drop down on my knees and take that gun in the back of my throat if it means getting him inside me.

He withdraws. A cry of disappointment moves up my throat, but he cuts it off by flipping me on my back.

My stomach twists. At some point, he took off his coat, leaving him in just his button up. The front is soaked in sweat and open halfway. Revealing his upper chest, covered in dark hair and tattoos.

His bare forearms are so thick, so corded with muscle from hard labor. I want to drag my nails down them so hard he bleeds. I want to lick his blood and sweat off his skin just to taste what he's made of.

Maybe that's the only way to get close to him.

"This wasn't in the contract," I moan, unsure why I'm even speaking.

He leans in and his fingers wrap around my throat.

"We're not playing anymore," he says. "*Mrs.* Garrison."

Fear thrills up my body and my head spins. He gently lifts me by the throat until I'm a foot from his face. Hanging from one of his enormous hands. I should be shaking, I should be fighting him, but all I can think about is the night we met. The way he looked at me in Clint's office, eye-fucking me in front of my husband.

The question lurking on the back of my mind feels so much more real. Clint went to Sovereign Mountain and never returned. And somehow, despite all the strange coincidences, I've ended up in this man's bed.

His grip tightens. Stars spark and my pussy throbs. I'm leaking and I know he can see it wet the pool table.

"Why did you call me that?" I manage.

The cold barrel of the handgun drags up my outer thigh. Down over the soft flesh of the underside and up again. My lids flutter and heat scorches my cheeks as he pushes it between my legs and up against my clit. Electricity shocks to my deepest point and my eyes fly open all the way. My breathing comes heavy and fast.

"You call yourself that," he says from between his teeth.

My hips twitch, and the sight on the barrel touches the soft entrance of my pussy. It's cold, but it's delicious. Like having an ice cube touched to my sex.

"Are you just a Garrison slut?" he growls.

I feel the venom in his words when he says my surname. The gun presses a little lower and angles. Fear spikes and my survival instincts threaten to take over and make me fight him. But the need to release is far stronger.

I lock my eyes with him and hitch my hips and hump the barrel of the gun.

His jaw twitches.

"Fuck," he breathes.

My head spins and I feel the steel tip of the gun enter my body. Oh God, I'm going to come or die. Just like the first time he put that enormous cock into my body and fucked me until I bled. What kind of man made someone bleed when they weren't even a virgin?

He thrusts the barrel once. "Answer me."

The grip on my throat eases just enough I can speak. Stars pop as air floods my brain, sending even more blood thrumming between my thighs.

"I am a Garrison," I gasp. "Neither of us can change that."

He tilts the gun and I feel it push against my G-spot. The entrance of my sex throbs, so sensitive it aches as my tight muscles grip the weapon.

"It should have been me," he says, jaw tight. "I should have been the one to fuck you first."

I'm rising higher and higher. Pleasure is a hot itch deep in my hips and I can't keep my body still. He thrusts the gun into my pussy and I thrust back onto it.

"You had enough blood," I gasp.

He growls in his chest, his forearm flexing and fingers tightening on my neck again. "He might have fucked you first, but I'm going to ruin you for any other man."

My head rolls from side to side. My eyes are wet and my hips are shaking so badly they're rattling the table.

I can feel his rage. This is bigger than me...and yet here I am right at the center of it.

"Come for me, little redbird," he says, his voice dropping until it rumbles. "This cunt was made to come for me. Give it what it wants."

Pleasure bursts around the barrel of his gun, now warm from being inside me. My eyes snap shut and my spine goes hard as steel. Arcing and locking. He pumps the weapon up into me and I hear how wet I am past the sound of our panting breaths.

The gun is jerked from me and the euphoria of not being dead from it hits my brain. Better than when he released my throat while I was coming in the hall. I hear his zipper and then he's inside me. So hard and fast that the pain splits like a knife through my hips.

Will I ever get used to his size? Or will I always scream like this?

Bang.

Bang.

Bang.

The pool table shakes as he takes me. Relentlessly, the heavy, slow strokes thudding against my hips. It has to be bolted to the floor, otherwise he'd be moving it easily.

My lids flutter and I roll my head. Still coming around his length. His narrowed eyes are fixed on me, a spark of triumph in them. He said he would ruin me and he has. I'm drenched with my wetness and his cum is still dried on my face. I can feel where it stuck to my skin.

He thrusts one last time and I feel him paint the inside of my pussy. I'll feel everything tomorrow. I'll get up in the morning and he'll trickle down my thigh. I'll smell the faint scent of his cum when I go to clean myself. Every time I slip my panties down, I'll remember the high of coming for him.

I hope every time he sees his gun tomorrow, he thinks about my pussy wrapped around the barrel.

Pushing myself up on the heels of my hands, I stare up at him. He looks so good that somewhere in the depths of me, I twitch. There's nothing like the feeling of our bodies joined. And I want it endlessly.

But I'm still jarred by the things he said.

Neither of us know what to say.

He picks me up. I grab his hat and he carries me down the hall. In the shower, he washes my body and gets down on his knees. I rest one leg on his shoulder and let him inspect me.

The tip of his rough fingers are surprisingly gentle on my sex. When he's done, he kisses my clit.

And despite everything that just happened, I melt for him.

CHAPTER TWENTY-FIVE

GERARD

The contract was supposed to protect us both from what happened last night. She wasn't supposed to see that side of me.

I know how to be her Dom, but I don't fucking know how to be her man.

Or at least I thought I did. I've never broken the rules with anyone before. But with her, all the things I've held sacred are changing.

I wake the next morning and she's lying with her eyes wide open. The blankets are pulled to her chin, the top one made of white fur stark against her red waves. I slide my hand up to brush a tendril from her cheek. She watches me. Her lids flutter and her tongue darts out to wet her mouth.

"I want to work with Angel today," she says.

"You can do whatever makes you happy, redbird," I say.

She sits up, moving to the edge of the bed. Quick as a flash, I wrap my arm around her waist and pull her back to me. She yelps as I flip her body around and set her in my lap. We sink back against the headboard. Her nails dig into my shoulders and her breasts heave.

My eyes rove down.

She's got a little mark around her throat where the belt bit her skin. Otherwise, she's flawless. Entranced, I run my palms over the inward curve of her waist and relish the way her hips widen.

"What is it?" she whispers.

I feel my throat bob. "Our contract isn't what I anticipated it would be."

My words hang in the air. She twists, but I keep her still.

"I'm sorry," she says. "Maybe I'm not very obedient."

I touch between her breasts with the tip of my middle finger. She shudders as I trace it down to her navel. The little dip is warm, and I gently push my fingertip in. Exploring each part of her with the slowness it deserves.

"No," I say, not looking into her eyes. "I'm going to rewrite the contract."

I glance up. Her brows arch.

"You want something...different?" she says. There's a trace of unease in her voice.

"I'm going to limit it," I say. "But not take it away."

"Oh," she says. "Why?"

How can I tell her the truth when I can't speak it myself? I needed to be her Dom because I have to protect her from my darkness. Maybe that simple, safe dynamic would work with another woman. But despite having met less than a year ago, there are tangled threads surrounding Keira and I that go back decades. Outside of our contract, we're two people with complicated histories.

Our pasts are shadowed with secrets. With deceit and death.

Last night, the past caught up with me. I looked down at her, and remembered who she was, and the darker side of me came out.

She was the wife of my enemy.

And yet, I have no right to hold that against her. She's a helpless player in this game. I saw her from my place of wealth and privilege and wanted her, so I took her as mine.

A better man would regret that.

But I don't.

One of us won the war. Clint is in the cold ground and I have his warm, naked wife in my lap.

She puts her hand on my chest, right below my collarbone. Her touch sends tendrils of heat through my torso that find their way to my groin. My cock hardens slowly beneath her ass and I know she feels it.

"I don't want to hurt you," I say finally. "We both lost control last night, but you're inexperienced. This is adding a layer of complication you're not ready for."

"You knew I was inexperienced going in," she protests. "You're thirty-eight. I'm twenty-one. What were you expecting?"

"I know, but I think this is for the best."

This part is real. She is inexperienced and I'm wondering if we should have a dynamic outside sex for that reason. I can tell she's second guessing the boundaries, unsure if we're playing or not.

That can't happen if there are feelings involved. And I have some strong feelings about this woman.

"I want to keep some aspects. I love rough sex," I say.

She bites her lip. "I...like it too. I don't want to stop that part."

"I'd never deny you a good fuck. We can still play during sex," I promise. "I'm still your Dom, you will call me sir. You'll continue to journal and be truthful and communicate. Or you'll be punished. Is that fair?"

She chews her lip. I tap her chest.

"You be you for right now," I say. "And I'll just be me. Alright?"

She nods, her hair falling over her shoulder. Brushing her left breast. I push it back and cup the soft roundness of it. Running my finger over her nipple until it hardens. Her hips move in a slow rotation, brushing against my erection.

"You're a needy slut," I murmur.

She lets her head fall back. I spit into my hand and rub it over her already wet sex. It takes a moment to work my cock into her tight pussy, but it's all worth it as she sinks down and her eyes roll back. A husky moan rises from her lips and she humps her hips against me.

"Ride your man, little redbird," I urge.

I'm not sure where that came from, but it feels right. Her mouth tugs back in a quick smile and her hazy eyes lock on mine. "What is it they say? Save a horse, ride a cowboy?"

I can't keep back my smile. My hand cracks across her ass and she clenches around my cock. Tight, hot muscles working me from base to tip. She grips my shoulder and braces herself, grinding those pretty hips hard. Like she's starving.

Something changed last night. She trusts me enough to show me some spine.

Maybe letting down my walls wasn't a complete mistake.

Her submission is beautiful, but her confidence is breathtaking. She's so confident in her soft, curvy beauty and she's hungry enough for pleasure that she's taking it.

No hesitancy, no asking if she can come. Just fucking my cock however it feels good.

I grip her body and fuck her back. The bed shakes against the wall. Outside the window, snow falls gently over the lake and the mountains are barely kissed with the rising sun. I should be outside starting chores right now. No doubt Westin is wondering where I am. But I can't pry myself from bed until I see her come.

I stroke her clit with my thumb. The combination sends her over the edge with a silent cry. Her body shudders and I follow her, pleasure shooting down my spine. When I pull from her, my cum slips out and trickles down her thighs.

She falls back onto the pillows and watches me get ready for the day.

CHAPTER TWENTY-SIX

KEIRA

We broke some rules last night. I can't tell if he regrets it or not.

I feel like I should regret it. But I don't.

I feel like I should hate what he did to me. But I didn't.

All I know for certain is that the further we fall together, and the more I see of him, the more I realize I had no idea who I was getting into a contract with.

Last night, when he got in from chores, he said they found my horses on the other side of the ranch. It's far away, so it'll take two days to round them up. There's a cabin on the other side of the property and he said he'd be gone overnight there.

I begged him to let me go too. He said no. I hate hearing that word from him because he doesn't elaborate. He just says no, and it doesn't even sound unkind, so I can't be mad at him.

But this morning, he shook me awake and said, "You can come with me, redbird." I don't know what made him change his mind, but I'm already packed.

He said he'd be back from chores by noon.

CHAPTER TWENTY-SEVEN

KEIRA

We ride up to the northern side of Sovereign Mountain Ranch later that day. Gerard has two saddlebags and I brought a backpack. He says the cabin is stocked with enough food for a week in case of emergencies. I'm imagining a shack, but he laughs and says, no, it's just a small version of the main house.

He rides Shadow and I take Bluebell. I wanted to take Angel because she's finally allowed me to ride her around the paddock without trouble. She trusts me more every day. But Gerard shakes his head when I ask if I can ride her out. He says no, he doesn't trust Angel not to throw me if she spooks.

So I take the painted mare instead, pushed deep in the pocket of my coat.

"Do you think I'll ever get Angel to the point where I can take her out?" I ask.

I turn in the saddle. We're out beyond the pastures, heading up the gradual tilt of the highest northern point of Sovereign Mountain. He's riding behind me, hat pulled low over his face. In the last few days, he's let his beard get thicker. Last night after we talked, he fell asleep on his back and I ran my fingers over his face and down his chest. Enjoying the way he feels when he's rough like this.

"What's that, redbird?" He lifts his head.

"Do you think Angel's confident enough to be ridden out?"

He considers it, squinting up at the mountain looming closer. "She's unsure of herself, never been allowed out beyond a fence."

It feels like he's not talking about Angel. I chew the inside of my cheek until a bit of blood stains my tongue.

"You're good at being patient," I say.

"Some things are worth being patient for," he says. "If you really want Angel to be your horse, you'll work at her pace. If she feels forced, she'll always be nervous."

My chest feels strange, like there's something sitting on it. My fingers tighten around the reins.

It would be a lie to say he hasn't forced a great deal onto me since we met. I wouldn't be here if he hadn't offered me a contract. Or showed up at my door when my house was burning and rode off with me on Shadow.

So why haven't I shied away from his touch?

Perhaps because I trust him. Like it or not, when I look up and see him coming, I feel safe.

We don't talk for a while. The path leads higher until we reach a flat area that winnows down to a wide path between twin mountain cliffs. My stomach freezes as I realize where we must be. When Clint died, they'd said he'd been trampled when a herd of cattle stampeded through a narrow opening between two mountains. I look up at the solid gray walls on either side and a shudder moves down my spine.

"Did you want to ask something?"

I turn and he's taken off his hat. His dark hair is tousled by the wind. His hat rests in his hand, on his thigh. His winter-blue eyes are washed out until his pupils are two black dots against ice. There's a hardness to his face that scares me, like he's thinking about something that conjures loathing in him.

It hits me right then that I'm alone with him.

Completely isolated.

The wind whistles through the opening. It smells like winter and on it I catch his scent. An odd sensation follows, a feeling like I've known him before this. In another life, a long, long time ago.

The hair on the back of my neck raises.

There are secrets like ghosts on his ranch. I have a feeling Gerard knows where each one is buried, because he put them six feet under.

"How far are we from the cabin?" I ask, my mouth dry.

Shadow moves up beside me and we fall into step together. Gerard's jaw works grimly.

"Not far," he says.

We move silently between the cliffs and the landscape opens up. The further we go from the mountain pass, the better I feel. When it's just a smudge in the distance behind us, I look up and see the cabin at the top of the mountain. It's barely peeking from the trees, but I can see it's simple, but comfortable. There's a small barn beside it with a paddock big enough for several horses.

"We built this ten years ago," he says. "That way if we have to be on the far side of the property, we've got a place to spend the night. And it makes a good hunting cabin."

"Do you hunt a lot?"

He shakes his head. "Maybe once, twice a year. All the meat on the ranch is from the cattle. But a couple times a season we bring in elk and deer. Do you hunt?"

I shake my head. "I've always been too busy on the ranch."

His eyes linger on me as we climb the hill, but he doesn't speak. I know he's thinking of my life before him—I see it in the grim line of his jaw. I know he disapproves of the way Clint treated me and that look in his eyes reminds me of the one I saw at the mountain pass. For the first time, a horrible, dark thought creeps into my mind.

No, Gerard might be intimidating, but he's not a murderer.

A chill moves down my spine and even Bluebell feels it and prances to the side. Gerard leans in and catches her right rein, steadying her. His brows crease in an unspoken question, but I'm speechless. He hated Clint, that's obvious, but...no, I should be ashamed of entertaining such a thought.

And yet...it was so convenient that Clint died the day after Gerard met me.

I shake my head hard. My husband was killed in an accident. That was verified by the coroner.

The coroner who's close friends with Gerard.

Damn it.

We pause outside the cabin and barn. He swings down from Shadow and the sound of his boots hitting frozen ground jerks me back to reality. Gerard isn't evil. He's rough, obsessive, and maybe a little controlling in some areas, but he's not that twisted.

He looks up at me, his dark lashes and brows making his pale eyes stand out like the sky against snow. My mouth goes dry. He moves close to me and lifts me down and I feel his hands on me for a fleeting moment. Strong, warm, safe. The first time I've felt safe since my father died.

My body wouldn't feel safe with a murderer. The wilderness is making my mind go down dark paths. Perhaps it was seeing the place where Clint died that triggered it.

I make the conscious choice to stop these thoughts in their tracks.

He takes both horses by the reins and walks between them to the barn. We brush them down and put them in their stalls with grain and water. Then he leads the way to the cabin and unlocks the door.

It's all one room inside except for the lofted bedroom upstairs. He taps the thermostat and the heat kicks in. Then he crosses the living area and crouches by the fireplace to stack logs and kindling inside.

I peel off my coat and flannel and let them drop to the ground. The clock above the stove shows it's almost six. I know he's probably hungry and for the first time in a while, I actually want to cook something. I pull off my boots and pad into the kitchen in my socks and start going through the cabinets.

"What's this, redbird?"

I turn. He's standing in the hall, looking down at my coat and boots with a faintly amused expression. My stomach flips and I gather my things up. His eyes follow me as I back down the hall and I'm at a loss for what he's thinking.

"Where do I put my things?" I whisper.

He jerks his head towards the loft.

I scamper up the stairs and place my coat on the bed and my boots by the bathroom door. The mattress is covered in a white quilt and a thick fur blanket. The floor has a southern style print rug, and there's a little lamp by the bed. Otherwise, it's bare. I stand on my toes to look out the window. The view is astounding. I think I can see the ranch in the distance. A tiny speck.

When I return, he's taken off his coat. His Henley is rolled up to his elbows and he's kneeling by the fireplace, nursing the flames.

"Are you hungry?" I ask.

He nods. "I could eat."

I go to the kitchen area. There's everything I need in the pantry for biscuits, even dry milk, and I get to work. He leaves the fireplace crackling and comes over to lean on the island counter. His eyes burn like his touch as they watch me cut biscuits and arrange them on a greased tray.

"You're good at that," he says.

"I'm a good cook," I say.

He runs a hand over his jaw, short beard rasping. "I wasn't snubbing your skills, you're just not on my payroll. Take your clothes off."

My head whips up. "What?"

"Remember our contract is in place right now."

My jaw is slack. "You want me to cook naked?"

The corner of his mouth jerks up. "Strip, redbird."

I freeze and he circles the counter until he's right behind me. His heat washes over me and his big, rough hands slip under my sweatshirt and pull it over my head. My pulse quickens. He unfastens my jeans and tugs them off. Leaving me in nothing but my bra and panties.

He slaps my ass, gripping it. "You can keep your bra and panties. For now."

I flush to the roots of my hair. He goes upstairs and I hear his boots in the loft and when he comes back down, he's in just a pair of sweatpants. The bull skull on his chest looks at me first, but I can't look away.

He sinks down in the chair by the fireplace and leans back, spreading his knees.

The oven beeps. I slide the tray inside and wipe my hands. There's maple sausages cooking on the top. I'm making biscuits, gravy, eggs, and pancakes.

I've never met a man who didn't get excited about breakfast for dinner.

"Can I get you a drink?" I ask, looking around.

He cocks his head. "For me?"

"Yeah." I put one hand on my hip. "You want some whiskey or something?"

The corners of his mouth turn up. There's tempered amusement in his eyes. "I'm sober."

He is? I run through our interactions and try to remember if I've ever seen him drink before. I recall having wine with him...but now that I look back, I don't remember ever seeing him pick up a glass and take a drink.

I wonder why I didn't notice until now. I've never lived with a man who didn't at least have a shot of whiskey at night when the work was done.

I wonder what he does to unwind, and then realize that's a stupid question.

Me—he does me to unwind.

I pad barefoot across the room. "I guess I didn't know."

He pats his knee once and my stomach flips as I sink down onto it. His palm rubs a slow circle on my lower back before gripping the swell of my ass. I can feel the heat coming off his body and I have to resist sinking against his bare chest. He's so big and solid and when I'm with him, I don't mind feeling weak.

That part caught me off guard. I never liked showing weakness before. It made me a target for Clint's ire. With Gerard, I feel myself reverting to a state of dependency that would have horrified me weeks ago.

It feels natural. He's got a wild mind and a cold heart, but for me he's willing to forgo both. The least I can do is not question his authority in the world he built.

"Yeah, I got the liquor before the liquor got me," he says.

There's so much about him I don't know. Never in a million years would I have imagined Gerard Sovereign had weaknesses. I reach out and skim my fingers over his tattooed chest. Does he have more secrets hidden behind his hard front?

"Can you tell me about it?" I ask.

"There's not much to say. I had some shit happen to me when I was nineteen. I was young and couldn't hold it together, so I started getting fucked up. Then Westin cleaned me up and I lived with his family. Stayed there a while, got sober. Been sober ever since."

My brows rise. "You've been sober since before you could legally drink."

He dips his head. "That's true."

I shift so I'm facing him. He puts his other hand on me, encircling my waist.

"Can I ask...what happened?"

His lids lower. For a moment, I think I've gone too far. But he lets out a slow sigh and I think I feel his walls come down. Just a little bit.

"I was engaged," he says. "About to get married. Then she died."

My stomach drops. I wasn't in love with Clint, so I don't know what he felt. But I did lose a spouse so I know how disorienting it is to be the one left behind. I know what being suddenly untethered feels like, and it's not pleasant.

"I'm so sorry," I whisper.

He looks at the ground. "It was a long time ago, redbird. And I was so young I thought it was the end of the world."

"And it wasn't?"

He shakes his head. He raises his eyes to mine and I can't read them.

"I'm not the same person I was back then."

"But it still hurt you," I whisper.

"It...destroyed me," he says. "But I moved on."

I try to find the right words, but my brain is still trying to wrap my head around the concept of a nineteen-year-old Gerard. Who was he then? Why was he so alone that there was only Westin to save him from his grief? What had happened to his parents?

I know nothing about the man who has total control over me.

I open my mouth to speak, but he pulls me in by the nape of the neck and kisses me. My stomach curls with heat and my brain goes silent.

From the first time his mouth touched mine, I've craved being kissed by him. He's slow, thorough, and deliberate. Like he's got nowhere to be and nothing to do but make sure his taste is burned into my lips.

My lower spine arcs. He pulls back an inch and our breath mingles.

"Put your tongue out, redbird," he says, his voice husky and quiet.

Hesitantly, I obey. He bends in and spits onto it.

"Swallow," he says.

Pussy aching, I swallow for him...because what else am I supposed to do?

He tells me what to do and I do it without thinking. Especially after that night in the game room. When he slipped the barrel of his gun into me and called me a Garrison slut. That night made me understand why everyone on Sovereign Mountain obeys him without question.

Because he might not be evil, but he's not good either.

He's a lot like the wilderness surrounding us tonight. Placid, breathtaking on the surface. Wild and harsh, deadly underneath.

I glance up and our gazes clash.

"Can I ask you something?" I whisper.

"Anything," he says. "But I might not answer."

"The game room...what you did to me there...what would you have done if the gun went off?"

He tilts his head, sinking back. "It didn't go off."

"But what if it had?" I press. "You risked that to...prove a point?"

His grip tightens on my hips until it hurts. "I wasn't proving a point about me, redbird. It was about you."

"Okay...what point?"

His other hand goes to my knee, curling around it. Yanking me closer in his lap until my palms are flat on his chest.

"I discovered that my redbird has an appetite," he says. "One that I can satisfy."

He's talking in riddles again. I've grown to realize that's how he hides his secrets. He flips every answer into a question or statement about the inquirer.

"But what if?" I whisper.

"What if, redbird?" he says softly. "You tell me what if?"

I can barely breathe when he's close like this. My eyes flick over his face. Noting the few bits of gray at his temple. It's only a few hairs, but it reminds me with a sharp jolt that I'm only twenty-one.

"What if another man put his gun in my pussy?" I say, knowing my words are explosive.

His eyes narrow. "Do you think I've never killed before?"

My jaw drops and my body tingles. I don't know what I expected, but it wasn't for him to go right for the throat. I stare at him, waiting for his face to crack. For a smile to appear. But his expression is set in stone.

"You...um...have you?" I whisper.

He grips my chin and pulls me in for a rough, open mouthed kiss.

"Better get to that gravy," he says.

The food—I forgot it's still cooking. Dizzy, I scramble out of his lap and head to the kitchen. My face is bright pink, I can feel it burning down my neck, and my legs are unsteady. I pull the biscuits from the oven and take the gravy off the low burner. I know he's looking as I pour leftover grease into a cast iron skillet and start frying eggs. When I turn around, his pale eyes are fixed to me.

"What are you staring at?" I whisper.

I get a hint of a smile.

"Just you," he says.

Why?

Why does he stare at me like he's eating me alive with his eyes?

Why does he hold me like he never wants to let me go?

Why does he care at all?

And did he do something so terrible I can't let the thought form in my head without guilt?

Pushing it aside, I set the table for two and fill our plates. He makes coffee and we sit opposite each other. He tries the gravy and his brow goes up.

"You're quite the cook," he says.

"Thank you," I say. "I know."

The corner of his mouth turns up. We eat in silence, and I manage to sip half a cup of his coffee even though it's so strong it could stand up on its own. When our plates are clean, he puts them in the sink.

"Can I ask you something?" I say.

His gaze flicks up and holds. "Depends."

"What...what did the Garrisons do to you?" I whisper.

The towel he's drying his hands on slips to the table. My heart beats against my ribs like a scared bird. Have I ruined everything?

"Why do you want to know?" he says finally.

I hesitate, chewing on my lip. Once upon a time, when I was young and hadn't tasted how cruel the world was, or how harsh men could be, I was braver.

Now I know life is so much colder and lonelier than I could have imagined. But I hope there's a spark of warmth in Sovereign.

I've felt it. I swear I have.

"I feel like you're a tangle of threads...it all leads back to the Garrisons," I whisper. "Clint was my husband and that means something to you. But I don't understand what."

His eyes flash. "Sir. When we're alone, you call me sir."

His walls are back up, good and hard.

I stand, tired of him being evasive. "Alright. I don't understand what the Garrisons mean to you. *Sir*."

He hears the bite in my tone. His hand comes up and he beckons me with two fingers. I go, but only because I signed my name on a dotted line. His big hands wrap around my waist and he lifts me onto the countertop.

I'm still shorter than him. He brushes back my hair and goosebumps rise down my arm and his fingers skim around my back. He unhooks my bra and slips it from my breasts. Methodically, he lifts my hips and takes my panties down my legs, pushing them into his pocket.

He's going to fuck me because he doesn't want to talk. I'm not doing that tonight.

"I want the contract completely off," I blurt out. "Just so I can talk to you without anything between us. Just for tonight."

His gaze snaps to mine. "No, you don't."

"Yes, sir, I do."

His hand closes around my throat and my hips tighten. The countertop is cool beneath my bare pussy and I know I'm wet.

No, fuck being wet, I'm soaked.

Our eyes lock.

"Did you like being fucked with my gun, redbird?" he says, jaw tight. "Is that who you want me to be with you?"

I swallow past his grip. "I want you to stop being afraid. Stop hiding behind your contract."

His head cocks. Slowly. I'm on the thinnest of ice.

"What are you going to do? Put a gun inside me? Fuck me until I bleed? You've already done both," I breathe.

His jaw tightens. "I've never done anything to you that you haven't begged for with that sweet, perfect mouth and body."

I grip his wrist, just below where his hand is wrapped around my throat. His other hand comes up, heading towards my sex, but I slap it. Battering it away.

My pussy aches deep inside, drenched at the feeling of his hand around my throat.

What does it say about me that I want this side of him most of all?

"Don't fucking deny me," he says.

That's when I realize the contract is off for the night. He's looking at me like he wants to devour me whole, and I know we're off the edge of the map.

Do safewords still count here?

I want him like this...raw and threatening. So I do the stupid thing and lift my gaze to his. Even though I know that when faced with a big, dangerous animal, I should avoid eye contact, drop, and cover myself as best I can.

"Don't fucking touch me," I shoot back. "*Sir.*"

His hand moves between my thighs again and I lash out at his forearm with my nails. Blood wells up in two, short stripes from my pointer and middle fingers.

We both go still with shock as it drips once onto the counter.

"Fucking wildcat," he breathes.

I'm horrified, but still angry. He's drawn blood from me before and now we're even. He pulls me closer by the neck and his bleeding arm slides between us. I cry out as two fingers plunge into my pussy. Filling me with a shock of pleasure and pain.

"Fuck you," I hiss, arcing my hips.

His eyes flash like a thunderclap. "This is what you want, isn't it, redbird? You want to make me lose control? Hit me, you dirty little bitch."

My jaw drops. His words sting, but I don't know why. His jaw squares and his fingers flick my G-spot hard to remind me who's really in control. I swear I'm going to come just from being fucked on his hand.

"No, sir," I burst out.

"Fucking hit me," he orders.

"Gerard—"

"Do not use my name when I'm knuckle-deep in your cunt," he hisses. "Fuck me up, redbird. I'm already so fucked up for you there's nothing you can do that'll hurt me."

I backhand him across the face. The sound is like a whip cracking. I gasp and clench my smarting fist. He freezes, his face slapped to the side, a mark blossoming on his jaw. Then he whips his head around like an animal and lifts me by the neck, pulling me so close I can taste his breath.

Mint and Sovereign.

The slap doesn't phase him any more than the blood on his arm. I doubt he felt the sting.

"Did you do it?" I gasp.

I can't believe I let the thought that's been weighing on my mind out of my mouth.

Fuck.

I have to find a way to backtrack so I don't have to explain myself.

"Do what?" he says, eyes on my mouth.

His grip tightens and my vision flashes. Into my mind rushes a torrent of images from the night we met. His eyes burning into me as I confessed that I was frightened of Clint.

"Is your husband a mad dog?" he'd asked.

The cliffs—they're haunted by something. The mountain pass is stained in blood, and I wonder if seven months ago, that blood also stained the hand around my neck. His fingers tighten and my head spins.

"If you're going to accuse me, be a big girl and do it to my face," he says.

"Did you kill my husband?" I whisper.

He withdraws abruptly and I sink back, gasping. His chest, covered in that black and white bull skull, heaves. God, I can't get away from those sightless eyes. Sweat breaks out on his neck and trickles down between his pecs. Catching in the hair.

"You and I, redbird, our interests aligned," he says.

"Don't." I'm raising my voice and I don't mean to, but I can't stop. "Don't talk in riddles. Give me a fucking straight answer. Sir."

He comes back to the counter and his palms slide up my waist. Touching me so gently I want to crumble. He's cradling me and it's a stark contrast to the anger pounding through his eyes. He wants to break something, but he's touching me like I'm made of glass.

"I saw you," he says, his voice low and husky. "I wanted you. And now you're mine."

My stomach goes cold. This time, I understand what he's saying without him spelling it out. He saw me, he wanted me, so he killed Clint to make me his. My stomach turns. This is the dark undercurrent I feel when it's just us. I felt it on the pool table, his gun against my pussy. And I feel it now.

My lips part. My mouth is so dry.

"I don't like your riddles," I whisper. "But this time...I know the answer."

He bends in and kisses the side of my neck. My nipples go hard and my hips tighten, my lower spine arcing towards his body. His hot mouth trails down to my shoulder and he bites it gently. I gasp, letting my head fall back.

The ceiling spins. How can I still want him?

"I will never let you go, redbird," he says.

His words are soft, like a declaration of love, but chilling like the cold wind through the pines.

CHAPTER TWENTY-EIGHT

GERARD

I lift her in my arms and she doesn't struggle. We sink to the kitchen floor and her hair pools around her head. My hand goes down to the tie of my sweatpants and she shakes her head. Her wet lashes flutter.

"Don't," she whispers.

I slide my hand up her inner thigh and my fingers meet warm slickness. Coating her sex and upper thighs. When I part her with my finger and thumb, I can see how flushed and ready to be fucked she is. Her lower back arcs and I graze my touch over her clit. Her mouth parts and she whimpers.

"Please," she begs.

My cock is so hard it aches. Every move I make, I feel the fabric of my sweatpants rub against it. Threatening to set me off before I can get inside her pussy. I push the waistband down and unleash my length, sinking down until our hips meet. Our mouths are inches apart.

"Sovereign. Don't." Her eyes are wide.

If she were locked up, I'd get off her. But she's drenched and her hips ride up, rubbing her wet cunt along the underside of my cock.

From the base all the way to the tip, pelvis tilting like she's trying to get me inside.

"Are you ashamed to be fucked by the man who killed your husband?" I breathe.

Her eyes roll back and her hips stutter. Maybe she hasn't put the feeling into words yet.

"This changes nothing," I tell her. "You've already come on my cock, my face, my hands."

"I didn't know," she whimpers.

I shift my lower body to press hers down against the floor. Pinning her body beneath mine to keep her still.

"And now you know," I say. "And nothing has changed. You're mine, little redbird."

I'm being cruel, I know that. She was innocent—she doesn't know what the Garrison family did to mine or what they took from me. She wasn't there for all the years where the only thing that kept me going was the fantasy of looking in the eyes of each Garrison son before I put a bullet in their heads.

She doesn't know that Clint's murder was just one chapter in the dark story I've shielded her from. All she knows is that she had a shitty husband, but not one that deserved death. And now the man who killed him has her pinned to the kitchen floor, ready to take the spoils of war.

Of course she's fighting me.

I lift her thigh and wrap her leg around my waist. The soaked heat of her pussy touches the head of my cock and feral need erupts in my chest. So strong I have to bit my tongue to keep from devouring her right here. She shakes her head from side to side and her hand pushes against my chest. Her palm is flat and her nails pierce my skin.

The pain makes my eyes roll. Fuck.

"Wait," she begs.

Her hips push up against mine. Seeking the head of my cock.

"You're telling me no, but you're rubbing your pussy on me like a whore," I spit. "Do you even know what you want, redbird?"

"Fuck you," she pants. "Fuck you, Sovereign. Fuck you for everything you've done to me."

"I did you a favor," I say.

Her lids flutter. "You're a murderer."

"You know what to say if you really want me to stop."

"I hate you."

"That doesn't sound like your safeword to me."

She just shakes her head again. I take her hands and gather them in one fist and pin them above her head. Her hips rise and fall like she's begging to be filled. But when I slide up between her thighs, she moans and jerks back.

"I'm not yours," she pants.

"Can you hear yourself moan for me? Your body already knows who it belongs to."

"Fuck you—"

I put my hand over her mouth and push into her pussy. It welcomes me easily, soaked and hot as it pulls me in deep. Her eyes go wide and she cries out as I draw back.

Then I thrust to the hilt and her blue irises roll back as she takes me all at once.

Without warning, she comes so hard her body convulses.

Her stomach shudders beneath me and she wails against my hand. Tears soak her lashes and stream down her face to her temples. Arousal floods my groin, the wet sounds loud as I grind myself against her clit.

It hits me all at once.

The dark part of me I was afraid to show her...she gets off on that.

She wants me, as I am.

The realization should throw me off, but it doesn't. I've seen her come from having her breasts whipped. She needs pain and humiliation to feel pleasure. And whatever it is we're doing on the kitchen floor, she's soaked from it.

Her inner muscles tighten around me. I release her mouth and she gasps. She wails aloud and I let her because no one will hear her up here at the top of Sovereign Mountain. She can cry and beg, but there's no mercy at the edge of the world.

Just darkness and monsters like me.

She lashes out and I catch her wrist, flipping her onto her belly. Her ass lifts, begging for me even as she writhes under my hand. I gather her breathtaking hair in my fist, a river of soft red, and pin her to the floor with it.

Then, my other hand braced beside her head, I sink back into her cunt. Filling her until she gives a quiet sob and gives up.

"That's a good girl," I praise.

She's loose now. Her body goes limp and soft beneath mine. Instead of hissing like a cat, she's moaning as I fuck into her sweet pussy. All her fight is gone, and her acceptance drives my desire to new heights.

I slam into her hips and her ass shakes beautifully. Her head falls back and as I thrust in hard, I bend and kiss her forehead. Breathing in the pomegranate scent of her hair. Intoxicated, I rut my hips against her ass and find that sweet place where her throat connects to her shoulder with my mouth.

She gasps as I bite down. Her skin is so fucking soft.

Her nails scrape the floor. Her body shakes under me.

Then she comes again and I feel the wetness against our bodies and the kitchen floor. She gives a harsh sob and starts fighting again. Arching her back and lashing out with her claws. Unperturbed, I grip her wrist and pin it down, subduing her rage.

She doesn't know what she needs. She's just fighting blindly because she's never been safe until now.

My hips stutter and I know I can't hold back for long. The scent of her hair fills my nose, the taste of her skin between my teeth, and the hot pulse of her pussy are too much.

I fall over her, hips bucking as I empty myself. My hand grips her around the throat, forcing her back up against my chest. My hips ride out the final pulses of my orgasm against her cervix. My mouth hovers just over her ear. I can feel her lungs flutter in her chest.

"Is this what you want, you pretty whore?" I whisper through my teeth. "You want to be forced like this? On your knees on the kitchen floor?"

She twists, but I have her firmly in my grip. Holding her down like an animal in a trap.

"Answer me," I press, kissing down the side of her neck.

"Fuck you, Sovereign," she hiccups.

"Why?" I urge.

She sobs, her whole body shaking. "Because...because you are a monster. And I'm...I'm falling for you."

My entire body goes numb. Like I've been hit with a bolt of lightning. I'd dreamed of those words in my unconscious mind. But I've only ever hoped to hear her speak them. I pull from her and flip her onto her back.

She's flushed and her big eyes are stained with tears. She bit her lip and there's a spot of blood.

I bend in and kiss it. Licking the crimson from her skin.

"Fall for me, redbird," I breathe. "I'll catch you."

She shakes her head hard from side to side. High from desire, weak with emotion, and still limp from the aftershocks of her pleasure.

"You are...not a good man," she whispers.

"So what?" I brush a strand of hair from her forehead.

"I thought you were giving me a choice with the contract. You never gave me a choice." Her fingers curl into her open palms. She has my blood under her nails.

I study her, focusing on a little strand of red hair that's stuck to her temple with sweat.

She's right. I never gave her a choice.

I should have, and if my life had gone much differently a long time ago, I would have taken a gentler route. But that's not who I am anymore.

The problem is, I'm struggling with the moments and memories and people that made me the man I am. I haven't done that in years.

Not since I built a fortress at the top of Sovereign Mountain and locked myself in it.

Then she came, my redbird.

My little spark of color in a lifetime of winter.

Does she deserve to know why I'm all fucked up inside? I know the answer already. If I'm going to be her man, if she's going to fall for me, she deserves the truth.

We're so embedded in one another it's only fair I tell her what the Garrisons did to me and the ones I loved most.

CHAPTER TWENTY-NINE

KEIRA

I'm so ashamed I can't move. I'm not sure what he just did to me. The word that bounces around my mind doesn't fit. A part of me knows that if I'd started crying in earnest, if my body had locked up, he would have stopped.

If he didn't force me, then what did we just do?

He's a sadist.

So that makes me his masochist.

Does that mean what we did was play? Because it felt deadly serious.

I don't have time to unravel my feelings because I'm angry that I told him I was falling for him even though he killed Clint. I'm so fucking angry that even though I said no and I meant yes, neither of those words meant anything to him in the end.

And I'm so ashamed because I should hate him, but I don't.

Tears spill down my temples. Catching in my hair. He picks me up and I sag against his naked chest as he carries me up the stairs. We're both a mess. Both sticky with his blood and our cum. He pulled his sweatpants back up, but I see the wet stains seep through the front.

I must have been soaked.

Distantly, the shower runs. Then he lifts me and we're standing on cold tile with steamy water running over our bodies. He tilts my chin up and all the anger is gone from his face.

"Do you want the truth, redbird?" he says hoarsely.

I swallow hard. The last time he told me the truth, it was horrifying. But I have to know, so I nod weakly.

"The woman I was engaged to...Clint Garrison killed her," he says. "She was twenty, I was nineteen. There was an ongoing feud between myself and the Garrisons. Clint ran into her at a bar one night. He offered to drive her home, but instead he crashed his truck outside the lodging house I was staying at with Westin. We heard the noise from the house. I pulled her body from the vehicle, but she was gone."

My jaw is slack. He's staring at the wall, his thumb moving over my chin in a slow circle.

"I'm so sorry, Sovereign," I whisper.

"She was pregnant, about seven weeks," he says. "After that, I got snipped. I thought if I couldn't have her babies, I wouldn't have any. I regret that."

"You can get it reversed," I whisper.

He shrugs. The slow realization of what he said is sinking in hard. Clint did that. My dead husband killed his fiancée.

It was no wonder he'd wanted revenge, or that he had a chip on his shoulder about me being Clint's widow.

"How did Clint survive?" I whisper.

He clears his throat. All I can see is that black and white bull skull swimming in my vision. Dotted with dark hairs and water droplets.

"The police said it was accidental," he says. "But he ran the passenger side of the truck into a wall. The rest of the car was fine, he barely had a scratch."

"Do you think it was an accident?" I manage.

His eyes go dark. "It doesn't matter to me."

I'm still aching from what he did to me on the kitchen floor. But I lift my hands and lay my palms on his hard stomach. He feels like life, like warm flesh and blood. I want to close my eyes and pretend everything leading up to this moment was a dream.

Pretend there was no Clint.

No contract.

No death.

My breath hitches. He pulls me against him and strokes my soaked hair.

"Don't cry, redbird," he rumbles. "No one will hurt you again."

"No one, but you," I whisper.

He doesn't answer, he just washes me and turns off the shower. We lay down in the bed in the loft. His mouth finds my neck and he's so gentle this time when he kisses me.

His tongue soothes the place where his bite mark is imprinted in my skin. I stroke over the scabbed scratches on his arm as his finger and thumb tease at my nipples until they're hard.

He doesn't fuck me even though my sore pussy aches again. His mouth moves down my stomach. Kissing lightly until he gets to my sex. Desire roars back to life, and I find myself spreading my thighs wide to beg for his touch. His tongue slips hot and wet over my clit and I let my head fall back into the pillow and give in.

My hand weaves in his hair.

"I hope you're being honest with me," I whisper.

He kisses the inside of my thigh. "I will always protect you."

I know that means he's still not telling me everything. Maybe because it's too ugly for me to see. My heart thumps and I'm so ashamed.

Am I so starved for love that I'll swoon over my husband's murderer?

A part of me wonders...did Clint kill that poor woman on purpose?

Or was it really an accident?

Because to me, the truth would change everything. But to him, it means nothing. He's got a black and white view of justice. He's the sort of man no one wants as their enemy because he won't stop until the scales are balanced.

I look down at him and his hard eyes are soft for the first time. He's looking at me like there's no one else in this world. My throat tightens and tears gather in my eyes. He dips his head and licks slowly over my entrance. Soothing the sore places with his tongue.

"You taste like mine, redbird," he says hoarsely.

My eyes smart.

Maybe I'll tie him to a chair and call the police and make him confess. Maybe I'll slip away and catch a train up north to Ontario and never see him again.

But I know I won't do either of those things. Just as I knew I'd sleep with him without a contract, I know I'll follow him anywhere. We're a swift train heading into darkness and only he knows what's up ahead.

CHAPTER THIRTY

GERARD

I feel so naked I can't sleep. I'm not used to letting anyone see my scars and I feel almost guilty for having shown them. Part of me wishes I could take it all back. It's not her responsibility to bear my burdens.

It's not anyone's but mine.

She sleeps fitfully beside me. In the early morning—or is it just late at night—I pull her body back against mine and trace the full curve of her naked hip and the sharp dip of her waist. I kiss the back of her neck until she stirs and her eyes flutter open.

"I need you," I murmur. "Open your legs."

She arcs her back and her eyes slip shut. "Do what you want to me, Sovereign. I'm going back to sleep."

I push my hand between her thighs and stroke her pussy and listen as her breathing deepens. She doesn't stir again as I wet her sex with saliva and push my cock into her entrance. I'm hard, but my desire to come wanes as I bask in the feeling of being inside her.

She feels like home.

More than Sovereign Mountain ever has. The ranch is my fortress, but she is the warmth, the heart, inside.

I nestle her soft ass up against me and exhaustion finally hits my brain. Outside the wind howls and bits of freezing rain bounce off the windows. Beneath the quilt and fur blanket, I'm so deep in her I can feel her heartbeat around my cock. Her scent has gone from something I notice to something so familiar it's just the air I breathe now.

There's no going back.

No letting go, no giving up now. We were meant to be like this, I feel it in my bones. I'm certain of one thing. This woman and I were made from the same kind of stardust.

CHAPTER THIRTY-ONE

GERARD

It's late when I roll over to find her still sleeping. She's relaxed and her hair covers the pillow in a soft cloud. She has a mark on her throat where I gripped her, a bruise on her knee from the kitchen floor, but otherwise she's unharmed. Bending, I kiss her thigh. Moving up to kiss just above her clit. I can smell my cum on her pussy and it's so fucking satisfying.

I slip from the bed, pull on my clothes, and leave the cabin to check the horses.

It snowed, but not heavily enough to impede our trip back.

Bluebell and Shadow are ready to be out of their stalls and they both do several laps around the fence. Kicking up snow and dried grass. I break the ice on their water and toss a bale of hay into their paddock.

She's awake when I get back inside. Naked and frying eggs on the stove. I linger in the door just to look at her perfect, heart-shaped ass, but she hears me and turns around.

She swallows, her throat bobbing hard. Then she lifts her arms out.

"Hold me," she whispers. "Please."

I shed my coat and gather her in my arms, lifting her onto the counter. She buries her face in the cold front of my shirt. I feel her give a shudder and I run my palms down her spine. Soothing her with gentle strokes.

I kiss the top of her head. "I've got you, baby girl."

She pulls back and kisses my mouth and, fuck, she's sweet. I dart my tongue in between her lips for an extra taste and she moans. Her lids are lowered when I pull back.

She's still hungry.

"I have something for you," I say.

Her brows go up. "What?"

"Stay," I tell her.

She sits still on the counter as I retrieve a small package from my saddlebags. I open it and take the discreet collar out first. It's a fine silver chain with a matching circle at the center.

She lifts her hands, opening her fingers. Then she flicks her gaze up and pulls back, waiting obediently for me to make the first move.

"What is that?"

"Your day collar," I say.

Her tongue darts out and wets her lips. "Is the contract...still what you want?"

"Yes," I say, without hesitating. "I need a place where I can fuck you the way you need fucked without hurting you. If you want to keep it in the bedroom, that's fine. But I want you collared."

Her naked breasts heave and her pink nipples contract. I put the discreet collar around her slender throat and click it into place, rotating the latch. If she wants it off, she'll need a pair of wire cutters. Her fingers come up and touch the little silver ring between her collarbones.

Satisfaction floods my chest. She drops her hand and I touch the chain, playing with it between my finger and thumb.

"How do you feel?" I ask.

I slid my grip loosely over her throat. She looks up at me through her lashes.

"I feel like you are not a good man, Sovereign," she says. "And I shouldn't want you."

My mouth turns up. "But you do."

"I do," she whispers.

That's all I need to hear. I pull out the leather play collar next. Her eyes widen as I unfurl the rows of bluebells engraved and polished into the dark leather. The edges are smoothed and the inside is soft fabric so it doesn't irritate her skin.

I fit it around her throat, over the discreet collar, with the soft inner lining against her skin. She shivers and her eyes widen. It's engraved and sealed so it looks like glossed wood. In the front is the Sovereign Mountain Ranch insignia and at the nape of her neck are my initials in gunmetal gray.

A little tag hangs between her collarbones. I tap it and it jingles.

"What is that?" she asks.

"Name tag."

"What does it say?" Her gaze is wary.

"Sovereign. I want my whore wearing my name."

Heat floods her face and she tugs the metal tag. "Is that how you think of me?"

"When you're on your knees with my cock down your throat, yes."

I'm trying to keep things light. But seeing her in my collars is pushing me to the point she was at when she said she was falling for me.

Feelings aren't my strong suit. I know how I feel for her, but I'm not good at saying those words aloud.

So I swallow past the lump in my throat. And take her own words.

My hands come up, cradling her face. Her eyes are huge.

"Maybe...I'm falling for you," I say.

Her lips part and her breath catches. Her lashes flutter and I know tears simmer right on the edge.

"Really?" she whispers.

I open my mouth to tell her more, but I find I don't have the words to describe what I'm trying to say. She doesn't know everything I've done to get her, and when she finds out, she'll know just how obsessed I am.

But for right now, I just kiss her. So hard I swear I feel her heart beating in my mouth.

When I pull away, she's flustered. She pushes her hair back.

"That's it?" she asks.

"That's it, redbird," I say. "For now."

I put her on her feet and slap her ass hard enough the recoil shivers down her thighs. She gives a little huff, but when I swipe my finger over the seam of her pussy, it's soaked.

She makes eggs, naked except for both my collars. I wash up and sit at the table to soak in the view. She's so fucking beautiful it feels like a physical ache in my chest just looking at her.

Every little dip, every curve, every soft line, every dimple in her thigh—a work of art.

I could spend my lifetime tracing the lines of her body with my tongue and never get tired.

We eat and then we fuck. In the loft, the bed thudding against the wall so hard it leaves a dent in the wood. I wrap my belt around her wrists and bind her to the headboard. Her hips barely touch the bed while I eat her out until she comes over and over. The sheets are soaked after the fifth orgasm.

"Stop," she begs, trying to kick me off her. "Fuck you, Sovereign, I need a break."

I kneel and push the front of my pants down.

"Fuck you too, sweetheart," I tell her, slamming my cock into her soaked pussy. "You can take it just fine."

She cries and comes, then we eat leftovers and have coffee. The horses are somewhere in the mountains, but we both forgot why we're here. Instead of leaving at noon, we go back to bed and she pushes me on my back and sinks down on my cock.

Her lip quivers and she bites it as our bodies join. I know she's in pain, I fucked her raw last night and this morning. But she's insatiable, and she digs her claws into the tattoos on my chest as she grinds her hips. Her eyes roll back in her head.

"You're a fucking wildcat," I pant.

She grins breathlessly, white teeth flashing. It's cold downstairs, but it's hot in the loft and sweat etches between her breasts. I grip the soft swell on either side of her hips and work with the rhythm of

209

her body. Rising and falling, grinding until she shudders and her head falls back.

Her tits heave.

A warm flood soaks my groin. The tag on her collar shakes.

"That's right, redbird," I pant. "You fucking come all over this cock."

She's so weak she can barely sit up, so I flip her over and stroke her clit and fuck her until she comes again. I'm in no hurry to finish. As long as I can stay hard, I'm keeping her on my cock. And I've never had a problem staying hard.

She cries. That's fine, she can safeword me when she's had enough.

CHAPTER THIRTY-TWO

KEIRA

I don't ask him when we're leaving. The afternoon wanes into night. He goes out before dark and takes care of the horses. I stand by the window and watch him whistle for them to come back to their stalls. It's cold out, but he's just in his shirt. The muscles ripple across his back as he pulls the bar over the door.

Cold comes in on his skin as he returns. I shut and lock the door, turning to lean against it.

"Is there any meat for dinner?" I ask.

"There's a freezer in the kitchen pantry," he says. "But it won't be defrosted until tomorrow."

"Are we staying that long?"

He's by the sink, washing his hands. He pauses, wiping down his forearms with a towel, and his eyes snap to mine. That faintly amused expression is back.

"Yes, we'll stay," he says. "I'll ride out tomorrow and locate the horses. We'll leave the morning after."

He spanks my ass lightly as he walks by, gripping it hard through my panties. There's a driving possessiveness to the way he touches me and, my God, it keeps me wet.

I hear him rummaging in the pantry and then he sets a pack of frozen meat in the sink. He watches me, leaning on the kitchen counter, while I cook breakfast again. His stoicism is attractive, but it's also frustrating. After everything we've done together, I assumed he'd be more open.

Maybe there's nothing left to be open about. Maybe it died with the woman he loved first.

I swallow past my dry throat.

"What was her name?" I ask.

His expression doesn't change. "Mariana."

"Was...was she pretty?"

He nods.

"Do you...do you still love her?"

He's somewhere far away. I can see the mist settle over his face. Finally he shakes his head.

"No, I stopped loving her a long time ago. Young love only stays if it has a chance to turn into something more," he says finally.

Bacon spits in the pan, leftover from the morning. I turn, leaning on the counter and grip the edge so hard it bends my nails. My heart picks up.

"When did you start falling for me?" I whisper.

He doesn't look up for a moment. Then he finally lifts his azure gaze to mine and my breath hitches. For the first time there's something there that looks like peace.

His jaw works. "When I saw you in your husband's office."

Deep inside, I knew this already. He upturned our world for no reason. He could have taken revenge on Clint at any point, but he chose the day after I confessed I was scared. He opened the gates of his fortress and let me into his bed despite how deeply he'd been hurt before.

I bite my lip, worrying it hard.

He picks me up and sets me on the counter. It should bother me the way he likes to move me around whenever he likes, but it doesn't.

"Do you love me?" he asks.

I don't know the answer to that yet. "I'm falling for you," I whisper.

His mouth thins. He takes my chin between his finger and thumb. I reluctantly shift my eyes up to meet his piercing gaze.

"You might not love me yet, redbird, but you will."

"Do I have a choice, sir?" I sigh.

"No." He kisses my forehead and I close my eyes.

"What are you going to do about the Garrison brothers?" I ask.

He rumbles, like he's laughing somewhere in his chest, and pulls back. "You let that up to me. I know if their parents were still alive, I'd skin them slowly before I took mercy on them and put a bullet between their eyes."

My jaw goes slack. "What did his parents do to you?"

"That's an ugly story."

"I want to hear it."

"My parents were tenants on their land, back when my family had nothing," he says. He's using the same flat tone he used when he talked about his fiancée's death. "Abel Garrison tried to rape my mother and my father defended her. After that, the Garrisons evicted them. They had nothing. My father started drinking...my mother got cancer and passed away. My father died of hypothermia. Drank too much, it was winter, he fell asleep in a ditch and never woke up."

My entire body tingles with shock. When he said he had a dark and bloody history with the Garrisons, I'd expected a feud over land.

"How old were you when your father passed?" I whisper.

"Sixteen." He lifts his chin. "After that, I went to Colorado to train. During the summer, back in Montana, I thought it would be a good idea to go after Avery Garrison at a bar one night. He shot me in the leg."

"He shot you?" My voice rises.

He releases me and unfastens his belt, pushing his pants down enough to expose his upper thigh. I didn't notice it before, but there's a faint scar there. Round and silvery. He pulls his pants up, but leaves his belt hanging.

"I told you, redbird, you and I, our interests aligned."

I touch his cheek, his short beard coarse under the heel of my palm. His skin is so warm with a little bit of roughness from being tanned in the Montana sun. His lids fall halfway and he leans into my touch. Like he's starved for it.

"Maybe we were destined to be tied together by all of this," I say quietly.

"No," he says firmly. "I chose you and made you mine. Despite you having that son of a bitch for your husband."

"Does it bother you that I slept with him?" I whisper.

Flame flickers in his eyes and he leans in and takes hold of my throat. His fingers encircle it and hold me firmly as he kisses my mouth. When he pulls back, I feel my nipples harden. My chest heaves and he puts his hand between my breasts.

"Do you remember how he felt?" he says softly. "Inside you?"

He's so jealous and it's giving me a tender ache between my thighs.

"Sometimes," I admit.

His lip curls. "So you need fucked harder if I want that memory erased."

"It's not a good one."

He puts me on my feet and strips my panties off. Not taking his eyes off mine, he spits into his hand and pushes it between my thighs.

My head spins as he sinks two fingers into me and finds that sweet spot. I feel more tender than usual, maybe because he's used me so hard the last twelve hours.

His mouth meets mine.

When he pulls back, my lips tingle.

"I shouldn't be jealous of a dead man, but I am," he says hoarsely.

My hips ache, but it's not pleasant this time. I push back and he pulls his fingers from me and I clap my hand over my mouth. His pointer and middle finger are stained red, a little rivulet dripping down his wrist.

He glances down, but his expression doesn't change.

"I'm so sorry," I rasp. "I guess I started my period."

He lifts his bloody hand and studies it. "I've never been with a woman who wasn't on birth control. It's the first time I've had period blood on me."

I wish I could crawl into a hole and live there forever.

"Here, let's wash it off."

He lifts his hand to his mouth and I panic, slapping his wrist away. His brow shoots up.

"What the fuck is wrong with you?" I hiss.

"It's just blood," he says, but he lets me grip his arm and wash his fingers in the sink.

I'm so mortified I can't speak. He's on the brink of laughter—I can feel his chest shaking. I order him out of the kitchen. Face burning, I slip upstairs and grab my panties and tuck a handful of toilet paper inside. I return to find him leaning on the counter with a glint in his eye.

"Go wait in the living room, please," I whisper.

He bends, kissing the side of my neck. "Whatever you like, redbird."

He sits on the couch. I feel his eyes follow me as I finish making dinner. When we're done eating, he carries me upstairs. I stand with my arms wrapped around my body, wondering what he's doing as he disappears into the bathroom. I'm too sore for sex, so I hope he's not expecting it. But he walks out with a towel, which he lays over the sheet. Our eyes meet as he kneels down and slips my panties off and lifts me into the bed.

He pulls me close, stretching his body out against mine. He's like a furnace, wrapped around me. It soothes my aching muscles and I feel myself relax into him. His fingertips move softly through my hair to my scalp, massaging gently over my temples.

I've never been comforted on my cycle. It's strange—I'm used to concealing it and pretending I'm not in agony. But I feel so safe wrapped up in his arms with his hand in my hair.

"Thank you," I whisper. "Sorry, I didn't mean to put a damper on things."

He rumbles in his chest. "Don't apologize for being in pain. Just lay there and rest."

His lips brush my hair. My lashes flutter shut.

I haven't felt this safe in a long time.

CHAPTER THIRTY-THREE

GERARD

I wake early the next morning and she's still sleeping soundly. Rolling to my side, I tuck a strand of hair behind her ear. She doesn't stir, even when I peel back the covers to reveal her bloody thighs. Maybe she needs more rest when she bleeds.

I fill up a hot water bottle, wrap it in flannel, and lay it over her lower belly. She stays still, her breathing even as I part her thighs and tuck a folded towel between them.

Then I write a note and leave the cabin. I know exactly where the horses are, so I saddle up Shadow and we take the main trail over the mountains. They've been less than a five minutes ride from the cabin this entire time. I see their backs huddled in the three sided shelter near a round hay bale.

I rope them, one by one, and bring them to the paddock. It's crowded, but we won't be here long and they'll fit in the open barn tonight. When I return to the cabin, she's still upstairs. I climb the stairs to find her standing in the shower, steam clouding thick between us.

"You alright?" I ask.

She turns, her arms wrapped around her body. "Yeah, I just...um, I forgot to bring pads. I didn't think about it."

I lean against the sink and cross my arms. "There's extra flannel sheets, but that's about it. We don't get too many women up here at the cabin so you won't find pads."

"I think I can make flannel work," she says. Her gaze darts over me and fixes on the shower wall. "I'm not feeling great. I don't know how much use I'll be in rounding up the horses."

"Already done," I tell her.

She brightens. "Are they all okay?"

"They're fine, I put them in the barn. And they have enough space to wait until you're ready to leave."

"Maybe I'll go out to see them."

I shake my head. "No, you're getting back in bed."

She's not used to being taken care of. I see her struggle to accept my words, but finally she nods. I linger while she dries off and runs a comb through her hair. It takes her a while, but she finally gets her hair hanging in a wet curtain down her back.

She goes to braid it over her shoulder and I stop her.

"Let me," I say.

She watches me in the mirror, eyes wary. Gently, I gather her hair and braid it down her back, tying it off with the rubber band she hands me. When I'm done, she turns to inspect my handiwork.

"I've never met a man who can braid hair," she says. "Why did you learn how to do that?"

I take the braid in my fist, wrapping it twice around my grip. Immobilizing her head. Her breasts heave and our eyes meet in the mirror.

"Okay, I see," she whispers.

I release her and she lays back down in the bedroom. I feel her curious eyes on me as I rip strips of flannel to fold and put between her legs. When I refill the hot water bottle and place it on her lower belly, her lids flutter and sink down.

"Thank you," she whispers.

I kiss her forehead and leave her resting while I find breakfast. When I return to the bedroom, she's sitting upright with her back against the pillows. I lay the tray of reheated biscuits, jam, and coffee on the end of the bed and sit down at her side. My boot catches on her coat on the floor by the bed and something tumbles from the pocket.

It's the little painted mare she hides from me.

I pick it up and her eyes widen, her hand darting out to snatch it up, but I hold it back.

"Why do you carry this with you?" I ask.

"I don't," she says.

I give her a stern look. "No lying, redbird."

She twists her hands, picking her thumbnail. "My mother was from Sweden. She died right after I was born and that's all I have left."

I turn the wooden horse in my fingers. It's about four inches tall and the craftsmanship is impressive. Every ripple of muscle or knob of bone is visible. The body is painted with chestnut red and white markings. It reminds me a lot of Angel.

"You hide it from me," I say. "Why?"

Her finger digs harder. "It's a child's toy," she says, glancing up. "Clint said it was stupid that I carried it with me."

My brow rises. "Grief isn't stupid, redbird. The way you grieve doesn't have to make sense to anyone else."

She swallows and her eyes are wet again. "Thank you," she whispers.

I take her wrist, flipping her hand, and put the painted mare into her palm. "It looks like it was repainted. Did your father do that?"

She nods, a little smile gracing her lips. "He did it before he died."

"You must have loved him a lot," I say.

She never volunteers information about her past. I don't pry because I know so much about it already. Everyone she's ever trusted was bought for a blank check. Doctors, lawyers, judges—they gave up her secrets easily.

The only ones who didn't spill are dead.

"He was amazing, but he was pretty sick," she says quietly. "That's all I remember...this weight on my mind that he didn't have a lot of time. He got really ill near the end, that's why we sold our cattle and

219

equipment. I wish...I wish I'd focused more on him and less on thinking about how he was going to die. I feel like his life is just...a blur in my memory."

A tear slips down her cheek.

"But you remember him," I say. "And the land he loved, that's still yours."

She blinks hard, wiping her face. "No, it's yours."

"Whatever happens, Stowe Farms will stay in the family," I say. "Break my heart, redbird, and I'll still give you what you're owed."

She sniffs and meets my gaze shyly. "Really?"

"I know what it feels like," I say simply.

She's quiet, turning the painted mare over and over in her fingers. Then she sets it aside and pats the bed.

"Have breakfast with me," she says.

I sit beside her and she tells me about her girlhood. Her words are colorful, filling my head with images of bluebells, sunsets, evenings by the fire while the winter wind tore at the farmhouse. She tells me how her father taught her to ride and shoot and rope cattle. How he always brought her candy or a book from South Platte when he went on errands.

She tells me about the little fragments her mother left behind. The Swedish dessert she baked from an old recipe. The burning wreath her father wove and put on her head for St. Lucy's Day and told her she was the most beautiful girl in the world. The book of fairy tales she read so often it fell apart in her hands.

She's lived her life in the shadow of death.

Maybe we're not so different, my redbird and I.

We sleep for a few hours in the afternoon. I wake before her, disoriented. It's been decades since I took a nap during the day. She's still sleeping soundly when I go to put the venison roast into the oven.

Then I go out to the back porch because I found a cigar that's still good and I want to have a fucking smoke. I never get a chance to unwind, so I'm taking it while I can.

The ground is dusted with snow. The entire world is silent.

I lean on the railing, the earthy tobacco taste on my tongue.

When I first met her, it was an instant attraction. A scorching hot lust that nothing could satisfy but her body. But now, what I feel for her is so much softer and deeper than anything I've felt before. I thought I loved Mariana, but now that I know Keira, I'm not sure I've ever been in love before now.

I'm never coming back from this obsession.

Westin told me once that I'm like a dog trained to fight. Once my jaws are locked in something, I'll never let go. He's right, especially when it comes to my redbird.

I smoke for a while, looking out over my ranch. Around two, the door opens and she steps out. She's in sweats, her bra, and my extra jacket. It's slipping off her shoulder, the light making her freckled skin glow.

"You feeling alright?" I ask.

She leans against my body, pushing her arm around my waist. "The meds kicked in. I didn't know you smoked cigars."

"One of my many vices."

She turns her face up, a little crease between her eyes. "You have no vices."

She's so fucking sweet. I kiss her forehead and she bends into me.

"I'm a hedonist for you," I say.

She smiles. "You are pretty dirty in bed," she admits.

"I've gone easy on you."

Her brows rise and she turns, leaning against the railing to face me. "What else do you want to do to me that you haven't already?"

I release a stream of smoke and lean over her, a hand on the rail on either side of her body.

"Choke your perfect throat. Fuck you until you pass out and fuck you to wake you back up. Find out how much fucking your mouth can take before you tap out. Paint your ass with bruises until you can't sit on it."

Her eyes widen, lids fluttering.

"You're a painslut and I want to know how far I can take that," I say.

221

Her lips part, her tongue flicking out. Her throat bobs.

"Why are you a sadist?" she whispers.

I consider feeding her some bullshit like I usually do, but I'm starting to think we're past that. I bend in and her breath washes over my face. Our lips brush, our bodies tense, and then our mouths come together.

I kiss her slowly, thoroughly. Until she moans and I break away.

"I need a lot to feel," I admit. "I'm just...numb. I have been for years."

Pain flickers through her eyes. "You can change that."

"Do you want me to?" I ask.

She takes a second to respond, but then she shakes her head.

"I want you as you are," she whispers.

This time, when I kiss her like it's the first and last time our mouths have touched. If I had the words, I'd tell her that she's the only cure I need for all the numbness in my heart. But I'm not good with words. So I let my body do the talking.

And I think she knows.

CHAPTER THIRTY-FOUR

KEIRA

We get back to the house at noon and Gerard disappears into the barn to get the horses settled. I drop my bag in the hall and walk through the quiet house. It's the middle of the day so everyone is out, even the dogs. I slip off my boots and pad up the stairs.

"Miss Garrison."

I turn to find Maddie standing in the living room. She looks almost nervous and that makes me nervous too.

"What's wrong?"

She climbs the bottom few stairs and holds out an envelope. "This is from your late husband's lawyer. I wasn't sure to give it to you or Sovereign."

"I'll take it," I say, pushing back my irritation. Has he been telling his staff that I'm not the point person for my ranch? "Thank you, I appreciate it."

She nods, frowning, and turns to go, but I clear my throat.

"Maddie," I say.

She pivots. "Yes?"

"Did...did I do something wrong to you?"

Her brows shoot up and I can see regret flicker through her face. "No, I'm sorry if I gave you that impression. I'm just...with you being a Garrison, I'm never sure what I can say. You know how Sovereign feels about your family."

I don't fault her for that.

"I'm not really a Garrison," I say in a rush. "I...it's hard being a woman up here. Would you be interested in maybe having lunch together sometime? Gerard said you eat with your husband, but if there's a day he's busy, I'd like to."

Her face softens. "Sure, he'll be gone this weekend."

I can't hold back my smile. "I'll look forward to it."

She smiles, and this time it's genuine. I skip upstairs and I think I hear her hum lightly as she heads back to the kitchen.

I push the bedroom door open and stop short. On Gerard's desk is a cardboard box with a lid, the kind used for storing documents. I push the door shut and pad silently across the carpet. There's black marker scrawled across the top that takes me a minute to work out.

Mrs. Clint Garrison.

I open the envelope so quickly it rips down the side and the paper inside falls open. It's a typed letter with Jay's name printed at the bottom.

Mrs. Garrison,

Enclosed is the remainder of your late husband's personal items left in my possession. If you have any questions regarding these or any other legal matters, I am handing his account off due to the unpaid balance detailed here.

My eyes skim down to the phone number below. And to the second number that's almost the same length.

Fuck. Why did I not realize I had to pay his lawyer?

The door opens behind me and I turn to see Gerard taking his coat off. I've never been good at finances because I never had access to my own money until Clint was gone. The impending doom of unpaid bills scares me. I turn and meet his eyes, panic tearing at my throat.

"What's wrong, redbird?"

Speechless, I hold out the paper. He takes it and there's a short silence before he hands it back.

"Don't worry about it," he says.

Don't worry about it? What the hell is that supposed to mean? I'm on the hook for over a hundred thousand dollars and I'm just supposed to not worry about it?

My hand shakes as I grip the paper. He removes his coat and pulls his shirt off. He goes to unfasten his belt, but he sees the tears spilling down my cheek and stops short.

He's beside me in a moment, pulling me against his bare chest. "I've got it, sweetheart. I'll pay it this afternoon."

"I'm sorry," I manage. "I feel so stupid."

He pulls back and wipes my tears with his thumb. "Stupid for what? They're not your bills."

I laugh weakly. "I don't know why it never occurred to me that I had to pay his lawyer. He did a bunch of work after Clint died and I guess I thought it was prepaid."

He lifts my chin and I sniff, trying to pull myself together. I'm not weak, but I cry as easily as turning on a faucet, and it's embarrassing. Clint hated it at the beginning, and then he liked to goad me until I burst into tears.

Gerard just wipes them from my cheek and kisses my forehead.

"What's in the box?" he says.

I go to the desk and lift the lid. Inside, there are stacks of folders and dozens of papers shoved between them. He leans over my shoulder as I grab a handful and pull them free. The top file falls open to reveal some tax documents from a few years ago.

"I think it's just some paperwork," I sigh.

He nods, but just before he turns to walk away, the files slip from my hand and thud to the ground. Papers fly everywhere and we both kneel down at the same time to catch them. I'm scrabbling on my hands and knees, burning with embarrassment, when I realize Gerard is perfectly still.

I look up.

He's holding a black business card and his eyes are dark. Not the way they are when he's angry with me. No, this is so much more terrifying. He's got an expression that could wither the skin off a person.

Cold and sharp like ice breaking over the lake. Dark ink spilling from his pupils.

The card is tiny in his fingers. Yet he's looking at it like he's holding a venomous snake.

"Gerard," I whisper. "What's wrong?"

He turns the card over. There's nothing on the black matte paper except a little silver terrier dog. His eyes narrow and jump to me and back to the card.

"You're scaring me," I whisper. "What's wrong?"

He shakes his head once. Then he rises and pushes the card into his back pocket and reaches for his shirt. I hate being ignored, especially when I'm panicking because he looks like he's going to murder someone with his bare hands. I scramble to my feet and cross the room to him.

I never had the courage to confront him before. But after the last few days, I'm not scared of him. My hands fall to his chest and I realize I'm cold because his bare skin burns my fingertips. He stops, his shirt half buttoned, and studies me.

"Sovereign," I whisper. "Please talk to me."

He shakes his head once.

My hands twist in his shirt, but he ignores them and finishes buttoning it. His hat sits by the bed and I make a grab for it before he can. He goes still, eyes crackling.

"Please," I beg. "I thought we promised to communicate."

His jaw works. I know what I said isn't true—I promised to be honest, he didn't—but I hope he doesn't point that out.

"You shouldn't know everything," he says finally, his voice a low rumble.

That pisses me off. I came here under the impression that my husband's death was an accident. I slept with Gerard, I signed a contract to share his bed, not knowing he had murdered my husband. He kept so much from me and I can tell he has more secrets buried behind those eyes.

He's good at being silent—too good.

"If you don't stop lying to me, I'm not going to be here when you get back," I say, my voice shaking.

His brow raises. "I thought you were falling for me, redbird."

Hot tears spill over. "I am, but you can't do this. You fucking killed my husband. You trapped me here on Sovereign Mountain, and now you look...you look like you're going to kill again. Please, just tell me what's going on. I can't do this, I won't."

His lashes lower. "You're not a coward."

"I am," I say. "I am a coward. And I'm not ashamed of it because not everyone is like you...you sit up here like a god and decide who lives or dies. I'm not like you. I'm not numb."

I regret it as soon as the word leave my mouth—that was his word, the one he used when he opened up to me on the porch of the cabin.

He winces.

"I didn't mean to...say that," I stammer. "I meant...heartless."

"You think I'm heartless," he says quietly. "If I'm heartless, then why does the thought of losing you feel worse than death?"

I reach for words, but come up with nothing. His dangerous eyes have softened. Maybe because he knows that I'm right, even if I never meant to hurt him.

"Redbird," he says. "My scars aren't thick enough to protect me when it comes to you."

I'm not sure how it happens, but somehow I'm up against the door. His warm, broad body is against mine. His mouth moves against my lips, filling me with his familiar taste. I'm molten lava in his arms. Blood pumps through my body in a frantic rush and pools somewhere near my heart. Filling me with the strongest warmth.

He pulls away, his mouth an inch from mine.

"Keira," he breathes. "I've lost everything, but I can't lose you."

My throat is dry. My entire body tingles.

"You're not just falling for me, you love me already," I whisper, tears pouring down my cheeks.

"Always." His gaze is steady.

"Where are you going?"

"I'm going to see a dog about a man," he says.

"I hate your fucking riddles," I manage.

"I know."

His final kiss is so soft it breaks my heart. He pulls back and puts his hat on, tugging it low over his eyes. Then he walks out the door without another word.

It doesn't occur to me until hours later that I didn't tell him I loved him back.

CHAPTER THIRTY-FIVE

KEIRA

I hate him. I love him. I want to kill him.
I want to be his forever.

CHAPTER THIRTY-SIX

GERARD

I go to see Jack Russell.

He's a friend and business partner. We both have a mutual understanding that he stays on my retainer for when I need someone taken care of, and I'll stay out of his business.

If our agreement stands, there's no good reason that my personal hitman's calling card should be in a box of Clint Garrison's things.

I take the truck south. Jack lives outside South Platte, that's all I know. But he's got a contact at a bar in West Lancaster, a large town that falls an hour's drive below the city. When I need to speak with him, I know I can find him there.

It's late when I pull up outside the bar. The lights are on and music thrums from the lower level. I make sure my gun is fastened to my belt and get out of the truck, putting my hat on and pulling it low. I don't like being recognized, it gets the rumor mill moving.

I push open the front door to reveal a packed front room. The bar has men lined up all the way down and there's a crowd at the pool table.

My eyes skim over the room until they fall on a platinum blonde head of hair and a heart-shaped face. She turns and I recognize the bright red of her lipstick.

The crowd parts for me, one of the benefits of being tall. I slide into the last empty seat at the end of the bar and rap my knuckles on the table. The woman turns to cuss me out and stops short. Her red mouth falls ajar and her eyes dart over me.

"One second," she says.

I lean back. The room smells faintly of whiskey, but after all this time, I don't find it tempting. I've tasted addiction too thoroughly to go back to it.

The woman returns and leans on the counter, tapping her red fingernails on the shiny wood. She's wearing a cropped shirt that shows the tattoo coiled on her lower belly. A blue snake surrounded by black flowers.

"What the fuck are you doing in my bar, Sovereign?" she says quietly.

"I'm here to see your brother," I say.

She narrows her eyes, cocking her head. "You still single?"

I shake my head. "Locked down."

"Good for you," she says, clearly taken aback. "Lucky woman."

I glance over the room. "Where's your girlfriend, Lisbeth? I thought she worked with you."

She rolls her eyes, shaking back her hair. "We broke up. She quit. It's fine. Want a drink or still sober?"

"Still sober," I say. "Is Jack upstairs?"

She jerks her head to the back of the room. "Go on up, I texted him the minute you walked in."

She goes back to pouring beers and I push through the suffocating crowd to the back stairwell. The roar of voices dulls as I turn the corner to reveal a dark hallway with a cracked door at the end. It's been a while since I met with Jack, but he knows we have an agreement to uphold.

I knock once on the door. He clears his throat from somewhere inside.

"Come in, Sovereign."

I enter, my boots loud on the glossed wood floor, and shut the door behind me. It's a dimly lit room decorated a lot like the main house back at Sovereign Mountain. A bull skull glowers down from above his enormous fireplace. A thick bearskin rug covers the floor beneath the couch. Against the far wall is a bar, a shelf of whiskey, and a stockpile of barrels.

Jack stands by the fire with a whiskey in hand. He's in his late thirties and his glossy black hair doesn't have a speck of gray. It's slicked back over his head, complimenting his clean shaven face. The eyes that fix on me are usually bright green, but in the dark, they're two glittering points.

"What can I do you for?" His voice is low and smooth as silk.

I take the card and cross the room, holding it out between two fingers. His eyes dart down and snap back up.

"I didn't give you that," he says.

"No," I say. "You didn't."

"So where did it come from?"

I take my hat off and smooth back my hair. "You tell me, Russell. I thought I was paying out the nose for a non-compete clause with you. So why was that card in Clint Garrison's possession?"

His brows rise. He flicks the card around and in between his fingers quick as a flash. In another life, Jack would have made an excellent magician.

"Clint is dead," he says. "How did you come by this?"

I sink into the couch and cross one ankle over my knee. He stays by the fire. The tension between us is palpable. There's a short silence and he realizes I'm not going to answer so he sets aside his whiskey and crosses to the other side of the room. There, he rolls the top back on his desk and sets the card down.

"Clint approached me two years ago with a job," he says.

"And you took it?"

"Yes and no."

He turns around, sitting on the edge of the desk. He crosses his arms and the miniature silver terrier around his neck glints between his open collar. My eyes dart down to his wrist. There's a leather band with an O-ring barely visible under his cuff.

He follows my eyes and the corner of his mouth turns up.

"I'm not sharing this one," he says.

"I'm not looking."

I met Jack when I was young, in my mid-twenties, and just discovering that my tastes ranged outside the regular. We started talking at a bar one night and he offered to share his sub with me. Watching him guide her through fucking me without touching her once made me realize I wanted that too. They were my gateway drug to the intricacies of BDSM.

"Are you locked down?" he asks. "Is she your...girlfriend?"

"She's my sub," I say. "But I'm going to marry her, just haven't told her yet. Back to the calling card."

He blinks. "The card...so Clint hired me...sort of."

Anger surges in my chest. "You broke our agreement."

"I was playing both sides. I didn't intend to follow through."

He doesn't look like he's lying, but I've learned enough not to trust anyone. Especially not men like Jack Russell. I sink back on the couch and cross my ankle over my knee. The amount of debt Clint was in is starting to make more sense. Jack Russell's services are expensive, and he would have charged thousands just for a consultation. I've seen his accounts. Most of his debt was bad investments, years where he was in the red, and a fuckload of money on cheating and gambling.

But this explains some of the gaps in his receipts.

"Who did he want you to kill?" I ask grimly.

He sighs. "Well, my confidentiality agreement is over because Clint is dead. It was his wife."

Deep down, I knew the answer to my question and I knew it from the moment I saw the calling card. But that doesn't keep white hot rage from pouring through my chest and making my vision flash. I don't move, but I feel my nails pierce my palms.

"Did he tell you why?"

Jack saunters over and sinks down onto the coffee table a few feet from where I sit. I'm on high alert because he doesn't have my trust anymore. Or maybe it's because when it comes to Keira, I can't be too careful.

"It's pretty obvious."

I stay silent.

"Clint married his wife because her father left her Stowe Farms," he says. "He annexed her farm into his ranch and got what he wanted. Now, all he had to do was get rid of his unwanted wife."

It feels like my heart is beating in absolute silence. Thump, thump, the way it does when it's just me standing at the edge of the frozen lake at the top of the mountain.

In my head is a stark image of Keira, painted in high definition with every detail seared into my mind. She's curled up in bed, the way she was the first night she slept with me. Bright hair spilling over the pillow, eyes closed, body relaxed.

If I hadn't brought her to Sovereign Mountain when I did...what would have happened to my redbird? It's not Jack's way to kill women, but that wouldn't have stopped the Garrisons from doing it themselves.

I clear my throat. "Was anyone else involved?"

He leans in, resting his elbows on his knees.

"That would be breaking confidentiality." he says.

"So the people who hired you are still alive?"

"Very alive."

"Both of them?"

He nods and then his jaw clenches, his narrowed eyes flashing a poisonous green. Now I know there are two more people involved in this plot. And I have a pretty good idea of who they are.

"Would these people happen to go by Garrison as well?" I ask.

He presses his lips together, but I already have my answer. Silence stretches on until he releases a heavy sigh and sits back.

"I shouldn't have gone behind your back," he says.

"Our contract is over." I'm on my feet, reaching for my hat.

"Wait."

I'm halfway to the door when that word rings out. I pivot on my heel, gracious enough to offer him one more opportunity to explain himself. He lifts his palms.

"What we have is a non-compete clause. At that point, you weren't competing with Garrison Ranch."

"I'm their biggest competitor," I say.

"But not their enemy. You were doing business with Clint."

Darkness and rage seep through my veins like ink. Inside, my anger simmers low. Waiting for when I can release it.

"I was, but only because behind the scenes I've been buying up their land," I spit. "Why do you think I own the banks? I've been squeezing the life out of those Garrison fuckers with interest until they had no choice but to start selling. You know these things, Jack, it's your job."

"No one knows anything unless you want them to, Sovereign," he snaps.

"That woman...the one I said I was going to marry," I spit out. "She's Clint's widow. So forgive me for distrusting you."

He pulls back, his brows drawing together. I see the gears turning in his head as he soaks in this information.

This changes everything because that makes Keira my family. And a long time ago, I'd agreed to finance his underground business in order to get Lisbeth away from her ex-husband and out of debt. He owes me for saving the two of them, and the weight of that debt makes his shoulders sink.

"I was never going to see this job through," he says finally. "I don't kill women, but I was curious why he wanted her taken out, so I gave him the card."

He has me there. We both know that's over the line for Jack. It might be a rough, wild country out here, but he still has his decency. Maybe he's telling the truth.

Jack releases a long sigh and rubs his eyes. "Jesus...fuck, Sovereign," he mumbles. "What do you want from me?"

"What I've always wanted from you—a hitman."

He swallows hard, throat bobbing. His hands go to his hips.

"Avery and Thomas?"

I nod.

"That'll be six million for both," he says. "That's a fucking deal too. Friends and family discount."

I hold out my palm and he locks eyes with me. Giving me a piercing stare, like he's trying to split me open and look inside my head.

Then he shakes my hand and I feel the balance of the world shift. I suppose this could be considered signing a death warrant. But I prefer to think of it as doing the Lord's work.

Jack goes to his desk. There's a wooden card box printed with a little silver dog that he slides open and takes two black cards from. I keep still as he walks over and tucks them into my shirt pocket.

"I'll collect them when it's done," he says.

I shake my head. "Pack your shit," I say. "We're doing this together."

He freezes. "I work alone."

The image of Keira in my lap, riding me with her crimson hair falling down her back, bursts into my mind. She's so fucking alive, so warm and real. When we first met, I'd wanted her...perhaps I'd thought I loved her. But the realization I could have lost her before I even got a chance to be hers shakes me to my core.

She looks like forever now.

Like, if I can undo the bindings of the past, the mother of my children.

My eyes shut and against my eyelids I see our entire future laid out. Sons, maybe a daughter, running free on Sovereign Mountain. My name and hers together on the deed to our ranch. Hot summer breeze coming through the open window at night while I fuck her beneath the quilt after the children are asleep.

My throat closes.

A long time ago, the Garrison family took that dream from me. They broke my heart and my pride and as good as killed my parents. At their hand, I tasted grief before I had a chance to become a man.

They tried to break me, to erase my name all because my father did what was right and defended his wife. It's time to close that chapter.

I am the only son of the Sovereign line and their death is my birthright.

I waited long enough.

It's time for retribution.

"Jack," I say, my voice quiet. "This is your expertise, but it's my blood to spill. We do it together."

He knows what they did to me. He knows how long I've waited for justice. There's a short silence and then he gets his hat.

"Let's go kill some Garrisons."

CHAPTER THIRTY-SEVEN

KEIRA

I cry again after Gerard leaves. There's a sense of foreboding in my chest and I tell myself it's just the oncoming snowstorm. In the evening, I creep down the hall and push open the game room balcony. I'm wearing the sweatsuit from my first night at Sovereign Mountain. It smells like him because it was in his dresser drawer, folded with his things.

The sky is black. Snow starts to swirl, but I know the storm won't hit until tomorrow at noon.

The feel of it on the wind reminds me of being a girl. The world was simple then, and I looked forward to storms because I never had to go out into them. I'd wait by the fire for my father to burst through the door, covered in ice and snow. Chilly from putting the horses to bed.

My eyes sting.

I never really had time to grieve for my father. But in the last several weeks, some of that sadness has tugged at the edges of my mind. Maybe because I feel safe now, safe enough to stop masking everything.

My feet are numb by the time I stumble back into the bedroom. All the papers that fell earlier are still in a heap on the ground. I flick on the fireplace and pad over to clean them up, but the memory of his reaction to the card stops me short.

I shiver. There are so many secrets at Sovereign Mountain that sometimes I wonder if I really know anything at all.

But I do know one thing for certain—he said he loves me.

I want to believe him.

He has nothing to gain from me. He already has my ranch in the palm of his hand. I'm drained dry by Clint's debt. I'm powerless against him and that's my saving grace.

Clint used me, but Gerard can't do the same because I have nothing left to take.

After his confession, I know he never intended on it.

My eyes are wet again as I sink down to my knees to clean up the papers. It's just a bunch of shit. Weeks and months I wasted with Clint right here on the floor at my feet. Receipts, faded bills, folders of paperwork. I wish I could stuff it all into the fireplace and watch it go up in a blaze.

I gather it all up and shove it back into the box and go to slam the lid.

There's a plastic folder wedged in the corner. Something about it draws me in, so I pull it free and flip it over.

Last Will & Testament.

My heart picks up. I never saw the will, I just signed everything Clint's lawyer put in front of me because I was too numb to care. I let him fight everything out in the courtroom without ever showing me a document. Now that I'm sitting here, I realize how stupid and naive I was not to oversee everything he did. I'd been groomed to be quiet and let men handle this kind of thing.

I simply hadn't known better.

My hand shakes as I unfasten the folder and let it fall open.

My eyes skim over the contents, but they halt at the date scrawled over the top.

The day Clint died. The time is four-thirty in the afternoon. An hour after the coroner came to take his body to the hospital.

What the fuck?

My eyes dart over the paper. Down to the bottom where Clint's signature is scrawled. Clear as day. Below it are two lines marked for witnesses and on those lines I see two names that make my heart go still.

Gerard Sovereign.

Westin Quinn.

My breathing comes fast and my vision flickers. This is the original will, this is notarized. My fingertips skim over the bumps where it's been stamped. But there's no way this can be real because it has my husband's signature on it, and by four-thirty that day, Clint was dead.

I stumble back to the bed, sinking down.

The will was a fake.

It was always a fake. Avery and Thomas were right to fight it in court.

I was wrong.

The folder spills onto the bed as I scramble for my phone. It has a solitary bar of signal. Shakily, I tear down the hall and burst out onto the cold balcony.

Now I have two bars.

I call Clint's lawyer. Snow falls in soft spirals and lands on my face. Melting on my cheeks. The phone rings three times and cuts out. I dial him again and wait.

"Hello?"

He sounds confused, and he has good reason to be. It's almost ten at night.

"Jay," I whisper. "This is Keira."

"Is this about the unsettled accounts?" he asks. "They've been paid up as of this afternoon."

A sob pushes up my throat.

"No," I whisper. "I have something I want to ask."

"Okay, but there's a consulting fee."

"No," I whisper harshly. "There's not, not for this. If you or the judge in my court case have ever taken money from Gerard

Sovereign, I want you to tell me that you can't answer this question because it pertains to confidential information."

There's a long, long silence. My eyes burn with hot tears threatening to spill down my cold cheeks.

"I'm sorry, Keira," he says finally. "I can't answer that question as it pertains to confidential information."

Everything changes. It feels like the sky shatters, and I close my eyes and let the tears flow. My hands shake as I lift the phone from my ear and hang up. It takes me almost five minutes to jerk myself from my reverie. My face prickles with cold and my feet are totally numb.

He didn't just kill Clint and disappear for seven months. No, he'd orchestrated everything from the beginning.

Nothing that had happened was by accident.

He bought out the bank to get ownership of Clint's mortgage. He'd put pressure on my husband until he started selling off his land to Sovereign Mountain.

He forged a will so everything was left to me, he bought out Clint's lawyer, and South Platte's judge to ensure it passed the court system.

He handed my land back to me knowing it would force me into his arms. Knowing I would have no one to turn to for protection but him.

He set a trap, laid the bait, and I'd walked right into it.

My mind whirls.

I can't make sense of this. The threads are so tangled I can't find my way through.

My eyes fall on the second name signed to the will.

Westin Quinn.

I run my hand over my face to wipe the tears. I cry too much, I always have, but tonight I'm going to find out the truth, even if I'm sobbing the entire time. I have to know if he's being honest about his past and if he means it when he says he loves me. Because nothing else will make me forgive him.

I put Gerard's coat over my sweatsuit, snatch the painted mare from my bedside table, and slip downstairs to find my winter boots.

Then I lock the dogs inside and go out into the yard and head for the gatehouse.

CHAPTER THIRTY-EIGHT

KEIRA

Westin opens the door after a solid minute of knocking. He's disheveled, his belt undone and his shirt unbuttoned. When he sees it's me, he turns and hastily finishes doing up his clothes.

"What are you doing here?" he says, scowling.

"Gerard left," I whisper.

He stares at me, eyes narrowing. "Okay?"

"Something's wrong," I say, unable to hide the tremor in my voice. "I was going through a box of my husband's things and there was a black card with a silver dog on it. He got really quiet when he saw it and left."

Westin freezes. His eyes dart behind me and he reaches out, grabbing my elbow and pulling me inside. He shuts the door and locks it, glancing around the room before pointing at the kitchen table. I sink down, looking around at the open concept interior. It's masculine, but clean, with dark wood and leather furniture and blue plaid accents.

He puts his hands on his hips. "You want something?"

"Whiskey," I say.

He pours two glasses and sinks down opposite me. Westin and I don't talk often, but he's close with Gerard. If anyone can answer my questions, it's Westin.

"What did that card mean?"

He swirls his whiskey, watching me critically. "That's Jack Russell's calling card. Everyone knows that."

"I didn't. Who's Jack Russell?"

"He's a hitman."

"Like...an assassin?"

He nods once, swirling the whiskey some more. "Yep, just like that."

My stomach sinks. Clint had that card locked in his safe at his attorney's office. Which meant, my husband had done business with a hitman.

But...why?

Westin sets aside his glass and steeples his fingers. "When you hire Jack to take someone out, he gives you a calling card. When the job is done, he brings you a receipt. Maybe it's a finger, or a tooth. And he takes the calling card back. Leaves no trace."

Sickness passes over me in a wave and leaves me weak.

"So if my husband...he paid Jack Russell to kill someone?"

"You don't get a calling card unless Jack gives it to you," Westin says. "So yeah, he had a deal...that looks like it didn't pan out. Stroke of good luck for the bastard he paid to kill that he happened to die."

I stare at him, anger flickering.

"I'm not dumb, Westin," I say coolly. "I know Gerard killed my husband and forged the will."

Westin's brows shoot to his hairline. He gives an uncomfortable cough.

"Oops," he says.

"And I saw your name was on it. I think Gerard meant for me to find out eventually, it wasn't hidden."

He swallows and lets out a heavy sigh. "Everything Gerard did was justified. Did he tell you about Mariana? About his parents? Your husband had that coming to him. It's not murder, Miss Garrison, it's fucking justice."

"I know he was engaged," I whisper. "And she was pregnant."

Westin shakes his head, downing his whiskey in a single gulp. I take a large sip of mine and shudder as it slides down my throat and burns in my stomach. My nerves buzz, but they're less fragile.

"That wasn't his baby," Westin says.

My jaw goes slack. "What?"

He runs a hand over his face, scrubbing his eye. "Mariana was cheating on him. I showed him evidence. But he just shoved his head up his ass because he treated her like she was a saint. She stopped wanting to fuck him and he chalked that up to her being scared off by his...interests. But she was fucking Clint and the baby was his. Sovereign admitted he hadn't slept with her in months when she told him she was pregnant. She kept going on about how she was further along than the doctor said. Bullshit."

My stomach turns for the most selfish reason.

If Clint took Gerard's fiancée...does that mean I'm just compensation? An eye for an eye?

My throat hitches. Tears start in my eyes and burn down my face.

"Fuck, Keira, don't cry," Westin mumbles.

I scrub my face with my sleeve. "Does Sovereign even love me?" I whisper.

His face softens. He reaches out and awkwardly pats my elbow.

"He's fucked," he says quietly.

My head spins with whiskey. If Gerard turns out to be a liar using me to get revenge, I know my heart will die in my chest. He told me once I was too young to be so hurt. And he was right.

"I hate this," I whisper. "I just want him to love me. That's all."

Westin sighs and leans back. I watch him refill our glasses and my hand shakes as I lift it to my lips.

"He does love you," he says.

"Then where the fuck is he?" I sob.

"Sovereign is a proud man," he says. "If he doesn't see justice through to the end, it'll break him. He watched his mother die, his father drink himself to death. He pulled his fiancée from a ditch. The Garrisons did that to him. This isn't about land or money or hurt feelings. It's justice for his family, his future children."

I'm too drunk to tell him Gerard can't have children without a reversal. I shouldn't have had so much whiskey, my body isn't used to it. I cover my face with my hands and let my body sink down over the table.

It feels like Westin and I are on a seesaw, rising and falling, both washed by the tides. By the powerful force of one man who isn't even at this table.

"This isn't about pettiness," Westin says quietly.

I lift my head and wipe my eyes. "He won't be at peace until he balances the scales," I whisper. "I get it, but I don't understand it. I wasn't raised with principles like that...I was raised to survive. Sometimes that means doing humiliating things like signing my body away in a contract with a man I don't know."

Westin looks at me and his brows furrow. He has a habit of scowling hard when he's thinking. There are faint lines left around his eyes from it.

"I don't know everything about your situation," he says. "But, I think Sovereign gave you back your dignity."

I open my mouth to argue that he'd made me sell myself for a mortgage, but then I remember his involvement goes further back. When I met Sovereign, I had no future. I was living in the house of a man who hated me. I'd told him I was afraid of Clint, that I was powerless, and he'd delivered me from evil.

Something that feels like hope flutters in my chest.

Maybe...maybe trusting him isn't the same as when I trusted Clint.

Westin sits across from me with his hands loosely folded. He's got scars on his knuckles the way Sovereign does. I study them, wondering if they're from bar fights or barbed wire. For men like them, either is likely.

"You've known Sovereign for a long time," I whisper. "Do you trust him?'

"With my life," he says. No hesitation.

"How...how do I know he's not just using me?" I'm struggling to get the words out. They feel like a betrayal after everything that's happened between us.

His eyes soften. "You're the only woman who's slept in his bed. He's not using you, Keira."

My eyes shut and tears seep down my face. I want to just give in. God, I want to surrender myself to Gerard Sovereign. And I would if I just knew what lay on the other side of all his darkness and need for vengeance.

Who will he be when this feud is over?

Does he know how to live without pain?

We hear a faint slam in the distance. Westin's gaze snaps to the door and we listen to the faint rumble of tires come up the drive. The engine of Gerard's truck dies away and I hear boots hit the gravel. Low voices rumble and a pang shoots through my chest as I recognize one as his. The other I can't place.

"He's back," Westin says.

I nod, wordless.

He looks to the side and in the corner of his eyes, I think I see something. Fear...maybe? Or is it hunger? Does he want this vengeance just as much as Sovereign?

I shiver, wrapping my arms around my body.

He stands. "Trust Sovereign and you'll be safe. Understood?"

The wind whistles through the trees. He pushes open the door and I see the shape of two men coming in from the yard. Walking side by side, their hats pushed low on their heads. Pistols on their hips. Heading for the gatehouse.

"Do you want to go out the back?" Westin asks.

I shake my head. "I want to talk to him."

CHAPTER THIRTY-NINE

GERARD

Jack and I step into the gatehouse and our conversation dies. Keira sits at the table, engulfed in sweats and her oversized coat. Her hair is tied up and her face is blotchy from tears. That doesn't alarm me because she cries often, but what I don't like is the half empty whiskey bottle before her. Other than the few drinks she's had at dinner, I've never seen her reach for a bottle before.

She drags her sleeve under her nose.

Our eyes meet.

And right then, I know that she knows.

Everything.

"What are you doing here, redbird?" I ask.

Her chin quivers. "I came to talk to Westin."

I know why, but I don't want to air out our dirty laundry in front of Jack and Westin. I jerk my head at Westin and we step to the far side of the room, out of earshot.

"You let her drink?"

"She was fucked up already. She knows everything."

I nod. My eyes wander back to her hunched shoulders. It hurts to know that I did this to her, regardless of my intention. I never wanted to cause her pain. If I had it my way, I'd build a castle at the top of the mountain and keep her safe behind a barricade.

"I need to talk to her alone," I say.

His mouth thins and he crosses his arms over his chest. "It's not my business...she's hurting. I hope you don't contribute to that, Sovereign."

I shake my head. He gives me a hard stare as he heads over to pour a drink for Jack and I beckon Keira. She gets up slowly and takes my hand, letting me lead her to the guestroom at the top of the stairs. The door shuts with a loud click.

"Where did you go?" she whispers.

"To see Jack Russell," I say.

"Westin told me what the card means. Who...who did Clint want to kill? You?"

I wish more than anything to protect her from all the ugly things in the world. But she deserves to know.

"You," I say.

The color drains from her face. Her throat bobs. She steps backwards and sinks down onto the bed.

"He...was going to kill me," she whispers.

I sit down beside her and she doesn't resist when I pull her into my lap. That's a good sign. She's not shutting me out after finding out everything I did to make her mine. The soft scent of pomegranate fills my senses as I bury my face in her hair. Her body shakes.

Fuck, I hate when she cries like this. I love her tears when they're from pleasure. But when they're from pain, it fills me with rage like I've never felt.

I want to gut the Garrisons. One by one. I want to burn everything they own to the ground, to wipe any memory of them from the earth.

"Redbird," I say. "No one will ever hurt you again."

Her body shivers in my arms.

"I swear it."

She wriggles back so she can look up at me. I brush her wet hair from her cheek and tuck it behind her ear.

249

"Is all that you want? Revenge?" she whispers.

I try to follow her train of thought and give up. "I've been waiting to take out the Garrisons for a long time," I say. "But what they were planning on doing to you...makes me realize it needs to be done. Now."

Her lip trembles. "You mean kill them," she says flatly.

My God, seeing her in pain hurts so badly, worse than anything that was done to me. My fingers grip her upper arms, pulling her back in as her face crumples. I rub her back and stroke my fingers through her hair while she shudders with sobs.

"I got fucking groomed," she bursts out. "They took my farm and they were going to kill me."

What I've known for a while is just now hitting her. Her body shivers and the whites of her eyes flash. I can tell she's right on the edge of panicking.

"Let me put you to bed and give you some sleeping pills," I urge. "You've been through a lot."

She wrenches from my grip and jumps to her feet. Her blue eyes, that are always so mild and beautiful, burn. I know that look—I've seen it in the mirror for years. She's starting to realize for the first time that she's a victim and she has been for years.

"No," she says sharply. "I'm not drugging myself so I don't have to feel this. I told Westin I didn't understand why you wanted revenge, but I'm starting to get it now. They don't deserve to live after everything they've done."

Her eyes are so wide her irises look small and her pupils are blown. She's frantic, trapped. I get up and she goes still as I rest my palm against her cheek.

"What do you want me to do to them?" I ask.

I let her take as long as she needs with the question. Her eyes are hazy and she's gazing up at me like she's never seen me before.

Maybe it's because until now, she never really has. Now she sees all my faults, my failures, my desire for justice and vengeance. She sees the lengths I went to make her mine and she has to know I'll do anything to keep her.

She pushes her face into my palm, her lashes fluttering shut.

"Tell me what you want," I murmur.

"I want you to love me," she whispers.

"Redbird," I say. "There's never been a question of that."

She pulls back from me, and for a second, I think she's angry. But then she turns and presses herself against the wall. Palms flat on the sanded wood. Her spine arcs like a cat and she pushes her ass out, just enough I know she's asking for my cock inside her.

Fuck. It's not the right time for that.

"Keira," I say, my voice hoarse. "Say it back."

Her eyes squeeze shut tight. "Let me feel you."

I close the space between us, mindful our steps can be heard downstairs. Her breath hitches and her soft ass pushes back against the front of my pants. Our breathing quickens in tandem. I yank her pants and underwear down to the floor.

"Please," she whispers.

I gather her hair with my other hand, dragging her head to the side. Then I take my cock out, pushing my pants down just low enough, and spit into my hand. Rubbing it over my length and her soaked entrance. When I enter her, she lets her head fall back against me and a little moan escapes her lips.

She feels the burn as I slide in. Her muscles fight, trying to adjust.

"Good girl," I breathe. "All the way for me now."

She whimpers as I bottom out. Her tight inner muscles clamp down around me. I drag out halfway and thrust slowly back in. I push my face into her neck, bracing my foot back to accommodate the difference in our height, and fuck her gently against the wall.

"Tell me," I pant.

She moans, her voice muffled. "I would have slept with you that first night. You didn't need the contract, I would have fucked you."

My hips move, pumping.

"Fucking isn't enough, I want to love you."

I don't say the rest—*let me love you, let me be your man, let me make you the mother of my children. Take my name and the land that I love.* She's not ready for me to say all those things to her yet.

But, God, they're right on the tip of my tongue.

"You could have just asked," she pants.

"Would you have said yes?"

She doesn't answer, but we both know. She wouldn't have accepted my terms if she hadn't been forced into it. We both know that whatever we have is born from desperation. Maybe that makes it taste all the better.

Like salt in caramel.

Pleasure from our pain.

She moans and I don't care that she's loud. I pull out and flip her, lifting her up and sinking my cock to the hilt in her soft pussy. She wraps her arms around my neck and her legs around my waist. She digs her nails into the base of my neck so hard pain sparks down my back. It sharpens my senses, giving me clarity.

"Tell me the truth," I order. "You swore to be honest."

Our bodies thump against the wall. I push her sweatshirt up and pull her bra down, baring her right breast. It marks pink when I tug her nipple hard enough to make her hips buck.

"If I kill the Garrisons, you can never leave me, redbird," I say. "We'll be tied together by that secret forever. So tell me you love me."

CHAPTER FORTY

KEIRA

He demands my love.

So I give it to him the way I've given him everything else.

My mouth is so close to his I can taste him. I wish he'd offer me more than just the grim set of his square jaw and the depths of his winter-blue eyes. He blinks slowly and his lids stay heavy, dark lashes stark.

"I love you," I whisper.

"You're mine," he says, his voice like gravel in his chest.

"I'm yours."

He kisses me and catches that word on his tongue.

CHAPTER FORTY-ONE

KEIRA

Maddie and I stand in the open front door. The barn light sheds a blue glow over the driveway. The men went into the barn and I can hear them talking in low tones.

My senses are sharp, the blur of whiskey gone from my brain after Sovereign fucked me. In the gatehouse, he put a blanket around my shoulders before he kissed me, using the edges to draw me near.

I pull the blanket close.

Hoofbeats sound and Shadow breaks from the barn and pulls to a halt, gravel spraying. Gerard is a silhouette on his back, his black cowboy hat stark against the clouded sky. Westin and Jack, both astride their horses, are at his heels. They loiter, talking in low tones.

I shudder.

"I don't like this," I whisper. "I feel like something bad is going to happen."

Maddie comes up behind me and pats my shoulder. It's the first affection she's shown me, and it feels awkward.

"It is," she says. "But Sovereign will come back. Hopefully before noon because there's a storm coming tomorrow."

They're all so confident in Gerard that it makes me want to turn my brain off and do the same. But I don't know him the way they do.

I'm a newcomer here in comparison with the years that Maddie and Westin have been by his side. They have a reason to trust him.

In the dark, he turns Shadow to look back. His eyes glint below the rim of his hat. For a second, I entertain what might happen if he doesn't come back and the pain that rips through my chest is almost unbearable. The blanket falls from my shoulders and I close the space between us, reaching up for his hand.

He's wearing gloves, but I feel the hard grip of his fingers around mine.

"I'll be back," he says.

I can't speak. He looks like a giant sitting astride his enormous horse, so tall I have to stand on my toes just to hold his hand.

Feeling silly, I kiss my palm and hold my hand up to him. The corners of his mouth turn up and he cradles my hand, letting my invisible kiss fall into his grip.

"Fuck," he says hoarsely. "You're so sweet."

"I do love you," I say quietly. "I really do. Please come back."

"Just give me time, just tonight. And I swear, when it's done, I'm all yours," he says.

I nod, tears streaming down my cheeks and neck.

He pushes his hat low. "I love you, redbird."

I pull back as their horses move past me and—damn it, I'm crying again. Big Dog and Small Dog circle my ankles, pacing. I feel Maddie's arms slide around me and lay the blanket back over my shoulders. Through my wet lashes, I watch their shadows disappear into the dark yard. Hoofbeats fade into the distance. I know it'll be the last night the Garrison brothers ever live through.

That doesn't bother me the way it would have before tonight.

If I love him, I have to love every part of him.

And that includes his darkness and desire for justice no matter how bloody the consequences. If I want to love this complicated, scarred man and everything that came with him, I have to be able to accept his past.

Maddie pulls me into the house, the dogs at our heels, and locks the door. The wind shrieks over the mountain and I feel the sides of the house shudder. I hate that they're out in the cold dark and I'm in here, safe and warm.

"Let's get you something to eat," she says.

She ushers me down the back hallway to the kitchen. The dogs are pasted to me, as if they sense my raging emotions. I wait in the doorway as she turns the lights on and starts taking things out of the cupboard. My head feels stuffy, and my eyes burn, so I lean my forehead against the cool wall. Maddie turns and her gaze narrows.

"You don't look very good," she says.

I shake my head. "I drank and now it's wearing off."

She takes my elbow and tugs me to a chair in the corner, pushing me down and wrapping the blanket around my shoulders. I'm having trouble telling how much time is passing. It feels like half a second later when she puts a cup of warm peppermint tea in my hand and sets a plate of strudel on the table beside me.

"Eat that, it's apple and cinnamon so it'll help settle your stomach," she orders.

Obediently, I push the fork into the flaky pastry and put a bite in my mouth. Warm butter and sweet apples melt on my tongue and my sickness ebbs as I eat until there's just a smear of cinnamon on the white porcelain. When I look up, Maddie is watching me with a hint of sadness in her eyes.

"Let's get you to bed," she says.

I stand to put my plate in the sink. "Are you okay?"

She nods. "I worry about Sovereign."

"Really?"

A slight smile crosses her lips. "Of course, I've worked with him since the beginning. When Sovereign Mountain was just a farmhouse and a stable."

"What...was he like then?"

"He was the same," she says, her tone soft. "He's always been stubborn. His head is as hard as a brick. And getting on his bad side was always ill advised. But he'd die for the people in his circle."

I swallow, brushing back my hair. "Was he always so...grim?"

Her eyes mist over. "No, but he's always been the type to look life straight in the eyes and get on with it. Nothing stops him, or scares him. He doesn't want much, but when he does...well, that's how you got here."

My neck is warm. I gather my hair, twisting it into a knot.

"I know it's not my business, but did he bring other women here?"

Her brow crooks. "No. He hasn't shared a room with anyone as long as I've known him. Now, I don't think he was celibate, but he never had anyone the way he has you."

Relief moves over me. I hate the thought of him with anyone else.

Hard head or not, he's mine.

I realize Maddie is looking at me and there's a faraway expression on her face. She notices me staring and she jerks her head, wiping her hands on the kitchen towel.

"You're good for him," she says. "I know I'm only fifteen years older than him, but he feels like a son. And I hope you choose him because he's one of the good ones."

"He's done a lot of bad things," I whisper.

She nods. "That's true. But what's that they say about casting the first stone? He who is without sin, and all that."

It hits me right then that I could cast a stone at him. I look down at my hands, twisted together. They're clean.

But they're untested.

I've spent my life being washed on the tides. Bouncing from one caretaker to the next, bending to their will. I had the luxury of keeping my head down, but Gerard didn't.

His hands are bloody so mine can be clean.

And that's enough for me to choose him.

And I do—I do choose Sovereign. Despite everything he's done, despite his cold mind, his scarred heart, and his calloused hands. I have a soft enough heart and plenty of tears for us both.

Which means, if he's not back in the morning, I'm going after him.

CHAPTER FORTY-TWO

GERARD

It's fuck-all cold at the top of the hill overlooking Thomas Garrison's house. We stand in a silent row, like grim reapers on our horses. At the bottom of the hill, with the road in the far background, sits the final third of the farmland that's been a specter at the corner of my mind for so long.

Tonight I'm laying that ghost to rest.

There's a light on in the kitchen. I glance at Westin because I know he's staring at it, painfully aware Diane is inside.

"She'll be free after tonight," I say quietly.

He snorts. "Like she'd fuck me after I kill her husband."

He realizes what he says as it comes from his mouth and Jack laughs. It's funny, but my chest tightens at the memory of Keira's tearstained face in the guest bedroom. She was so broken, and I hate that in order to extract her from her situation, I had to hurt her even more. I hope when the Garrisons are in the ground, the dust will settle and we can focus on healing.

I want to lick her wounds for her, to kiss her forehead, tell her she never has to hurt again.

I wonder if she feels the same.

Does love mean the same for her as it does for me?

Part of me doesn't care. So what if I love her most? I've always been cold until I find something that forces me to feel. And then I'm on fire, so intense I feel it course like blood through my veins.

When I saw the bare plot of land that would be Sovereign Mountain, I felt the future. I'll stand on this plot of earth until I die and am buried in it.

When I saw Keira, I knew she was the woman I'd sleep beside forever.

I don't know how to live in shades of gray.

"What's the plan?" Westin says.

"I'm going in after Thomas with Jack. I want you to go after Diane and make sure she doesn't get caught in the crossfire. We're here for the Garrison men only."

"And do what with her?" Westin frowns, barely visible in the dark.

"Whatever you want," I say. "I don't care where she goes, but she can't stay here."

The clouds part for a brief moment. The heavy wind blows them across the sky quickly, each one thicker and darker than the next. Through the opening, the moon is a pale silver disk.

It's the same moon that bore witness to what the Garrisons did to my parents. I look up and all at once I'm back there.

In that fucking room.

***

I'm laying on my back staring at the nearly full moon through the window. The cold air creeps in through the cracks of our employee housing. I'm a child, wrapped in the frayed quilt my grandmother gave me before we left Boston.

My mother is crying in the kitchen. Heavy, wet sobs like she'll never stop. My father's voice is a deep rumble. I hear his chair scrape back and her footsteps patter. I know he's holding her, probably stroking her hair. He always does that when she's upset.

Earlier in the day, I came back from school to find the house empty. The kitchen chair was overturned. There was something red on the floor, like dark red paint was dripped across the dusty boards.

I followed the drips to the back of the house and found my mother sitting by the laundry sink.

Ice cold fear gripped me. Her eyes were puffy and her nose dripped blood down her chin. My father knelt at her feet with a wet rag in his fist. Dabbing at her mouth and nose, trying to stem the flow.

"Dad," I whispered.

I didn't know what to ask. Is she alright? Who did this? Surely my father didn't do that. He's never even said an unkind word to my mother in my entire life.

My mother made a muffled sound and covered her mouth with her hand. Her eyes were so sad, so swollen with tears.

"Baby, go to your room," she said, putting on that fake happy tone that means she's trying to protect me.

I swallow hard because my throat is bunched up. My father nodded, jerking his head towards the doorway. I fled to my room and here I am, wrapped up in a quilt. Still in my school clothes and shoes. My lids are heavy despite my pounding heart.

I lie there with a sickening sense of dread in my small chest. Listening to them talk and cry until finally the moon winks out and I fall asleep.

For almost a year, I don't know what happened. I'm sure my father hit her, but I'm confused why she still kisses him and lets him hold her against his chest. And I don't know why we have to move into a cheap motel and my father has to go to work before dawn and return drenched in mud from the oil fields.

On my ninth birthday, I decide I'm a man now and I confront my father about it one night on the back porch.

How could he have hurt mom? Why is she so scared now? Why did she go from being soft and pleasant to rail thin and haunted?

He starts crying and I sit there, heart in my mouth, and wait for him to stop.

He tells me that Abel Garrison tried to rape my mother. He held her down and beat her face when she resisted. If my father hadn't walked in the door with a shotgun, he'd have gotten away with it.

He chased him down the road, shooting at him once and missing.

My father doesn't cry. He doesn't believe in it, but for my mother, he makes an exception.

The cold northern mountains make for hard men. My father only showed softness to my mother. He hit me at the end, after her death destroyed him. But I never hated him for it because I remembered, when things got dark, that he wept for her that day.

My first introduction to the concept of sex is through an explanation of rape. I'm innocent so he gives me The Talk with tears streaming down his face before he explains the rest. It's not lost on me that this isn't the way these things should happen.

He keeps his gaze on the ground.

Worn hands tangled together, eyes fixed on his boots.

He tells me why we had to leave Garrison Ranch. That while I was at school, the Garrisons evicted my parents at gunpoint. Driving them out with nothing but a few belongings in the back of their truck.

I'll never fucking forget that.

Not if I live a thousand years.

***

The wind picks up, cutting across my face, snapping me back to the present.

The memory of what happened all those years ago feels dim tonight. Learning that Avery and Thomas planned on killing my woman lights a different kind of fire in me. One that burns under my ribs, right where I hope I have a heart left.

At the very least, I can still protect my redbird before it's too late.

The waiting is over.

I shift my weight and Shadow begins moving down the hill. Jack and Westin fall into step behind me. We've never hunted together like this, but we all know what to do.

We'll work quickly, we'll get in and get out. We'll do the Lord's work and do it well.

CHAPTER FORTY-THREE

GERARD

Jack wants to be diplomatic. Westin is just here for a good time so he doesn't care how we do this. I open the door and walk right in.

No one locks their doors this far out.

Diane Garrison is in the hall in a slip and a terrycloth robe. She stumbles back, her mouth moving as she tries to scream. Westin skirts around me and snatches her around the waist. His hand goes over her mouth and he hauls her back against his body.

Her eyes widen, terror making her pupils blow.

"Hush, darling," he says. "We're not here for you."

Her hips buck and her bare foot kicks back into his shin so hard he lets out a soft, "Fuck!" under his breath.

"Where is your husband?" I ask, keeping my voice low.

Her eyes dart down the hall before she can stop herself. I lean in and I can see the shape of two men on the back porch. The cherry tips of twin cigarettes burns in the dark.

"Take her to the kitchen," I say.

He picks her up, hand still clamped over her mouth, and carries her into the kitchen to our left.

My eyes meet Jack's and he nods. He has his revolver at the level of his eyes, his hat pulled low. His face is covered in a dark bandanna. I took off my hat and my face is bare.

I want them to see—to know it's me—when I kill them.

Jack follows at my heels as I make my way down the hall. If we were going after anyone but the Garrison brothers, I would have used Diane to pull them out. But Thomas doesn't care if I put a gun to his wife's head. I've already witnessed how they treat their women.

Silently, I pull the glass door open.

Then I train my gun on the back of Avery's head.

"Keep still," I say.

They both whirl and Jack's gun whips up and points at Thomas. It takes a moment for their eyes to adjust, but then the color drains from their faces.

"Guns out of your belts and on the ground," I order.

They hesitate and Jack cocks his revolver. The sound spurs Thomas into action. He's always been the weak Garrison. He takes the pistol from the small of his back and drops it to the porch, kicking it behind him. Avery holds out a moment longer, but then he flicks his cigarette and throws his gun away.

"Walk inside," I say.

Jack keeps the door wide open. I back down the hall, my gun glued to them. The door falls shut and Jack takes the rear, his gun a foot from Thomas's head. The youngest Garrison is shivering.

Avery is stone cold. But he was always the meanest son of a bitch out of all of them. Even more of a motherfucker than Clint. I'm surprised he wasn't picked as the brother to marry and torment Keira until it was time to kill her off.

My stomach knots. The rest of me is numb.

We enter the kitchen. Diane is tied to the chair at the head of the table. There must have been a struggle because she's gagged and the terrycloth robe is on the floor, leaving her in just her slip. Westin stands in the open kitchen door, having a cigarette. When he turns, I see a bright red scratch across his jaw.

"Sit," I say.

Diane's eyes are wet, tears spilling down her cheeks. She looks to Thomas for reassurance, but he doesn't meet her pleading gaze. He just kicks a chair out and sinks down. Avery pauses by the table, narrowing his steel gray eyes at me.

"If you're going to act your little revenge fantasy, go ahead," he snaps. "I'm not letting you play with us."

"Sit the fuck down," I tell him quietly.

He sits.

I jerk my head and Jack ties their hands behind their backs. This isn't a fair fight, but it's never been a fair fight between the Garrisons and I.

They weren't going to have mercy on my redbird.

They were going to kill her, perhaps slit her throat while she slept. The thought of blood on her perfect skin, of her blue eyes open and lifeless, turns my stomach.

I sit down opposite Avery and spread my knees, gun still pointed at him.

"I found your calling card," I say.

His brow raises. He's got an angular face with tall features. He'd be handsome if he wasn't such an evil cunt. It seeps out in his narrowed gaze, in the harsh line of his mouth.

"What card?" Thomas asks.

"Mine," Jack says.

He flicks his wrist and a card appears between his two fingers. Black with a silver terrier. It flashes as he flips it between his fingers and then it disappears into thin air. He gets a lot of women with that trick.

"Who did you pay Jack to kill?" I ask.

Avery's face tightens. He darts a cold stare at his brother and Thomas shrinks back. I stand and flip my chair, sinking down and resting my arm across the top. This way I'm focusing on Thomas and he's squirming.

"Don't look at your fucking brother," I say. "Look at my face. Who did you pay Jack to kill?"

He's chewing on his lip so hard it's bleeding. Red trickles down his chin.

"Ask him," Avery snaps, jerking his head up at Jack.

Jack shakes his head. "I have confidentiality agreements. I can't squeal the way you can, Garrison."

Avery swings his head back to me and his lips curls. "I always thought you were smart, Sovereign. But after you picked that stupid bitch as your woman, I realized you're not as smart as you want people to think."

My jaw twitches. I've called Keira a bitch before, but not like that. When I use that word, it means I love her enough to degrade her and she still feels safe in my arms. The way Avery uses that word gets my blood moving.

"Who said anything about my woman?" I ask.

Thomas swallows hard. He's having trouble staying quiet. I can see the sweat etching down his temple.

"How does it feel having our brother's fucking leftovers?" Avery snaps.

He just can't help himself.

"Pretty good," I say. "Especially because I was the one who put him six feet under."

Thomas's jaw drops and Avery jerks at his bindings. I guess they're a lot slower than I thought, because I'd assumed all this time they put two and two together. But apparently they didn't because Avery is twisting, pulling at his ropes.

"You cunt," he barks. "I'm going to fucking kill you."

I sit back. "Let him out, Jack. Let's make this a fair fight."

Jack sends me a look and I can tell he disapproves by how his mouth thins. But he doesn't have to make a choice because Thomas clears his throat and the room falls silent. He lifts his eyes up to mine and hatred simmers, somewhere beyond the fear.

"This is because Clint fucked Mariana, isn't it?" he says.

I tilt my head. He's not going to get to me.

"That was your fucking fault," Thomas says, his restraint breaking. "Maybe you should've satisfied her and she wouldn't have opened her legs in someone else's bed."

I stand and push in my chair slowly. Two pairs of steel gray eyes, burning with anger, follow me as I circle the table to where Diane is tied. She's almost naked and her cheeks run with tears and makeup.

She trembles as I kneel beside her, resting my gun on the table.

"Diane," I say, keeping my voice soft. "Have you ever fucked another man while married to Thomas?"

I reach up and pull the wet gag from her lips. She gasps, her chest heaving.

"Come on, Diane," I urge. "You can tell Thomas all the dirty things you did. He won't live long enough for it to matter."

Behind me, Westin is frozen to the ground. He doesn't know that I know he still fucks Diane. It's never been my business up until now.

Was it a betrayal of trust for him to be sleeping with my enemy's wife? Maybe, but not a malicious one. So I let him think it was a secret, occasionally making remarks as if I didn't know what he was doing.

She sobs once, trying to twist her head to look at Westin. I reach up and grip her chin and turn her back around to face her husband. Thomas is shaking, his jaw set. If he wasn't tied down, he'd have his hands around his wife's throat.

She lowers her eyes.

"No, you look at Thomas and you tell him that Westin fucks you so hard I can hear you scream all the way from the gatehouse," I say.

I hope my relationship with Westin recovers after tonight. I'm going to need to give him a substantial raise and an apology tomorrow morning.

I glance over my shoulder and Westin has his arms crossed, but to his credit, he's not breaking eye contact with the Garrison brothers. Jack stares straight ahead with his brows up by his hairline.

"Shut up," Thomas roars. "Just shut the fuck up."

I tilt my head. "I thought you were interested in the topic of infidelity."

He spits on the floor.

"Now, tell me who you paid Jack to kill," I say.

The room is quiet for a second and Diane gives a short sob.

"Just tell him," she whispers.

"Shut the fuck up, you bitch," Avery snarls.

I stand up and shoot him in the foot. The sound is deafening in such a small space. Diane loses her shit, screaming and twisting her ropes. Thomas starts writhing so hard his bonds strain and I can see them loosening. Avery jerks forward and goes white. His body locks up and his eyes glaze over.

I cross the room, kneeling. My gun goes to his temple.

"Who. Did. You. Pay. Jack. To. Kill?" I breathe.

He shudders, his chest heaving.

"Keira," he breathes. "We wanted Keira dead."

I just needed to hear him say it—now I can close this chapter. I squeeze the trigger and the bullet blows a hole in his temple. He jerks to the side and his head flops. Thick blood drips from the hole and his body twitches. Convulsing as the life drains from him.

Diane screams, the sound ripping through the night. Westin has his hands on her thighs, on his knees at her feet. He's trying to calm her down, but she's going into shock. I can see the glaze over her streaming eyes.

Thomas's chair hits the ground and I realize he's not in it.

A knife falls to the kitchen floorboards.

Boots clatter down the hall.

The back door slams.

"Fuck," I snap, rising.

That motherfucker had a knife in his hand. He was playing the role of the cowardly little brother and the entire time he was just biding his time before he could make a run for it.

Jack swears under his breath. "I'll go after him," he says.

"No." I put my hat on and holster my gun beneath my belt. "Westin, take Diane out of here and get her somewhere safe. Jack, you're with me."

CHAPTER FORTY-FOUR

KEIRA

I almost fall asleep at the kitchen table, but Maddie shakes me awake around midnight and helps me upstairs. I crawl into bed on Gerard's side and pull his blanket up to my nose. It smells like him, and I can feel the faint indent in the bed where he lies. Big Dog curls up by the fire and Small Dog sneaks into the bed with me. I don't scold him, I just pull him close. Grateful for his warmth.

It's almost six-thirty when I wake abruptly and rush to the window to see if I can spot anyone in the yard. Everything is frozen over and snow falls lightly, not yet covering the grass. The world feels strange, like we're all stuck in a snow globe waiting for someone to shake it.

I know he's not back. If he'd returned, he'd be in our bed with his arms around me.

Which means...I'm going after him.

The Garrisons took my pride, they took my farm.

But I'll be damned if they take my Sovereign.

I dress quickly in my warmest clothes, stealing his warm wool socks and gloves from the closet. He has an extra black cowboy hat in there that's adjustable. I snatch that up too.

My boots sit under the window and on the sill sits the painted mare. Light glinting from the curves of her body, the reins thrown over neck glittering like starlight. My throat feels tight as I snatch her up and push her deep in my pocket.

There's only one more thing to take. The pistol Gerard hides beneath the bed. He thinks I don't know it's there, but I saw the free end of the strap of the holster poking out, one night when he had me facedown, ass up in bed.

I kneel down and feel for it, unhooking the fastening and pulling it free. It's loaded, the safety is on. I push it into my belt and tug my flannel down over the top to hide it.

I'm at the door when Small Dog lifts his head from the blankets. Big Dog lays on her belly by the fireplace, eyes glittering. They're waiting for instruction.

"Wait here," I whisper. "I have to go find Sovereign, but I'll be back."

Big Dog whines, but she stays put.

Downstairs, everything is quiet. It's late for the crew that does the first round of chores. They're already out in the pastures. Maddie is probably cleaning up breakfast.

I put on my boots in the hallway and slip out. It always smells fresh like pine at Sovereign Mountain, in the morning before the scent of horses and cattle creep in to overtake it. The lake is placid, the edges glittering with thin ice.

The whole world feels like it's taken a breath and held it.

Maybe it has. This ranch loves Sovereign back.

In the barn, I check each stall for a horse, but they're all taken or out in the secondary barn and pasture. When I get to the end, I hear a rustle and a soft nicker. Angel pushes her head over the edge and nuzzles me with her velvet nose. My stomach flips as I press my head against her neck. I haven't taken her out of the paddock yet. Doing that today seems like a colossally bad idea.

And yet...I take the painted mare from my pocket.

She's beautiful and delicate like Angel. I flip her upside down and lift her to the light. The words my mother put there so long ago, when the horse belonged to her, are barely visible.

Angel Stowe.

If anyone can bring me to Sovereign, it's them.

I lead Angel out and brush her down. Inside, my heart hammers like a war drum, but I keep my breathing even so Angel doesn't catch onto my emotions. We can't be at odds today. We have to work together as seamlessly as Sovereign and Shadow. He doesn't even use his reins or the heels of his boots to control Shadow, he just shifts his weight or clicks his tongue.

She stands perfectly still as I saddle her up and lead her around the back of the barn. She's small enough I can put my foot in the stirrup and swing up without a mounting block. When my weight hits her, she shies and prances. I breathe and let my center of balance shift with her. Riding out her nerves until she falls quiet.

"Good girl," I whisper, patting her shoulder.

She tosses her head, throwing that mane of bright red. Now that I'm ready to leave, I realize I'm not sure where I'm going. The world around Sovereign Mountain is vast. I could ride for hours and get nowhere.

I set my jaw, the painted mare still balled into my fist.

The only place to start is Garrison Ranch.

I pull my scarf over my chin and push my hat down, cinching the strap. It's bitterly cold, but deep in my layers, I barely feel it.

It takes me a half hour of hard riding to get to Thomas Garrison's ranch. I see the spiral of smoke before I even see the house. Angel throws her head and starts prancing as we crest the hill. Something is making her nervous. It occurs to me that perhaps Thomas was the abuser Sovereign rescued Angel from. From the flashing whites in her eyes, it seems like she knows this place.

That makes me fucking angry. On top of everything, he probably beat my horse.

The house is halfway burnt and still smoking. A spiral of dark gray creeping into the white sky. The dusting of snow is thicker here and I see a mess of footprints in the yard. Man and horse. Tire tracks etch their way down the drive to the main road.

I guide Angel along the crest of the hill. The hoof prints of two horses make a trail up over the ridge and behind me. Heading north, towards the cabin on the other side of the ranch.

Frowning, I turn Angel.

My stomach starts tightening the further along we get. We're heading north from a different route than the one Sovereign took me before. It's taking me through a flat, open grove of Ponderosa pines.

There's something about not being able to see all around me that's unnerving. Anything could jump out of the woods, or down from the trees. I glance up and scan for cougars every few yards.

I've never been afraid of bears, wolves, or elk, but I've always had a fear of cougars after seeing the wounds of a man mauled by one when I was a child. They're better left to themselves in the remote mountain peaks.

Angel prances and I breathe in, hold, and breathe out.

I can't let her throw me and leave me out here.

When we break from the pines, I feel a weight sink from my shoulders.

We're in an open grove with the mountains rising to the left and the hill curving up to my right. I can barely make out the cabin in the distance, right at the top. There's something in the field to the far left. I freeze, squinting hard. It's a black shape and it's moving fast towards Angel and I.

My heart thumps. Angel shifts and throws her head.

Fuck, what is that?

I glance over my surroundings. I can try to disappear back into the pines and hope they cover me. That's my only option other than stand and wait. The shape is between me and the cabin, so I can't go there.

It's getting closer. I turn Angel around and squeeze my thighs, sending her bolting into the forest.

She wants to run, she loves it. I feel her muscles loosen and elongate. She's quick and she darts around trees, keeping to the

271

loose trail up ahead. I barely notice that we're not going back the way we came until suddenly we're screeching to a halt. Faced with a wide, shallow river etching through the trees.

Where am I?

I cock my head and my whole body tingles.

A twig cracks and Angel rears back. I grip the saddle horn as she comes down. My teeth clash and my vision flashes as her hooves hit the ground. She whirls despite me trying to keep her restrained. Her ears prick forward and we both hear it this time.

Hoofbeats. Pounding the earth.

I stare into the empty pines as the sound grows closer. There's nothing I can do now except face whoever pursues me. My pounding heart begins to slow and my breathing evens. Angels stops prancing and falls quiet, ears pricked and eyes round.

I inch my hand closer to the pistol at my hip. I'm a good shot, my father made sure of that. But I've never had to aim at a moving target and I know it's not the same thing.

Thomas Garrison bursts into view, astride a deep bay horse. He sees me and veers to the left without missing a beat and he's gone.

Water sprays from behind me, but before I can turn, Angel rears hard. I don't have time to grip the saddlehorn. My feet come free of the stirrups and I'm falling through space. My teeth clack together and my head hits the ground hard enough to make stars pop overhead. My limbs are a tangle on the forest floor.

From the corner of my vision, I see Angel disappear through the trees.

I don't blame her. She wasn't ready.

Before I have a chance to recover, I'm grabbed by the collar of my coat and yanked upwards into a warm wall. My legs automatically wrap around his waist and my head lolls back. Sovereign is holding me with one arm, trying to shift to sit behind him.

"Get behind me, redbird," he says, his jaw clenched.

I wriggle to get into position and lock my limbs around his body. Euphoria bursts through my brain as the scent of leather fills my nose. He's here, he's warm, he's real. He didn't die last night.

"Sovereign," I pant, sliding my arms around his waist.

"Hold on," he says. "I've got one more thing to do and then we'll go home."

CHAPTER FORTY-FIVE

GERARD

Her arms wrap around my body so hard I can barely breathe. When all this is over, I'm going to bring her back and let her recover. Then she's getting punished. Not for fun. She's going to feel her disobedience across her beautiful ass and thighs.

Avery Garrison is dead. Thomas is the only one left. He ran out the back door, leaving his wife sobbing as Westin dragged her out to the truck. Leaving his brother's dead body slumped over the kitchen table.

I dropped a match in the living room and went after him with Jack.

It's been hours and I finally tracked Thomas to the north cabin. He crossed the border into my land, which pisses me off even more, but fair is fair. I entered his ranch last night and killed his brother and let Westin take his wife. I'll let him fight on my ranch if that makes him feel better about dying.

He's only loosely familiar with this part of the ranch. He'll move through the pines and try to get back down the ridge to the house. Probably in search of the main road. I have to head him off before he gets to the ridge.

I shift my weight and Shadow moves seamlessly from a trot to a canter. His big body winds easily through the trees.

My muscles ache. I've been hunting Thomas since after midnight. I thought this would go faster, I had lower expectations for him. But he's angry and he's fighting back.

I shift my weight and Shadow picks up speed as we break from the woods. We leave from the northeast side where the mountain flattens out to reveal the river winding through the center of a grove of pines.

Up ahead, I catch sight of the hind end of Thomas's horse. Spraying water as he fords the river.

Shadow senses my mood shift and he lengthens his stride. Rocks and dirt kick up from his hooves as we ride down the bank. Icy water drenches my boots and I hear Keira yelp softly as it hits her legs.

Shadow is tiring. The disadvantage we both have is that we're big, and carrying a lot of muscle tires us easily. And he's carrying us both. Thomas is lighter and so is his horse. They can go for much longer than we can.

We burst from the other side of the river. For a second, I think we're alone.

Then a bullet whizzes by, striking the ground behind us. Shadow shies back, and Keira's arm clamps around my torso like iron. I pull my gun free and spin Shadow in a quick circle, scanning the area.

I can't fucking see where he's coming from.

The underbrush is too thick at the edge of the pines. I need to get to them or he's going to take us out easily. If it were just me, I would have called on him to come out and fight fair. But I have Keira and the soft press of her body reminds me I have something to live for now.

My heart slows. I feel the bitter wind on my face.

There's a rustle from deep within the pines and it hits me that he can't get a clear shot. My senses sharpen and I pivot Shadow hard and urge him up the bank to the opposite pine grove. We're almost there when a huge crash turns our attention to the other side of the river.

Thomas erupts from the woods on his horse. He darts through the river so quickly I only have time to spin Shadow to make a shield of my body so Keira is safe.

His revolver glints. I see the faint puff of smoke. The sound cracks like a whip and a flurry of birds surge from the trees and take to the sky.

My body jolts. There's no pain, just spreading warmth in the side of my head. Something sticky seeps down the side of my neck.

Smells like blood.

Shadow spirals hard, spooked by the sound. The world spins in a circle and the ground rises up to hit my body hard. Forcing all the breath from my lungs.

I'm on my back on the rocky ground.

Up above, I see her take the reins. She's wearing one of my black cowboy hats and her brilliant hair whips around her face. Fear grips me and I try to force myself up, but my body won't respond.

My head lolls to the side. Thomas is riding hard at her, revolver up.

Her hand moves faster than I can follow. She flips the holster at her thigh, raises a black pistol, and unloads it. Jaw set and eyes narrowed.

Bang.

Bang.

Bang.

Fuck me, I didn't know my redbird could shoot like that.

For a second, I think she missed. But then a riderless horse surges past me and skids to a halt by the edge of the pines. It stands there, eyes wide and ribs heaving. Foam flecking down its neck.

My body tingles as I force myself up onto my elbows. The side of my head feels raw, like it got skinned, but I can't feel any pain.

I'm bleeding, I can tell because my shirt collar is soaked and rapidly freezing to my neck.

Over the brush, I can make out a dark pile of limbs on the ground.

My body gives out and I sink back against the dirt.

It's done. It's over.

276

A weight lifts from my chest for the first time since I was a child. They're gone, all of them. Keira is safe and my heart is free to love her without this dark weight on it.

No one ever has to put up with their abuse again.

No Garrison will ever rape, murder, or prey on anyone ever again.

The sky is gray overhead. Thick clouds crowd each other and snow begins to fall harder. The flakes are thick and they melt on my skin.

My revenge cost me everything. I'll never be the man I could have been.

The sky fills with the most beautiful woman I've ever seen. I must be high from blood loss because it takes me a moment to realize who she is. A pale freckled face, frightened eyes, and a river of crimson hair. It falls over my face and kisses my mouth.

No, it didn't cost me everything.

I can live without a heart or soul because I have her, and she's got enough for us both.

Her cold fingers brush my hair back and turn my head to the side. Her lips press together grimly and she takes off her hat and unwinds her scarf. She rips it in half and begins wrapping the thinner end around my head. Pain twinges as she ties it, pulling it tight.

"I got shot," I whisper.

Her eyes are full of tears. They're dripping from her lashes and the tip of her nose. One falls onto my lips and I taste salt.

"Don't die," she whispers.

I feel the corner of my mouth turn up. "I won't leave you, redbird. It's just a scratch."

She swallows hard. "You're going to pass out from blood loss in a minute. You have to stand up and get on Shadow *now*."

The urgency in her voice wakes something in me. I know what she's afraid of. If I pass out, she won't be able to lift me. I'll freeze to death while she's riding back to the house to get help.

My lids flicker.

I see her hand flash and pain explodes across my jaw. Suddenly I'm sitting upright with my eyes wide open. Blood seeps over my tongue and my heart hammers as adrenaline surges back through my veins.

"Fuck...you hit me," I spit.

"Don't pretend you don't like it," she whispers. "Now get on Shadow. We're going to the cabin."

CHAPTER FORTY-SIX

KEIRA

I killed Thomas Garrison and I'm not sorry.

That's the part that shocks me. I've always been sensitive and shooting a man three times should make me crumble.

But I didn't.

He had it coming.

Yes, I'm terrified. My hand shook so badly I had to shove the gun back into the holster to keep from dropping it.

All I know is he would have shot Gerard, and I was not letting a Garrison take from me again.

Still, I want to vomit or faint, but I can't. We have to get back to the cabin. My heart pounds as I scramble up to sit in front of Gerard on Shadow. He managed to pull himself into the saddle after I hit him, but he's pale, and sweat beads on his neck. The entire side of his head is drenched in crimson.

I hope it's just a flesh wound. I remember once my father told me even minor head wounds bleed the most.

He pulls me back against his chest, his broad arm locking over me. I shift my weight the way I've seen him do and Shadow breaks into a smooth walk. He seems to understand he has to be careful. I dig my hands into his mane and narrow my eyes, trying to see through the thickening snow.

It's almost noon. The snow is falling faster.

I can smell the chill moving in.

It feels like it takes forever, but somehow we get to the cabin. I halt Shadow by the door and I'm about to slide off when I hear hoofbeats. Gerard doesn't turn to look. I glance over my shoulder and his head has fallen back and his eyes are shut. He's breathing, but he just keeps getting paler.

I spin around and reach for my gun, but it's Westin and Jack who appear about the other side of the cabin. Relief washes over me.

"He's shot," I manage.

My voice squeaks. I don't realize until now, but I'm shaking like a leaf in high wind. Jack and Westin both jump from their horses and run to Shadow's side. Just in time because Gerard sways and slides to the left and right into their arms.

"Fuck, he's heavy," Jack grunts.

Gerard mumbles something incoherent. I hate seeing him like this, he's only ever been strong and in control around me. My stomach twists as I hurry ahead and tap the code into the door, pushing it aside. Westin and Jack haul him inside and lift him onto the countertop. He's so tall the lower half of his legs hang off the edge.

"What do we do?" I ask.

Tears stream down my face. Jack waves his hand, clearing us back.

"I've done this shit before," he says. "Get me wet and dry cloths. We need to get the blood flow stopped. Westin, get me all the first aid equipment you can find."

I run up the stairs and wrench open the cabinet door in the bathroom. The ripped flannel from when I had my period is washed and folded beneath the sink. I gather an armful of it and run back downstairs. Jack has his head propped on a rolled blanket and he's using a wad of paper towels to apply pressure above his ear.

"Get some of those wet," he says.

Westin veers around the corner with a large first aid bag in his hand. Jack empties it on the counter, sorting through. His jaw is set

280

and he's totally focused. I wonder if he's been through something like this before.

"Fuck...here we go," he mumbles.

He pulls out a bundle of gauze, tape, and sticky bandages. I finish soaking the rags and he takes one and starts dabbing the flowing blood.

"Shouldn't you apply pressure?" Westin asks.

"I don't think it's that bad," Jack says, not looking up. "But I need to get a look at it."

We gather around. He gently wipes the blood back, revealing a long wound about a half inch tall and five inches long. There's no sign of his skull showing through. Jack releases a low whistle and folds a strip of gauze, applying it to the area.

My throat clenches.

"We just need to get the bleeding stopped. That could be a problem," Jack says. "Westin, check the time."

"It's twelve-thirty," he says.

"Okay, fifteen on, fifteen off," he mumbles.

He puts one hand on the other side of Gerard's head and keeps gentle pressure on the wound. I sink over the counter, reaching for Gerard's hand. It's limp, but still warm and familiar. I turn it over and stroke up his palm, tracing a faint scar that runs to his knuckle.

My Sovereign.

I shot a man for him. I saw Thomas raise his gun and I knew he would kill Gerard without hesitating. Something hard and detached filled my chest. Muscle memory took over and I barely remember my hand going up or flipping the safety off.

I remember the sound. Thunk. The look on Thomas's face as the bullet hit him in the shoulder. He jerked and swayed. I emptied the next two chunks of metal into his chest and upper thigh. His lips parted and blood covered his teeth.

I slid off Shadow and hit the ground. Something snapped under me.

My heart sinks. I reach in my pocket and pull out the painted mare. In my open palm sits two broken front legs.

I lose my shit.

Tears erupt and my chest heaves so hard I feel like I'm being crushed. My nails dig into Gerard's palm. He twitches and turns his head, eyes cracking.

"Keira," he murmurs.

Jack stares at me, frozen. He can deal with a head wound, but not a hysterically crying woman. Westin springs into action, circling the table and prying my grip from Gerard. He ushers me out of the kitchen and into the living room, pointing me towards the couch.

"I'm sorry, I'm fine," I gasp.

"What happened, Keira?" he says, forcing me down on the couch.

My hands are shaking so badly I can barely hold onto the painted mare. "I went after Gerard and found him…he was in the pine grove. Then we were at the river and Thomas shot him and he went down."

"So Thomas is still out there?" he says, his jaw set.

"No, no, I shot him," I whisper, that sick feeling returning. "I shot him and blood came out of his mouth and he fell on the ground. He's dead, up by the river."

His brows go up and a slow smile moves over his face.

"Look at you, Mrs. Garrison," he says.

"Miss Stowe," I manage, wiping my face hard. I unfurl my hand and hold out the pieces of the painted mare. "I fell after I shot him and smashed my horse."

Westin stares down at the broken wood and I can tell this is above his paygrade. My fingers close around the piece and I hold them to my chest.

I'm not crying over the horse.

Everything changes, but this little piece of wood has been constant. It's my earliest memory. I held it when my father told me how my mother passed. It lay beside me the first night I slept at the Garrison house after my father was gone. I've been alone with nothing but wood and paint to keep me company for as long as I can remember.

And that's just so fucking sad I can't go back to it.

"Is he going to make it?" I whisper.

Jack looks up. His hands are bloody.

"He'll be fine," he says. "He's not in danger, the bleeding has slowed. The wound was surface level, but it was enough to put him into shock."

A wave of relief passes over me and the urge to vomit wanes. I'm cried out, and there's nothing left to do but be strong. Westin gets up and holds out his hand and I take it, letting him help me up. I go to Gerard and slip my hand into his, watching Jack apply a bandage to his head.

"He's fine," he says. "He just had a sudden loss of blood."

I nod, wiping my nose.

Westin blows out a sharp breath and goes to the door. He kicks it open and lights a cigarette. "He'd better live so I can kick his ass. Motherfucker didn't have to call me out like that."

Jack glances up. "He didn't say anything that wasn't true. You were fucking Thomas Garrison's wife."

Westin jerks his chin, blowing smoke from his nose. "Fair, but he was an asshole about it."

My tired brain can't comprehend what they're talking about. Nothing but the man sleeping on the table is important anymore. I lay my head on his shoulder and watch his chest rise and fall. He's going to live.

And the scales are balanced.

CHAPTER FORTY-SEVEN

GERARD

My head aches, my body is stiff. My lashes feel stuck closed and when I turn, natural light burns my lids. It takes me a moment to remember what happened and I roll onto my side, abruptly sending a shot of pain through my head that makes sickness roll through my body.

I open my eyes.

The outline of her face is blurry. I blink rapidly and she comes into focus. Beautiful face at rest, eyes shut. Pale lashes rested against her freckled cheeks. Relief floods me that she's safe, here in my bed where she belongs.

I push myself up on my elbows, using my fingertips to inch back against the headboard until I'm sitting upright. I'm in the loft in the cabin, which means Westin and Jack must be around because she couldn't have carried me up the stairs.

It's the middle of the day, I can see the pale sun glittering over the hills. I can't have been in the cabin long because the storm still hasn't fully hit. Thick, pale clouds gather on the edge of the sky, just above mountains touched with falling snow.

I can hear someone walking in the kitchen. Working carefully so I don't wake her, I slide from the bed. My head spins, but I manage to make my way across the loft and climb down the stairs. I'm shirtless and there's still dried blood on my chest, but someone put sweatpants and socks on my lower body.

Westin stands in the kitchen, holding a cup of coffee. Our eyes meet and it hits me right then what we did last night and today. For almost two decades, we've worked and lived together under the shadow of vengeance. And now it's suddenly gone.

We're free.

I wonder what he'll do with that freedom. I know what I'll do with mine.

"It's good you're up," he says, jaw working. "Storm is holding off, but we need to get back."

"Where are the horses?" I ask, leaning on the counter.

"In the barn."

"And Jack?"

He shrugs, leaning back to squint through the window at the mountains below. "He's gone. I expect he'll be back to collect what you owe him and take his calling cards. But he doesn't stick around."

"Jack's always been whatever the opposite of a fair weather friend is," I say. "When the storm's over, he's gone."

We sit in silence for a long moment.

"Where's Diane?" I ask.

His mouth thins. "I left her with Maddie. She was understandably upset."

"She was never in love with Thomas, that marriage was bullshit," I say, clearing my throat. "But I'm sorry for airing your shit."

I don't apologize unless I mean it and he knows that. He takes a second, I see his jaw work again like he's trying to wring out his annoyance. Then he takes a sip of coffee and shakes his head.

"It's all water under the bridge," he says gruffly. "But I want a raise."

"You'll get one," I say. "Are you staying?"

He frowns. "Staying? On the ranch? Where would I go?"

"I didn't know if you wanted to try things with Diane. Maybe move out of the gatehouse and get a real place."

He shakes his head, emptying his mug and setting it in the sink. "No, we're a long way from reconciliation."

"I think you can get there," I say.

He nods once, and I'm not sure if he believes me, but I do. Keira and I have been through just as much and now I know she loves me enough to kill for me. Westin puts his coat on and pauses in the doorway.

"I'm getting the horses ready to go. You should wake Keira."

He leaves and I climb the stairs slowly to find her up. She's still in her jeans and sweatshirt and she's braiding her red waves over her shoulder. She hears my steps and turns, relief evident on her face.

"How do you feel?" she asks, padding over in her socks.

"Like I got shot in the head," I say.

I pull her in and kiss her and she melds to me. Her fingers dig into my bare chest for a second before they slide around my torso and clench behind my back. I brush the stray bits of hair from her face, cradling it.

"You were so brave," I tell her. "Are you alright? You shouldn't have had to kill him."

"I wasn't going to let him take you from me," she says firmly. "I feel sick...when I think about killing him, but...I don't regret it. Does that mean I'm a bad person?"

"No, redbird. You defended us both."

Her lips quivers and I press my forehead to hers.

"Your father taught you to shoot like that," I say.

She nods, pulling back, eyes glittering. "I felt him there, telling me how to aim and when to shoot."

"You're never alone, redbird."

Her chin quivers and I kiss her mouth again to keep her tears at bay. When I pull back, she's smiling. It's a weak, brave smile and I know it's taking everything she has not to shatter. I kiss her forehead and go to put on my coat and shirt. She pulls on her boots and holds out her hand.

I take it.

"It's done, Sovereign," she whispers. "Let's go home."

CHAPTER FORTY-EIGHT

KEIRA

Westin, Gerard, and I managed to get back to the house upstairs. Westin went to the gatehouse, saying something about trying to fix all this bullshit. I helped Gerard upstairs and he took some painkillers and fell asleep.

He's in our bed.

Our bed.

That sounds like forever.

I'm sitting next to him, watching him sleep. The bull skull on his chest rises and falls. The sickness I felt at shooting Thomas is lessening.

Gerard is right. I defended us both.

The Garrisons are gone. After everything they did to us, it's over just like that. It feels like the tie that binds us together. We killed for each other and that feels more permanent than saying vows.

He never hesitated when it came to protecting me. I'm glad I didn't either.

I want to love him the way he loves me.

Without hesitation. Without fear.

That Evening.

I talked to Westin at dinner and he told me that Gerard demolished my house so I had to live with him. I'm back to watching him sleep, but right now I want to slap him across the face. Too bad it'll just turn him on.

God, he's such a dick. And I still love him so fucking much.

CHAPTER FORTY-NINE

GERARD

I don't want to lose my stride so I force myself to stick to my usual schedule. The wound on my head scabs over quickly. The pain resides. The only thing leftover a few days later is a lingering fatigue.

Then that's gone after a long afternoon nap. She wakes me three days after that morning on the mountain by shaking my leg. Her face fills my vision, like an angel. I clear my throat and sit up slowly. Now that I'm not bleeding, my clarity has returned.

I reach out and put my hand on her thigh.

She scowls.

"You demolished my house," she whispers wrathfully.

She's in just a slip. It's black silk and the top fights to keep her tits under control. Her brow arcs, but all I can see is how fucking pretty she looks sitting cross-legged in my bed. Slip hitched to the top of her thighs, and the outline of her nipples apparent.

"Come here," I say.

She shakes her head. "My house. You tore it down."

I shrug. "What do you need a house for, redbird? You live with me."

A dark cloud moves over her face and she scrambles down from the bed and stalks to the bathroom. The door slams so hard the bedside table wobbles.

I wait, listening. The lock doesn't click.

She wants me to come after her.

Slowly, I rise and I'm surprised to discover the world doesn't spin anymore. I pull on a pair of sweats and follow her, pushing open the door. She's standing in the shower with her back to me and her heart-shaped ass on display. I lean in before she can turn around and crack my palm across it.

She jumps, spinning.

"How could you demolish my house without asking me?" she snaps.

I strip and step into the shower with her, taking care not to get the bandage above my ear wet. She backs against the wall and her fists ball. I know she's trying to get me to take her seriously, but all I can think about it how much I fucking love this woman.

"You're an asshole," she grumbles.

"Hmm," I muse. "Tell me that again."

"Asshole," she hisses.

My hand shoots out and pins her by the neck to the shower wall. Her eyes widen and her freckled breasts heave. The pink of her nipples darkens as they tighten. She's on her toes, trying to keep her airway open as her claws dig into my forearm.

"You are still wearing my collar," I remind her.

I ease my grip enough she can speak. She's struggling with what to say, biting at her bottom lip until it's red. I bend and kiss it gently. Then harder, giving her a taste of my tongue.

Her body sags as I kiss her thoroughly, inhaling her breath, soaking in her taste. When I pull back, her mouth glistens and I lick it clean.

Her eyes are hazy. She fucking loves being kissed.

I slide my hand down over her stomach and delve between her thighs. Our eyes lock through the steam.

"If you talk back to me like that again, I'll wash your fucking mouth out with soap," I say quietly. "You're still my submissive. That's my collar locked on your neck. What happened on the mountain changes nothing."

"Get off me," she whispers.

I lean in and kiss her again, pushing my middle finger deep into her warm, wet cunt. It clenches and her lashes flutter shut as I pull back. Her tongue darts out to lick her lips and I catch it with my tongue. Biting her just hard enough to sting.

She moans, hips riding my hand.

"You ass—"

"Think carefully before you keep talking."

She glares at me even as she whimpers. I'm knuckle-deep in her beautiful pussy. My cock is so hard it aches and I can tell I'm leaking precum. It feels like it's been years since I was inside her. I'm not going to be able to hold back to argue the attitude out of her.

"You got that safeword, sweetheart?" I breathe.

She nods, a flicker of fear moving through her wide eyes. I turn the shower off and pull her by the wrist to the sink. We're both soaked and breathing hard. Her ass keeps brushing against my thighs and my cock rides up on her lower back.

"Bend over," I order.

She drops down. I take my belt from the chair in the corner and she turns, her lips parting.

"Keep your eyes on the mirror," I say, gripping her hair and turning her head back around. "I don't give a fuck what you want. You keep those pretty eyes open and watch."

Her hips buck against mine as she realizes what I'm about to do. She shakes her head frantically, but I tighten my grip to keep her still. Her body tenses, and I know she's getting ready to fight me again. Just like she did on the kitchen floor.

But she doesn't safeword me.

That's all the permission I need. One hand on her nape, I gather her wrists and bind them to the faucet. Drawing the leather tight and fastening it. It cuts into her freckled skin and locks her wrists into place.

She's not fucking going anywhere.

I step back and cock my head, ignoring the faint ache down my neck. Now that I'm feeling better, the deep, unquenchable need I have for her roars back to life.

I need to mark her body, to lash my signature across the back of her thighs, to leave my bite marks on her soft, round ass.

But she needs to be prepped if I'm going to punish her first.

I go to the cabinet and pull a black case down from the top shelf. It still has the plastic wrap on it and she hears me peel it free and cranes her neck to look over her shoulder. Her eyes fall on the slender white syringe and they widen.

"Fuck, no," she breathes.

I return to the sink. My palm strokes from beneath her arm to her hip. She's breathing hard enough to make her breasts shake.

Fuck, she's got good curves. Her body is thick, full, and so soft all I want to do is mark every inch.

I don't know what the fuck Clint Garrison was thinking sleeping with other women when his wife had an ass like this.

Satisfaction wells in my chest. She's mine now, my redbird. My pretty, perfect whore. I strike her hard across her right ass cheek and she yelps and bites her lip.

"Do you like humiliation?" I ask softly.

Her mouth trembles. Her eyes are wet.

"Use your words," I order.

Our eyes lock in the reflection. Her cheeks burn pink.

"Yes, sir," she whispers.

My palm runs over the hot mark where I just slapped her. My fingers trail down to her inner thigh and...there it is. A wet line of arousal dripping from her pussy. I scoop it up with my pointer finger and lean over her body.

"Open those pretty lips," I say into her ear.

She hesitates. My other hand comes down on her ass and her pupils blow. I grip her hair and draw her head back and she moans aloud. Her hips start working and her eyes roll back.

"Watch," I order.

She obeys even though she's burning with shame. Slowly, so she has to see every second of it, I put my wet finger to her lips.

"Lick it off, sweetheart."

Her tongue flashes pink and I feel it curl wet and hot around my finger. My cock throbs against her ass and I can't keep myself from riding her. Feeling the soft curve of her ass push back where I'm most sensitive.

I push my finger deep in her mouth. Tears spring to her eyes and she gags, but I don't relent. She's taken my whole cock before, I know she can do it. I pull my finger out and wipe her tears and make her eat those too.

"Stay still," I tell her, unfastening the belt and releasing her. "Palms flat on the counter."

She obeys, but she watches my every move as I prep the syringe. I've done this before, but it feels special this time. Maybe because she's so obviously dying of shame and I get off on her humiliation the same way she does.

Her fingers curl as my touch grazes her skin.

"Hands flat," I warn. "Unless you want me to spank your palms."

Her hands go flat right away. Satisfied, I gently spread her ass. Her pussy is soaked and swollen, so inviting I have to sink down and lick it clean. She tastes sweet and I want more so I push my tongue inside her.

She moans, biting her lip.

I kiss up the entrance of her pussy. Her hips tense, but I keep going. I know she wants it, despite how nervous she is because when I spread her wider and my breath hits her skin, she starts panting. She writhes as my tongue runs over her asshole. Her spine ripples and I hear the sweetest moan escape her lips. Fuck, she's trembling.

I lick her asshole slowly, circling around and around with my tongue. Until she's sagging over the sink. All her muscles relaxed and her eyes rolled back in her head.

I stand and slip the syringe into her and release it slowly. Her head jerks up and her lips part.

"Oh," she whispers.

Our gazes lock in the mirror. I pull the syringe free and toss it. Her lashes flutter and I know she feels the warm water inside. It's turning her on and I need to feel that too. I slide my fingers into her mouth to wet them, leaving a trail of saliva on her chin, and push them into her cunt.

It's tighter, if that's even possible.

"Gerard," she gasps. "Please."

I run my hand up her spine and grip her hair, dragging her head back. "You came after me when I told you to stay put," I say.

Confusion flickers over her face.

"I saved you," she whispers.

"I wouldn't have needed saving if I hadn't run into you in the pine grove. I had him in my sights. You put yourself in danger, redbird. You haven't apologized for it."

She swallows hard. "I'm sorry."

I shake my head and pick up my belt. Her thighs tremble and her hands shake as she tries to keep them flat. I don't draw this part out because it's not for pleasure. I just keep her still with my hand in her hair and bring my folded belt down across her ass.

I told her she was going to regret not trusting me.

The belt cracks.

She screams, a sob surging from her lips.

But she doesn't safeword me, even though I know she's in agony.

My cock aches, and I bring the belt down on her upper thighs. Hard enough to leave a pink and red mark on her freckled skin. Sobs spill from her throat as I lash her once, twice, three more times. Until I see creamy arousal on her inner thighs.

I drop the belt and pull her into my arms. She's warm, trembling. She cries quietly for a moment, rubbing her face into my chest. I wipe her tears with my thumb and kiss her forehead.

"You need to use the toilet," I say gently. "I'll leave you alone. But come out as soon as you're done."

She hiccups, wiping her face with her palm. Her eyes are glassy and her shoulders sag. When I run my palm down her spine I can tell her muscles have relaxed. It makes me realize how tense she is most of the time.

She's still stuck in fight or flight.

My mouth brushes her hair. "Is this what you want? For me to brutalize you, redbird?"

She gasps, pushing her face into my chest. "Yes."

"Beg for it then."

I turn her face up and she's deep in a submissive state. Her eyes are dreamy and swollen. She's breathing in little pants.

"Please," she whispers. "Please, Sovereign. Hurt me."

I stroke through her soft waves. She's so beautiful, so good. Too good for me, but I've always known that and it never mattered. If I'd listened to that voice in my head that said she was too sweet for a man like me, I wouldn't be here right now, holding her tight.

"I'll hurt you, but only if I can put you back together," I say.

CHAPTER FIFTY

KEIRA

My face burns as I shower and my hands shake as I scrub my skin until it's silky smooth. Of course, he's not embarrassed. Nothing seems to embarrass him. He got down on my knees behind me and licked the most intimate part of my body and he was rock hard.

Not even Clint touched me there. I'd always counted myself lucky he didn't want anal.

Maybe that's why I'm so nervous for this. When it comes to that part of my body, I'm a total virgin. I've never had a man touch me there until tonight.

I slam the shower door and scrub myself dry. I'm still wearing his discreet collar, but when I look down at the sink, I realize he left the leather one there for me.

My heart picks up. I wipe the steam from the mirror and fasten it around my neck. The little tag swings, glinting.

Sovereign.

There's no fighting that I'm his anymore. He never asked, never bothered to give me a choice. He just walked into my life and took what he wanted.

No apologies. No regrets.

I wish I could be truly mad at him for what he did. But for the first time since I was a child, I feel peace. I felt it the first time I set foot on Sovereign Mountain. And I didn't realize it then, but I felt it the first time his mouth touched mine.

I come out of the bedroom in nothing but the collar. The lights are out, and the fireplace sheds an orange glow over the room. He dragged a chair to the middle of the hearth, right below the bull skull. And he's sitting in it, shirtless, his knees spread. I can make out the hard length of his cock beneath his black sweatpants.

He lifts his head. His eyes glint.

"Come here, redbird," he says.

I feel small with him sitting there like that. My bare feet pad across the floor until I'm standing between his knees. He leans in and his touch burns as it drags down my waist to my hips.

He's got something wrapped around his fist. A silver chain.

"What is that, sir?" I whisper.

He doesn't answer, but I didn't expect him to. He's gotten so used to concealing himself that he'll always talk in riddles. He can talk around a question like an elite lawyer. Or just ignore it altogether.

"I want your full submission, redbird," he says. "No speaking unless I ask you a question or you need to use your safeword. Tell me you understand."

I nod, licking my dry lips. "I understand. Sir."

His hand circles to my lower back and he grips my left ass cheek. Squeezing it hard enough to hurt. Pleasure bolts down and tingles warm in my hips and thighs.

"You have the prettiest ass," he says, softly. Like he's just thinking aloud. "Turn around."

My heart flutters, but I obey. His fingertips brush over my ass, exploring the curves. He bends, and I feel his hot breath wash over me as he presses kisses to my bare skin. His tongue flicks here and there. My fist clench and I bite my tongue to keep from moaning.

He turns me back around. Then he leans in and unwinds the silver chain from his hand. It's got three long strands with a little clip that looks like a hairpin at each end. He cups my right breast, and before

297

I know it, he's sliding one of the clips over my nipple and pulling it tight.

It aches, and pleasure starts in my clit.

My eyes widen. I want to moan, but I promised to be good.

He moves to my left nipple, flicking it first to get it fully hard. I jolt and squeeze my thighs together.

He glances at me, amusement in his eyes.

He loves torturing me.

When he fits the other clip onto my left nipple, I have to bite my lip to stay silent. Then he lifts me onto his lap and spreads my legs. I keep perfectly still even though I can feel his cock against my thigh. Hard, blood pulsing. My core clenches, begging to feel him inside me.

He licks his fingers and reaches between my thighs. I just finished my period and I shaved this morning. My hormones are at an all-time high, and my pussy is silky smooth. I've never felt so sexy, so desirable in my life.

He pinches my clit. My hips jolt.

"Fuck, your cunt is so perfect, sweetheart," he murmurs. His middle finger teases my entrance. "Soft, tight, wet. I'm going to fucking ruin it tonight."

Cold metal slides over my clit. My thighs tense. He adjusts it tighter and leans back to admire his work. There's a delicate silver chain connecting the clips on my nipples to the one on my clit. In the center is a little silver bell. He taps it with his fingertip.

"Are you going to be my pet?" he asks.

I nod, mouth dry.

"Use your words when I ask you a question," he reminds me. "Are you going to be my dirty, little pet and let me ruin your cunt tonight?"

"Yes, sir." My breath hitches. "You've already ruined me, sir."

His jaw tightens and he leans in. "Not the way you've ruined me for any other woman. I'll give you everything, redbird. You deserve to have the world at your feet."

I didn't expect him to get vulnerable, but it doesn't last long. He bends in and flicks the bell with his tongue Then he takes it in his teeth and tugs it viciously, sending little shocks of pain and pleasure through me. I moan, my hips riding his lap.

He slaps my ass. "Don't forget, this is punishment too. Now, are you going to be a dirty whore for me?"

"Yes, sir." The words are a gasp.

He stands and pulls the chair aside, revealing a padded kneeler before the fire. He points and I circle him and sink down. The fire is warm on my back, which is a relief because the night is cold. Wind and snow lash at the window.

He stands over me, running his hand through my hair. Gripping it to pull my head back. My eyes drift up his broad, muscled body. Up over the hard cock in his pants. The trail of hair going up to his naval, the ridges of his stomach. His pecs covered in ink and hair, his broad, scarred shoulders.

To his face.

My chest warms. I've grown used to the stern expression in his eyes.

"Stay there," he says.

I nod and watch him go to the bedside table. I didn't notice until now, but there's a number of implements laid out. I can't see what he's doing, but when he returns, I can tell he's got a plug in one hand. My cuffs hang from the other.

My thighs tighten.

"Put your hands behind your back," he orders.

I obey and he kneels down. I feel the cuffs slip around my wrists. He applies pressure to my upper back until I understand he wants me to lean over. He guides my chest over his knee and gathers my hair at the nape of my neck.

"Try to relax your body, redbird," he says.

I'm trying, but it's hard when I have so much tension between my legs. He slips his fingers over my pussy, dipping the tip of his middle finger inside me for a brief second. Then he drags it up to my poor clit, pinched in the clip.

My eyes roll back. Arousal shoots through me like electricity.

I bite my lip hard, but I can't keep from whimpering aloud.

He doesn't correct me. He just keeps stroking the strangled tip of my clit, teasing it in circles. An orgasm starts and he doesn't stop it. He lets it wash over me until it's throbbing hard and I'm moaning through my teeth.

"Good fucking girl," he praises. "That'll loosen that pretty asshole."

Cold lube splashes down my hip and I know he's putting it on his fingers. His touch slides over my ass and finds my most sensitive point. He rubs in a circle before slipping his middle finger in. All the way to the middle knuckle.

Pain sears. My breath hitches.

Fuck, he's got big fingers.

He starts moving it, just a half inch in and out. The pain ebbs and pleasure replaces it. My face burns, my nipples and clit ache. But nothing is more acute than the perfect humiliation of being bent over, tied up, and at his mercy.

"That's my girl," he growls quietly, the sound vibrating in his chest. "Now let's get the plug in and you can come again. How does that sound?"

I just nod, my head blank.

His finger slips out and I feel cool metal at my entrance. It works slowly, but I can't keep my muscles from clenching.

"Bear down, baby," he murmurs, stroking my back. "You can do it for me. You're such a good girl, you've done so well already."

I want to please him so badly. Eyes shut, I bear down and pain bolts through my hips as the plug settles inside me. To my surprise, it feels amazing. Like it's touching all the right places at once.

He shifts me back so I'm on my knees and leaves me sitting there. I watch his broad body disappear into the bathroom, I hear him wash his hands. Then when he returns he has something in his hand that I don't recognize.

He crouches in front of me.

"Open your mouth," he says.

I hesitate. His eyes narrow.

"It won't hurt you," he says, holding it up.

I inspect it. It's a rectangular tab of leather with a metal ring as a handle. There's a little silver tag hanging off it. He flips it and I can make out the word etched in it.

Painslut.

Oh God, that makes me shudder.

The corner of his mouth jerks up. "You like that, redbird?"

I nod hard.

"Then open that pretty mouth," he orders.

I part my lips and he slides the leather into my mouth. It's about two inches long and an inch wide, big enough to cover the surface of my tongue and pin it down. Right away I can tell it isn't just leather.

"Bite it with your front teeth," he says. "Hold it steady."

I obey. It tastes a bit like sour candy, but a lot more intense. Right away my mouth goes into overdrive, saliva pooling under my tongue.

"Swallow," he orders.

Automatically, I try to swallow, but the leather tab keeps my tongue down. I gag, barely keeping my teeth together. The sweet and sour taste is making me drool so badly it slips from my lips. His eyes follow it down my neck, spilling over my tits.

He's so turned on, I can see the vein pulsing in his neck.

"Fuck," he murmurs, touching my chin. "You're such a good slut."

My body trembles. Humiliation has me so wet it's slipping down my inner thigh. I wonder if it's soaking the kneeler or if that's just the saliva dripping down my chin and neck.

He circles me and I hear him crouch behind me. His breath grazes my neck. "You want out, drop your head all the way back. Understood?"

My heart pounds as I nod. Gently, he gathers up my hair and starts braiding it down my back.

Oh God, what is he going to do?

His mouth brushes kisses down my shoulder and upper arm. Then his fingers slide between my legs and my vision flashes as he slips a slender vibrator up into my pussy. My inner muscles clench, pushing it deep inside. So it moves against my G-spot.

I whimper around the leather. My eyes start running.

He stands and unfastens the ties of his pants. "Close your eyes, painslut."

I snap them shut. I hear him spit into his hand and start jerking himself off. I doubt it will take long. He's panting and I wish I could see him. I know he's beautiful, aroused, rock hard. Sweat etching down his carved abs.

He groans. Warmth hits my breasts and chin.

My eyes snap open and he's just as I imagined. So fucking sexy, standing over me with the firelight glinting off his tattooed chest. His hard cock in hand, still coming on my tits.

I shudder, unable to help myself. The pressure of the clip on my clit and vibrator inside me is too much.

An orgasm washes over me and I sink back onto my heels to keep from falling over. He tugs the leather from my mouth and pulls me back up, pushing his wet cock between my lips. His other hand draws me back by the braid. Forcing me to look up into his eyes as he feeds his length, inch by inch, into my mouth.

My throat convulses, saliva spilling down my chin. My nose runs and my eyes sting. His hand clenches against the back of my head and he pushes slowly. Forcing himself deeper until I have no air. Until we're way past worrying about my gag reflex.

I might pass out. My fingers clench in the cuffs. My head spins as a rush of arousal washes over my body. So strong it feels like that desperate moment before orgasm. Where the only thing that matters is pleasure.

My vision blurs and darkens. He's in my throat now because he reaches down and cups it. Squeezing it just hard enough I can tell he feels the bulge of his cock.

Then he pulls back and I suck in air, coughing around his cock. I have one moment of relief before he's back in. Pushing all the way until my face is against his groin.

I'm back to drowning. Falling through dizzying space where there's nothing but his ravaging touch.

Then he's out just enough I can inhale.

And back in.

He reaches down and tugs the chain connecting my nipples and clit. Arousal sears like fire, and I moan as he pulls back at the same time he releases the tension on the chain. It takes me moment, but I start to feel a pattern.

Air in my lungs.

Sweet release of the pressure on my clit.

Suffocation.

Tension that burns like fire.

He's building me back up, using my breath and the clip on my clit. An orgasm surges quickly and hits my hips hard. Making my toes curl and my legs stiffen until I rise an inch off my heels. As I come, he pulls his cock back and releases his hold on the chain.

I shake, arousal dripping down my thighs and calves.

He pushes back in one last time and comes with low groan. Dragging his cock out as he does so the first pulses go down my throat and the last spatter my chin.

"Fuck," he says hoarsely. "Pretty whore, mouth full of cock, covered in cum."

I'm so overstimulated I can't tell if I'm still orgasming or not.

"Tongue out," he orders.

Weakly, I obey, spilling saliva and cum out onto my chin. It slips warm down my breasts and stomach and the corner of his mouth turns up.

Euphoria bursts in my brain. He's pleased—I pleased him.

He studies my eyes, which I know are glassy, and his hand comes up to stroke my face. I push my chin into his cupped palm, not caring I'm filthy. I've never wanted anything more than to hear him tell me I'm a good girl. That I did exactly what he wanted.

His grip returns to the back of my head. His other hand fists the base of his cock.

"Clean me up, little whore," he says.

Eagerly, I run my tongue up the underside of his cock. Licking up all the wetness. When I get to the head, I swirl my tongue all the way around. Getting every bit. His grip tightens, sliding down towards my mouth. A drop of white appears at the tip.

"Get it all," he orders.

I push the head into my mouth and suck. His jaw twitches and his chest rumbles with satisfaction. When I pull out, I unfurl my tongue. Showing him without being asked. Begging for his approval.

His head cocks slightly and the corner of his mouth twitches.

"Good girl," he says softly.

CHAPTER FIFTY-ONE

GERARD

I saw the moment where she slipped into total submission. Her eyes went from bright to soft and dreamy. All the tenseness eases from her body. Leaving her soft and pliable to my desire.

It's so fucking sweet.

She swallows the last bit of my cum and her full mouth closes. I bend and gather her wet, sticky body up in my arms. She gasps as I lift her and carry her to the bed, ripping the blankets back.

This is going to get messy.

She's still got the cuffs on, her arms behind her back. The clips are still on her pink nipples and her swollen, overstimulated clit. I'll keep everything on her until I'm done.

"Stay on your knees," I order.

She nods, sinking back onto her heels. I know she's so overstimulated she couldn't speak if she wanted to. I lean past her and flip the headboard. There's a mirror on the other side positioned so she can look herself in the eye while I fuck her ass. I've been saving it back for a night like this.

Her jaw drops. Her eyes rake over her reflection.

I kneel behind her, pulling her soft ass against my groin. My hand slides up to her breasts, gathering my cum and rubbing it into her pinched nipples. She whimpers, but she's too weak to move.

I kiss where her shoulder meets her neck.

"Dirty fucktoy," I whisper. "I'm going to bend you over and fuck your ass and you're going to watch."

Her tits heave. Her eyes are so big. She's soaked as I push my two fingers inside her, finding her G-spot and tapping it hard. Her eyes rolls back, she clenches.

"Please," she yelps.

"Please...what?"

"Sir," she whimpers. "Please, sir, I can't take it."

Her inner muscles tense. She's going to come again, this time all over my hand.

"You can take this," I say through gritted teeth. "And then you'll take every inch of my dick up your ass too and you'll fucking thank me for it."

Her eyes roll back, she arches, and she shatters. Her eyes fly open and connect with mine. Lashes fluttering and mouth moving soundlessly until her blue irises roll back and she goes limp.

Fuck, that's a beautiful sight.

Wetness dripping down my wrist, I pull my fingers free of her cunt as her orgasm wanes. She slumps against my chest and I lift my hand to her lips, working her jaw open. Her lashes flutter and she cranes her neck to look up at me, but I grip her hair and jerk her head back to the mirror.

"No. I want you to watch yourself eat your cum off my hand," I growl. "Keep those pretty eyes straight ahead" —my hand comes down on her ass so hard she screams— "and lick it clean."

Her tongue pushes out and curls around my fingers sticky with her arousal. Twin tears overflow her eyes and make tracks in her messy, perfect face. When my fingers are clean, I slide my hand under her chin and grip it so I can feel those tears against my skin.

"Good girl," I praise.

I release her hair and she whines, clearly disappointed. She's turned her mind off, she's nothing but a blank canvas.

And she's doing it because she loves it, because she's a pretty, perfect painslut.

She trembles. My gaze flicks lower. I've waited for this moment, patiently. Giving her time to get used to being fucked rough before I take it a step further. But I'm not waiting anymore.

Taking a pillow, I lay it before her knees and lower her over it. She turns her head and her cum and tear stained cheek rests on the sheet. Her blue eyes follow my every move as I go to the bedside table and retrieve the lube. We're going to need a lot of it.

Her breathe hitches as I kneel behind her. My pants are pushed down to expose my already rock hard cock. I know she can't take me for long in her ass, so I'll fuck her pussy first, until I'm close to coming.

She'd let me do anything to her right now. But I don't want to hurt my redbird.

Her breath hitches as I dip my finger in her cunt and pull the vibrator out. It's slippery and smells like her lust. I grip her hair and drag her head back, pushing it into her mouth.

"Clean it," I order.

She gags as it fills her mouth. Holding it by the string, I pull it out enough she can get a breath. Her tongue works, cleaning up her mess.

That's my good girl.

I toss it aside and release her hair. Lining my cock up with her cunt, I brace the heel of my hand beside her head. And thrust into her slippery pussy.

Fuck, with the plug in her ass there's barely room for me to get my cock halfway in her cunt.

Her mouth parts. Her pupils blow.

"You can be loud, sweetheart," I pant, fucking the first few inches into her. "I want to hear you cry and beg."

Her lips part and a soft whine escapes. A little sob that makes those tears spill over and her eyes roll back in her head.

It doesn't take long for another orgasm to start in my hips. I pull out and work the plug from her ass. She's loosened enough I can drizzle lube into her and slip my middle finger past her opening. Her lips part in a silent cry as I fingerfuck her ass. I reach under her stomach and tug the chain gently.

Her hips shudder. She rubs her face into the sheet, leaving smears behind.

Wetness drips from her cunt as she comes again. I work my fingers harder and release the chain.

She's loose, she's ready.

I grip my cock at the middle and guide the head to her asshole. I've been fucking with a big dick for a while, and I know this should actually be easier for us both than the first time I fucked her pussy. There's more room, I won't hit resistance the way I do when I'm fucking up against her cervix.

Her fingers clench in the cuffs.

"Bear down," I tell her.

She whimpers, but I feel her obey. The head of my cock slides into her ass and she gasps, her eyes rolling back.

"Does it hurt?" I press.

"No—no, sir," she manages. "Yes…maybe."

She doesn't know what she feels yet. That's normal. I stroke my hand down her naked back and let her adjust.

She's being such a good girl and I want this to be a reward, not a punishment. Her hips tremble and I adjust the pillow, making sure she has support.

She needs it. She came so many times her muscles are limp.

I brace myself and push again. This time she opens for me beautifully and I slide in. All the way to the hilt in my redbird.

"Sovereign," she gasps.

I gather her red braid in my hand and wrap it around my fist. Pinning her to the bed, her cheek sticking to the sheet.

"I know, sweetheart," I murmur. "You're such a fucking good girl."

I don't make her come again, she's past that point. I'm not even sure we can tell if she's stopped coming from the last time. Instead, I focus on dragging myself out an inch and thrusting back in. Moving my cock just enough to get the friction I need, but not enough to hurt her.

She moans, twitching. Her face rubs into the bed. She mouths something, but I can't hear her.

"Speak up," I urge.

I lift her head with her braid and her lips tremble.

"You feel good," she manages, her voice breaking. "You feel so good, sir."

My cock throbs and she feels it, writhing those pretty, soft hips beneath me. My hips thrust faster and she moans like the sweet whore she is.

She loves this, she loves the pain, the humiliation.

Heat shocks down my spine. We're so perfect together, my redbird and I.

Cum spills from me and I push in and shudder. My groin pressed into her ass, my fingers in her hair.

"Take it," I grit out. "Take all of me."

She does, she lays there until I'm done. I bend, still inside her, and kiss the side of her head. Right on her temple.

"That's my girl," I tell her.

Her lashes flutter. "Did I do what you wanted, sir?" she whispers.

"Everything," I assure her. "You're so good, such a good girl. I'm going to pull out and clean up now."

She nods, wincing as I disengage my hips. My cock leaves her warmth and her chest constricts and releases.

A deep, deep sigh.

I take everything off until she's naked. She clings to me as I fill the bathtub and let her sink into the steamy water. When I return from cleaning up the mess on the hearth and in the bed, her eyes are heavy.

She reaches for me weakly.

"Hold me," she whispers.

I sink into the water and pull her into my arms, facing me. Her legs wrap around my body and her arms drape around my neck. She burrows her face into my chest. I kiss the top of her pomegranate scented hair.

There's no place in this world I'd rather be than in her arms.

CHAPTER FIFTY-TWO

KEIRA

It takes a week for the snow to stop.

Everything between Sovereign and I is put on hold because he's gone so much. Winter on a ranch is hard, and it's even harder up on Sovereign Mountain. He leaves early and comes back late. Frosted with snow and smelling of the outdoors.

I spend a lot of time sleeping, exhausted from everything that happened. When I'm not out cold, I'm occupied with Angel in the barn or helping Maddie in the kitchen. She's a lot warmer to me now, she even told me she was impressed with what I did by the river.

We start decorating the ranch for the holidays early even though Sovereign narrows his eyes. He doesn't say anything, but he does leave a pile of cut fir branches outside the front door early one morning.

It's Sunday night when I finally get him to myself. The men finish the chores early and the main house clears out. The clock chimes. I'm laying in bed with my eyes fixed on the snow covered mountains through the window.

The painted mare lays on the bedside table. She doesn't stand upright any longer. I tied her broken legs together with a ribbon so they don't get lost.

Sovereign doesn't come in when he usually does around eight. I slip from bed, the goosebumps rising on my skin, and pad out into the hallway. I'm in my silk slip, the one I wore the night my barn burned. I scrubbed away the smoke stains and now it's back to its original white.

I don't wear it because I have to anymore. Just because I want to. Because Sovereign's eyes light up when he sees me in it.

I pad down the stairs. Maddie hung the fir branches over the fireplace and wound them with little white lights. The gas fireplace burns. Otherwise, the big main room is quiet.

Sovereign sits on the couch facing the fireplace, knees apart. He's got a glass in one hand.

My stomach tightens.

Is he...drinking?

Small Dog and Big Dog are sprawled out at his feet. Both flipped on their backs, paws in the air, snores rising from their slack jaws.

I creep down the curved staircase, my bare feet silent on the wood. He doesn't see or hear me until I circle the couch and sink down on the floor at his feet. Small Dog sneezes loudly and flips to his side. He cracks an eye.

"What is that?" I ask, taking the glass and lifting it to my nose.

It's water. My shoulders sag with relief.

The corner of his mouth turns up. He touches the side of my face, his rough palm cradling my cheek. I burrow my face into it. He feels so strong, so safe.

"It's Sunday night," he says.

"I know," I whisper.

His mouth thins, his eyes flick over me and rest on the fire. "I still want a contract with you, but I want it to be simple."

"That's alright with me," I whisper. "Contract or not, I still love you."

He bends down and kisses my forehead. My entire body goes still and my lids flutter shut. No one ever touched me this gently before he came along. My heart is tender and wide open like a flower reaching up to the sun. I feel his touch on my chin, tilting it, and I open my eyes.

"It took me a long time to settle my scores," he says. "I wanted the Garrison bloodline gone and now it is. It's time to close the book. I'm glad you were here for the last chapter."

My stomach flutters. His words sound so grim.

"What happens next?" I whisper.

He takes my hand. "Come here," he says hoarsely, lifting me to my feet and guiding me into his lap. I climb up and straddle him. We're eye level and I can make out the pale blue of his iris and the dark icy outer ring surrounding it.

"You're very young," he says. "I forget how young you are because...you've been through so much already."

I swallow, feeling awkward. I'm not even in my mid-twenties and I feel like I've lived half a lifetime already. But he's almost forty, even though he doesn't look it. There's over a decade of life between us, and I feel the weight of it tonight.

"I don't mind," I whisper.

He smooths back my hair, playing with a strand. "Tell me what you want for the future?"

The future has never been easy for me to imagine. I'd given up hoping when I realized I'd married a man who hated me and stole my family's farm. The future had always looked bleak and short.

But with Sovereign...I feel like I'm just waking up.

"I don't know," I admit. "But I'd like whatever it is to be with you."

His jaw works and his hand leaves my hair and trails down to my stomach. My body goes still as his fingertips skate across the curve of my lower belly. His lashes are lowered. His face is unreadable.

"Sovereign," I whisper.

He clears his throat. "I scheduled an appointment for a reversal."

My heart picks up. His eyes flick up. The air between us feels thick with tension.

"You...what are you saying?" I whisper.

"The reversal success rates are very high for what I had done," he says.

"You need to slow down," I blurt out.

He goes quiet and he can't hide the devastation in his eyes. I slide off his lap, unsure what to say. The fire crackles, the dogs snore. I back up to the bottom of the stairs.

"I...my painted mare is broken," I whisper. "I was hoping you'd fix it."

He stands and his face is strained. I know I hurt him, but I'm not sure how to get myself out of this situation without causing more pain. I grip the railing and back up onto the landing.

"Of course," he says.

I swallow past my dry throat. "Thank you. I'm going to bed."

Up in our bathroom, I splash my face with cold water. My hands shake as I dry them and tears push up past my lashes. I spread my left hand and lift it, studying the bare spot on my ring finger.

Is he expecting to get me pregnant without even talking about marriage?

I want to be married and I want it right this time. I want the ring and the wedding and the promises. And a husband who doesn't hate me. I take a shuddering breath and it hits me that I'm having a panic attack. My hands shake and my heart pounds. There's a sick sensation in my chest and my head spins.

I realize now that Clint fucked me up more than I care to admit.

I don't hear him knocking at the door until it's too late and it's being forced open. He crouches down and scoops me up, carrying me out to the bed. Dimly I'm aware that he's holding me and we're both propped on the pillows. And his boots are on the bed, propped on the folded fur blanket at the end.

I frown, rubbing my wet face against his shirt.

"Boots are on the bed," I whisper.

He laughs. "Hush, it's fine. We have a washing machine."

My lids feel sticky and I don't care what he thinks about me anymore. He's seen me in every compromising position. With my hair messy, my eyes swollen, gagging, begging. He's seen my rage, my wrath, my vengeance. And I've seen his, laid out in all its ugliness.

I've only loved him for a short time.

But I know him. I stood witness to his vengeance.

"Why don't you marry me, sir?" I ask softly.

He turns abruptly, flipping me onto my back. He leans over me and slides his hand up my forearm to weave his fingers through mine. Pressing my hand back against the pillow.

"I don't know what will happen in this next chapter, but I know who I am in it," he says. "I am your husband, redbird. I thought that went without saying."

Tears leak from the corners of my eyes. I wish I didn't cry so easily, it's so fucking embarrassing.

"Really?" I whisper.

His jaw works. "I killed Clint because he was sleeping in my bed with my wife."

My breath hitches. Deep down, I know I should be horrified. But instead, I feel the slow burn of arousal kindle between my thighs.

"What does that mean?" I whisper.

"It means, of course I'm going to marry you."

There's something about the intensity of his voice that's setting me off. That growl at the end of his words has me burning. I writhe slightly and his grip tightens, holding me to the bed.

"You are the mother of my children," he says. "My wife."

My eyes are wide. My lashes are wet.

How does he always get me like this? Aroused and in tears seems to be my default mode when I'm in bed with him. But I don't have time to think about it because he bends and kisses my mouth and my body sets on fire.

His kisses are always so slow and thorough. He takes his time to explore my lips with his. I distantly feel his arousal growing against my leg and it stokes the flames of mine. He breaks our kiss and uses his hard head to push mine aside and kiss the side of my neck.

He bites it gently and returns to my mouth.

"Give me your tongue, redbird," he murmurs.

My hips rise, rubbing against his body. I part my lips as his distracted eyes find my mouth. He dips down and captures the tip between his teeth. I feel his saliva slip into my mouth and I swallow without thinking. Our mouths draw apart and our eyes connect.

He's fucked up for me, just like Westin said he was.

"Do you want to be Keira Stowe or Sovereign?" he asks.

My breathe comes out in a slow shudder. He doesn't know how much it means to me that he's letting me choose. Clint just forced my hand down on the paper, his grip firm on my lower back. He took my name before I had a chance to realize what he'd done.

I never wanted to be a Garrison. But I do want to belong to Gerard Sovereign.

My dry lips part.

"Get me a ring and I'll be Keira Sovereign forever," I whisper.

He rumbles, moving to lay halfway atop me. His body is so heavy and it presses me down into the mattress. His knee shifts and I let out a little gasp as it lifts enough I can breathe. His hips move, gently humping against mine. He's got a satisfied, drunk expression in his heavy eyes.

"I can't get you pregnant tonight, redbird, but let's practice."

CHAPTER FIFTY-THREE

GERARD

The world gets smaller in the dead of winter.

We can't bring the trucks out until the snow has been cleared from the road. We spent all summer preparing for this though, so it doesn't matter. The freezers and cupboards are packed with food. We have enough gas and fuel to last till spring. Everyone on Sovereign Mountain hunkers down and slips into the slow wait until the first scent of spring touches the air.

Keira loves comfort and she thrives in winter. I find her curled up in the bedroom window wrapped in blankets. Hot coffee and a stack of books nearby.

She naps every afternoon in our bed because I keep her up late at night. She stays up till past midnight, usually cuffed in leather, on her knees. Letting me fuck her and force orgasms from her body until she collapses with exhaustion.

She's had a hard life, and I can give her comfort and pleasure.

So I do. More than she could ask for.

At the end of the month, I manage to get to South Platte to pick up an order I've had waiting for me since October. It sits silently in the passenger side of my truck all the way home. A flat cardboard box with her initials in silver across the top.

KS.

Except this time, the S isn't for Stowe.

She's out in the barn with Angel and Westin when I get back. I asked Westin to distract her and he dropped the bomb on me that he has something he's been waiting to tell Keira for a few weeks. Apparently Angel is pregnant, expecting in the spring. I slip past the barn door and head into the house, knowing Keira is completely distracted in the barn. Probably clinging to Angel's neck with tears running down her face.

Westin won't know how the fuck to deal with that.

The corner of my mouth turns up as I ascend the stairs. I love that she's soft and her tears flow easily. All the cruelty she endured didn't scar her the way it did me. She still feels everything to the fullest.

In the bedroom, I lay the package down and flip the lid. Inside is a little wooden box with the SMR logo burned into the top. It's tiny in my hands as I flip the lid open and reveal the ring I ordered back in October.

It's a diamond, the shade of the ferns that grow in the mountains, by the edge of the lake. The tall stone is surrounded by little diamonds that glitter like the stars on the bridle of the painted horse.

I knew it was the one for her the minute I laid eyes on it. The shade of green is beautiful against her auburn hair. I'm not sure how to explain myself, but it just looks like the ring of a beautiful woman.

And my redbird is the most beautiful woman I've ever seen.

I snap the lid shut and slip it in my pocket. Beneath it in the box sits a set of fern green lingerie wrapped in black paper and tied with a silver ribbon.

I know she's used to living in rough country, but she deserves to feel beautiful and spoiled now and then.

She never asks for anything.

I hear her steps, rushing up the stairs. I move fast, snapping the box shut and setting it in the dresser. The door bursts open and she's there, still in her coat and boots. Eyes glassy and lashes wet.

"Angel is having a baby," she bursts out.

She runs to me and I lift her in my arms. Her legs wrap around my waist and her arms encircle my neck. It's the first time she's done this and my heart is pounding. But I have to play it cool, I don't want her getting self-conscious.

"How do you feel about being a grandmother?" I ask.

She laughs, her head falling back.

Fuck, she's pretty and I'm getting hard at the wrong time.

She sobers, sliding from my arms and stripping her boots and coat off. I watch her shed the rest of her clothes, leaving them in a trail on the floor. This time I just gather them up and drop them into the chair without saying anything.

She climbs naked into the bed and pulls the blankets up to her chin.

"I'm so cold. Do you want to go out and see Angel after dinner?" she asks.

I shake my head. "No, I have an appointment tonight."

Her face falls and I lift my brow.

"Don't pout," I tell her.

She rearranges her face, but I can tell she's crestfallen. "Okay, that's fine. I'll probably eat with Maddie in the kitchen then."

"Maddie actually asked me if you would go down and help her out with dinner tonight," I say, trying to keep my voice casual. "She's finally admitted you make the best biscuits."

She smiles, although I can tell she's disappointed. But she's a good girl and she'd never complain about it. I cross the room and bend to kiss her waiting mouth and she grips the front of my shirt.

"Do you want a quickie?" she asks, a flush creeping up her face.

That's tempting.

I cup her right breast, rubbing her nipple until it's hard beneath my thumb. I should wait until tonight, after she's got my ring on her finger. But, fuck it, I can go as many round as she needs tonight.

She yelps as I flip her over the edge of the bed. Her spine arches and I can tell she's wet. She wanted to be fucked all along, that's why she stripped and got into bed. Holding her by the hair with one hand,

I take my cock out with the other and push it mercilessly into her pussy.

She yelps.

"You wanted it," I tell her, slapping her thigh.

I fuck her until I come, but I don't get her off. I want her needy and dripping so she has to think of my cock in her every time she feels her wet panties against her clit. She's panting, still bent over the bed, when I tuck my cock into my pants and kiss the nape of her neck.

"Good girl," I praise. "See you tonight."

I leave her there, naked except for my collar.

CHAPTER FIFTY-FOUR

KEIRA

Everyone is being unusually nice to me. Maddie never wants help in the kitchen, but tonight she has me cutting out sheets of biscuits. She has an ancient record player in the corner of the kitchen and we work to the muffled sound of classical music.

"Angel is having a foal," I say.

She glances up. "That's what Westin says."

"It's so exciting," I muse. "It'll give me something to look forward to. Spring seems far away."

"I'm sure there's lots to look forward to," Maddie says, banging the oven door shut as she sets the last sheet inside. She can't seem to look me in the eye.

"Are you alright?" I ask.

She nods, ducking into the pantry. When she returns, she has a picnic basket in her hand. She sets it down before me and I stare up at her, confused.

"This is your dinner," she says. "Yours and Sovereign's."

"Um...thank you," I say carefully. "Sovereign has an appointment tonight though."

She looks at me pointedly. "You are his appointment, Keira."

It hits me right then why everyone is acting strange. Why Westin took the time out of his day to stand in the barn with me for two hours. Why I've been cutting biscuits in the kitchen since four in the afternoon. My lips part and my heart starts hammering at the base of my neck.

Her brow arcs, she jerks her head towards the door.

"Better get upstairs, missy," she says. "And take your basket with you."

My eyes are already wet, but I blink hard. I can't think of words so I just grab the basket handle and make a dash up the hallway. Up the stairs and to our bedroom.

It's empty.

The fire is burning. There's a black box laying on the carefully made bed. But it isn't that that draws my attention.

My painted mare is back, sitting on the bedside table. And beside her is a dark brown, varnished wood stallion with a bridle made of painted stars. Between them is a little wooden box with the lid popped open.

And inside is a ring.

My entire body feels like it's made of air. I place the basket on the bed and float to the bedside table. My painted mare is whole again, her front legs seamlessly attached and painted over. My eyes fall back on the ring. I'm almost afraid to look at it. What if it's just my imagination?

Except for the sterling silver band Clint gave me, I've never had a piece of jewelry before meeting Sovereign. It always felt sad to buy my own, so I just pretended I didn't want any. He gave me the silver collar and that felt like a luxury.

But this ring is different. This is a delicate work of art. Like something I've seen on the fingers of rich women in movies.

I should savor this moment. The only useless pretty thing I've ever had is the painted mare.

And that had an element of sadness attached to it.

But this ring is the beginning of a new chapter.

"You like it, redbird?"

322

I whirl and he's standing in the doorway. He's in good clothes, a dress shirt and pants. His sleeves are rolled up, exposing his thick arms. He looks so good I can't think of a single word.

He crosses to me, tilting my chin up.

"I don't know if that ring is pretty enough to be on your finger," he says. "But I gave it my best shot."

I just nod hard. His mouth turns up as he takes my hand and leads me to the bed. I don't know what I expected, but it's not for Sovereign to sink down on one knee at my feet. We're still almost eye to eye, but I don't care. Nothing about my life has been conventional. I missed everything—I've been just an accessory until now.

He's giving me this because he knows it means something to me.

He takes my hand. I'm shaking so hard I can't speak. He picks up the ring and a laugh catches in my throat because it looks so small in his fingers. Our eyes meet.

"Marry me," he says.

He doesn't ask, but he's not the type. Those pale blue eyes demand the answer he knows he's going to get. Because he gets everything he fucking wants.

So I give it.

"Yes," I whisper.

He slips the ring on my finger. I lift my hand and turn it slowly to catch the firelight. It's stunning.

He gets to his feet, taking my face in his hands. When he kisses me, my heart beats so fast it feels like it's going to lift from my chest. He's so good at it and I'm fucked. Fucked for the slow, thorough way he kisses. Like I'm the most important thing in the world.

When he pulls back, I'm so choked up I can't speak.

"My redbird," he murmurs, running his fingers through my hair. "I have something else for you."

He releases me and flips the lid on the box on the bed. Inside is a delicate, moss green set of lingerie. I've never had real lingerie before, but I've always wanted at least one nice set. I bite my lip and glance up at him, suddenly shy.

"You want me to wear that?" I whisper.

"You will wear it," he says.

He strips me slowly and I'm glad I just took a shower and shaved everything.

The panties slip up my legs and the soft lace settles over my hips. They fit me perfectly, made for the curves of my body. I wonder if it's a custom set. There's no tags. He lifts the bra and it looks so strange in his big, rough hands.

"You're my wife and my submissive," he says firmly, eyes locking on mine. "You sit at my feet because you choose to. Do you understand?"

I nod shakily.

Somehow we both know what's on his mind. That first night we met, when Clint made me stand and wait in case he needed something.

He circles me and clasps the bra over my breasts. "Good girl."

He tugs my hair free, letting it fall down my back. His fingers skate over my throat and down between my breasts. His hand flattens, pulling my body back against his. He turns me and I find my gaze in the mirror on our headboard.

"I'll be your husband and your dominant," he says. "And the father of your children. Is that what you want?"

The light glints off my collar. My breasts heave as I take a quick breath.

"Yes, sir," I whisper.

"Good girl," he says again. "I want you to sign something for me."

Before I can speak, he releases me and goes to his office. He rarely unlocks it, so I haven't been inside, but he beckons me through the door. It's a small, plain room with a window that looks out over the lake. There's an office chair at the oak desk and a closed laptop. Gerard has never been one for frills.

"Is it an updated contract?" I ask.

He pulls the desk drawer open and takes out a black folder. "No, but we do need to rewrite and update our contract before the wedding."

I hover at his elbow. "So what is it?"

He flips open the folder and sinks into the chair. His hands are on my waist and he lifts me into his lap so I'm facing the desk. I'd be distracted by the feeling of his thigh between my legs, but my eyes are on the paperwork.

It's a surveyor's map.

My heart sinks. It's showing all the Garrison land and Sovereign Mountain Ranch as the same piece. Did he...did he annex all my land into his?

I feel like I'm sinking in cold water.

How could he do this after what Clint did?

"Sovereign," I whisper.

"Turn the page, redbird," he rumbles.

Hand shaking and eyes blurred, I obey. The second paper is a deed of some kind. I have to read it three times before it makes any sense at all. What does it mean? Is he giving me the Garrison land?

"Sovereign, what is this?" I ask, my voice trembling.

He leans in, his chest warm against my back. His finger taps the empty line at the bottom below where he signed his name.

"Dual ownership," he says. "Just sign your name."

I shift, turning so I'm sideways on his knee. He's watching me intently, clearly waiting for me to say something.

"So...we would have dual ownership of the Garrison Ranch?" I manage.

He taps the paper. "Read it again, redbird."

He flips the map so the paper is side by side and it hits me like a brick wall. The land is consolidated into one piece. There are two dotted lines on the deed. My entire body tingles and I whip back around, my hands going to his chest. At the base of his neck, where the vein pulses when he wants me.

"You can't do that," I manage.

"We absorbed the Garrison land, I paid for it," he says. "It's all Sovereign Mountain Ranch now. And when you sign there, redbird, you'll own it all with me. Is that what you want?"

He's giving me equal ownership of Sovereign Mountain and all the land that goes with it. Including the Stowe and Garrison farms. If I sign my name, I'll own it all alongside him.

My hand goes over my mouth.

"How's it feel to be a billionaire, sweetheart?" he asks.

"You can't do this."

Sovereign Mountain is everything to him, he can't just give me legal ownership of it. It's what lifted him up and kept him safe all those years. It gave him back his dignity when that was stripped from him by the Garrisons. It's a fortress in the mountains where he's king.

Where he kept me safe.

"I can do whatever I want," he says. "Now sign that paper so I can fuck my fiancée."

He turns me around and pushes a pen into my hand.

So I sign it.

Not because I know what I'm doing, or what this means for our future. But because it hits me right then that he's going to be my husband. His ring is on my finger. He's going to get his vasectomy reversed and make me the mother of his children. I'm going to wake up every day for the rest of my life with Gerard Sovereign's arms around my body.

With my head nestled against the bull skull on his chest.

And that's all I really want.

He flips me around and pulls me close. Our mouths meet, just for a second.

"You look like an angel," he says.

I cradle his face between my hands. His jaw is scratchy beneath my palms.

"Do you love me?" I whisper, just wanting to hear it in his words.

His lids are heavy. "I love you, redbird."

We kiss, our breath clashing. When I pull back, I hear him groan.

"Now fuck me like you hate me," I beg.

EPILOGUE

PART 1

KEIRA

EIGHT MONTHS LATER

I climb the stairs and turn the corner. My hand wraps around the doorknob, but I don't turn it. Instead, I take a deep breath and close my eyes, smiling.

This summer has been perfect. Beyond anything I could have imagined.

He married me in the springtime on the front porch with Westin as the officiate. The whole ranch was there and Maddie cried loudly into her handkerchief the entire time. The dining hall was decorated in bluebells and silk ribbons. Everyone ate there and we cut the cake in a white tent in the lawn under the pine trees. Music was still thumping and everyone was thoroughly drunk by the time Gerard and I stole upstairs.

After that, we sat down together and negotiated a contract.

A few nights out of the week, we set aside time to be completely immersed in our dynamic. Outside of that, I still call him sir and he still calls me his redbird, but the lines are clearer now.

It's the perfect balance.

I blink, jerking from my reverie. The clock downstairs strikes seven and I slip into the bedroom. In the upper dress drawer, he laid out a black silk set of lingerie. I put it on and pad into his office to make him a cup of black coffee. The curtain is still open and I can see him walk through the barn doors with Shadow at his heels.

My heart flutters.

The coffee machine beeps. I carry the mug out to the chair in the corner I ordered for him as a surprise on his birthday. It's dark leather, plush, and big enough he can sit in it and have me over his lap.

We've gotten a lot of use out of it. Especially on Sunday nights.

I set the coffee on the table beside it and fold a clean pair of sweatpants over the back of the chair. Faintly, I can hear him talking in the yard. My pussy tingles as I hurry into the bathroom and turn the shower on for him.

On the sink sits my collar, the leash attached.

I lift my eyes to my reflection and braid my hair so it's out of the way. It took me a while to get used to the feeling of voluntary submission. At first, it had always been initiated by him. It's a different feeling to act it out as part of our daily routine.

The collar slides over my throat. The feeling is so familiar now that my body reacts to it. Heat sparks deep inside and aches as I leave the bathroom and circle the bed. At the foot, in the wooden board, he attached a metal anchor. I sink to my knees and clip the free end to it.

And wait.

I hear his heavy footsteps on the stairs. The door creaks open, but I keep my gaze lowered. From the corner of my eye, I can see him take off his boots and deposit them into the hallway.

He walks by me and into the bathroom.

The faint scent of his soap fills my lungs. It reminds me of giving him oral because he's always clean and smells like soap. Now the scent triggers a Pavlovian response and heat pours through my body and makes my toes curl.

I squirm, noticing I'm already soaked.

The door opens. I hear him put on the sweatpants I laid out for him. Then he's beside me, and his fingers are under my chin. Lifting my face up, giving me permission to drown in his pale blue gaze.

My heart thumps.

"Good girl," he says.

He has a soft, firm way of saying it that makes me feel so safe. I keep still as he sinks to a crouch and unhooks the leash from my collar. Then he takes my hand and leads me to his chair. I wait until he's settled, my hands interlaced over my lower stomach.

I thrive in this environment.

It's so exciting, and yet completely predictable. I never wonder what he'll do next, if he'll be angry, if I have to walk on eggshells. He's got an even temper, a short store of words, and endless affection.

We had a rocky start. There's no denying that.

But we made it through, and he's so at peace. I was worried that without the need for vengeance that drove him for years, he would start drifting. But it's the total opposite. He's so calm, so grounded. I still taste his darkness and the brutality that he's capable of, but only when I want to, only when he fucks me rough, makes me cry, and then puts me back together again.

He pats his knee once, and I sink down, wrapping one arm around his neck. We sit in silence for a moment while he drinks his coffee.

"How was today?" I ask.

"Good, we're ready for auction next week," he says.

He's been out for days doing inventory. Taking stock of losses, estimating what we need to make a profit this year. In the spring, we had a huge crop of Quarter Horse foals and Gerard confided in me that if we sold all of them, we'd be set for the first two quarters.

He had.

I never doubted him. It's such a good feeling to trust my husband.

He sets aside the empty cup and turns me to face him. His hands rest on my waist. I smooth back his dark hair and bend, kissing him slowly. When I pull back, his eyes are heavy with desire.

"I want your opinion on something," he says.

329

I nod, a little unsure. After he gave me dual ownership of the ranch, he started roping me into big decisions. I was hesitant to do more than offer advice, and when I told him that, he respected my choice. As much as I appreciated that he was gifting me autonomy, I was not ready to help run the biggest ranch in the state.

"The strip of land on the southern side of the old Garrison ranch just went up for sale," he says. "I was thinking of purchasing it."

I know what he's talking about. It's a rocky strip of earth where the river bottoms out and turns southeast. The land isn't suited for pasture or farming, but it's got a solid water supply.

"Why?"

He shrugs. "The earth needs restoration. In a few decades, we could have it back to pasture. Maybe plant some pines."

"Do you have the extra money for that? It sounds like a project rather than an investment," I say.

"It is. But I can afford it," he says, nodding. "But it's worth it if the land recovers. Nobody's worked it in a long time."

I know how deeply he cares, and I care too, so I nod. "I think you should buy it then."

He leans in and kisses me again. Slowly, thoroughly. His tongue grazes mine, tasting faintly of coffee. My body warms and I lean into him, winding my arms around his neck. When we break apart, we're both flushed.

"Get up on the bed, redbird," he says hoarsely.

His hands roam over my body, his fingers digging into my thighs. The roughness of his palms drags over my skin and catches at my silk panties and garter. He kisses my mouth again, and the side of my neck, and between my breasts.

"Fuck, redbird, get up on that bed." he says, setting me to my feet.

I turn and he slaps my ass so hard it sends a rush of heat between my legs. He's behind me as I climb up on the bed and sink to my back. Spreading my thighs for him.

His eyes roam my body and I can see the heavy ridge of his erection in his pants. My pussy throbs, aching for the warmth of him inside me.

"Please, fuck me," I beg.

He shakes his head, eyes glittering. "Get on your knees and hold onto the headboard. I want your pretty, wet cunt on my face."

Oh my God. My stomach flutters as I scramble to my knees and turn. He slides up behind me, slapping my thigh and gripping my ass so hard I whimper. He kisses the back of my neck, gathering both wrists and putting my hands up on the headboard.

His breath spills hot over the nape of my neck.

"I'm going to eat your pussy until you come all over my face, redbird," he breathes. "I want to taste you, until you're begging me to stop. Can you be a good girl for me and come until you can't come anymore?"

My throat is so dry I have to clear it.

"Yes, sir," I whisper.

He slaps my ass again and my head falls back. My nails dig into the headboard.

"That's a good girl," he says.

His warmth disappears and I close my eyes, knowing he's laying down between my thighs. His fingers grip my hips and he pulls me down onto his face. The moan that sounds in his throat makes my toes curl.

His tongue drags from my pussy to my clit.

And I give into him.

My Sovereign.

EPILOGUE

PART 2

GERARD

I get in early from chores one night in late summer. It's warm and dry, so we keep the cattle in the lower pastures. They spend their days sleeping at the edges of the woods or standing in the river and pond to keep cool. Most of the time, I feel like doing the same.

Keira's not at the house when I get in, and Maddie tells me she took Angel out to the top of the hill that overlooks the old Garrison Ranch. I mount Shadow bareback and go after her. The late afternoon shadows lengthen. The sun spills its light like molten gold over Sovereign Mountain.

She's in the grass, laying on her back. Angel grazes a few dozen yards away. Silently, I slide down from Shadow and give him a light slap on the shoulder to send him walking to Angel.

Keira hears my footfalls and she rolls to her side, lifting her head. I sink down on my hands and knees over her, bending and kissing her temple.

"What are you doing up here, redbird?" I ask.

She smiles, her nose scrunching. Her freckles multiply in the summer and her hair bleaches until there are strands of gold intertwined with red.

"I was hoping you'd come after me," she sighs.

I sink down until we're laying side by side. She touches my temple and her soft mouth twists, like she's trying not to smile. I let her stroke through my hair and down my neck to my shoulder. She doesn't hesitate when she touches me anymore.

She's so confident now.

She's not afraid.

And she never will be again.

Her fingers skim down my jaw and she presses them to my lips for a kiss. Our eyes lock and I have to pull her in and press my mouth to hers, letting her taste fill my senses. When I release her, she reaches down and takes my hand, stroking my palm with her thumb.

"Gerard," she whispers.

I lean in closer, our bodies almost touching.

"What is it, redbird?"

Her throat bobs. Her eyes are glassy with tears as her fingers tighten on my hand. Then she moves it down and presses the heel of my palm to her lower belly.

Fuck.

My entire body freezes and my brain goes quiet. I got the reversal in March, but I kept my expectations low on purpose. I want children with her so badly, but I kept myself open to the possibility that might not happen.

That didn't stop me from carving a little wooden foal one night in the barn. I painted it deep red and sealed it so it was shiny and smooth. It's in a sitting position so the delicate legs don't break and written on the underside is our names.

I've carried that foal in my pocket for months.

Hoping.

Now, I clear my throat and realize my hand is shaking. When I look back at her, she's smiling past the tears sliding down her face and falling into the dry grass. I've imagined this moment before, but now that it's here, I'm frozen in place.

"Well...say something," she whispers.

"Are you...pregnant?" I manage.

Her mouth shakes as she laughs, reaching up to wipe her face. She nods hard and the strangest sensation fills my chest. Like something broke and now it's bleeding inside me, flooding me with warmth.

I'm not crying, but it's the closest I've come in decades.

"How far along?"

I can't keep my voice steady and she's so sweet she pretends she doesn't notice.

"I've missed two periods," she says, sniffing. "I wasn't sure the first time, but then I missed another so I had Maddie get me some tests and they were very positive."

"So eight weeks," I say. "We need to get you a doctor's appointment."

"Maddie has me set up for next week," she says.

She rolls onto her back and her fingertips skim over her lower stomach. She's wearing a plain cotton sundress with a slit up the middle so she can pull it aside to ride Angel. I stretch out on my side and slide my hand through the opening to grip her thigh.

Her eyes flicker up and lock to mine. I bend and kiss her the way she deserves. Slowly, enjoying her taste, her scent, the feel of her mouth. I pull away and use my head to push hers aside and kiss her neck.

"Thank you," I say.

"For what?" she murmurs.

"For being my wife, for having my baby. Thank you for seeing me for the man I am and loving me anyway."

"I love you," she whispers. "And Sovereign Mountain."

"And the children we have here."

She's trying not to cry again. I push my hand in my pocket and take the little wooden foal out. Her eyes widen as I gently place it on her lower belly, on the little rise between her hipbones. The tears break through and trickle down her temples into her brilliant hair.

"I made that in the spring," I say. "I wanted to hope."

She turns it over and over in her fingers. "It's perfect."

I kiss her forehead. When I lift my eyes, I see the sun is setting over Sovereign Mountain. In the distance, I can make out the cliffs where Clint died. I know beyond it runs the river where she shot Thomas and his body bled out into the dirt.

I'm not haunted by what could be anymore.

Or what has been.

Soon the snow will come and cover Sovereign Mountain. Then it'll melt and flow into rivers that make green grass cover the pastures. And bluebells will grow over earth that was once stained in blood.

There will be a new Sovereign—perhaps a little boy with my eyes or a girl with her brilliant hair.

Sovereign Mountain will be new again.

And I owe it all to this woman I call my own.

THE END

OTHER BOOKS BY RAYA MORRIS EDWARDS

The Welsh Kings Trilogy
Paradise Descent
Prince of Ink & Scars

The King of Ice & Steel Trilogy
Captured Light - Lucien & Olivia
Devil I Need: The Sequel to Captured Light
Ice & Steel: The Conclusion to Captured Light & Devil I Need
Lucien & Olivia: A Christmas Short

Captured Standalones
Captured Desire - Iris & Duran
Captured Light - Lucien & Olivia
Captured Solace - Viktor & Sienna
Captured Ecstasy - Peregrine & Rosalia

Acknowledgments

Thank you to my husband. This was the hardest book I've ever written that hit the closest to home in my heart. Your support during late nights, early mornings, and everything in between got me through to the last word.

A special thank you to Corinne who read this book before anyone else. Your insight into this story and wonderful advice was truly invaluable!

Thank you to my editor, Lexie, for your hard work on this story. Thank you to my cover designer for another amazing cover. Thank you to my MIL (who is never allowed to read this book) for her extensive, firsthand knowledge of horse and cattle ranching in Montana.

And thank you to everyone I spoke to in my research who provided their insights, opinions, very thorough contract examples, and thoughts regarding BDSM dynamics and relationships.

A huge thank you and shout out to my beta and ARC readers, you are amazing! Thank you to everyone on Booktok and Bookstagram who is so supportive and wonderful. I will always be grateful for your support in my author journey.

Made in the USA
Monee, IL
27 October 2024

68773755R00203